Elder cleared his throat. "I don't know what we're afraid of here. We do business with people just as bad. We've financed many a stock grab and proxy fight and insider takeover. The minutes of this meeting are not going to show that Harry Elder said we should let the mafia buy into UBCO. But I honestly don't know what there is to be afraid of."

Kinch sniffed. "I had a helluva union problem till I met a man who cured it. You remember that nationwide metal tubing shortage last fall? A man asked me if I cared where he got the stuff. I said 'hell, no.' It was standard stuff like the Christmas gift booze we get at half price. And when it comes to entertaining congressmen, we support half the casinos in Vegas. The mafia's just businessmen doing business. They supply what we want."

Harry Elder said: "It boils down to this: is there any real difference between them and us?"

LESLIE WALLER

The Family

Mandarin

A Mandarin Paperback
THE FAMILY

First published in Great Britain 1969
by W. H. Allen Ltd
This edition published 1991
by Mandarin Paperbacks
Michelin House, 81 Fulham Road, London SW3 6RB

Mandarin is an imprint of the Octopus Publishing Group

Copyright © Leslie Waller 1968

A CIP catalogue record for this title
is available from the British Library

ISBN 0 7493 0703 X

Reproduced, printed and bound in Great Britain by
BPCC Hazell Books
Aylesbury, Bucks, England
Member of BPCC Ltd.

For Pat, always

"Draw your chair up close to the edge
of the precipice and I'll tell you a story."

F. SCOTT FITZGERALD

PART ONE
Saturday

The needle on the station wagon's speedometer crept past seventy. Palmer eyed it with irritation. Ever since he'd driven out of Manhattan over the George Washington Bridge, he'd been quite lost in a maze of New Jersey roads. While this annoyed him, it bothered him even more that he was in some irrational way trying to compensate for being lost by speeding.

He realized now that instead of briefly scanning the map at home he should have taken it along. The single comforting factor, he told himself as he let up on the accelerator, was that he was the only one in the car who knew he was lost.

It reminded him abruptly of a moment in time more than twenty-five years before, on a hot, dusty Sicilian road leading up into the mountains from Licata on the Mediterranean. Palmer had been heading up a T-Force of twenty men in those first days of the Allied invasion. It had been about D-plus-1, roughly July 11, 1943. The American, Canadian and British troops, having swept Rommel out of Africa, had launched the first invasion of European territory. It had been Palmer's very secret assignment to dash up to a small mountain town near San Cataldo, there to make contact with a man most important to the Allied victory in Sicily.

There had been trouble getting transport for his men. In the last-second rush to move off on his mission, Palmer had left behind both map case and survival pack, which contained a map of Sicily printed on silk. Instead, he managed to get his whole T-Force lost for several precious hours by relying on his recollections of the maps he had studied during the trip by LST from Tunis on D-minus-1.

Of course, Palmer reminded himself now, that had been a matter of life and death. Today's mission came under the heading of pure trivia.

He and Edith had been planning such a Saturday as this for several weeks, without having found the time to do anything about it. The New York winter had been unkind to some of the hundreds of plants with which Edith had filled their double brownstone house in the sixties off Fifth Avenue. Now that March had come – and almost gone – Edith had wanted to visit several nurseries in New Jersey to find replacements for the dead and dying.

"The cut-leaf philodendron on the third floor," she had announced that morning at breakfast, "has gone into shock. This town does weird things to plants. It's the air, I believe, or lack of it. The old leaves have turned gray, and the new leaves are yellow."

Watching her mother with huge, mock solemn eyes, Gerri had put down a piece of toast from which she had bitten an exact semicircle. "If you want, Maw," she murmured solicitously, "I'll lead the poor thang behind the barn and put a forty-five slug through its skull."

"See?" her older brother, Woody, grunted. "This town doesn't only do weird things to plants."

He gave Gerri a giant fake smile, pushed back from the table and got to his feet. At eighteen, he now stood three inches over six feet, which gave him an inch on Palmer. Woody already outweighed his rather thin father by fifty pounds.

Watching him gallumph out of the room, Palmer found himself thinking that the line between a growing oaf and a mature slob was getting narrower. He turned to Edith.

"Can we put him in the Youth Corps this summer?"

Edith frowned. "Woods, I believe today actually is the day."

"For what?"

"For driving to New Jersey. Have the bank send around a big car for us."

Palmer considered for a moment. Only the custodial people and a three-man audit team were on duty at the bank's main office this Saturday. He would have to telephone his driver, Jimmy, at home and have him waste part of his day off. Palmer would go to any length to avoid doing this, not because Jimmy would complain or feel put upon, but rather because Palmer held very strict ideas about off-duty time. He had held them now for at least six months and, like any new idea, he was overwhelmingly devoted to it.

Roughly phrased, Palmer believed he owed it to himself, now that he was nearly forty-six, and to Ubco, the bank he served as president, to Take It Easier. This meant cutting down on the deadly social-business events of nearly every evening, the interminable political and charitable dinners to which executives of banks as huge as Ubco were invited. It meant not bringing paperwork home. It meant keeping weekends free. And if it meant this to Palmer, he was determined to extend the concept to his employees, or at least to those whose lives, like Jimmy's, he directly controlled.

Thinking all these things, he had said: "We'll need a station wagon, and the bank has Continentals. I'll rent a car."

The way it finally sorted itself out, the two boys voted to stay home. The youngest, Tim, was to do the schoolwork he had neglected all week. Mrs. Gage would give both boys lunch. Gerri, who not only kept up with her schoolwork but was usually a week ahead of the teacher, would drive to New Jersey with Pamer and Edith.

And now he had gotten them lost. It didn't really bother him that much, Palmer realized now as he turned onto N.J. 4 for perhaps the third time. The sky was a deep, brilliant blue, nicely accented by white clouds on the horizon. The sky in Sicily that day had been the same brilliant Mediterranean blue, but there had been no clouds, and the July air had been hot and chalky. Today the March weather was still chilly with the dying taste of winter. Nevertheless, Palmer had opened the window on his side to inhale immense drafts of cold, clear air.

If one had to be lost, he reflected, it was a good day for it. And he was still the only one who knew they were lost.

"Dad?" Gerri's voice from the back seat was an uncanny imitation of Edith's.

Palmer glanced into the rear-view mirror. Because he had neglected to adjust it before they started out, instead of seeing Gerri he saw himself. His face seemed somewhat more drawn than usual. Palmer knew he normally looked a bit gaunt; he preferred it to being overweight. But the hollows under his high cheekbones looked deeper than usual. The wind had ruffled his blond hair and thrown a lock of it down over his right eyebrow. He watched his dark gray eyes in the mirror, wondering why they looked so odd, almost empty, as if they led back into nothing at all.

Grimacing, he twisted the mirror to its proper setting and eyed Gerri. "What is it?"

"Is this the second or third time we've passed that furniture store?"

Palmer's thin, wide mouth twisted in a crooked grin. Of all his children, only Gerri would notice such a thing, and only Gerri would have enough confidence in herself to say it aloud.

"What furniture store?"

"You know. The one we keep passing."

"Woods," Edith asked, "are we lost?"

"In a manner of speaking."

11

"What is that supposed to mean?"

Palmer sighed, so softly and with so little force that Edith could not know he had sighed. In the last year since he had settled down to the running of United Bank and Trust Company as its chief executive officer, his relations with Edith had improved only very slightly, if at all. The family was pretty well settled in New York, after having spent most of their lives in Chicago. The frenzy of their first year or two was behind them now. Uprooted, they had rerooted and seemed to be flourishing. It was high time, Palmer felt, that the coolness between Edith and him began to thaw, at least enough to improve her temper.

He supposed now, as he often had in the last year, that she had somehow gotten wind of his one big extramarital affair. It had been messy enough that some inkling could have reached her. Palmer had no training whatsoever in the East Coast mode of infidelity. He had bulled ahead, Midwest style, to the very brink of disaster. He knew better now. He understood how Manhattan marriages were managed and the crucial role discretion played in them. He felt that Edith should have sensed this change in him and in some way forced a change in herself. So that when she spoke sharply, as she had now, with that steely edge of venom to her voice, it pained him to realize that they were still as far apart as they had ever been.

"What does 'in a manner of speaking' mean?" she persisted coldly. "One is either lost or not lost."

"Sort of like being pregnant," Gerri put in helpfully.

Palmer pulled the heavy station wagon off the road onto the grassy shoulder. After he braked to a halt, he sat without speaking for a moment, trying to remain as coherent and as calm as possible. It seemed very important to him, in line with his recent decisions to Take It Easier, that he remain as cool as he could under the circumstances.

"First," he began, "we are lost only in the technical sense. That is, we know generally where we are but have not yet zeroed in on our precise destination. Second, we —"

"Spare me," Edith cut in. She began looking through her handbag. "I have written directions here somewhere. Agnes gave them to me over the phone."

"We can forget Agnes' directions," Palmer said flatly. "We have no need of them. I said I would get you to this accursed place, and get you there I will."

"Shall," Gerri edited.

"What?"

"*Shall* means more than futurity. It connotes necessity or a sense of predestination."

There was a rather long pause. "The question is closed," Palmer said then. "I *shall* not speak again."

Silently he reviewed what little he remembered of the map. Then he shifted into drive and moved out onto the highway again. By his calculations he was heading north. The particular nursery Edith hoped to visit was known simply as Amato's. Friends had recommended it as having a greater number and variety of plants than any other in the area. Palmer tried now to recall every scrap of information Edith had given him.

From a peaceful, relaxing Saturday in the country, Palmer realized he had somehow turned it into a test of his ability. He wondered whether he had deliberately done so, whether he had purposely left the map at home and forgotten to ask the Hertz people for another.

"Stop at this filling station," Edith suggested. "They'll give you directions."

Palmer said nothing as he drove past the filling station. He rarely asked directions of any local. Few of them knew enough to more than confuse the driver passing through. But he especially would refuse to ask directions on this particular morning.

He felt his breathing speed up. Something peculiar was happening to him. His mind had started to race back and forth over the meagre clues he could remember. The name of the nursery, Amato's. The road it was on, something like Old Country Place or Old Country Lane. The town, something like Cloverdale or Clovertown or Cloverville or something else. The direction, north from the bridge, then west. The distance, under ten miles.

"There's a police car," Edith said. "Stop and ask him."

Palmer drove past the car. He checked the position of the sun and at the next big intersection turned left. He sincerely hoped that left meant west. All of a sudden a lot seemed to be riding on inane decisions like that.

He found himself remembering that July morning in Sicily. He wondered if he were cracking up in some subtle way. Men did at his age, the male climacteric and all that nonsense.

He almost never thought about that mission in Sicily. He hadn't remembered it in perhaps ten years or more. It was not a good memory. Nothing had seemed to go right that day or in the week thereafter.

But it would go right today.

Palmer wondered why he attached so much importance to the trap he had worked himself into on this sunny Saturday. He wondered how he could square his sudden eagerness to take chances with his determination to Take It Easier. Was it his way of showing up Edith? Showing off for Gerri? Why had he need to do either? Or was it change of life, for God's sake?

Out of the corner of his eye, he saw a small sign set far back in the scrubby underbrush along the roadway. Old Something.

Palmer tramped on the brakes and swerved off onto the shoulder. He checked the rear-view mirror, found the road empty in both directions and put the station wagon into a screeching 180-degree turn that sent it careening back in the direction from which they had come.

"Woods!"

"Whoo-ee!" Gerri hooted.

Palmer spun the wheel again and made a sharp left turn into a two-lane road called Old Furnace Drive. The rear wheels of the station wagon dug into the gravel and howled wildly before they gripped. The car shot forward in a sudden burst of speed. Within a few seconds Palmer caught sight of a small white sign with green lettering. He braked to a halt.

"Amato's," he read, pointing. "I have spoken."

The three of them sat there staring at the sign and, beyond it, at the immense complex of greenhouses rising slightly into the distance. The clean air of March let the sunlight pour down unchecked on the whitewashed glass windows, touching off an intense glare in which patches of clear glass glinted like snowflakes. The surrounded greenery, softly pale with tiny new leaves, seemed to vibrate with the intensity of the sun.

"Let's hear it for Dad," Gerri said. "Hip-hip –"

"Sarcasm will get you nowhere," Palmer cut in.

He surveyed the brilliant landscape. Then, directly overhead, a cloud passed across the face of the sun. It hovered for a moment in the wind. All warmth seemed to be blotted out of the scene. The crisp blacks, the blazing whites, the pale greens went muddy gray. The air grew chilly.

Palmer shuddered.

2

Ben Fischetti sat down cross-legged on the thick earth-red pile of the rug in his living room. He was wearing chino slacks, a heavy, off-white Irish knit sweater and dark brown loafers. An immense picture window allowed the bright sun to shine directly on Fischetti's close-cut, glossy black hair. At the age of twenty-eight he had begun to find an occasional gray hair, but he told himself this was normal for a brunet. Now the Saturday sun of March made the crisp mat of hair seem to crackle with electric brilliance.

He winked at his son, Barney, who sat cross-legged on the floor beside him. ("Barney?" Papa Fischetti had asked. "What da hell kinda name is Barney?" But his baptismal certificate read Bartolomeo Gaetano Fischetti, the Gaetano for Papa. It was Fischetti's hope that Bartolomeo would shorten nicely later in life, the way his own name had. Born Benedetto, he had been just plain Ben since his freshman year at West Point.)

"All set, buddy-baby-boy?" Fischetti asked Barney.

"All set, Pop."

Fischetti attached the leads from the transformer to the clips at the edge of the miniature racetrack. He carefully fitted his own car, a model of a Shelby GT-350 no longer than a matchbox, onto the racetrack. The delicate wire brush under the car's nose made contact through the slot to the electrical conduit hidden beneath.

"What do you want this time, Barney, the Jag?"

Barney's fingers were fairly deft for a seven-year-old's. He fitted the long, lean Jaguar XKE to the slot, picked up the speed control and triggered off the car, sending it hurtling around a bend and dashing down a straightaway.

"No fair," Fischetti said. He gunned the Shelby and sent it chasing after the Jaguar.

The two dueled for fifteen minutes, one gaining, then the other. Finally, with Barney's car in the lead, Fischetti called out "Last lap!" The two tiny autos whirred around another circuit. Fischetti eased off his speed control slightly, not too much. Barney liked to win, but he knew when a race was obviously being thrown.

Ben Fischetti found himself wondering whether he was doing Barney any favor letting him win this way. His own father had never in his life deliberately lost a game of cards or *boccie* to his son. Fischetti could remember very clearly his father's excitement when his son, Ben, had beaten him for the first time. Ben had been damned near seventeen, he recalled now, before he got good enough to beat Papa. And the event had been all the greater for being so long in coming.

Fischetti sat back and looked around the living room. The bright March sun filled the entire place with pale yellow light, setting the Etruscan red of the carpeting on fire and igniting the salmon of the upholstered furniture to a bright, burning orange.

Typical wop taste, Fischetti thought, salmon pink and terra-cotta. He wondered for a moment why Rosalie hadn't gone all the way and papered the walls in a bright green.

Immediately he felt guilty, even though he knew Rosalie wasn't his responsibility, not really. Uncle Vincenzo had chosen her for Ben. Rosalie and Celia were his only children, given very late in life by his second wife. For him to confer one of the girls on a young man was to confer knighthood. Goddamned incestuous xenophobic greenhorn nonsense.

Not that Uncle Vincenzo was a real uncle, or Rosalie a cousin. True, they were all related back in Palermo or Catania, but Vincenzo Biglioto could not be any closer than a third or fourth cousin to Ben's father. That was close enough, Fischetti recalled now.

But the whole thing was ludicrous. He helped Barney pack away the little cars and dismantle the racetrack.

To think that cute little Rosalie Biglioto, who graduated from Sacred Heart with a respectable C-plus average and promptly jumped headlong into marriage, could ever make it with Ben Fischetti. Forget it. Not possible. The odds against Fischetti making it with Rosalie were even worse, he reflected. How many West Point graduates could you name who resigned their Army commission a year out of college and took a master's in economics at the University of Chicago's School of Business Administration?

("Of Chicago?" Papa had asked. "What da hell kinda school is Chicago?" Later, of course, they told Papa Gaetano about the school. He had friends check up on it for him, or something. "My Benny, he goes to a genius school, is what. To get in, you gotta be a genius. My Benny." Which helped make up for resigning his commission in the Corps of Engineers. He had never been quite sure why Gaetano Fischetti had schemed

16

and muscled his son into West Point. Nor did he want to examine the connections necessary to have a New Jersey boy appointed to the college by a Senator from Nevada. All he knew was that the Point was one hell of a wasteful way to get an engineering degree.)

Ben glanced at his watch. It was nearly time for lunch. He'd promised to take Barney into town. Rosalie had left with the girls earlier in the day, and they were all supposed to meet at Casa Coppola for lunch. It would be a big family picture. He and Rosalie still had their looks, and the kids were all winners. The elderly gents at the bar or in the back room would beam at the five Fischettis and mutter, "'At's Don Vincenzo's grand-kids." They seldom referred to the children as Tano Fischetti's grandkids. Or, for that matter, Ben Fischetti's daughters and son.

("Ben Fischetti? What da hell kinda Fischetti is he that anybody should notice him?" What did he ever do except run the ball thirty-seven yards against Navy for a touchdown in a game Army won 7–0? That's all, just beat Navy single-handed. What did he ever do except cop a master's at the U of C in a year and a half, all As at that? And get to be the youngest bank V.P. in Westchester County.)

He and Barney put away the slot-car racetrack, changed to more somber clothes and left the house by way of the side door in the kitchen that led into the garage. Rosalie had taken the Buick Riviera for herself. Fischetti and his son got into the Karmann-Ghia (which Ben preferred), put the top down and roared off along the side streets of Scarsdale to the Saw Mill River Parkway.

As they drove down a winding street heading west, Fischetti saw one of the Old Man's trucks backed up in the driveway of an immense estate. "Amato Nurseries," he told Barney, point-ing.

"Great-grampa's." The boy sounded either bored or smug, Fischetti couldn't tell which. He wondered how Don Vincenzo would feel about Barney's reaction to the fabled forebear, the Old Man.

("What da hell kinda respect is that for a snotnose to show his great-grandpa? You teach him wrong, Benny. You don't show enough respect yourself. Not for your father. Not for me. That's enough of a mistake right there, Benny. But when it comes to the Old Man, you better unteach that kid of yours and learn him right.")

17

The open Karmann-Ghia swerved around a ramp and fed into the traffic heading southward along the parkway to New York City. Ben Fischetti turned and grinned happily at Barney. "This is the life, huh, Barney baby?"

"Great," the boy responded.

He seemed sincere enough about that, Fischetti thought. Maybe Uncle Vincenzo was right. Maybe he hadn't taught Barney enough respect. So what? Respect for whom? Why?

A bunch of greenhorns, still clinging to their old life in Sicily? Some of them were even born here, but the deadly vinegar of Sicily ran in their veins. What could you say about his father, Gaetano Fischetti, who came to the States as a boy of six and still spoke with a Palermo accent? They were laughable, even the grandest of them. Uncle Vincenzo Biglioto, the archetypical Sicilian father-in-law, was as funny as the rest. The newspapers never failed to refer to him in parentheses by his nickname, Vinnie Big. The hilarity came from the fact that in the old days Uncle Vincenzo had a sidekick named Guglielmo Smaldone, nicknamed Willy Small.

He braked the little car hard to avoid being cut in on by an immense Olds Toronado. Baring his teeth, Fischetti tramped on the accelerator and heard the iron stroke of the Volkswagen motor in his car change to an urgent roar. The open car picked up speed and howled past the Toronado. Fischetti cut in front of the monster and slowed down to make his opponent brake suddenly, as he had had to do before.

Finito. Paid in full.

Ben Fischetti glanced at Barney. The boy's eyes were bright. He hadn't missed a second of the interplay.

"Great, Pop. Great."

Barney digs the same things I do, Fischetti thought, but I don't dig anything the way my father does. There had to be a break in the chain, he decided, and it had come when Gaetano Fischetti maneuvered his Ben into West Point.

So it's a whole new Fischetti family, Ben thought now. Good-bye, you smelly old bastards with the oily paper bag full of roasted peppers in your baggy suit pockets. Good-bye, respect for respect's sake. Let all respect be earned from now on.

Fischetti patted Barney on the head. He intended to see to it that what he did from now on would earn Barney's respect.

3

It took only a moment for a salesman to identify Edith and begin Mrs. Palmering her. It seemed that she had telephoned ahead to Amato's nursery, quite as if making a reservation at a hotel. Although the man was dressed rather informally in blue denim dungarees and a sports shirt, he approached Edith with the same ambivalent air, Palmer noted, that most salesmen had when about to lock horns with a knowledgeable female customer, part deference, part flirtatiousness, part hatred.

Palmer stood there like a vestigial appendage for several minutes, listening to Edith and the salesman set down the ground rules for today's shopping expedition. Palmer noted that Gerri's eyes had already begun to glaze under the thunderous drone of rhododendrons and philodendrons and icosahedrons.

Palmer sidled over to a wall display demonstrating in aggressively unretouched photographs the results of seeding half a lawn with ordinary, unfortified grass seed and of planting the other half with Agrivade, containing five different seed types, four antibug nostrums, three growth hormones and two kinds of manure.

And a partridge in pear tree, Palmer told himself, sidling still farther from Edith's incessant murmuring about smilax, taxis and clematis. How could there ever be more than one kind of manure?

He knew, even as he wandered away from the office area, that he was behaving rather strangely. He had no real reason to be peeved at Edith. Her wifely digs at Palmer's navigational troubles were pretty much just what he had deserved. Only luck and his own sense of direction had saved him from the usual comic-father fate. Deserting her now, while it didn't bother her in the slightest, was a rather childish rejection counterplay she didn't deserve and he almost never employed. Besides, it was rude to both Edith and Gerri.

Nevertheless, Palmer noted, he continued to drift away from Edith. He was not only out of sight but certainly out of earshot. As a matter of fact, he was out of the building entirely, staring at the parking lot from a new angle of view. He noted automatically that of the dozen cars parked there, including his, eight were station wagons. He wondered, again automatically, if Amato's Saturday morning customers usually ran over 66 percent to station wagons.

Christ, he thought, once a banker always a banker.

He hated the idea that on a calm, quiet Saturday devoted to Taking It Easier, he could still not stop himself from the automatic computation of what he still could not stop himself from observing.

He sat down on a sample cast-concrete bench, noting the price tag – "$78.89, inc. delivery." Sitting forward, hands on kneecaps, he watched another station wagon pull into the parking lot. Up from 66 to 75 percent. A family got out and trailed into the main office building, youngish father and mother, preteen children, and finally, an extremely elderly woman who seemed to be the parents' grandmother, rather than mother.

He watched her struggle to get out of the station wagon. Her family had already disappeared inside the office, as if not suspecting and certainly not wanting to suspect that Great-Grandma needed a little help through the badly engineered doorway of the station wagon. The twisting seemed to cost her quite a bit of pain. Palmer started to get up, then realized she had finally extricated herself.

He watched her make her way along the uneven gravel path, grimacing now and then when her foot turned slightly as she stepped into a depression. Hell to get old, Palmer thought. Who is there to care?

He felt his lips tighten in a grimace that mimicked the old woman's gesture of pain. And she hadn't accomplished any of the things she'd planned in her youth. Nobody does.

He'd had his own plans. He'd never been a particularly unrestrained or imaginative boy. His older brother Hanley, who'd never returned from a training flight out of Pensacola early in the war, had been the brother with a flair for gaiety and roughhouse. Where Hanley had imagined great conquests – a flight around the world like Wiley Post or perhaps a secret war against the crime lords who ruled Chicago – Palmer had been content to see himself as a doctor, saving the lives of grateful thousands, or a statesman carefully guiding his countrymen through troubled waters of political intrigue.

As he sat on the concrete bench, Palmer realized his boyish dreams had been pretty dull stuff. Hanley had said as much and razzed him unmercifully about it. In retrospect, Palmer understood now that there was something faintly comic about a young boy wanting a career in politics. He might as well

20

have chosen sewer engineering or actuarial statistics.

But of course, he'd not done any of the things he'd planned. He'd studied neither medicine nor law. Instead, and with only the B.A. to his name, he'd simply done what he was told. Bankers' sons usually end up bankers, Palmer realized. Too much was at stake to let them freely choose their destiny. They might choose to flee the bank. Then father would be forced to leave his prized possession in the hands of strangers. No, blood is always thicker than money.

Palmer got to his feet slowly, feeling as aged and infirm as the old woman who had gotten out of the station wagon.

There was nobody to care, Palmer repeated to himself. Suddenly one day you were finished, over the hill, no more time left to do any of the things you'd wanted to do, no time left to be the man you'd wanted to be.

He started back into the building. He was thoroughly chilled now, and it seemed to him that the tremor in his jaw would soon start his teeth chattering.

He pulled himself up short, aware that he was maundering. Leaning against a rough wooden wall, he tried to tell himself that he had, in fact, become the man he'd wanted to be. Was there any question, for example, that he was an immense success as the world counted successes? In all the country no bank was as large as Ubco, and he was its chief executive officer, not at age sixty or sixty-five, damn it.

To have accomplished something worthwhile, he told himself; that was success. To have, in a corny phrase, left the world a better place; that was success. To have placed one's mark on the world for all to remember with pleasure or wonder or joy; that was success.

But to manage to slip blandly through life in one piece, skin whole, pores open and mouth shut, the very model of a modern major organization man, was not success. It was too cheap. And it left the world without a mark of any kind to say that someone named Palmer had passed through it and would not be forgotten.

Palmer began to wander around the labyrinth of the greenhouses, searching for something. It wasn't Edith or Gerri, he knew, nor was it the office. And it wasn't fame. And it wasn't youth.

He had no idea what it was. But the absence of it seemed to squeeze his heart into a gnarled black thing.

He wandered from room to room. There was no sound

behind him, yet he seemed to hear the footsteps of something following, something inanimate and hostile.

In twenty years, Palmer thought, I may be dead, in twenty-five, certainly. And meanwhile, what is it all about?

4

Harry Klaman told himself it was tough enough doing business in the New York area, what with the unions and the politicos and the *gonifs*. And on top of all that, no matter what, you couldn't keep from getting all balled up in interstate commerce, too.

Harry had left his family fast asleep in the ten-room apartment on the penthouse floor of the building his company had put up a few years before on Park Avenue in the low seventies. Having left the house rather early this Saturday morning, hoping to beat the rush out to Long Island, Harry now found himself, an hour later, squeezed behind the wheel of his Thunderbird, the car motionless in a bumper-to bumper jam up between exits 36 and 37 on the Long Island Expressway.

Harry sneered at a sign that read: "Speed Limit 55." Then he stared for a long moment at a large group of one-family detached homes, row on row of them, that had been built almost, but not quite, up to the very edge of the parkway.

Kids living in those houses, Harry thought, died young.

He blinked, realizing he had himself built this particular subdivision nearly ten years before. He grimaced and turned away to survey the triple line of stalled cars, bright sunlight shimmering on their roofs.

Harry switched on the radio and, for the second time, heard the helicopter spy-in-the-sky tell all the boobs in radioland that traffic on the expressway was "moderate to heavy, but moving freely."

"Another *gonif*," Harry muttered aloud as he turned off the radio.

Under the warm March sun, with all the car windows closed tightly against the exhaust and dust, the air in the Thunderbird had grown unreasonably warm. A coarse dew sprang up on Harry's forehead and the patch of scalp above it where his hair was in steady retreat. His temples grew moist, and so did the carefully brushed-back hair over his ears.

He dabbed automatically at all these spots with a large, clean

22

handkerchief. The gesture was unconscious. As a fairly heavy man, Harry had learned to live with sweat. Blotting it away seldom distracted him from the main problems of his life, nor did it now sidetrack him long enough to think of turning on the car's air conditioner. In a lifetime devoted to solving more major problems than the One on High had ever visited on Job himself, Harry could not remember more of them, and more pressing ones at that, than he had right now.

The man driving the car behind him leaned hard on his horn. Harry flinched, then realized that a space some two cars in depth had opened up ahead of him. He had committed the most unpardonable sin of the jammed-up motorist. He had Left a Gap.

Harry took his foot from the brake pedal and let the Thunderbird inch slowly, tantalizingly forward. This teasing earned him a wild fusillade of hoots and yelps from the congestion-maddened drivers behind him. He swiveled weightily around in his seat and glared at them.

"Honk, *gonifs*, honk! And when you get tired honking, play with your windshield wipers."

He turned back, glanced at the dashboard clock and picked up the telephone from the spring-loaded clip under the front ashtray. Harry asked the mobile operator for a number and waited. Traffic had come unstuck somewhere up ahead, and the cars were beginning to move.

"Klaman Company. Good morning."

"Harriet, this is Mr. Klaman. Get me maintenance."

"I'm sorry, Mr. Klaman. There's no one in the department yet."

"Where's Healey?"

"He called in sick a little while ago."

"Schwartz?"

"This is his Saturday off."

Harry paused for a moment. "Tell me something. Do any of our tenants have a Saturday off? Are they busting pipes and clogging up toilets and blowing main fuses only on weekdays?"

"I'm sorry, Mr. Klaman. I could –"

"You could call Healey at home and tell him to call me in the car."

Harry slammed the phone back in its clip. The cars were moving now. The Thunderbird's speedometer crept all the way up to five miles per hour.

23

The big trouble with doing business in New York, Harry told himself now as he settled back in the car, was the clogged-up physical layout of the damned thing.

Manhattan was like the hairy body sac of one of those tropical spiders. The brains and the guts were there. But the way Harry operated, the arms and legs were spread over three states without even half trying. One leg, he thought, sprawled to the south-east, via Brooklyn and Queens, into Long Island where all the speedy parkways were. One leg drooped south into Staten Island. A third extended north through the Bronx into Westchester. Fine, so far, and all in one state. But the spider had more legs. There was a short western leg that straddled the Hudson River and landed in New Jersey. And there was the north-east leg that reached into Connecticut.

If a man did business properly, smartly, successfully, actively and expandingly – and if any words accurately described Harry Klaman's operation, these were the ones – then he ended up in interstate commerce. Everyting got more expensive, riskier, more subject to the idiot whims of under-educated public servants who, because they were on the federal level, couldn't be approached in the normal way through the normal channels with the normal bribes.

To overall problems like these, Harry had recently added a new and unsettlingly immediate one. He could sense a growing uneasiness at certain levels of the management of his prime lending institution, the People's Bank of Westchester. They seemed somewhat reluctant to set up a new round of home-improvement loans for Harry's one-family-home customers in Mamaroneck and Greenwich, a growing number of whom were defaulting.

Now as everybody knows, Harry told himself, the builder who loses his prime lender loses the entire collection of crown jewels, balls and all. No lender, no builder. No credit, no construction.

He saw an opening ahead and rammed the Thunderbird through between two cars.

The reluctance at People's Bank, Harry knew, was only temporary. The top brass was trying to set things straight before the long-discussed merger with Ubco took place. Ubco was United Bank and Trust Company, the largest bank in the country, larger even than Bank of America. It had taken Ubco almost exactly one decade to fight its way through a maze of contradictory rulings by state and federal banking agencies and

24

the Justice Department before it had finally received a very grudging go-ahead on its plans to buy People's.

Now that the deal was actually going to begin to start to commence, Harry recalled, People's had a lot of sloppy odds and ends that needed cleaning up or, more likely, sweeping under the rug.

It was true, of course, Harry told himself, that People's did an awful lot of consumer lending on the poorest kind of collateral. But so did a lot of banks. Without shit as collateral, half the lines of credit in this country would have dried up long ago.

And mine along with them, Harry thought.

He would have to goose them a little at People's. Merger or no merger, he wanted money for his customers, and People's had goddamned better supply it. He picked up his phone and gave the operator another number.

After many rings, a man's tight voice answered. "Yeh?"

"This is Harry. Gimme Vinnie."

"Yeh."

After a pause, a richer, deeper, more generous voice: "Hello, Harry, goombar. How's my *paisano* Harry?"

"Vinnie, I gotta see you for lunch. I got a date at ten thirty in Babylon, and then I'll take the Throg's Neck Bridge back into Westchester. Lunch about one fifteen?"

"Sure thing, Harry."

"*Ciao.*" Harry hung up the phone. A lunch date was all right to make over the mobile telephone. Everybody knew he and Vinnie were friendly. But at lunch, Vinnie had better promise a few results.

And that little *gonif* son-in-law of his at the bank had better pay off on the promises.

5

The greenhouses stretched on for miles.

Palmer had no way of knowing how large Amato's actually was, how many acres or square miles were under cultivation. But just the acreage under glass was impressive enough.

Knowing he was lost, but not particularly caring, Palmer wandered idly from one greenhouse to the next. They were laid out like teeth on a double-edged comb, with a long spine building that connected with each along a dark corridor.

25

The air was rich with a loamy smell, part earth, part mold, part moisture and part the very faint perfume green leaves put forth. Diffused light filtered down from the whitewash-spattered glass overhead. Here and there, unattended sprinklers sent a fine mist over a particular row of tables on which stood plants in pots.

Not all the individual bays were empty of people. In a place this large, Palmer decided, an army could disperse almost openly. But from time to time he came across a single person, or a pair of them, working at some small, peaceful task. He stopped behind a pair of old women who, despite the moist heat, where bundled up in sweaters, with faded babushkas on their heads and woolly knit lap blankets draped over their shoulders.

They stood before a long table set against a wall. At some previous time in the slowed-down, leisurely tempo of this place, Pamer realized, someone had dumped several barrow loads of rich, black earth on the table, shoveling it back against the wall to make a steep hill. Now the hill was covered with profusion of tiny green shoots, each of them no more than two inches high, all bearing twin serrated leaves at their very tips.

The women worked with a pile of tiny terra-cotta pots at their elbow. They would fill a pot with as much earth as their gnarled hand could scoop up, pat it down in the pot and poke a hole in the center. Then the same crooked fingers, joints knobbly with arthritis, would delicately ease a single shoot from its own earth and gently tease its white taproot into the hole in the potted earth. A few downpressings to secure the stem and the pot was placed on a large, flat wooden tray.

Palmer stayed there no more than a few minutes. Neither woman worked terribly quickly. They were both too old for that. Yet in the time he watched them, they had peacefully potted a dozen shoots between them.

He moved on, believing himself unobserved. Behind him the women began to speak quietly in clacking Polish.

He frowned, trying to remember what little Polish he had once known in the war. As a major in Army Intelligence, Palmer had headed up T-Force units on various fronts in Europe. His job had been to race in just ahead of advancing Allied troops and scoop up as much material and key people as the Nazis had left behind. G-2 had given Palmer short courses in such wildly varied languages as Polish, German,

26

Italian, Norwegian and Dutch. But of course, the choice of languages had been no wilder than the choice of theaters of action to which Palmer had been assigned.

Strolling from one greenhouse bay to the next, totally ignorant of all plant and flower names, Palmer began to feel a great sense of peace. The brooding quiet of the place helped, he realized. Its tempo was keyed to the slow growth of greenery. And with nothing but an occasional hiss of water spray, how much noise did plants make growing? But the color was immensely peaceful, too. Green and black, black and green extended along endless vistas, light yellowish greens and deep bluish ones, dark black shadows under the long potting tables, striped zebra patches under the roofs of glass. It all seemed remote and out-of-date and peaceful.

"Jimmy G., Jimmy G., wanted at the front office."

Palmer stood still, his wandering arrested by the woman's voice from some hidden loudspeaker. The peace was shattered.

"Jimmy G., Jimmy G., front office, please."

Resuming his stroll, Palmer decided that a place as scattered out as this one had obviously to be tied together with some kind of intercom system. But the intrusion of the sound had broken the spell. Palmer was back in the second half of the twentieth century and not at all happy about it.

Now, too, he became aware of the amount of time he had spent wandering. Edith and Gerri would long ago have concluded their shopping tour. They would be waiting impatiently now.

Palmer turned on his heels and started back along the way he had come, trusting to his sense of direction. He passed the two women potting shoots. He passed a spraying room he remembered. Then he reached a cross corridor that forced him to make a choice of left or right. He took the right instinctively and walked past dozens of greenhouse bays, looking exactly like all the others he had seen.

After fifteen minutes, Palmer acknowledged that he was no closer to the front office. He had, as a matter of fact, passed the two Polish ladies twice. Catching sight of a telephone, he picked it up and jiggled the hook.

"Yes?" a woman's voice asked.

"I'm a customer, and I'm lost."

The woman laughed. "What's the number on the phone there?"

"M-seventeen."

"Okay. Just stay by the phone. We'll send somebody." Palmer could hear her laughing continue until she unplugged his line.

Smiling slightly, Palmer sat down on the edge of a wheelbarrow near the telephone. After a while he heard a sound in the distance that was new, neither the hiss of spray nor the murmur of women. It was a high, grinding sound, thin at first, then fuller. He stared along the green and black corridor. Then he saw it.

A small, wizened old man sat at the wheel of an electric golf cart, his faded eyes squinting through tinted glasses as he moved cautiously ahead. The whine of the cart's motor filled the corridor. Then the cart wheezed, squealed softly and came to a halt in front of Palmer.

"*Buon giorno,*" the little old man said.

Palmer smiled and bobbed his head. A faint aroma of garlic and roasted green peppers began to reach him.

"*Smarrito?*"

"Yes, I'm the one." Palmer got onto the front seat next to the old man. "Thank you very much for finding me. You got here very quickly."

The old man's mouth turned down at both corners in a grimace of self-deprecation. "Is the cart *batteria*, she need *caricare*. Recharge. *Capito?*"

"*Si, capisco.*"

The old man's large, pale eyes glanced sideways at Palmer as he put the cart in motion. "You come with you family? Palmer, Mr. Palmer, *si?*"

"Yes."

"*Bene.* I am Biglioto."

The old man extended a small hand toward Palmer. The aroma of stale roasted peppers grew stronger. Palmer shook the hand and found it unusually dry, with a surface like slightly crumpled tissue paper.

"Mr. Biglioto," he repeated, pronouncing it as the old man had, Bil-yoto, the vowel sounds closed, Beel-yaw-toe. Palmer's mind clicked back through its files and miraculously produced a phrase. "*E un piacere vedervi.*"

Something further crawled very faintly in the back of Palmer's mind, something from long ago, mixed up with Italian. But what?

The cart stopped at the intersection of two corridors. Biglioto gestured down one to where Palmer could see people near

28

the front office. "Easy from here," the old man said. *"Venite a trovarci ancora."*

Palmer jumped off the cart. "Many thanks."

The old man mumbled something and steered the cart off along another corridor, leaving Palmer alone. When he got to the front office, the girl at the switchboard was talking to someone over the telephone.

"He's got to be near the M-seventeen station. Keep looking."

"I'm here," Palmer said. "Mr. Biglioto brought me back in his cart."

The girl turned to him. "Who?"

Palmer gestured meaninglessly. "You know, the little old man, Mr. Biglioto."

The girl's eyes widened slightly. Then her face went dead. Into the telephone, in a flat, noncommittal voice, she said: "Forget it, Frankie. Don Girolamo picked him up." A pause. "You heard me," she said and cut off the conversation. Then she glanced up at Palmer. "I believe your family is waiting for you in the car." She eyed him curiously, but said nothing more.

Palmer nodded and left. Girolamo Biglioto. Something bothered Palmer all the way back to New York, but after a while he forgot about it.

6

Sean O'Malley's reddish-blond hair had begun to recede along two paths on either side of his lengthening widow's peak. They had retreated so rapidly over the past year that Sean pictured leprechauns with power mowers giving his scalp the final once-over-lightly.

Since he had arrived in America three years before, Sean had so assiduously cultivated fake Irishisms that now he often found himself thinking in outrageous Ould Sod conceits. Today, alone in the office on Seventh Avenue near 38th Street, the workrooms closed for Saturday, Sean went over some sketches for cocktail numbers. He sighed unhappily.

The sketches were fine, but business wasn't. He got up and walked slowly to the window, his gait lethargic and uncertain, not at all the bright, twinkling step he showed the world on weekdays. Looking out the windows and down at the almost empty streets, Sean wondered who else was in as much trouble as Mod Modes, Inc.

In the garment center, he reflected, the buildings were almost as tall as hotels. And despite the fact that they had businesses as tenants, the check-in, check-out traffic was as brisk as a hotel's. Companies were born, flourished, withered and died in bankruptcy with such regularity that about the only workers in the garment center absolutely certain of year-round employment were the sign painters who lettered doors.

The bright March sun hit Sean head on and put a reflection of his head and upper torso in the window. He automatically adjusted the elf-lock fringe of near-bangs which he had recently cultivated to hide the ravages of the Little People with the power mowers. The bangs made him look even more faggoty, of course, but by now he was beyond caring.

In the garment trade a little faggotry went a long way, especially if you were a novice designer fresh from London with a lumbering name like Edward O'Malley Cranksworthy, Jr. Even if your mother, née Mary O'Malley, was only half Irish, you did a little fancy footwork and out came a name that sounded like something more ... uh ... creative.

Sean simpered at his reflection, hating it. He had just gone through the whole thing for the past two weeks with Dr. Apfelshpein, painfully retracing his name change in terms of father hatred and mother fixation, getting nowhere and finally giving up because Dr. Apfelshpein, for all his degrees and his certificates on the wall, couldn't grasp the simple fact that when you designed dress, you wouldn't get anywhere in life as Ed Cranksworthy.

As a matter of fact, Sean had been meaning to point out to Dr. Apfelshpein that even in his line of work he'd do better slimmed down to Dr. Apple or something that was less of a gob of spit that landed on your lapel. Sean giggled. And ditch that hokey goatee, too, he told Dr. Apfelshpein mentally.

His face went dead, and he turned away from the reflection in the window. How crazy could you get, he wondered, paying Dr. Apfelshpein thirty-five dollars an hour twice a week just so you could poke fun at him.

"And these episodes of homosexual fantasy," the doctor would begin, ponderously, slowly.

"Ah, yes, well, as to that," Sean would hedge, "you see, we don't quite make as much of them at home as you people seem to do in the States. More of a kind of way-of-life type thing,

30

you know."

And so on. And on. Sean told himself now, as he sat down at his drawing table again, that one always had to pay the admission price. His admission to the designing field had been to let one or two of the better connected designers work him over for a few months. June and July he had spent with Phil in a remote Fire Island community called Talisman. August and September he'd been Augie's guest at Ischia, in the jolly blue Med.

And really, there hadn't been such a hell of a lot of bad scenes after all, since he was playing the passive role and had little more to do than lie there and let it happen. Most of the time, really, people carried on too much about it. What seemed to bother Dr. Apfelshpein most was that Sean didn't seem to care much whether he was being blown by a boy or a girl. And of course, having gone into it mostly to get useful business entrées also shocked the doctor's insulated little Jewish middle-class soul.

"*Gottenu*," Sean muttered, staring at a thin sheaf of shipping orders.

He wouldn't be able to understand what was happening if he lived to be a hundred. None of it made sense. Augie had recommended him as the designer for this new concern, just starting up. The financing was good. The mills had extended solid lines of credit. The contract with the union was a living doll. For more than two years Sean had come up with one line of winning designs after another. The salesmen had sold like demons. The advertising had been gorgeous. Sean smiled at the memory; he felt it was the only decent thing he would be able to remember in years to come.

The ads had feature full-color photos of a girl in one of his dresses. But Sean also appeared in every photo, looking faintly fey and brooding. He had become, in two years' time, one of the few designers people could recognize on sight. Soon the discotheque photographers zeroed in on him. The other fag designers flocked around, but Sean had been smart enough to realize that in this business loyalty was so rare as to be price-less. So he had remained fairly loyal to Augie, except for those few falls from grace with showroom models and Mrs. Brad-smith's eldest daughter, Pussy, who worked on the *Herald Trib* fashion staff and that one night with the drunken dyke from *Vogue*.

Who did what to whom? Sean repeated the old punch line

31

and smiled slightly. They had been two years of discotheque notoriety, and he had enjoyed that part of them immensely, coming on the scene when the British thing was in full swing and all that.

Well, he mused, the British thing is still going strong, but Mod Modes, Inc., is not.

No one could give him an answer that made sense, not Murray, his accountant, not Marv, his head salesman, not Seymour, his foreman, not even Mr. Fischetti, his backer. Such a friendly man. Why, he treated Sean as well as he treated his own son, Ben, taking the two of them to dinner at least once a week, often twice. Even with someone as close as Mr. Fischetti, even there the answers made no sense.

Only Augie made sense, but a confusing kind. "Sweetie, the party's over. Dig, baby? Like, they have all they want, and it's good-bye, Mod Modes, hello bankruptcy."

None of it made sense to Sean. Who would want to build up a concern and then let it fall apart, almost wilfully? What would be the sense in that?

The telephone rang. He picked it up at once. "Sean, it's Ben."

"Just thinking of you, luv."

"I got the matinee itch. Can you round up that blonde for me?"

"Gretchen?" Sean frowned. "I think she's in Miami this weekend."

"Out of season? Not Gretch."

"I'll find something. My place in half an hour?"

"Where else?"

Sean paused for a moment. "You sound real up tight, luv. What's bugging?"

Ben hesitated, too. "Family troubles."

"Thank God mine are on the other side of the Atlantic."

"You've got something there." Another pause. Then: "Will I see you at the apartment, Sean?"

"No, I'm stuck here for a while. Use your own set of keys."

After he had hung up, Sean continued to frown as he leafed through his address book. Gretch had to be out of town; he knew the manufacturer she'd flown down with. So Ben would have to make do with another big blonde. Having seen Rosalie Fischetti, Sean understood Ben's craving for tall, skinny blondes.

Edith watched her husband leave the nursery office and head for their station wagon. She sat in the front seat of the car and noted that although his thin face seemed somewhat pre-occupied, he looked in no way anxious about having left her in the lurch.

She decided it was fairly typical of Woods, as he had done during the more than twenty-five years of their marriage, to go haring off without warning on some entirely unimportant and completely inconsequential thing.

"Here's your father," she remarked.

"Looking properly concerned about the state of the universe," Gerri added.

"Don't take that tone, young lady."

"Sorry."

Edith knew she had thoroughly confused Gerri in the past two years since they'd moved to New York. Everything had seemed to happen to the poor girl all at once. She'd finally begun menstruation, finally conquered acne, finally started to show some faint signs of a figure, finally begun to shed child-hood and crystallize her attitudes toward men. And, Edith realized, to Gerri's immense disservice, her own mother was going through an equally unstable, unsettling time.

It wasn't that change of life had arrived, Edith knew, al-though the time could not be that far off. It was something else, something hard to admit, a hidden thread in herself that had begun to show for the first time and at the most in-opportune moment for Gerri, who probably depended rather heavily on the stability of her parents at this moment in her life.

"Sorry I'm late," Palmer said, getting into the car.

Edith noted the smooth, one-piece movement that carried his slender body through the door and onto the front seat in a single complex series of individual postures. Few men his age could move that way, she knew. She also recognized the fact that her husband could by now be about as physically repellent as so many men in their late forties were, bald, fat, coarse-skinned, awkward, slow-moving.

"Yes," she heard herself say in a flat voice devoid of warmth. "Now let's try to get back to town without getting lost again."

33

She immediately hated herself for saying those words in that way. It was not, she reminded herself now, that she owed Woods any loyalty. After that shocking near-scandal, she owed him nothing. But she owed Gerri at least the believable simulacrum of a decent, civil relationship. She owed her a model of feminine behavior a great deal warmer toward men than the one the poor girl was seeing.

Of course, Edith told herself, that was the peculiar part of it. She definitely did not feel unfriendly or cold toward men.

She had once, she realized. Certainly before she married, as a virgin, she had deliberately avoided experiences with men. She had seen to it, too, that sex was kept pretty much in its place during the years of their marriage. She had flatly refused to wear any disgusting apparatus down there, throwing the burden of contraception on Woods, where it belonged. He was the one who got enjoyment from the act. Let him take the precautions that had to accompany the pleasure.

For the last few years, of course there had been little sex at all. And since his revolting disloyalty of last year, there could be no question of sex between them again, ever, unless he paid a great deal in apology, humiliation and renewed respect and consideration. He showed no signs of this, much to Edith's relief, and she considered the question of sex between them a closed issue.

Edith watched the New Jersey landscape reel past her side window, the pale greens of March giving a very faint blurriness to the scene, as if viewed through the water of a swimming tank.

No, she repeated to herself, sex was out of the question.

And yet, lately, she had begun to think more and more about it. It might be out of the question with Woods, both to punish him and because it was unthinkable after what he had done. But it was by no means out of her mind.

Edith's first inkling of this had come last year, when the news of Woods' adultery had finally reached her, long after the affair had ended. She had realized, with something like a pang of jealousy, that he had adapted much more quickly to their new environment than she had. They had both been fish out of the water of their native Midwestern background, but only Woods seemed to have learned to enjoy their new style of living.

Edith watched him out of the corner of her eye for a moment as he steered the heavy station wagon around a long

34

curve in the road. He seemed completely oblivious of her thoughts, which was just as well.

In fact, Edith thought, it's just as well no one's privy to my thinking. It had started last year in long, complicated dreams, vaguely disturbing to her. She would awake in the middle of the night, breathless with an excitement that had no name. The dreams were never explicit at first, nondescript scenes in art galleries, museums and the like. It was a long time before Edith realized she was actually dreaming of statues.

They were statues of men, nudes. After a while she would wake up remembering details, the smoothness of a penis, the incurve of a buttock, the bunched scrotum tense with power.

At first Edith had told herself this was a natural, if aberrant interst. The Palmers had, in their time, commissioned a few works of sculpture. One of them, a heavily modern impression of the three children, was at the moment on loan to a State Department traveling exhibition somewhere in the Pacific. Edith had always taken an interest in the arts, and she told herself that this unusual interest in statues was simply a subconscious reflection.

Sitting in the station wagon now, as Palmer threaded his way through the approaches to the George Washington Bridge, Edith realized the whole idea had been self-deception of the most fraudulent kind.

She really had no greater interest in art than anyone else of her background, experience and class. Perhaps she had even less than some of her former college classmates who had taken up a variety of artistic causes over the years.

Edith told herself now that she had always been a little different from the rest of the girls in her milieu. For one thing, she stood nearly five-ten in her stockinged feet, which made her quite tall for her generation, although not for Gerri's. For another, she had always considered herself an ugly duckling, awkward, unfeminine, gangling, too boyish, too athletic, too everything that was the opposite of the petite, rounded, soft girls with whom she had gone to school.

It was only now, in her forty-forth year, with menopause waiting behind the next curve in the road, that she realized her type had enjoyed quite a tremendous vogue, both then and now. Gazing at herself in the mirror – something she had never done too much of before this year – she saw that she could pass for beautiful.

At cocktail parties and dinners, Edith knew, there were men

who had found her attractive. This had been going on for many years without her wishing to be aware of it. But lately, she could not avoid awareness. It had now become most centrally important to her that she become aware of such things.

She stared ahead now through the windshield of the station wagon as they sped over the long, down-curving span of the bridge toward Manhattan's West Side.

Edith wasn't at all sure she enjoyed what was happening to her. It was disloyal to her children for their mother suddenly to become someone else. And it was terribly sinful, of course, that someone else had become obsessed with sex.

Edith smiled slightly. For a woman obsessed with sex, she certainly hadn't done much about it. She sighed, again very slightly, to avoid being detected. It was probably all too little and too late. Other women, women who had taken a strong, active interest in sex from the very beginning, knew how to handle it and enjoy it. Edith knew that to many women, sex was enjoyable. She was painfully aware, too, that she had missed all of it, and she suspected that at forty four it was far too late to do anything about it.

Ahead of her, to the right through the clear, merciless March air, she could see the immense towers of Manhattan thrusting skyward like clusters of thick, powerful mushrooms or ...

Edith shut her eyes, waited, opened them again. But the skyscrapers were still there.

8

Ben Fischetti hung up the telephone in the booth. He stared out through the closed glass doors at the corner table where his wife, his three daughters and Barney were seated. Rosalie couldn't be that stupid, he told himself. She had to know something was up just by the fact that he used the pay phone, instead of the one in Vito's office.

"I don't want to bother Don Vitone," Ben had said as he pushed away from the table and went to the booth.

Which was a silly excuse, Ben thought now, because Don Vitone Coppola existed for the purpose of being bothered. He loved bother, and when there wasn't enough of it around to suit his bustling, gabby temperament, he created bother out of thin air.

Watching his family through the booth's glass doors, Ben tried to think of an entirely new and original excuse for copping out.

Usually, when they spent a typical Scarsdale Saturday at home, he could plead office work as a cover for his visits to Sean's apartment. A staged call would reach him at home between about ten in the morning and two in the afternoon, and he would go through a wonderful one-sided act while Sean tried to keep from laughing at the other end of the line.

"What? A shortage in the mortgage balance? You can't close the book without me? Why does this have to happen on Saturday? Oh? You only check the mortgage book on Saturday. Well, all right, but just for an hour or two." Click. "Rosa, baby, it's the office. They're all fouled up again, honey. I'm afraid I'll have to..."

This worked perfectly when they were at home in Westchester, Ben reflected now. But all of them were down here in Manhattan, and if such an emergency call from the bank reached him here, they would all pile into their cars and head back up. Which didn't suit his plans at all.

Without a creative thought in his head, he surveyed the restaurant. Casa Coppola catered to several distinct classes of eaters. Its mainstay customers were mostly prosperous Italo-Americans who liked the fact that in one good restaurant they could get both the hot, oily dishes of Sicily and the south and the tart, delicate, ryish dishes of the north. These eaters who on one day might tantalize their palates with sophisticated tastes and on another drench them in a frantic orgy of garlic provided Vito Coppola with about a third of his business. Another third, roughly, was compromised of eager-to-impress-each-other expense-account diners from the world of communications who kept the place crowded during the lunch hour. Their eagerness allowed Vitó to turn his tables over at least once during lunch, unheard of in a restaurant that charged such high prices. The remainder of his customers were the usual mixed bag: local strays and affluent out-of-towners who swiped dozens of the giant color postcards from the counter and stuffed them in their handbags along with paper lobster bibs and oversized matchbooks.

The decor tried for a compromise that would please all three classes. Although the walls were flocked in crimson fuzz to please the ethnic diners, everything else was Spartan plain to keep the communications boys from getting too jumpy. Lush,

Ben Fischetti decided, but not *busy*.

He tried to see someone at the bar who might become the occasion for his having to leave his family for a few hours. The usual group of sawed off, pounded-down, middle-aged *Sicilianos* and *Napolitanos* in dark pinstripe stuits and white-on-white shirts stood around eyeing the clientele and passing remarks in careful voices. Some were waiting for their lunch dates to arrive. When this happened, the maître d' would sweep them to a choice table with a great flourish, assign two waiters and make a tremendous fuss with the drinks. But others at the bar were merely waiting, watching and, Ben felt, making notes for a report at some later time.

He observed Rosalie for a moment, trying to gauge her temper. She looked, at a distance, only slightly larger than her children, more like one of them than their mother. But then, he mused, no one would ever accuse Rosalie of being an adult, except in the psysiological sense.

She was a short girl, not much over five feet in height and, although at the moment she had slimmed down some by drastic starvation, she was normally plump to the point of being fat. Ben wondered how many girls that short wore 38-C bras.

Married at nineteen and pregnant for most of the next six years, Rosalie was only now beginning to stand apart as an entity separate from the welter of her own children, her father and mother, her sister and her other relatives.

Her first act as a separate individual, Ben noted, had been to try losing weight. Although she took great pains to conceal her actual weight, Ben knew that she had managed to drop from 170 pounds to about 135. Her second act had been to have all the long, glossy black Sacred Heart-schoolgirl ringlets chopped and straightened into a modern bob with bangs. Her third act had been to have each girl's hair redone as a replica of hers so that when they sat together, as they did now, they resembled a pop singing group. When she tried to have Barney's hair done in the same style, although he recognized that it was a very mod thing to do, Ben had stopped her cold. He didn't mind his son looking like a pop singer; he minded him looking like his mother.

As he watched his family finish their spumoni, Ben tried to remember when he had first set up one of these Saturday matinees for himself.

It had to have been within the past two years because it had been through Sean that the whole thing came about. Ben's father had introduced the two young men at dinner one night, and something about the way Ben's glance followed women who walked past the table inspired Sean later, with the older man out of the way, to suggest some interesting possibilities.

And of course, it had been in the past two years that Rosalie had stopped honoring her contract as a tractable wife, Italian-style, eternally flopping down on her back with legs spread wide. Four children in six years had done something to her libido, Ben decided. It might affect anyone's.

He often wondered how the wife felt in these arranged political marriages. He imagined that somehow she couldn't possibly feel as used or as resentful as the husband. Rosalie was pretty enough. Her round face somewhat resembled one of those hackneyed cupids usually seen hovering around the periphery of a Renaissance painting. But at the time Don Vincenzo had pressed her hot, wet hand in Ben's, she had been a tub of lard about as wide as she was high. What she got out of the bargain was a young man of great prospects and already great achievements, Ben told himself, who was also not too hard to look at. So, all in all, the former fat girl hadn't done badly with the arrangement.

And the young man, he thought now, will do all right if he can keep his Saturday afternoons clear. He pushed open the doors of the booth and made his way back to the table.

"Da-a-dy," his eldest girl, Tina, said. She had an accusing way of drawing out the word that implied all sorts of unnamed guilts.

Ben sat down at the table and helped himself to Rosalie's untouched spumoni. "I wanted to see if the Ubco people were available today."

"What Ubco people?" she asked.

"Ubco, United Bank and Trust. I told you. The merger's finally going through."

She nodded her clean, straight hair bobbed up and down with the motion. Automatically she adjusted the napkin around Barney's neck, slapped Tina's wrist for stealing sugar cubes, lifted the baby, Graziella, up straighter in her high chair and wiped a smear of marinara sauce from Anita's cheek. The oldest girl made another try for the sugar cubes.

"Augustina," Rosalie snapped, "I'll tell Don Vitone you're stealing his sugar." The girl's hand withdrew. What the slap had been unable to enforce, the name succeeded in doing.

"So, anyway," Ben picked up, "they want to talk to me this

39

afternoon about the —"

"Vrroom!" Barney burst out, grabbing the imaginary wheel of a racing car. "Vrroom-rroom!"

Rosalie rapped the top of his head, spooned some spumoni into Graziella's mouth, shoved Anita's feet off the upholstered chair and gave Tina a terrible warning frown when she started hiding stolen sugar cubes in the pocket of Ben's jacket.

"So I'll have to leave you guys for a while. I'll take the little car. And I'll see you back home before dinner." Ben paused. "Right?"

Rosalie wiped Graziella's mouth, pulled Anita's water glass back from a precarious perch on the edge of the table, straightened Barney's collar and tie and brushed Tina's bangs out of her eyes. "Right," she said.

9

The drive back to New York from Amato's was unnaturally quiet. Palmer didn't really notice how quiet it was until long after they'd crossed the bridge and were threading their way through the irrational traffic tie-ups and slowdowns of Manhattan.

He himself had very little to say to anyone. Edith, he realized now, had probably decided to take as an insult his desertion of her during their stay at the nursery. And Gerri was miffed that she had, in a sense, to do Palmer's job for him in his absence.

Typical happy family gathering, he told himself, waiting patiently for the line of cars ahead to begin moving now that the light had turned green at the intersection. Just as the traffic-drugged drivers realized it was green and started forward, the light turned red again. Nobody seemed to care one way or the other. It was just a part of life in Fun City.

Resignation. Palmer nodded as the word came to him. Resignation is the key to life.

He frowned, knowing he had never felt this way before and worried that he suddenly did. To resign himself, he realized, was too profoundly an Eastern concept all mixed up with predestination and kismet and the swooning masochism of submission to divine will.

And yet, what the hell else could one do?

Palmer banged on the horn as the light up ahead turned

green. By dint of producing short, peevish barking sounds, he managed to jolt the line of drivers into enough alertness to recognize the color green. The line of cars shuddered sluggishly and began to creep ahead. This time Palmer's station wagon gained four car lengths toward the intersection.

There. Didn't that prove the fallacy of resignation? he asked himself. Wasn't it better, more morally correct, more affirmative of life to pitch in and take a hand at changing destiny? On the next green light, he would get through.

He watched the parade of pedestrians crossing in front of the lead car in the line. Saturday strollers, shoppers, women with baby carriages crossed both ways in unbroken lines. Although he had lived less than two years in New York, Palmer had visited the city many times over the years. He could not remember ever before there being such a sheer press of humanity. He knew the statistics as well as anyone, and he was aware that the city's population hadn't really increased. But there was definitely more traffic, more cars, more people, more trucks.

The light turned green, and Palmer did his little wake-up obbligato for electric horn. The first car heaved convulsively and stopped. The line of pedestrians crossing in front of it remained unbroken. Now horns behind Palmer were joining in a kind of free-form tone poem, some producing long, anguished hoots, others vehement, percussive honks. The pedestrians' nerve broke at last, and Palmer eventually made it to the corner as the light changed to red.

No, really, he told himself, it's better to resign oneself.

Someone who fought back, who tried to take charge, who continued to act out the whole Western myth of free will – such a person was definitely not going to Take It Easier.

Palmer watched a sports car snake in alongside of him, its narrowness barely fitting between his station wagon and the side of an immense, double-parked truck. A take-charge guy. Nothing mystical about him, Palmer thought. He'll have his motor revving and his car half out into the intersection by the time the light goes yellow. And he's got a fifty-fifty chance of not colliding head on with another take-charge guy running the yellow light against him.

Palmer realized suddenly that in places of great human congestion life was possible only through resignation, only by queuing up, only by waiting patiently. Free will was for the great open spaces America hadn't been for several decades.

Those contemplative, resigned philosophies of the East,

41

where people swarmed all over each other like maggots, were now the obvious models on which Western man should base his life. So a man's choice is clear, Palmer thought, at least in a cauldron of humanity like New York. He either submits, relaxes and lets it happen, or he moves to Wyoming.

But to return to the splendid American isolation of the frontier, Palmer reflected, to the underpopulated America that once had room for eccentrics and individualists of every stripe, one had either to go it alone or make one's life with people one really loved very deeply.

"The light's been green for ages," Edith said coldly.

Palmer blinked and stepped on the gas.

10

"Yeah, right, Sean. *Arrivederci.*"

Tippy hung up the phone and glanced at the red leather traveling clock propped at an angle on her dresser. From there her glance moved slowly to the mirror on the wall above. She leaned closer and painstakingly examined the lines under her large gray eyes. Even in her oldest photographs, snapshots taken of her as a five-year-old on the beach at Winnetka, she had this well-defined line – this *bag*, really – under her eyes. Now that she was well into her twentieth year, the line – the goddamned bag, yeah, right – was still there, especially when she smiled or laughed or, as on this Saturday, hadn't had enough sleep.

She popped her eyes at her reflection, flared her nostrils and began hurriedly brushing her long, straight, pale yellow hair. All her actions began to speed up now. It was getaway time.

Never a dull moment when you were a friend of Sean's, she thought, quickly making up her mouth and eyes. In the past year since she'd moved to New York, she had come to rely on Sean for her entire social life. All her friends had been met through Sean, except those who were the children of her parents' friends. The places she frequented had first been shown her by Sean. He had gotten her her first job as a stylist for a gay fashion photographer, and through a friend of Sean's she had gotten the job she now held as a kind of correspondence-answering ghost-writer for one of the big disc jockeys.

Whenever she felt alone and needed cheering, she could call Sean, and he would find a party for her somewhere, even if he had to organize one on the spur of the moment. Whenever she needed an escort, Sean would oblige or, if busy, would provide a perfectly neat, lovely and charming fairy boy who made just the right impression without being obliged to grab her in the cab coming home. And finally, when she felt in need of that kind of thing, Sean seemed to know so many single or unhappily married young men, all as straight as the escorts of the evening were gay. No strings, just flings. And the loveliest part of all, of course, was that Sean had never, ever, laid a hand on her. There was nothing between them, only mental, she decided now.

A blessing in this town, Tippy told herself, to be able to get *just one thing at a time* from a man. Yeah, right.

It was an age of specialization, and perhaps even of overspecialization. Tippy rushed through putting on her underclothes and a yellow tent dress that reached to the middle of her thighs. She needed a well-mannered, remote escort for those few formal events connected with her work. She needed a full time jester in attendance for her blue days. She needed a sex-mad bedmate for a really frantic blast. She needed a calm, wise father-brother for advice. But she did not need any or all of them rolled into one. Such a combination would be just a little too menacing, if not downright disgusting.

Glancing at herself in the mirror again, she checked the hang of the dress, the look of the sunglasses in her hair, the straightness of the checkered stockings on her long legs. Then she ran out of the room fast, without looking back at the bedside table. She let herself out of the apartment and rang for the elevator. It arrived within seconds, as if everything had been perfectly timed in advance, like a bank robbery. With three elevators, a fast getaway like this was always possible.

With any kind of luck, Tippy thought as she strode off toward the cab stand, the man she was meeting at Sean's would be good for an entire evening and perhaps an entire night. It really didn't matter too awfully much who he was, she told herself, as long as he was even moderately attractive. Perhaps he had the whole weekend?

Just as long as she had a good excuse for not going back to her apartment. Just as long as she had a good reason for not having to stare at the squat, yellow-topped bottle of sleeping capsules. Just as long as she could get through the weekend to Monday.

Yeah, right.

11

It was past two in the afternoon by the time Harry Klaman's Thunderbird returned to Manhattan, roaring in under the East River through the Queens-Midtown Tunnel, then down Second Avenue to Ninth Street. He turned west and tried to make time on the crosstown street as he drove through Greenwich Village from its scruffy east side through its respectable center to its somewhat less respectable west side.

In the block between Fifth and Sixth Avenues, as he waited for the light, he watched a tall, slim blonde in a yellow dress and checkered stockings jump out of the cab ahead of him and dash a few houses along the block before she ran up the steps of a very sleekly remodeled old brownstone.

Crazy legs, Harry thought. Real eating stuff. He moistened his lips and watched her long legs as she stood in the doorway of the brownstone.

Up ahead the light turned green, but the car at the head of the line was having trouble with pedestrians who refused to stop crossing. By the time Harry got to the head of the block, the light at Sixth Avenue was red again. His fingers drummed impatiently on the steering wheel of the Thunderbird.

Vinnie Big would be patient, he told himself. Vinnie was a patient man. At the thought, Harry started to sweat again. Harry being half an hour late – so far – wouldn't get Vinnie mad. Harry had once seen Vinnie mad, and he knew why Sicilians made such a point of cooling it, giving no clues to their inner turmoil. Once a Sicilian blew, he blew all the way, right through to the finish. So on the whole, it was smart of them to cool it most of the time.

Harry had spent a very discouraging morning in Long Island. He had visited a few of his sales managers in some of the developments he was promoting along the Nassau-Suffolk County line.

He had houses to suit anybody's taste, or so he had told his salesmen. In one area or another, you could get a Klaman house for anywhere from $12,900 all the way to $48,800. You could get a clapboard Cape Cod. You could get a split ranch. A patio split. A ranch plunge. A plunge split. A patio ranch. You could also get it in one, two or one and a half storeys, with or without garage and/or carport, flagstone walk, all-electric kitchen, complete air conditioning, color TV installed, dishwasher and garbage disposal unit, ceiling-light dimmers, sliding window-doors, integral shopping center with kinder-garten-through-third-grade school on premises and nearby house of worship, post office, theatre. You could live in solitary splendor on an entire quarter-acre of your own, iso-lated from all of humanity. If you were the gregarious type, you could buy one of Harry's semiattached two-family houses where the rental unit was supposed to pay your carrying charges. Or if you really loved people, you could live in Klaman Korners, a nine-building high rise co-op project com-plete with its own veterinarian, art theater, TV repair shop and wall-to-wall grass in the collective fun-a-rama patio.

But money was tight, goddamn it, Harry thought. And all of this abundance was just lying there while prospective cus-tomers fished around for mortgages. The lousy bank *gonifs* had him by the short hairs and didn't mind twisting, Harry decided bitterly.

A tall young man with dark, glossy hair turned the corner of Sixth Avenue and started walking along Ninth Street, in the direction Harry had come from. Harry frowned. The face was familiar, very familiar. If he weren't so upset about financing, he told himself, he'd know the kid's name.

The light turned green. Harry squinted at the young man, trying to place him. He swiveled his bulky body and tried to continue watching the man, who turned in at the same brown-stone as the blonde had.

Behind Harry Klaman horns were honking. Muttering to himself, Harry tramped on the accelerator, and the Thunder-bird jolted across Sixth Avenue. He guided it west on Chris-topher Street toward the office on Bleecker Street where Vinnie Big would be waiting.

He still couldn't place the young man. It bothered him.

12

Palmer dropped Edith and Gerri at the house, then found a parking place nearby. He got the garage attendant to help him with the potted plants. They carried them around the corner and down the block toward Park Avenue. Halfway along, Palmer stopped in front of a house that had once been two brownstones. It had been gutted and rebuilt with a pierced con-

45

crete facade behind which lay four storeys of picture-window facade, shielded from the sun and curious passers-by by the pierced concrete.

"This where you live?" the garage attendant asked. The tone of his voice implied an additional phrase, something like "In this nutty-looking joint?"

"Right," Palmer grunted.

He led the way down three steps that took visitors from the sidewalk level to a kind of moat planted with ivy before they reached the main entrance at what had once been the basement level of the old brownstones.

"You like it?" the garage man asked. Again a slight New York upturn on inflection added an unspoken "How could anybody like it?" to his question.

"Love it," Palmer said, putting down his plant and fumbling for his keys.

"Which floor you on?"

"All of them."

The garage man's face twisted into a caught-with-the-hand-in-the-cookie-jar expression, brow wrinkled, eyes popped, mouth downturned. Palmer grinned at him, noting the man's resemblance to the celebrated picture of Eisenhower snapped as he was told that Truman had just fired MacArthur.

"You own it?" the man wanted to know.

"Yes."

"You loaded?"

"Comfortable," Palmer responded in New York vernacular, "comfortable."

The man's mouth opened and closed a few times. He was having difficulty articulating his next thought. Then: "So tell me, Mac, you're so comfortable, how come you drive a Hertz?"

Palmer relieved him of the plant he was carrying, "It's more comfortable that way," he explained. Then he dug in his pocket and gave the man a dollar bill.

"Thanks." The garage attendant seemed unable to leave. "You want I should help you carry them inside?"

"I'm okay," Palmer assured him.

"Okay."

The man backed up the three steps to the sidewalk. He still seemed terribly reluctant to leave. "Them hole-type things," he said, indicating the apertures in the concrete "screen" that shielded the building, "is that the way you wanted 'em? I

46

mean, was it planned like that?"

Palmer surveyed the holes. They were actually interstices between the concrete blocks of which the screen was built. The masons had arranged the blocks so that two kinds of apertures were formed, a kind of diamond with curved sides and a lopsided rhomboid which was actually the diamond rotated 45 degrees and set on one side. These two shapes had been laid out in a random way with no discernible pattern of repetition.

"My wife planned it that way," Palmer said at length.

"Your wife," he said. "Whyn't you explain that before, Mac?"

He turned and disappeared, humming the tune of a television commercial jingle for mentholated cigarettes.

Palmer flipped a switch on the vestibule intercom panel and said: "Woody? Get down here to the front door and help me, please."

After a moment he distinctly felt a slight, regular tremor in the floor beneath his feet, the kind of vibration caused by trains running underground or a pile driver in a nearby open lot. A moment later Woody clumped into view.

"You're wanted on the phone," he said. "I'll put the plants away."

Palmer walked up the broad set of wide oak-plank stairs that led from the front hall to the second floor, then up another flight to the room at the back of the house where Edith had laid out his "office."

In the past six months, during which he had tried not to bring work home, Palmer had found uses for the office other than those for which Edith had originally planned. He had had the very efficient, very straight-back desk chair removed to Woody's room. In its place Palmer had put one of those insidious loungers that looked like an ordinary armchair upholstered in black glove leather. The only difference was that when Palmer leaned back, a support came up under the calves of his legs, and in no time at all he was the nearest thing to prone. Sleep followed quickly. It was, all in all, the best investment he had ever made if he planned the rest of his life as a downhill slide.

It was seated in this lounger that Palmer now picked up the telephone and pushed down the lighted button. "Palmer speaking."

"I'm terribly sorry to be disturbing you this way, Mr. Palmer."

47

Palmer listened to the man's voice, high and prim and fussy. He tried to place it. The bank? Yes. "Is that Elston?"

The voice sounded terribly pleased. "Yes, sir."

"What's up, Bill?"

Palmer listened to Elston dither along for a few minutes. The man was an assistant secretary or something fairly low on the executive scale. A youngish man, still in his thirties, but with all the vocal tricks of a crochety old lady, Palmer thought. What's more, he noted, Elston had the mental outlook of an old lady. And further, he absolutely couldn't get to the point.

"Yes," Palmer cut in. "Speed it up, Bill."

"It's up over twenty percent," Elston said.

"What is?"

"Their loan delinquency rate."

"Whose?" Palmer persisted.

"People's Bank of Westchester."

"How can you tell?"

"Well, of course, we don't know for certain." Elston and two other men had spent the Saturday going over all fiscal material the other bank had published for its stockholders in the past few months. "But their bad debt reserve has dropped almost out of sight, and there doesn't seem to be anything covering these delinquencies except the usual over-the-weekend kiting these little banks always do."

There was a world of disdain in Elston's voice, as if he had caught the other bank dealing in Confederate money or Czarist bonds. It was the self-protective disdain of the small man in a big pond who, no matter what cruel ways life might find to cuff him about, could still draw himself up and say, "But I'm an Ubco man."

Palmer caught the faintly smug overtone. He wondered how much Elston or any of the other timeservers at Ubco Really knew about the kind of freewheeling banking that had built the country and was now destroying it.

It was the style of operation that in San Francisco before the quake would lead a bank to write a favorable mortgage on a whorehouse and gambling hell. Nowadays it took the form of totally unrestrained personal credit. Nobody financed brothels anymore, Palmer reflected, but bankers were still underwriting gambling by lending money on signature loans so that investors could cover margin calls on stock. They weren't shelling out anymore for fancy houses where errant husbands could

48

go broke on a Saturday night. But they were making it attractive for the whole family to go up over its eyeballs in irreversible debt.

"What kind of loans are going bad for them, Bill?" Palmer asked.

"Personal loans. Home improvement loans. Conditional sales contracts on cars and boats. Renegotiated open-end mortgages. College tuition loans. Small business loans. Accounts receivable—"

"Hold it," Palmer cut in. "What's left? I'm not talking about how many different kinds of loans can sometimes sour on them. We all know that. I'm talking about where the biggest bulge of delinquencies is."

"Home improvements. Also these renegotiated mortgages."

Palmer nodded, almost as if Elston could see him. He'd already known the answer before asking the question. From the abstract financial viewpoint, there was little difference between the two types of loan. Both were secured by real property, a house the borrower lived in and owned. Both were negotiated to get money for some reason ostensibly connected with the house. But the bank and the borrower both knew that most of these loans were for something else.

Stock purchases in a bull market were a favorite need. Another reason for taking out such a loan was to consolidate small debts, usually money owed on charge cards and at department stores, and get straight. The borrower traded a lot of long-past-due small debts, confusing in their quantity and diverseness, for a single debt to a single lender, the bank. In this way the typical successful suburbanite hocked his home to pay for last year's fly-now-pay-later vacation, this spring's clothing, last fall's sweet sixteen party, miscellaneous restaurant bills, repairs on cars and appliances, money owed the cleaner, the liquor store, the orthodontist, the pediatrician, the psychiatrist and the man who manured the lawn.

"Any foreclosures?" Palmer asked.

"None that show up."

Palmer nodded again. The pattern was typical, and not just for a suburban bank. No lender wanted to reclaim a house and have it on his hands. Foreclosure was a move of desperation for all concerned. "What about this over-the-weekend kiting?"

"Usual stuff. They cover Friday withdrawls with money they hope to take in the following Monday and Tuesday. Real bush league," Elston sniffed.

'T.F.—3

Palmer smiled lopsidedly and leaned back in the lounger. He found himself being gently adjusted until he was looking at the ceiling. He wondered what smug little prigs like Elston would say if they knew that several big Manhattan banks were at the moment caught in the same kind of kiting operation?

He sighed. He found it difficult to concentrate on Elston's news, now that the lounger had eased him into a posture of sleep. He closed his eyes.

"Sir?" Elston asked after a long moment of silence.

Palmer blinked and sat up straight. "See me at nine Monday morning, Bill. And have all the figures ready."

"Right."

"And thanks for calling."

"Not at all, sir. I just felt sure you might like to know."

Palmer replaced the telephone in its cradle and let himself drift back into a prone position. The insurance actuaries would place him at forty-six, he mused, because although he hadn't reached it yet, it was his nearest birthday. Let someone else mull over Elston's news. There would have been a day when he would have started digging into it like a terrier who suspects a large buried bone. Before the merger, it would have to be cleared up – if there was going to be a merger. But this was Saturday and he was forty-six, and all he wanted to do now was to lie here with his eyes closed and think long, green thoughts.

His attention slipped its moorings and fled down a corridor of dark greens toward row upon row of plants in pots. At the far end of the corridor a little old man in a golf cart came toward him.

Palmer lay deep in sleep. The smell of roasted green peppers filled his dream.

13

On Bleecker Street, not far from Seventh Avenue, the Thunderbird sat at the curb in a "NO PARKING ANY TIME" zone.

Where the thoroughfare met Cornelia Street, Riordan, the beat cop, eyed the car for the third time and glanced at his wristwatch. He had seen the Thunderbird park there half an hour before. He had watched the heavyset, balding man wrestle himself out from behind the wheel, pat his forehead dry with a handkerchief and disappear inside the storefront building.

Riordan had seen the Thunderbird parked there twice before, although this was the first time he'd seen its driver. Checking the time again, he told himself he'd do the beat once more, which would bring him back in another thirty minutes. If the fat sheenie still had the car there...

He walked slowly up Cornelia toward Sixth Avenue, wishing Vinnie Big would have a little regard for appearances. After all, how could you keep the snotnosed guinea kids in line around her if they saw you let Biglioto's visitors get way out of line?

At Sixth Avenue, by appointment, he met Patrolman Hoover. They moved west on Fourth Street toward Sheridan Square.

Hoover was black. His teeth shone brightly as he grinned at Riordan. "Great day, man. That sun is really something."

Riordan nodded coolly. He only had to be civil to niggers, not friendly.

The storefront on Bleecker Street was among the older buildings in Greenwich Village, but certainly not in line for preservation as a historic site.

Two storeys in height, the building had been constructed, mostly of brick, somewhere around 1840 or 1845. At the moment the buildings to the east of it had been demolished to make way for a high-rise apartment house. For several months now, passersby had been able to see the unimaginative outline of the original brick. The walls of the first floor rose vertically but at the start of the second began to slant to a peak. On the facade facing Bleecker this slope, pierced by two dormers, had originally been covered with terne sheet, a tin and lead alloy of the pewter family that during World War I had been ripped out and replaced by asphalt tar-paper shingles. The terne had probably been sold at a good price, the lead for bullets, the tin for the brass then employed to make shell casings. Somewhere in the earth of Verdun, perhaps, in an Army and Navy store on 42nd Street or in an American Legionnaires's buttock the Bleecker Street terne might now be found.

From about 1930 to 1945, the building had lain vacant. It had been bought about then by someone for use somehow, but the neighborhood people weren't sure of the who or the what. Minimal sprucing-up took place. The rotted tar paper was replaced by horizontal clapboard, painted white. The dormers that jutted out of the front slope were painted a reddish brown. So were the fluted wooden pillars that stood at each corner of the facade and the two that flanked the door in the middle.

The two windows, because they had been boarded over during most of the Depression and World War II, remained intact. They might even, for all anyone knew, be the ones put in sometime in the 1890s when the place had been a tavern with a free lunch that attracted every poet, painter and pimp on Bleecker Street. They had probably been washed at least once during that first year of new ownership. But by now they had been etched, fogged and caked over by New York air so that even scrubbing would have failed to restore their original transparency.

At night one could dimly see what the inside of the storefront was like. The original stand-up bar at the rear still existed, a tiny thing no more than two yards long. On it an ancient gas-heated *machinetta* dispensed steaming espresso through a spigot. The bar held a few odd bottles and glasses. It seemed to be a self-service arrangement now, mainly for the members of the club. Across the left-hand window, probably back in 1945, someone had lettered in the kind of whitewash used for temporary signs that can be washed off: "Bleecker Str. Soc. Club." The right-hand window carried the legend another way – "Bleeker St. Social Clb." – in a slightly different printing style. Since the lettering had been done backward from inside to escape the rain's erasure, the unsteadiness of the letter forms was excusable.

Three tables filled much of the building's front room. Castoff chairs from various eras of design were drawn up to these tables every night, and cards were played. Sometimes only one table was used. On certain nights, all three were kept busy.

At the back of the room, a doorway covered by some black material – or what seemed through the windows to be black – gave access to another part of the building and logically, by stairway, to the second floor. No one in the neighborhood was sure of this. They only knew that an occasional light was seen through the second-floor dormer windows. They also knew that whatever it seemed to be from the outside – private cardplaying club or what have you – none of the players remotely resembled Vinnie Big. Obviously, therefore, there had to be a back room for Don Vincenzo.

There was. Harry Klaman found it stuffy on this warm March Saturday, but he knew that this room was one of the few places where he and Vinnie could have a secure discussion. Harry glanced at his watch. He had been here almost an hour, and he was sure his car had a green ticket on it. He was unhappy about that and also about the fact that he was hungry. Since he'd arrived an hour late, Biglioto had eaten without him.

"You in a hurry?" Biglioto asked.

He had a deep, furry voice, a kind of husky rumble. The deepness had always been there. The huskiness was a legacy from an attempted garroting in a speak on Houston near Sullivan one day back in the late 1920s.

Harry Klaman smiled unhappily and shook his head. "The car's in a no-park zone."

Vincenzo Biglioto turned his hands palms out and shoved them lightly back and forth in Harry's direction as if warding off malign spirits. Now in his sixties, he was still a fine figure of a man, Harry thought. Harry seemed to recall that Vinnie had gotten those shoulders in the construction trade, but it didn't seem possible. He'd been an important man right from the beginning, what with his father being who he was, and it hardly seemed very likely that Vinnie had ever carried a hod or swung a trowel or hammered home a rivet.

Nevertheless he gave the impression of a much younger man, hardly fifty, who spent a lot of time out of doors. Harry knew for a fact that Don Vincenzo Biglioto was rarely seen out of doors until long after the sun had vanished. He might expose himself to daylight on a Sunday, perhaps, in the privacy of his immense weekend estate across the river in New Jersey. But there was no other way to account for the browned ruggedness of his high cheekbones and the Indian-chief bridge of his nose.

Harry had once let his wife, Esther, drag him to some cockamamie place up in the Heights, the Cloisters, they called it, to see some half-assed show of old stuff, paintings, tapestries, furniture, wormy-looking shit like that. He had wandered unhappily behind her, wishing he were anywhere else, when suddenly he had come upon a tiny framed painting of Vinnie Big.

It had to be him, no question about it, Harry recalled now. You couldn't mistake the cheekbones or the big beezer or those thin lips that had no red in them at all, sort of like knife-sharp creases in the skin of Vinnie's face. You couldn't mistake the big chin, shaped like a spade, or the long vertical dent in it.

But if you gave away all that, Harry remembered, the eyes would still let you know this had to be Vinnie Big's portrait. They were exactly the same as the real thing. The most start-

53

ling fact about them was that they were blue. From the side Vinnie's eyes had no depth at all, like a doll's eyes, painted on and hardly deeper than a layer of paint. But from the front...

Harry shifted uncomfortably and tried to get a look at Vinnie's eyes without being impaled by his glance. The eyes were terrifying, in a way. You felt as if they weren't eyes at all, but tongues of blue flames. You had the feeling Vinnie Big could with a single look turn you to a blackened cinder. And this picture up in the Cloisters had the same eyes.

Harry remembered he had checked the number of the painting in the catalog Esther had bought. He hadn't done this until they'd gotten home because he didn't want to betray any undue interest in the crap she had forced him to see. The painting had been done in the fourteenth or fifteenth century, Harry couldn't recall exactly which, and it had a long name, some monsignor or cardinal or pope or some other *goyish megillah* with a ginzo name. In other words, Don Vincenzo Biglioto it wasn't.

"What're you thinking, Harry?" Vinnie wanted to know.

"Me? Nothing."

"You're so quiet. Thinking." Vinnie's great nose swung about like a weather vane until it pointed due Harry. His eyes narrowed slightly in the papery brown skin that surrounded them.

"I'm worried," Harry admitted. "That much you knew already."

"Did I tell you to stop worrying?" Vinnie asked. "Did I say, 'Harry, your worries are over'? Did I do that?"

"Sure."

"But still you worry." Vinnie's eyes widened almost menacingly.

Harry winced. "Okay, Vinnie. I just stopped worrying."

Vinnie's thin mouth seemed to grow, if anything, thinner as it stretched sideways in a narrow, crooked smile. "See? Now, if you could stop sweating, Harry, I'd even believe you."

Harry nodded miserably. "I always sweat, Vinnie. Summer and winter. You know that."

"That's because summer and winter you worry too much."

Harry shrugged with one shoulder only. "That's because I haven't got your advantages, Vinnie."

Biglioto's palms went up in the air like birds fluttering. "How can you say that? What I got, you got. We're partners, goombar. We're closer than partners, we're brothers."

Harry nodded again. "So, that makes this kid up in Westchester my nephew, right? This kid who's gonna pull a rabbit out of the hat? What's his name, my nephew, Benny?"

"*Si*, Benedetto, a nice boy, my Rosalie's husband, three fine girls and a fine grandson. Here."

Swinging around in his chair, Don Vincenzo unlocked the roll top of his dark oak desk. The top made a whining noise as it swung up. In among the papers stood a rather elaborate set of picture frames. Each was an oval no more than an inch and a half high, edged in gold metal and joined to its neighbor by a gold band. There were ten ovals in all, arranged in a kind of pyramid with four on the bottom, three above, then two, then one. Don Vincenzo took Harry on a tour of the pictures.

A thin woman of about forty with a cherub's face looked out of the top oval. This, Harry knew, was Mary Biglioto, Vinnie's third cousin and second wife. The first had died of cancer during World War II.

Beneath Mary's face, in the row with two frames, were pictures of Rosalie and Celia, the daughters who had come late in life to Don Vincenzo. Below Rosalie, in the row with three frames, were pictures of a small boy who had to be the celebrated grandson. Barney and the oldest girl, Tina. The frame under Celia's picture was empty. She had not yet married. In the bottom row of four, another blank had been left under Celia. Two ovals showed pictures of baby girls. The third, low man on anybody's totem pole, bore the face of the dark, good-looking young man who had more or less followed that leggy blonde into the remodeled brownstone on Ninth Street.

Harry smiled pleasantly and sat back in the creaking swivel chair reserved for guests. He toyed very briefly with the idea of raising the subject of seeing Ben on Ninth Street. After all, Vinnie had said he and Harry were brothers.

In all the years he had been doing business with Vinnie Big, Harry had never before been shown the golden ovals. He had never been introduced to any photographic likenesses of Vinnie's family. What he knew of the Bigliotos he had gathered from newspaper accounts, nothing more, and the newspaper morgues were notoriously shy of Biglioto pictures.

So, as the young man's brand-new uncle, Harry might be justified in raising the matter, especially since Ben was supposed to help him at the bank. It was a simple, matter-of-fact thought. Oh, that's Ben. I thought I recognized him. I was on my way here when I saw –

Harry's smile grew even sweeter as his mouth remained firmly closed. Herschel, he told himself, when you're a member of this family, you learn how to keep it shut tight.

14

The intense Mediterranean sun pouring down out of the hot blue sky like a fiery runnel of molten yellow steel seemed to have parched the dusty streets of the mountain town, sucking up all moisture and leaving powdery dust over the tiled roofs and thick stucco walls. The streets were deserted.

Asleep, Palmer worked his mouth slowly, tasting the acrid dust of the Sicilian town he had now resurrected in a dream.

Awake, he would probably have been able to resurrect its name, too. But there had been so many of them during the war, so many hot, dusty towns in Italy, France, North Africa, so many cold, soggy towns in the Low Countries, Denmark and Germany.

He dreamed he was seated in the front, right-hand seat of a jeep he had commandeered from a Royal Air Force colonel in Licata, who in the frenzy and confusion of the landing had refused to recognize the superior priority of Palmer's T-Force counterintelligence requisition. Palmer had seemed to submit to the colonel's idiocies. When his back was turned, Palmer and his men had liberated the jeep and two trucks, 300 gallons of gasoline and extra ammo. Intact, Palmer's T-Force of twenty men had roared off up-country for an urgent rendezvous.

Because he had forgotten his maps, they were arriving in this dusty little town too late by several hours for the rendezvous. Palmer's instructions had been to make contact with a certain Don G. Or rather, his instructions were to arrive and let Don G. make contact first, since none of the brass at Palmer's counterintelligence office knew Don G.'s name or physical description.

"He's the top bigwig in Sicily," Palmer's briefing officer had explained rather airily. "That's all we know. He signaled us about two weeks ago when he felt sure we were going to invade. He signalled us, instead of the Limeys, because he's done business with Americans before."

"Why is he willing to defect?"

The briefing officer shrugged. "No capeesh, buddy. They tell
56

me his organization was on Il Duce's blacklist. Maybe that's the angle. Or maybe he knows Mussolini's had it and wants in on the winning side."

"We don't really care which, right?" Palmer asked, not trying very much to conceal his disapproval.

"Right, buddy. He's been cleared in the highest quarters."

"Even if this guy is some kind of hood?"

The briefing officer's mouth turned up at the corners in a gorgeous fake smile. He raised his hands on either side of his head and, wide-eyed, wiggled his fingers in mock glee. "Ain't nobody here but us chickens, boss. You got to apply much higher up for answers to them deep philosophical-type questions."

"How high? The Pope?"

"Naughty." The officer handed Palmer several sealed pouches. "Letters of accreditation, money, the usual shit. Go to it, stalwart warrior."

Aware what something had gone wrong. Palmer stepped down out of the jeep and felt his boot soles crunch in the parched whitish earth. He could hear sounds of a crowd in a nearby building that might be the town hall. Motioning his T-Force to deploy as skirmishers, Palmer unsnapped the leather guard on his holster and made sure the Colt .45 would slide out easily.

In the dream he moved slowly, too slowly, as if the burden of molten air and powdery earth were an immense sea of heat through which he had to wade as if through water. He was aware of himself in the dream, of his own body moving with solemn slowness like a ritual gunfighter along a Western street, ready to slap leather and gun down the man in the black hat. Which was the villain?

The door to the town hall was open. Palmer paused to one side of it and listened for a moment. Inside, a man's high-pitched voice was excitedly spitting out great, jerky torrents of words. It was as if the words had been imprisoned within him for so long that, with the freedom to release them now, he had lost full control of their formation or the speed or rhythm of their utterance.

"Lowest criminal..."

Palmer squinted, trying to pick out the significant words despite his lame grasp of Sicilian. "Conspiracy of black mail..."

Palmer turned around, looking for his interpreter, a California kid named Fusco. Seeing him holed up 200 yards away with his squirt gun resting in the crotch of a tree, Palmer decided not to wave him forward. He listened to the man inside the town hall.

"Added yoke from our necks..."

It sounded vaguely political to Palmer, even with his poor command of the language. He edged sideways around the corner of the door and surveyed the hall inside.

A group of about a dozen men, well-dressed and well-fed, were chained together on the dais at the front of the hall. They seemed neither abject nor arrogant, but unnaturally calm in the face of what was apparently about to happen.

A thin young man, the one with the high voice, stood at the lectern and gestured jerkily as he harangued first the prisoners and then the several hundred townspeople seated on the pew-like benches as an audience. A Mauser carbine was slung over the young man's back. Several other armed men, all carrying German weapons, stood about the hall. They were poorly dressed, some of them in rags, all of them even more gaunt with hunger than the townspeople. On their left arms they wore red bands of cloth. Guarding the prisoners were two women, also wearing red armbands.

Palmer ducked back out of sight. The situation was getting clearer. No soldiers or police had greeted his arrival, either from ambush or openly, for purposes of surrender. The red armbands were Communist partisans from the high country. The prisoners were probably local Fascisti. And if Palmer's guess were right, a search of the militia barracks and police station would reveal nothing but corpses.

His instructions had said nothing one way or the other about interfering with local wrong-rightings. Palmer took a breath and stepped into the doorway. One of the women guarding the prisoners saw him and raised her rifle. She took dead aim at Palmer's head.

"I am American," Palmer called out loudly. "*Sono Americano.*"

The tiny black eye of the rifle wavered slightly and lowered to cover his abdomen. The woman holding the gun peered over the sights at him.

The young man at the lectern pulled a pair of steel-rimmed spectacles from somewhere in the dirty jacket he was wearing. One lens was cracked. He peered through the other at Palmer. The people in the audience began to mutter softly.

58

"Americano?" the young man asked.

"Si, Americano." Palmer took two steps into the hall. Then he put out his hand as if to shake that of the young man. Holding this gesture, he continued up the middle aisle to the lectern. The woman's rifle followed his progress closely.

There was a moment of confusion in which the leader tried either to hook his spectacles properly over his ears or else dispense with them completely. In the end he let them drop to the floor and shook Palmer's hand. His Adam's apple bobbed violently.

The people in the hall began to laugh and talk. The woman let the rifle swing sideways until it was covering the prisoners again.

Palmer noticed an odd change taking place. The people had been absolutely still before, as if afraid of irritating the partisans by any idle chatter or signs of easy amusement. Now the atmosphere seemed much freer and, in some strange way, relaxed. Even the prisoners seemed more at ease.

"You are partisans?" Palmer asked.

"Si. Yes. Partisans. Yes." The young man nodded several times with such vigor that Palmer was afraid he would snap his frail neck. "From de hilles," he managed to mispronounce.

"You speak English well."

The leader seemed to blush beneath the dirt on his face. "I receive master's degree in literature," he said, speaking very slowly to make certain of his pronunciation and vocabulary, "and prepare thesis on poetry of Lord George Gordon Byron."

Palmer felt his own face grow red. He nodded several times, as if verifying a personal acquaintance with Byron. "You know, of course, that we have landed."

"Si. Yes. I have heard."

"And that we will now be administering civil affairs on behalf of the Sicilian people? Until qualified local and national governments can be reconstituted, naturally."

The Byron scholar's lips moved in time with Palmer's words, as if simultaneously translating them. *"Si.* I understand. But here in this town we have ... special problems," he said then.

Palmer indicated the prisoners by cocking his head in their direction. "Local Fascisti?"

"No." The young man seemed reluctant to go on.

"Collaborators with the Germans?"

The partisan leader shrugged.

"Then what?"

In the silence that followed, Palmer turned to look more closely at the prisoners. They were watching him quite as intently. A young one finally spoke. "Hello, major."

"*Silencio.*" The woman holding the rifle jabbed it in the speaker's back. Close up, Palmer saw, she seemed to be about twenty or twenty-one year's old.

"Hello from Don G.," a disembodied voice said. No one seemed to hear it but Palmer. He squinted at the group, trying to find the souce of the voice. The young Byron scholar watched the prisoners and then regarded Palmer more closely. Finally, he moistened his dusty lips.

"This is a, um, personal affair, *Maggiore*," he said, speaking even more slowly, as if desperately anxious to be understood. "Not personal so much as, um, internal? No. Communal. *Si.* Communal affair. These men have raped our young women. They have stolen property. They have blackmailed us. They have extorted money by threats. They have levied illegal taxes on our very lives. On our grain, our water, our wine, everything."

He paused for breath. In the moment of silence a voice from behind Palmer, from the audience itself, from someone not on the dais, murmured, "Hello from Don G."

This time everyone heard. The effect was uncanny. Palmer felt as if the town hall, humming with whispers and chitchat, had somehow been quick-frozen, the people like living statues, by the thin, disembodied voice, now here, now there.

He felt the sweat start out under his armpits. He pulled off his helmet and placed it carefully on the lectern.

"Here is the problem," Palmer began, speaking as slowly as the young partisan leader had. "The word you were searching for was 'civil'. These men have committed civil offenses of a nonpolitical nature. They will be punished. But they must receive civil justice from a civil court. There will be one soon in this town, a qualified civil body which will rule on these matters. You do not pretend to be such a body. I suggest that these men be locked up in the local jail. They will be well guarded by my own soldiers. This I guarantee."

One of the women guarding the prisoners shook her head violently and sent a volley of fast Sicilian at the partisan leader. "That may be," he replied confusedly in English. Then he recovered and spoke in the local dialect again, leaving Palmer clinging to isolated words and phrases.

The argument among the partisans seemed to drag on. A

young man at the far side of the room, Schmeisser machine pistol held carelessly on his hip, seemed to side with the women. Palmer began to sort it out dimly. The woman and several of the partisans did not trust any outsiders, American or not. The young leader seemed to be willing to trust the Americans, but perhaps not with these prisoners. Palmer took a long breath.

"I guarantee these men will be well guarded," he said loudly. "You have the guarantee of the government of the United States of America and of President Franklin D. Roosevelt."

He paused, trying to gauge the effect of his promise.

Then he noticed that his men, worried by his absence, had begun to appear one by one in the doorway of the town hall. They listened for a moment to the course of the discussion and slowly filtered along the side aisles.

They took up listening posts around the perimeter of the hall until they outnumbered the red armbands by nearly two to one. In firepower, Palmer's T-Force of twenty men was the equivalent of a hundred partisans. The squirt guns, the Garands, the Colt sidearms and the Thompson submachine guns glinted quietly beside the rows of hand grenades. In the intense silence the T-Force men regarded Palmer and the partisan leader with grave attention, as if trying to answer Palmer's own question. Which was the villain?

Palmer knew his men had enough power to kill every partisan, prisoner and townsperson in the hall. The logic of the unvoiced argument was deafening. The partisan leader gave in, and Palmer ordered the prisoners marched to the jail. They spent the afternoon under armed guard clearing out corpses and hosing down the interior. Then they docilely submitted to being locked in the three cells.

Within forty-eight hours a large force of infantry had moved into the town, freeing Palmer's T-Force for duties elsewhere. By the end of the week the dozen prisoners had been released. Four of them were subsequently appointed to the new governing board of the town. One became mayor, two were named magistrates. The rest melted away into the countryside in search of the partisan band that had originally captured them.

Most of the partisans were never found. But before he left the Mediterranean theater for an assignment up north near Peenemünde, Palmer heard of the Byron scholar again. At a Sicilian crossroads not far from Catania he had been nailed to a crude crucifix, castrated and disemboweled. His genitals had been stuffed into his mouth, but he had been left alive. He had lived nearly two days in a cloud of buzzing flies before a passing infantry patrol had cut him down, shot him in the head and buried him in an unmarked pit.

"Hello from Don G."

Palmer came awake in his chair, heart thudding wildly.

His mouth tasted brassy and dry with guilt. He sat up in the easy chair, forcing it to change back from a lounge to a more businesslike piece of furniture. Which was the villain?

"Hello from Don G."

He had never actually met the man he was supposed to find, the man he was supposed to protect, to whom the safeguarding of Allied-held Sicily was to be entrusted. He had heard later that Don G. had been, as he assumed all along, a very high-up gangster of some kind with American connections.

One could not call it a meeting, then, if both parties had not recognized and certified each other's identity. Over the years, Palmer rarely thought about that day in Sicily. It still had the power to unnerve him. He swallowed twice, trying to wash down the metallic taste of his memories.

One of a dozen prisoners in that town hall obviously had been Don G.

Palmer's mind went over the logic of it again for the first time in many years. One of the men whose life he had saved, whom he had helped to elevate to power under the protection of the American flag, had clearly been this Don G. Palmer wondered now whether it had been Don G. himself who supervised the crucifixion of the Byron scholar. Probably not. Bigwigs are always miles away from such scenes.

So, in the end, it didn't matter if the scholar's glasses were broken. He had little need of them. It had been his partisans who had cleared out the town so that Palmer's T-Force could safely, almost casually, enter it. And Palmer had handed him over to his enemies. Which was the villain?

If they had met that day in the town hall – Palmer and Don G. – it was a one-sided encounter.

Palmer had the strong feeling now that they had just met again.

15

Tippy stretched out full length on the bed and reached for one of Sean's Gauloises. She listened to the radio for a moment, then lighted the cigarette and blew smoke at her feet. Sean always kept his bedroom too warm, with the result that blankets and sheets that were flung to the floor in the heat of fornication usually stayed there.

It was a terrible room for anything but swinging, Tippy decided. She found it hard to picture someone actually living here, going to bed, waking up, brushing their teeth, all that jazz.

It was too fussy for either man or a woman, that was the trouble, she told herself. I had been designed by Sean's former friend Phil, that soft little suit-and-coat designer who'd had him first, before Augie. Augie, now, was a different breed. He, uh, how did it go in those homo magazines? – he did not make a statement, either by the way he dressed or his style of talking. But this room had been done by a Phil in a style you could only call Flaming Faggot.

For one thing there was really no necessity, Tippy thought, for all those yards and acres of narrow fumed Mediterranean oak shelving with spool-leg brackets. When you'd seen one shelf loaded with knicknacks, jars and whatnots, you'd seen them all. For another thing, there was no living with magenta, puce *and* shocking pink walls, not when the window shades were olive green.

Beside her, Ben stirred slightly, grumbled and fell back to sleep. Tippy turned on her side in Sean's immense king-size bed. He was the handsomest of the lot to date, she decided. Yeah, right.

He had this great crisp hair, with highlights that vibrated even when he was motionless, as now. Tippy stroked his breast hairs and made them stand up slightly. She leaned over and licked his forearm. He tasted of her.

It was hardly to be expected, Tippy thought, after their calisthenics of the last three hours, that he would taste or smell of anything else. She licked the back of her hand and found the same thing, the salt-and egg-yolk taste of all the juices they had been squandering on each other during the long, hot afternoon.

She rolled over on top of him. He awoke very slowly. Her mouth plucked at his with hard, blind mumblings. She could feel his toes wiggle under hers. Because of his football-hero build, he had looked much taller than she, but they were probably almost the same height.

"N-n-n—" he was trying to say. Her tongue kept him from uttering a "No." Then his arms came up, and he tried to lift her off him. She dug her nails into his palms and forced his arms out to the edges of the bed. He lay there, spread-eagled, and started to laugh.

"You flatter me, baby," he said then. "You don't honestly think in this world or the next I could get it up again?"

His voice sounded somewhat remote to Tippy. The fifteen minutes' nap had cooled him, she decided. He already had that Homesville look. His next words would be, "Gee, look at the time."

"Get off," he said, only partly disappointing her.

"Yeah, right," she said, rolling over to her side of the bed. "Your wife's waiting dinner."

"Ah-ah."

"Go on, get dressed and split."

"Did I say anything about having to leave?" Ben said.

"You didn't have to."

"That's unkind, baby."

"You mean," she pounced, "you can stay?"

"Ah-ah-ah."

"Shit." She retrieved her Gauloise and blew clouds of Turkish-reeking smoke into the air.

"You know, Ben," she said then in a calmer voice, "for a guy who's as good in the sack as you are, you really don't dig sex, do you?"

This was a line Tippy had heard her second week in New York at a publisher's cocktail party. A man had used it on a woman. She knew neither of them, nor what became of them after the line had been delivered. All she knew was that it had reverberated in her head for days. Her selective use of it on subsequent occasions had more than justified her hopes for this line. It proved to be everything she expected and often more.

"I don't?" Ben asked in a shocked voice.

"Yeah, right."

"After what's been going on here this afternoon?"

"I said you were good," Tippy reminded him. "It's just that you're really not *with* sex, are you?"

64

"'Jesus H. Christ, lady. We just made it twice on this here mattress here." Ben swung his legs over the edge of the bed and sat up. He reached for his underwear shorts.

"What are you afraid of?" Tippy pounced.

"Huh?" The shorts hung in midair from Ben's suddenly motionless hand.

"What're you proving?"

The shorts dropped to the floor. Ben turned on her. "You're putting me on, right?" he asked. His voice had a faint note of urgency about it.

"I'm just saying what I feel, what I sense."

"You're not making sense."

"To you," Tippy said. "A girl understands these things better."

"Understands what?" Ben had climbed back on the bed now and was kneeling over her as she lay back on her pillow. He seemed to feel the superior posture somehow strengthened his position.

Tippy made a face. "If I have to explain it, it's no good."

"Try."

She shrugged and put out her cigarette. "Lie down." She waited for him to relax into a prone position beside her. The radio was playing a slow number. She began to stroke his belly and down into his groin.

"That's some explanation," he said. His voice sounded thicker.

"Yeah, right."

She was stroking his penis with a long, slow pull, watching his face and the tightness of his closed eyelids. The mounting pleasure-pain would begin to show soon enough. She slid along the rumpled sheets and took a mouthful of the hair on his chest, pulling it slowly from side to side.

"Hurts!"

"But you love it."

She worked her way down until she could reach his kinky black pubic hair. She struck suddenly, clamping her teeth into the flattish mound of flesh. Ben's body jerked upward off the bed in an arc. His howl sounded like the anguished yelp of a kicked dog.

Tippy began to nip at the soft skin inside his thighs. "You adore this kind of pain, don't you?"

"Not so hard. Please."

"Nobody's really gotten rough with you, have they?" She

65

could feel his penis stiffening. "But now you're going to get it, baby." She squeezed him hard to test his capacity for pain. He writhed silently.

"We're absolutely made for each other," she said.

"Wha'?"

"I said, we—" She pounced like a snake, biting in to keep her hold. His scream was thin and died away quickly. He tried to push her away, but she grabbed his buttocks and held on.

After a long moment she felt his body soften and sink back into the sheets. His thigh muscles relaxed slowly. His legs spread apart enough to offer himself fully to her, unprotected.

"That's a good boy." Her words were hard to understand.

"Wha'?"

She spit him out for a moment. "Lie there and take it like a good little boy," she said. "You're going to suffer deliciously."

His eyelids flickered.

Tippy watched a pearl of blood rill up on the tender skin inside his right thigh. She licked it off. It seemed to have no taste at all. She got off the bed and poured some vodka in a glass. She sipped it slowly, then gulped a mouthful.

She dipped a fingertip in the vodka and touched a bead of it to the open bite on Ben's thigh. A twitch of his scrotum showed that he had felt the burning pain. But he lay absolutely silent now, his breathing hoarse with desire and anticipation.

Good, Tippy thought. With any luck at all, I won't have to turn this one back to his wife till Sunday night.

By which time, of course, he won't want to go.

16

Sean carefully, quietly, made his way through the vestibule of the remodeled brownstone, let himself in the downstairs door without making the latch click, tiptoed gently up the stairs to the second floor and very cautiously eased open the front door of his apartment. He stepped out of his black loafers.

Tippy and Ben had the radio on in his bedroom. They had turned it down, but the thud-slump of the rock 'n' roll number it was playing was loud enough to mask any small noises Sean might make sliding around the apartment in his stockinged feet.

Sean crossed to the foyer closet, removed his tight-fitting double-breasted suit jacket with its narrow waist and flared

66

edge. He hung it away carefully in the closet and put on a bright madras sports jacket he found there. Then he stepped into a pair of patent leather dancing pumps, checked himself in the foyer mirror and let himself out of the apartment as quietly as he had entered.

He paused for a moment on his threshold, listening to the radio in the bedroom. He could hear Tippy's light, full voice, then Ben's lower, harsher one. Christ, Sean thought, don't tell me they're lying there talking?

He met Augie a quarter of an hour later in a small, musty old bar on First Avenue in the fifties whose name had been unknown a year ago except to people like Augie, who had gone there for years. Now anybody who read the "People Are Talking About" column in *Vogue* or Eugenia Sheppard's new fashion reportage knew that this smelly little hole was the new groovy place for in-people and swinging singles.

"Are we swinging singles, luv?" he asked Augie as they sat there in the bad light and sipped Sazeracs made with Pernod rather than absinthe.

Augie had crossed one skinny, long leg over the other and was studying the way his ankle flexed in the half darkness. The light from the street had almost gone on this March afternoon. It was nearly dusk. The tiny votive candle on the table picked out yellow flecks on Augie's high brown cheeks. He blinked several times quickly.

"I'm hip we swing, doll," Augie replied, not caring too much how the sibilant came out, "but singles we ain't."

Sean could tell Augie had had a hard day by the way he let his carefully controlled diction and grammar go as campy and raunchy as any other of the boys who frequented this place. Agosto Del Gaudeo was a very respected name in the magazines, the fashion columns, on Seventh Avenue and in the most expensive stores. For a young Negro who had been born almost exactly thirty years before on 137th Street off Lenox Avenue, né August Thigpen (his mother had had a thing about names of the months; Augie had sisters named April and June, and a brother named March), Agosto Del Guadeo had done extremely well for himself.

Nearly everything Augie was he owed to his own talents and efforts. Unlike Sean, whom he had greatly helped, Augie had had no one to ease the way for him. Unlike Sean who, being A.C.-D.C., could make professional hay swinging either way, Augie was a homosexual who had gone to some pains to camouflage his inclinations, thus getting little or no professional benefit from what was, in his line of work, an asset.

"You look like way down, baby," he remarked to Sean.

"Business."

"Yeh-ass," Augie drawled. "What year is Mod Modes in, sweetie?"

"What?"

"I mean, is the company a year old, two years?"

Sean's forehead wrinkled under the crisp fringe of reddish elf locks. "First year's over. We're into our second."

Augie nodded. He started to say something, then thought better of it and kept nodding.

"Spit it out, ducks," Sean urged him.

"Why should I be the one to tell you, man? Like, let Fischetti do his own explaining."

"What can he tell me?" Sean asked. "He's the moneyman, he is. Bit if a proper dago, very serious and formal, you know. But the chap who puts up the money is the last to know why business stinks."

"Not this chap, old dear. I've slipped you enough hints, baby."

"What?"

Augie sighed. "How much do you know about Tony Fish?"

"Who the blazes is Tony Fish?"

Augie patted Sean's arm apologetically. "Gaetano Fischetti is Tony Fish."

"Tony Fish?" Sean repeated dubiously. "It's positively grotesque."

"Leave me hip you to the man," Augie said. "His business is money. You straight there, baby. But it's money both ways. Dig?"

" 'Fraid not. What's money both ways?"

"Tony Fish has two businesses," Augie explained, "making money and losing money."

"Come off it, luv," Sean said.

"Matter of fact, Tony Fish happens to be their number one money-loser. And with the income they got, honey, it ain't easy to lose as big as Tony does."

"Who's they?" Sean asked.

Augie's eyes widened as they watched him. Then his heavy lids lowered halfway, and he seemed to lose interest in Sean, the bar, the world and perhaps even life itself.

"Augie, baby, you're nodding."

Augie made a noise halfway between a snort and a laugh. "You came a long way from St. Louis but, baby, you still got a long way to go," he sang in a soft undertone. "I always thought you Limey cats was the hippest."

"If we know what you Yanks are blathering about, yes."

Augie shrugged his thin, bony shoulders. "It ain't up to me to clue you to the scene, sweetheart. That ain't my shtick. But I can kind of hip you around the edges so's you ain't quite so square."

He sighed and glanced quickly about him. The bar at dusk had begun to fill with youngish men, all thin, all extremely well dressed, all tired. It would take two or three leisurely drinks and the mounting excitement of new faces, new chances, to revive these tired customers. About now, the single girls and heterosexual pairs would start arriving, legitimizing the scene, offering topics for gossip and providing additional possibilities for coupling. By dinner time, having paired off in ways that seemed promising, the boys would be as vivacious as terriers again.

"You see," Augie began, his voice dropping so low that Sean had to lean forward to hear him, "they get two kinds of take, legit and not so legit. The legit kind comes from all sorts of operations, but what they dig best is the type business where you have low capital investment, high return and not much plant or inventory. With me, baby?"

"Only barely, luv," Sean admitted. "You're beginning to sound like one of those perfectly dreadful articles in *Women's Wear Daily*."

"Maybe you should of read some of them there articles, doll. You sure is ignorant." Augie batted his eyelashes in mock severity. "Anyway, the kind of legit operation they dearly love best is, like, loan-sharking, if you call that legit. What they don't like the worst is something that only earns a nice steady amount. With them it's either a low-cost, high-profit deal, or else it's a loser."

"They like losers?" Sean could feel the muscles of his neck tightening.

"They love losers. This is Tony Fish's speciality, setting up losers. He puts together a company, like, say, a small café. Let's say it's one more English-type pub, or one more French restaurant or one more drug-on-the-market-type thingie. He sets up tens of thousands of dollars of legit overhead and capital investment, rent, salaries, equipment, supplies, all that.

69

Then he lets it go broke."

"Ow!" Sean yelped. "You mean like Mod Modes?"

"Finally you is hip, baby. When Mod Modes goes bust, Tony Fish has himself maybe two hundred thousand in legit losses. He moves that loss back through Mod Modes ownership to half a dozen other operations that are not so legit. The cash the ownership takes out of these other operations would all go to Uncle Samuel as taxes, except that Tony Fish sets them up with legit business losses like Mod Modes."

"In other words," Sean said, "I'm nothing but a deduction for a bunch of wide boys I've never even seen." His neck felt as stiff as wood.

"Wide?"

Sean gestured aimlessly. "Forget it." He stared into his drink.

"What you bitchin' for, baby?" Augie asked. "You had a run for your money, and you ain't finished yet. You had it all, sweetie, money, photos, your name in the columns, the chicks and studs flopping on their knees every time you swish past. What more did you want, baby? Annuities? Old-age benefits? You the most ungrateful bitch I ever saw, and that's a fact."

Sean was forced to grin lopsidedly at Augie. "If you put it that way, luv, you don't leave me a leg to stand on. But where do I go from here?"

"You got another six months before Tony Fish pulls the chain on Mod Modes. By then the two of us can scheme up a little something."

"Like what?"

Augie pretended to think for a moment. When he spoke, it was obvious to Sean that this was no spur-of-the-moment idea. "You got the exposure, baby," Augie said, "I got the contacts. I think we should just lift up Sean O'Malley and shove another company in underneath him. Same ads, same clothes. Only we extend the line. O'Malley keeps on doing his low-end line for mod swingers, but we add the Del Gaudeo line for better party frocks, sportswear and separates. Dig?"

Now their voices grew very quiet. Their heads touched as they murmured details of pricing, ditribution, promotion. Augie pulled an old envelope from his inside pocket and began scribbling on it. Sean began to feel a little better. The muscles in his neck and shoulders were still knotted hard, but they no longer ached with tension.

It was good to have a friend like Augie, he thought, only

half listening to the business details. Aside from Tippy, Augie was his only friend in this huge, confusing city where nothing was what it seemed. Augie would do anything for him, just as he would do anything for Tippy. Sean found himself wondering who Tippy would do anything for.

After a while, sensing that Sean had not exactly lost interest but had plainly retreated from the responsibility of planning the business side of the venture, Augie stopped and put away the old envelope. He called over the reedy, blond waiter and ordered to more drinks.

"I thought you'd never stop, old thing," Sean confessed.

"Money details bore you, baby?"

"Horribly."

"Nothing about money bores me."

"I find myself wondering about dear, sweet Mr. Fischetti," Sean said. "There's a man money doesn't bore." He finished off the last of his old drink in one sip. "He must be fabulously wealthy."

"Well-heeled, anyway."

"Only well-heeled? His son, Ben, is well-heeled. I should have thought the father a veritable Croesus."

Augie frowned. "Get that Limey talk." He accepted the new drinks and paused until the waiter had left their table. "Your buddy, Tony Fish, he's only a little fish, sweetie. It's Ben's father-in-law who's the big fish. Vinnie Big Fish." Augie giggled.

"I'm sure I don't know what you're havering about, Luv. It only seemed quite clear to me that anyone who handles the kind of money Mr. Fischetti does has got to be fairly high up in things."

"Tony Fish is about two notches above a button man," Augie said.

"A what?"

"A soldier, a private, a low man on the totem pole."

"And this Vinnie Whatshisname, he's the top of the pole?" Sean asked.

Augie shook his head. "Don't you ever read the newspapers, baby? I mean, after you read the women's page?"

"To depressing."

"Well, Vinnie Big is up there, but he ain't all the way up there." Augie sipped his new drink. "There's somebody over him, over all of them."

"Mysterious mastermind sort of thingie?"

71

Augie's smile was sour at the edges. "Back in the woods in Haiti there's these old papaloi cats. They make big magic. They put curses on people. Turn people into zombies. Ooh, they ba-ad niggers." He giggled again, but softly. "Now this papa of Vinnie Big's, he live back in the woods, too. He a regular papaloi, for sure."

"The big boss, eh?"

Augie popped his eyes very wide and broadened his watermelon accent. " 'Fore Gawd, massah, he sho'ly Big Magic."

"Ah, come off it, luv."

Augie turned his hands palms out and reverted to his Agosto Del Gaudeo voice. "Have no fear, Augie's here." He patted Sean's hand.

Sean turned his hand over and gave Augie's a quick squeeze. That was as far as it ever got in a public place.

17

All afternoon, Palmer's attention had kept wandering away from the various events of family life. It was true, he realized as he watched his children in their own common room on the third floor, that he loved them. It had to be true or nothing else made any sense. He was instantly gnawed by the realization that this ponderous cliché would simply not stand on its bottom.

He had to love them, he repeated to himself, or nothing else made any sense. But this was just not so.

Palmer watched Gerri working her way rather quickly through six back issues of *Punch* she had borrowed from the Donnell Branch of the public library on 53rd Street. He watched her eyes race over each page, pause for a cartoon, move quickly on. She could read in excess of 900 words a minute without any special training, and Palmer had steadfastly refused to have her I.Q. tested because he was afraid it would be too high. Desirable in a boy, he believed this information was too deadly accurate for a girl to know.

Right here, Palmer saw, the fallacy of loving one's children became obvious. He did not love all his children equally, far from it. He could hardly stand Woody, now that he'd reached the stage of oxlike, stolid complacency. He felt Tom was just too bland to be real sometimes and too damned querulous at others. But Gerri, with her fast repartee, her fantastic powers of observation and her sometimes too mordant wit, was obviously his pet. Gerri was turning out to be exactly the kind of girl Palmer would have married.

He winced at the Freudian overtones of the thought and transferred his attention to Woody, hulking in a corner, lips moving, as he spelled out a required reading assignment he was supposed to have finished a month ago. This June, with a strong personal assist from God, he might just barely graduate from high school. Most likely, according to the warnings they'd gotten from his advisers, he would get a delayed diploma if he took summer make-up courses ... and passed them.

Palmer found it almost shocking that a son of his was still in high school at eighteen. He himself had graduated at sixteen from New Trier in Winnetka, and it seemed in retrospect that all of his classmates had been sixteen. He was well aware that eighteen had now become the more common age. But it still surprised him, especially since he firmly believed that what Woody and Gerry were learning in high school he had been taught in elementary school.

It didn't matter in Gerri's case, he thought now. She's teaching herself more than I'll ever know.

He frowned and stopped watching his children. He glanced down at the newspaper on his lap and then looked away from it, too. He was in a very peculiar frame of mind, had been all day, and the damned dream hadn't helped one bit. He wished Mrs. Gage would announce dinner.

Palmer understood that it was easy to love Gerri. He also knew he was being vastly unfair to Woody and Tom for not being like their sister. It didn't bother him too much that he was being unfair. Parents are always unfair, he thought now. His own had been, or his father, at any rate. And when it came to fairness, neither of his own sons would have any complaints. They would inherit enough in money and connections to be as stupid as they pleased in their later lives.

But Gerri deserved more, didn't she? Or, he wondered, was it wrong to make the girl carry the load of his own unsuccessful marriage?

It was odd how marriages went wrong these days. In Woody's generation, marriages blew in six weeks and were wiped off the books within a year. Zap. As Gerri would put it. But in Palmer's own generation marriages generally waited fifteen or twenty years to go bad. Perhaps when Woody's children reached marriageable age, the pendulum would have

73

swung back again. Or perhaps Woody's children would never reach that age. Perhaps the whole thing would have blown off in a giant fireball, third planet out from the sun, blasting the rest of the solar system with deadly radiation from what had once been called earth.

Palmer got to his feet with an undisguised grunt of pain. Only Gerri looked up. "Going to dress?" she asked.

"For what?"

"Didn't you say you had that thrilling, icky political dinner tonight?"

Palmer groaned. "Couldn't you have managed to forget it?" He rubbed his right eye. "I had."

"You're in a real thing today."

"What kind of thing?"

"Mood. Study. You're bugged."

Palmer turned to leave the room, then paused. "When one is cursed with the power of observation," he said then, "one must also practice the art of discretion."

"Dig," Gerri said. "But what bugs, anyway?"

"Grown-up stuff."

"Yech." She put away the magazines and stood up. Her figure at fourteen, Palmer saw, was more like his than Edith's. He hoped she might fill out some as she moved into the more frenetic social life of senior high school.

"Sounds to me," Gerri went on, "like undifferentiated *Weltschmerz.*"

"When was the last time I washed out your mouth with soap?"

"Never."

"Always a first time," Palmer said. He twinkled falsely at her and left the room. There were times when even Gerri was too much.

18

Harry Klaman stepped out into the cool evening of Bleecker Street. Farther down, the Italian sausage shops and bakeries gave forth strong, fresh odors. Mothers with baby carriages and strollers paused in front of Our Lady of Pompeii and gossiped. Girls with tall beehive hairdos flirted with boys in tight trousers. Riordan, the beat cop, stood beside Harry's Thunderbird and eyed it, then Harry, then his wristwatch.

"Sorry, officer," Harry said. "Am I overtime?"

Riordan pointed silently to the NO PARKING ANY TIME sign.

"Jeez," Harry intoned, his eyes wide.

Riordan stared at him for a long moment, then turned and walked away.

"Mick prick," Harry said, not loudly enough for Riordan to hear, but just enough for him to know something had been said.

Having indulged himself in this bit of childish play, Harry cackled soundlessly as he unlocked the door of his car on the side away from the curb. The grin on his mouth froze, then faded. Someone had scrawled in orange crayon: "Viny Big eats cok." Sweat broke out on Harry's forehead.

Some Sicilian kid had written the insult, of that Harry was certain. Only a Sicilian kid would know what a mortal sin he had described, a sin that someone of Don Vincenzo's stature would know was punishable by death. All forms of this kind of sexual fooling around, Harry recalled, were totally beyond the pale. He pulled out of his pocket the damp handkerchief with which he had been keeping his face partially dry. Hurriedly he scrubbed the insult from the side of the car door.

Then he got behind the wheel and drove away, heading uptown on Sixth Avenue, drifting with the traffic, not trying to make time. Funny, he thought, how you had to be as Sicilian as any of them if you wanted to stay in one piece.

He reviewed for the twentieth time Vinnie Big's complete assurances that the People's Bank of Westchester would delay no further in reopening credit lines for Harry's customers. For the twentieth time, he felt the whole promise was hot air.

It just wasn't possible, Harry decided, that even Vinnie Big, with or without that good-looking son-in-law of his, could swing People's around that fast when it was on the eve of a merger with Ubco. You could say what you wanted about the promises of Don Vincenzo Biglioto, regardless of who his father was, and still you knew he couldn't pay off on each and every one forever.

In Harry's opinion, Vinnie had bitten off more than he could chew. It would've been different if he'd promised financial support from Gaetano Fischetti's bond and mortgage company. Everybody knew Vinnie controlled Fischetti, the father of his own son-in-law. Gaetano was Vinnie's second cousin, which made his son a third or fourth cousin of the daughter of Vinnie's he had married.

Harry made a disgusted face at the idea of marrying that close. Of course, his own Uncle Motke had married a second cousin, Hannah. Let's face it, he thought, Jews make the best Sicilians.

But when it came to Vinnie Big's promise today, Harry was pretty sure it couldn't be kept. Vinnie might intend to keep it, might even work hard to keep it. But Vinnie, even Vinnie, would fail.

So, even Vinnie was allowed a failure. True, you did business with someone of Vinnie's stature because he more or less guaranteed success. But everybody was entitled to goof now and then. This would be Vinnie's goof.

Except, Harry reminded himself, that I can't goof.

Things were stretched to thin for anything to go as radically wrong as they were about to go. If Harry couldn't sell scores of his split-ranch-plunge-type homes and bring in a cash flow to pay his lumber and masonary creditors, to meet final payments on land-acquisition purchase contracts, to pay electrical wholesalers for major appliances and to meet the interest payments on his previous indebtedness, then Harry would go bust in a spectacular way, bringing down a real estate and construction empire worth, conservatively, a quarter of a billion in assets.

Never mind creditors, Harry told himself bitterly. I need cash just to meet payroll.

It was imperative that his customers get mortgage money. It was equally imperative that old customers looking for home-improvement money be allowed to renegotiate their mortgages and grab off the few gees they needed.

So, finally, it became imperative that Harry Klaman get Vinnie Big in a box.

At the very thought of boxing in Don Vincenzo, Harry broke out into tiny rills of sweat. They started in his receding hairline and ran down his forehead and sideburns. He pulled to the curb at Ninth Street and stared a long time down the block. He could hardly breathe.

Harry could feel his heart hammering away at his rib cage. Even through the layers of fat, Harry could feel the violent knocking of fear.

Box in Vinnie Big? It wasn't possible. The Balestrere brothers out in Queens had tried it three years ago. Carmine Iandole had tried it in 1954. J. Edgar Hoover had been trying it for thirty years.

Who am I to think I can get away with it? Harry wondered. Just a fat mockie in a big sweat.

But it was just barely possible he might succeed, Harry decided. The Balesteres had wanted Queens and Brooklyn, half of Vinnie Big's territory. Carmine Iandole had wanted everything, beginning with Vinnie's life. Hoover wanted Vinnie behind bars. All of them wanted something big and final, something Vinnie Big could not give them and go on being Vinnie Big.

All I want, Harry told himself, is a little crumb, less than the sweat off Vinnie's balls, a drop of nothing, almost. I'm willing to pay for it. I'm willing to pay anything up to 12 percent, even 13, he added hurriedly to himself.

He stared along Ninth Street, ideas swarming wildly. Biglioto and Gaetano Fischetti in one box. Unlimited funds from Fischetti's bond and mortgage company. His lungs ached.

Harry Klaman licked his lips. They tasted of salt. He got out of his car and walked unsteadily along Ninth Street to the remodeled brownstone he had seen Ben Fischetti enter. Standing in the vestibule, he started to copy down the four names on the mailboxes. A private cop would do the rest for him.

The sweat pouring down his forehead nearly blinded Harry.

19

Graziella had been asleep in her crib since seven o'clock. Tina and Anita had gone to their room at seven thirty and would surely, by now, be asleep. Barney had wanted to wait up for Ben, but at a little after eight in the evening Rosalie had sent him off to bed.

The Saturday evening schedule was now in effect. As she had since she was a small girl, Rosalie followed the same routine. Seven thirty belonged to Jackie Gleason. People said he was coarse, and the way he talked about women and booze sometimes, well ... But Rosalie liked him. He was something constant. The years he had been away from television, she had missed his big, moonlike face with the dark eyes full of hurt. When he came back, she vowed never to miss him again if she could help it.

By nine o'clock Rosalie was sure something terrible had happened to Ben. Nine o'clock was no time to be getting home for dinner. The whole roast couldn't be eaten now, anyway. It was overheated and overdone.

She sat upright in the upholstered chair across from the television set and watched the start of the nine o'clock movie. Usually it was a good one, with a star like Clark Gable or Jimmy Stewart or Cary Grant. But if in an hour's time it failed to hold her, Rosalie knew that *Gunsmoke* was waiting to save the evening. You could depend on Marshal Dillon. People said Kitty, who owned the bar, was too much for a family show. After all, some of those girls in her bar, well...

But Rosalie liked Kitty. She liked Doc. She missed Chester, the cripple, but she enjoyed Festus. Most of all, she adored Matt Dillon. She had long ago decided that whatever was going on between him and Kitty, it took a woman as rough as Kitty to match Matt Dillon.

At nine thirty the phone rang. Knowing it was the police, Rosalie hurried through the long living room to the kitchen, where the downstairs phone was kept. "Yes?" she asked in a tense, high voice. "This is Mrs. Fischetti speaking."

"I'd never have believed it," Ben said.

"You're all right?"

"Not bad." He paused a long time. "These Ubco people are long-winded as hell, honey. Now they want to take me to a late dinner."

"All right."

"And by the time we're done, it'll even be later, maybe midnight."

"That's all right," she said. "Sophia Loren is on the eleven o'clock movie."

"Too late, I'm afraid," Ben continued. "I think I'd better stay over in town, honey. Okay?"

"Stay over?"

"In town."

"With who?"

Ben paused. "At a hotel, sweetheart."

"Papa will put you up."

"I don't want to bother him so late, honey."

"It's no bother. He's your family. I'll call him and tell him to expect you."

"No," Ben said. "I'll call him. You go to sleep, baby."

"All right. You know Papa's number? It's unlisted."

"*Ma*, shu'," Ben joked.

"If he isn't in, tell Annunciata, the maid, you want the guest room on the second floor. It's my old room."

"*Si, bambina.* Good night."

"Good night, Ben. Oh, Ben?"

But he had hung up.

Rosalie walked slowly back into the living room. She discarded the high-heeled mules and sat down in the chair across from the television set, her ankles turned out, her bare feet pigeon-toed on the carpet. She watched the film unfold for another reel, then suddenly got up and switched off the set. Just like that.

She had already walked back into the dining room and was removing the two place settings there when she realized that she could not remember ever doing such a thing before — switching off the television in the middle of a program. Her parents had done this on occasion when she and Celia had neglected their homework. Or she might have tuned in another channel. But Rosalie herself had never before, in all her years of watching the television tube, actually turned it off before the end of whatever program she was watching.

She glanced nervously at the set in the other room, as if the baleful glance of its single blind eye would somehow strike her down. Then she laughed nervously at herself, collected the dishes and silverware and walked into the kitchen.

Mrs. Traficanti had left everything very neat and clean on Friday night. Saturday and Sunday she had off this week, and Rosalie was determined the kitchen would be as neatly arranged Monday morning as Mrs. Traficanti had left it.

She took the roast out of the oven and sniffed it. She had done it English style, plain, with a little salt and a bit of powdered mustard on it. Now it was overdone. Rosalie quickly cut three slices and stored the rest of the roast in the huge double-door refrigerator.

Her short, plump fingers worked automatically as she put a pan on the range, oiled it, diced half a small onion into it, some green pepper and a small garlic clove. She stirred the mixture till it started to brown, cut the slices of beef in pieces and folded them in. Then she dished the whole thing out, ten minutes after she'd started, carried her plate to the kitchen bar and sat down on one of the tall stools.

Three hundred calories? Rosalie asked herself. Tops, three hundred. There hadn't even been half a teaspoon of oil. She started to reach in the breadbox, then checked herself, her plump, full lips pressed in a hard line of determination.

"No starch," she announced out loud.

She sighed as she ate. Not that the food didn't taste good. Just that she hated eating alone, seldom had. But tonight was apparently some kind of turning point, she decided. First I turn off the TV, she thought, then I eat alone. The last time she remembered eating alone was in the hospital with Graziella. Even there, they had brought the baby in to nurse almost as soon as lunch was over.

Halfway through her sparse meal, Rosalie reached into the breadbox again. This time her hand encountered the heel of a loaf of Italian whole-wheat bread. She broke off a shred of crisp curst with sesame seeds clinging to it. Desperately she stuffed it into her mouth. I'm fooling everybody, she thought dejectedly.

Stealing the crumb of bread depressed her. She made herself unhappy doing things like that. She knew better. And Ben not coming home only made her lust all the more for bread or pasta or something to go with the beef. Crazy, she told herself. Starve all day, starve all week, starve for a month now. Then cheat with a piece of bread? Just crazy.

The sisters at Sacred Heart had her number, all right. Gluttony. At lunch Rosalie would always sit next to Sheila Keefe, who hated desserts. That way Rosalie got two desserts, at least until the sisters caught on. She glanced down at the food in her plate now and, faintly sickened, pushed it away from her, another first.

Rosalie got to her feet and wandered back into the living room. She supposed the smart thing would be to put on her nightgown, go upstairs to bed and watch the Sophia Loren movie till she was sleepy. Instead she sat down on the couch and picked up the magazine she had bought that afternoon in Manhattan. They sold the magazine in Scarsdale and, in fact, in virtually every town in the country, but Rosalie had never bought it before. It was a magazine for women, and somehow being in Manhattan today had gotten her all reckless and daring, and she had bought the magazine for the first time in her life.

Three new things today, she remembered now.

She scanned some immense color photographs of beautiful young models in short, straight hairdos. One had hair like Rosalie's, but shorter, the English mod look, like a waif boy's hair, carefully ragged and half covering her eyes. The model looked absolutely great, Rosalie thought, but you had to have that pinched face to get away with it.

Instead of a face like *gnoccos*, round and wide and white. Dumpling head.

She would spend more time in the sunshine. Brunettes should look brown and healthy like her father, not white and sickly, the way she did. She read further in the magazine and was soon choked up with fear and excitement, reading a long article about birth-control pills. None of the language made sense – menstrual cycles, ovulation – she understood none of it. But the fact that they would write in a magazine about *that*, just come right out and write about it, made her heart pound and her cheeks feel hot.

She knew it to be a sin, of course. The article mentioned some Catholic doctors who weren't sure it was a sin. But Rosalie knew you didn't go to a doctor to know what was a sin; you learned such things from a priest. And who in her right mind would ask a priest about this? She could always ask her mother, of course, but she shared her father's and her grandfather's view of her mother, pretty, skittish and unsteady. The fact that there had only been Rosalie and Celia and no other children was always a little suspicious. Mamma was from Turin, not a *Siciliana* at all, and thus unable to show proper respect. Not that the north Italians were frivolous by nature, but they had no sense of values of any deep seriousness. She couldn't blame Mamma for being that way. But she had been forced many times, often reluctantly, to admit Mamma's grave shortcomings. After all, when two respected men like her grandfather and her father both felt the same way ... So this was one thing Rosalie didn't want to ask her mother. She was afraid of the answer she might hear: use pills.

Well, why not use the pills? Rosalie frowned and let the magazine drop in her lap. Had she actually thought that? Was it her hidden idea that the pill was not a sin, or perhaps only a small one? Was she as frivolous as Mamma? It didn't matter what a magazine said some doctors thought. The Pope had been clear enough about it.

She was on her feet, going into Ben's study, heading for the big dictionary he kept in there on a stand. Ov-u la-tion.

Later in the evening, in her nightgown, Rosalie lay in bed wondering what it would be like to have Ben in bed and not worry about getting pregnant. She really didn't want any more children, not for a while, and it killed her to refuse Ben except for those certain times of the month. But to do that any night, every night, and not worry, that would be something wild and new.

The magazine had mentioned even crazier things, things you didn't have to remember to take, intrauterine devices. That meant something they put inside the uterus. The uterus was the womb. The womb was where the baby took form and grew. Rosalie had looked all of it up in a frenzy of discovery. The intrauterine device had to be inserted through the cervix. The cervix was the opening from the vagina into the uterus. In an hour with the dictionary she had learned all the words.

But that meant a doctor had to go in there and ... but why not?

Old Doctor Scaffidi had been in there, and so had Ben. It was only nature, after all. And to be honest, with their quick, grimy fingers, Frank Gagliardi and Charley Gioe and Dennis Horgan had all three been in there that night everybody got drunk in junior year after the church dance. And on their way out, so had Barney, Tina, Anita and Graziella. A regular public thoroughfare.

She needed a traffic cop down there, that was it. Thinking about it, Rosalie grinned and turned off the bedside light.

She had a lot to learn about all of it and all of everything else, too. They had schools for grown-ups. She ought to have a night or two out. If there wasn't anything in Westchester, she knew there was a place on Twelfth Street in Greenwich Village, near Papa's house. They called it the New School, and they had evening classes for adults and gave college credit. Rosalie found it strange to think of herself as an adult. Maybe after being a full-time mother, she could get back to being a schoolgirl again. Maybe she could get a bachelor's degree. Maybe some day a master's like Ben.

She yawned. It was only eleven o'clock, but she was very tired. So many new things had happened to her all of a sudden. Ben could stay away overnight more often. She seemed to think better with him gone.

20

Woods Palmer had played with his shrimp salad, ignored his potage St. Germaine, picked at his breast of capon with green peas and duchesse potatoes. Now he toyed with his cherries jubilee. The stench of burnt cognac made his nostrils twitch.

He turned to his left and nodded politely to the governor, sitting three seats down, spoon poised over the cherries jubilee without ever quite actually picking any up and carrying it to his mouth. Palmer gave a straight-line smile, no upturned corner of the mouth informing it with mirth, and got an identical pseudosmile in return.

He turned to his right and looked along the dais to where the mayor sat, neither his spoon nor his dessert touched. A man stood behind the mayor and whispered in his ear, holding a hand before his lips in such a carefully casual way that Palmer realized the man had been hiding his lips all his life.

Glad he was no lip-reader, Palmer returned his attention to the overflamed cherries jubilee. How he had ever gotten himself into the position of being unable to refuse yet another of these idiotic dinners – especially in view of the vow he had vowed never to let his job encroach on his evenings again – was beyond him. He wished he had pleaded anything up to and including mental illness to get out of this particular dinner.

Like most of the evening affairs in New York's leading hotels – at least those which weren't bar mitzvahs, convention dinners or golden anniversary celebrations – this one was a testimonial with a strong political odor. Like those testimonials that were given not in honor of an organization but rather of an individual, this dinner celebrated some perfect nonentity Palmer had never heard of, whose accomplishments still defied analysis despite the fact that they had already been trumpeted skyward by the rabbi who had blessed the dull evening and the priest who had blessed the cliché meal.

Palmer knew, and the knowledge caused his leaden heart to sink still farther toward his shoes, that his blessed ignorance of the guest of honor could not last long. Within a few moments, with the burnt-caramel tang of the dessert still fresh in his mouth, a toastmaster would arise to quip, to introduce the dais guests and to present the main speaker.

It was this speaker, whoever he might be, whose existence freighted Palmer's heart with heaviness. This man would spend not less than thirty minutes praising the life and the works of the honored guest. To spend twenty-nine minutes would be to insult him. But every minute over thirty during which windy platitudes and immense empty generalizations soughed down upon the audience was an additional leaf in the crown of laurels being plaited for the honored guest's brow.

"Can't go the cherries, either, huh?" the man on Palmer's right asked.

He turned to see his neighbor more clearly. He recognized him as a state senator of some broad influence. "I think they're burnt," he said.

"This hotel couldn't cook its way out of a paper bag," the senator announced mysteriously. "How's everything at the bank?"

Palmer placed his spoon on the rim of the plate. "In and out, in and out."

"Hear you're buying that Westchester bank finally."

"Looks that way. It's only taken ten years to get the application okayed."

"That would have started before your time at Ubco, wouldn't it?" the senator wondered.

"Much. This is only my second year with the bank."

"Then you're not too familiar with the bank you're buying."

"I will be, by the time we actually sign the papers."

"I hope so." The verb held more than casual emphasis. The senator seemed to shift gears suddenly and veer off at a different speed on another road. "Lovely warm day for March, wasn't it?"

"Yes. I – what did you mean, you hope so?"

The senator shrugged. He had a big, florid face built up out of a few slabs of healthy-looking suet, a small mouth and wary eyes. The mouth grew all but invisible as he spoke. "Nothing. You're not originally a New Yorker, are you?"

"Chicagoan." Palmer wondered why the man refused to pursue the original line of thinking.

"You learn to treasure these good spring days. They're rare. Then all of a sudden it's summer, and we're sweltering in this soup kettle of a town."

"We took a spin in the country this morning," Palmer said. "Whereabouts?"

"New Jersey. My wife needed some plants at a nursery. Place called Amato's."

The senator nodded slowly. "Amato's." His eyes, as he watched Palmer for a long moment without saying anything, grew even warier. Then he opened his mouth to speak.

"Ladies and gemmun," the toastmaster brayed. "Have yr attention, please?"

Looking almost relieved, the senator turned to face the

speaker's lectern. He said nothing more to Palmer for the rest of the evening.

21

The night sky was cloudless. Having risen at about ten o'clock, the moon shone clearly down through the whitewash-spattered glass roofs of the greenhouses.

Inside, all green had turned to black. The moist warmth of the day had grown clammy with cold. Sprays had been shut down. Along row after row of greenhouses, all was silent.

In the distance, the faint whine of an electric motor accompanied the nervous beam of a small head lamp jittering about weakly in the darkness. The golf cart moved slowly, very slowly. The batteries had all but run down after the long Saturday of use. They would have to be recharged while Don Girolamo slept.

The trouble was, he thought, *no ha sonno*. He hadn't felt sleepy for many nights now. Normally he slept *come un ghiro*, but tonight his brain was spinning like a top instead of sleeping like one.

The golf cart bumped slowly along the corridor, its pale headlight doing little to illuminate the path. Don Girolamo knew the way, even with his eyes closed. He had spent every hour of the day and night in this place for more years now than even he could remember.

It wasn't, he told himself now, that he was *un solitario*. He was, if anything, *un uomo socievole*, always welcoming whoever came to him. But that was just it. Everyone came to him. He had no need to go anywhere outside his greenhouses.

The clammy cold had begun to chill the marrow of his bones. He steered the cart around a corner. He touched a button on the dashboard of the golf cart. A silent signal electronically opened a door that lay in darkness.

"Santo?"

There was a rustling from somewhere inside. Beyond the open door, another opened and a crack of light showed. "*Sì, padrone?*"

Don Girolamo edged the golf cart into the room. Behind him the electronically controlled steel door slid shut on noiseless nylon bearings. He watched Santo shuffle across the room and double-lock the steel door. Then Santo helped him from the golf cart, through an inner door and to the easy chair by a small wood fire. Don Girolamo sank into the chair and felt the fire's warmth. He watched Santo roll the golf cart into a corner and connect it to the battery charger. He wished there were a way to charge his old bones, too.

Aching bones. Don Girolamo sighed heavily. If he could not sleep tonight, he would feel the pain through all the hours of darkness. He could stand pain in the day, with so many things to distract him, *ma nel cuor della notte*, alone and sleepless, never.

Day was so much more different than night for him. By day the plants poured out their life-giving *ossigeno*. The air was thick and rich with it. He could feel his lungs heavy with the strength of its life.

But at night the plants turned to murderers. They filled the air with death. The night itself crawled with killers. And all the vitality Don Girolamo had greedily sucked from life during the day became at night the poisonous kiss of death.

PART TWO
Tuesday

22

Jimmy pulled the Lincoln tightly against the curb at Fifth Avenue in the fifties, and Palmer got out of the car. He dismissed his driver and stared after the long black car as it pulled into early morning traffic and disappeared, heading downtown.

Had he told Jimmy about picking him up early for lunch? And about working late tonight?

Palmer glanced at himself in the plate glass of the bank's facade. The look was quick and veiled, but it was enough to assure him that he was all right, tall and thin with a dark gray hard-finish herringbone tweed coat and no hat, his thin blond hair slightly ruffled by the March wind. He rarely looked at his face. It had not changed materially in the last ten years, except perhaps that the hollows under his cheekbones had grown somewhat and the skin around his dark blue eyes showed a few more tiny wrinkles.

Palmer frowned at the traffic, glanced at his watch and started toward the immense upthrusting structure of aluminium and glass that housed the main office of the largest private commercial bank in the country. It being not much past 8.30 in the morning, the doors were locked. But the guard had been watching for the Lincoln, and before Palmer could touch the push plate of the right-hand door, the guard had it unlocked and open wide. In accord with procedure, his gun holster was unbuttoned and his right hand rested on the butt of his .38 special.

"Thanks, Ed."

"Good morning, Mr. Palmer."

Palmer strode quickly along the gray and white terrazzo floor toward the automatic elevators at the rear of the banking floor. A few tellers looked up. Those who were women smiled. Most of the floor officers busied themselves at their desks with meaningless fidgets. Another guard pressed the elevator button and had the door open as Palmer reached him.

"Thanks, Harold."

"Good morning, Mr. Palmer."

The doors started to close as Palmer's leg cleared the electric-eye beam. Officiously Harold opened the doors again, reached into the elevator and pressed the "PH" button.

"Thanks, Harold."

"Have a good day, Mr. Palmer."

His smile, which seemed to have been slashed into his bony face with a straight razor, lasted until just before the elevator doors closed. Through the space of barely an inch between the doors, Palmer saw the smile fade. Click.

Officious bastard, Palmer thought, and wondered how difficult it could have been for Harold to hold that assassin's smile of his another half a second. The elevator shot upward, and Palmer closed his eyes as a means, admittedly unsuitable, of keeping his stomach from rising with equal rapidity. Having once mastered Newton's various laws, he knew that his stomach was, if anything, sinking as the elevator car rose. But it wasn't his fault, he decided, if his stomach felt as if it were trying to crawl up his esophagus.

This was going to be one beaut of a Tuesday.

Elston, the officious, smarmy little bluenose who had first uncovered problems in People's Bank of Westchester's loan situation, had yesterday taken him through the various pieces of printed literature in which the bank had divulged some few faint inklings of its position to its stockholders. Even from the neat evasions, omissions and half-truths that made up the bulk of this literature – as it did most stockholder communications – Palmer could only agree with Elston that something was very wrong up in Westchester.

Rather than alarm the top management at People's Bank and give them time to scrape together some kind of plausible story, Palmer had let the matter entirely alone until today, when a meeting had already been scheduled on several other matters having to do with the prospective merger. It was at this meeting, to be held in the bank's dining room downtown in the financial district, that Palmer planned to spring one or two rude questions on old Phelps Lassiter, who had been president of People's since the Bank Holiday of 1933.

He knew Phelps had no answers. Phelps was like too many of the titular heads of these smaller institutions; he knew very little about his own operation, about business in general and about banking in particular. In most of the cases where a smaller bank suddenly got aggressive, someone who knew as much as there was to know in all three categories was keeping the front man up front. In Phelps' case, Palmer thought, it was probably one of his senior veepees, whichever had managed to buy up the most stock through the various highly favorable option plans People's had made available to its management.

That stock, after nearly a decade of waiting, would soon be worth its weight in Ubco shares. Whoever had been building toward this moment would exchange some undistinguished stock for a nest egg of probably the most respectable blue-chip bank shares ever issued.

Running over the list of People's officers he knew, Palmer decided it might be Ralph Fenger, who functioned as an exec veepee, or it might be the head of the board's executive committee, Charley Kornbluth. Either one was greedy enough, but neither had the brains for it. Someone else, then, some unknown quantity.

The elevator door flew open, and sunlight burst in on Palmer as he left the elevator car. The large bubble skylights set into the penthouse roof allowed the March sun to hammer down directly onto the deep maroon carpet.

Squinting at the glare, Palmer walked quickly along the corridor to his office. Ubco was a two-headed bank, in that it had this extremely modern main office in midtown Manhattan and a very fusty old-style main office on Broad Street in the financial district. Both were "main" offices, but only one was the "head" office, the one in which Palmer found himself at any given moment. Today was a split session; the morning would be spent midtown, and from lunch on, Palmer would work at the downtown office.

Although Palmer suspected the worst, he could never prove to his own satisfaction that his secretary, Miss Czermat, actually sold advance copies of his weekly itinerary to junior officers at both banks. Nor could Palmer prove that junior officers made no advance dates for long lunches until they had checked Palmer's weekly schedule to find out which main office would be home base during what lunchtime. Palmer, of course, refused to ask any of the senior officers if this were true. Instead, he contented himself with giving Miss Czermat detailed itineraries, down to the last fifteen minutes of accounted-for time, and then deliberately being somewhere else from time to time on an irregular basis. It kept the juniors on their toes, and it amused the seniors to watch the progress of the game.

The penthouse floor was deserted at this hour. Palmer entered his own office and, as sometimes happened on a particularly sunny morning, winced.

The immense sweep of the room, the glassed-in roof, the rising ceiling line that followed the upswept configuration of a bird's wing, the far end with its twenty-foot high plate glass windows always gave Palmer the feeling that he had somehow entered the small end of a megaphone and that if he so much as cleared his throat, the sound would emerge at the far end as thunder capable of shattering glass.

He hung his coat away in a closet that stood behind a teak door that, like the windows, went from floor to ceiling. Then he opened his brown leather lawyer's satchel on the desk and took out the papers Miss Czermat had given him last night from his "in" box. These he laid in his "out" box, snapped his satchel shut and put it away in the closet with his coat.

He sat down at his desk, another immense expanse of teak, and stared at the "out" basket. For a man who had sworn to Take It Easier, he was engaged in a rather elaborate ritual of self-deception.

Saturday night had been totally squandered on a political dinner at which he had learned nothing; nor had he communicated anything of import to anyone else. At the predinner reception, he had picked up the usual gossip about who wanted what nominations and who was getting what contracts. But during the past few months Palmer had more or less kept aloof from that kind of chitchat, especially during the current period of tight money when any banker in any social situation was an instant target for half a dozen businessmen in dire need of sounding off.

Even so, Palmer reflected, he hadn't cut down nearly enough on evening socializing. And here he was now, taking work home and bringing it back the next morning, all neatly finished.

He tried to look away from the "out" basket but only succeeded in staring at its filled twin next to it, which Miss Czermat had filled with a variety of statements, letters, reports, memoranda, requests, forms and the like.

He found himself wondering how many other people had jobs like this. It was beadwork. As casual acquaintance at a cocktail party, a man named Spitzer, who had been some kind of advertising executive, had once explained the beadwork concept to Palmer. You came in every weekday morning, the man had said, and your desk was covered with beads of all sizes, shapes and colors. By the end of the day you had strung them all carefully, efficiently, perhaps even artistically, into a pattern. Next morning when you came in, your desk was covered with another random assortment of unstrung beads. And so on.

Palmer wondered if anybody ever gave the whole assortment of backhanded sweep of the arm and cleared every last bead off the desk. But if one did that, Palmer realized, one had nothing to do for the rest of the day.

He glanced at the clock. Eighty forty. This was going to be a grand Tuesday. About the only way Palmer could think of to get rid of his load of frustration was to dump it on the group from People's Bank whom he was meeting for lunch.

That, he reflected, was going to be some lunch.

23

"*Si*, Mamma,' Rosalie was saying.

She had put on her nicest, warmest dressing gown. It was not more than nine in the morning, but she had been up since six with the children and getting Ben to the office. She had looked forward on this windy Tuesday to staying in the nice, warm house and playing mamma in her nice, warm dressing gown. Now her own mamma had telephoned.

"Call Mrs. Traficanti. She can come early," Mamma was saying in her hard Torinese accent. "She can give the kids lunch. You have lunch in town with Celia and me. What do you say, *ragazzina*?"

"At Casa Coppola?" Rosalie asked. "But we were there Saturday, Mamma. And we're seeing you this Friday. Besides, I'm on a diet. For real."

"Diet? Don Vitone has good diet food for you."

"Don't make fun of me, Mamma. I'm trying hard to lose weight."

"*Si, figuri*. Everybody's trying to lose weight."

Rosalie took a long, steadying breath. She could never before in her life remember being this angry with Mamma. Not this way. Not so that she found it difficult to keep from saying something sharp and ... and without respect. But why did Mamma try to keep her a fat little baby, the way she kept Celia?

"Mamma, it's easy for you to say. You have the figure of a young girl."

Rosalie could hear the self-satisfaction in Mamma's voice. "*E vero*. And I eat all I want of Don Vitone's pasta. This dieting is one of your new ideas, Rosa, like the way you had they chop off your hair like a boy's. It's not womanly."

93

Rosalie closed her eyes tightly, as if to shut out the sound of the rich, self-indulgent, heavily accented voice coming over the telephone receiver. The nerve, she thought, the nerve of this woman who had never done anything at all in her life except live like a parasite off Papa. She was only that, nothing more, not even giving value for the money she spent. It was almost as if in some fit of melancholy madness after the death of his first wife, Don Vincenzo said to himself: now that the war is over, send to Italy for a doll; all I want is a petite brunette doll with a pretty face who will lie around all day and look pretty. It isn't necessary that she give me a big family; it isn't even necessary that she give me pleasure in bed whenever I desire. I don't require that she give the children love or even attention because I have the money to hire the finest governess and send the children to the most exclusive convent schools. It isn't even necessary that she instruct the children in the ways of the world or of humanity or of womankind or show them how to dress or talk. And when they are grown women, my daughters, all I require of my petite wife is that she parade them around where my friends and associates can see them like two gnocchi, two dumpling-faced fat girls whose only role in life is to show the world of Don Vincenzo Biglioto, by contrast with their own puffy bodies, how petite, how ravishingly youthful his young, young, young doll-wife is. .

"Rosalie?"

"*Si*, Mamma."

"Well? Are you coming?"

"I t-told you." Rosalie hated to hear her voice begin to break that way. "I'm on a diet."

"*Perchè?*"

"To l-lose weight, Mamma."

"*Che sciocchezze!*"

"It's not nonsense. I'm tired of being fat so you can look thin."

At the other end of the line there was a silence of a second or less, and then Rosalie heard a sharp intake of breath. "*You* no blame *me*," Mamma said then, her accent worsening. "I am no the one."

Not listening now, Rosalie began to shake her head, as if to erase what had been said and what was being said, "I'm on a diet, Mamma," she repeated doggedly.

"I am no the one who want you *una pingue ragazzina*," Mamma insisted. "It was no me."

"It was no me," she said again.

"It was no –"

Rosalie hung up the telephone.

She was breathing so hard and so fast that her lungs began to ache. Her heart pounded wildly, as if trying to twist its way out into the daylight, where everything could be seen clearly and in truth and people were what they seemed to be.

The telephone rang.

By reflex alone – knowing it was her mother, knowing she didn't want to talk to her mother, but unable to suppress the habit of being open to her mother, being "in" to her – Rosalie picked up the phone.

"*Si*, Mamma."

"Rosalie, you hang up on me?"

"Si."

"We eat somewhere else, then, *bambina*. You want a nice steak? Some *insalata verde*? We go to that place Papa owns on Sixtieth Street? *Si? Kevin's* Dublin Chophouse?"

Rosalie could feel the nausea building in her throat. She swallowed nervously twice. "All I want to do is stay home with the kids, Mamma."

"And all I want to do," her mother said in a strange, wild voice, "is see my own two kids."

"All of us will be in town on Friday, Mamma. Ben must have told you."

"Friday? For dinner?"

"Did Ben forget to tell you?"

"But it's only Tuesday today."

"That's not long till Friday. Honest, Mamma."

There was a pause. They had quarreled, it seemed to Rosalie, for the first time as adults of equal rank. They had patched it up as two adults might. "So we'll see you on Friday," she said aloud. "And this way you'll see all the kids, too. It's better this way."

"*Si.* I didn't know."

"He should have told you Saturday night."

"*Si.*" A pause. "What Saturday night?"

"When he –" Rosalie stopped short. The path had suddenly forked. "Didn't he –?" Carefully, now. Being adult was a tricky business. "Didn't he, uh, phone you Saturday?"

"He's a good boy, Rosa. He can't remember everything."

"*Si*, Mamma."

"Okay. Friday, then. I wait till Friday."

95

"*Si*, Mamma."

"But we talk before Friday."

"*Si*, Mamma."

"*Arrivederci*."

"*Si*. Good-bye, Mamma."

When she hung up the phone this time, Rosalie was not completely aware of what her fingers were doing. Her mind clicked over the events of Saturday and Sunday, flicking rosary beads with the speed of an abacus worker. One, he had had to have a late dinner and stay in town. Two, he would stay at Papa's. Three, he would call to tell them he was coming. Four, he had arrived home in Scarsdale after lunch on Sunday. Five, he spent the afternoon reading the papers and saying nothing, to anyone, about anything.

Rosalie found herself in the kitchen, staring at the breadbox. She had opened the copper-plated front of the box. A half loaf of Italian white bread and a full loaf of Italian whole-wheat bread with sesame seeds lay in the bottom of the box. The loaves were from the same bakery on Bleecker Street whose bread Rosalie had eaten since she was an infant, teething on crusts.

She reached in and broke the heel off the whole-wheat loaf. She started to cram it into her mouth. Then she stopped, slowly replaced the heel, closed the breadbox and sank down on the kitchen stool.

She was still crying softly, almost to herself, when Tina found her there half an hour later. She wrapped her skinny arms around Rosalie's plump legs and hugged her fiercely. Then she began to cry, too.

Afterward, they both felt much better.

24

Tippy checked her face in Sean's bathroom mirror. Like the rest of this fag-ridden apartment, the bathroom had been gussied up with fumed-oak spoolwork. A complete frame of spindles, balls, pears, pineapples, acanthus leaves and spools surrounded the medicine cabinet mirror and, at the moment, Tippy's pale, narrow face.

Her features hardly showed the events of the weekend, she noted, nor did they reveal her matinee with Ben yesterday. He had gotten a ticket for speeding on the Saw Mill River Parkway at noon yesterday, racing into town to make a 12:30 date with her. She had no idea if he'd picked up another ticket on his way back to the office but, since she hadn't let go of him till three, she doubted that he'd actually returned to the bank. Funny thought: getting a ticket for speeding in that little Karmann-Ghia. Funnier thought: Ben losing his license after too many matinees. In his own best interest, Tippy thought, she'd have to move him out of Scarsdale and set him up in Manhattan.

She crinkled her nose at the idea. Her brain had to be turning to mush. Yeah, right.

All of a sudden she was getting possessive about him. The last man about whom she had gotten possessive had been the basketball captain and two years older than Tippy, and he'd been able, during their entire affair, to ball all night. Which was more than you could say for Ben.

Tippy gave herself a flat smile. She understood perfectly why older women chose younger men. The only thing she didn't understand was how long, now that she was nearly twenty-one, how long it would be before she started robbing the cradle. Five years, tops? Yeah, right.

She glanced at her wristwatch. Nine thirty. She was already half an hour late for the midtown radio studio where she worked. Fortunately her boss, a disc jockey named Big Billy Beanbag, was fast asleep and wouldn't arrive at the studio until noon at the earliest to tape tonight's show. Although the listener relations department had hired Tippy to answer Big Billy's mail, it had been Big Billy who'd told them to sign her on. And it'd been Sean who'd gotten the word to Big Billy.

Tippy knew how to handle her boss. Sean had given her the clues. And now, no matter how wretchedly she did her job, listener relations wouldn't dare fire her.

Even so, Tippy thought, as she left the bathroom and began looking for her coat, there were limits to wretchedness. She hadn't actually done any work at the office since Friday afternoon, and it was now Tuesday morning, and mail would be stacked up high enough to start falling off her desk. It always arrived in droves over a weekend because Big Billy Beanbag had some mad offer to make every Friday night. "And to the first fifty listeners who write in, five miles of Lackawanna Railroad track and a life subscription to *Collier's* Magazine. And now, here's Del Crema's latest ballad. Sing it, Del-baby." All the deejays were spinning Del Crema this month.

97

In a way, Tippy supposed, Ben Fischetti was the best thing to happen to her since she'd hit New York. He had money and looks. He dug her more than anybody had in years. And his being married made the whole thing safe. The big thing now was not to get possessive. It would drive him away and, if not, it would for sure make her sick of him. Whichever happened first, both were inevitable. Yeah, right.

Tippy pulled on her coat and glanced around Sean's living room. He was certainly the neat one, wasn't he? She supposed it came from being A.C.-D.C. and British, to boot. Everything tidied up just so, magazines in their rack, Monday mail sorted for answering, clothes hung away, table tops dust free, rug spotless.

Tippy felt a terrifying urge to spit on the rug. It passed over her like a wave of heat, as if close at hand the door of a furnace had opened. She was physically wrenched, as though someone had shoved her.

After the feeling passed, she was left with a sense of rawness in the back of her head. It was all very strange for a moment, and then she forgot about it and started for the front door, walking unsteadily but not aware of it.

Things were a little better for her these days, Tippy decided somewhat smugly. It was true she hadn't been back to her apartment since Saturday. The place gave her the grims. Of course, if any place was designed to keep you in fits, it was this Marseilles whorehouse of Sean's. And yet she felt at home and happy here, only here. Maybe it was the unreality of it. Nobody lived in such a place. Therefore she wasn't there, nobody was. And therefore, she could be happy.

Tippy walked out into the harsh sunshine of Ninth Street. She saw the man in the blue gabardine raincoat reading a newspaper in the entryway of a bar across the street. She did not see him fold the newspaper and follow her to Sixth Avenue, nor did she see him flag the cab behind the one she summoned.

When she got off in the mid-fifties, the other cab passed her and let out the man in the blue gabardine raincoat half a block from the entrance to the radio station. Nevertheless, he was able to see where Tippy went in.

25

The construction had all but demoralized the area of Lexington Avenue where most of an entire square block had been leveled and excavated, sending fleets of immense double-tired dump trucks trundling through the streets of Manhattan during the working day with thousands of tons of dirt and jagged chunks of igneous schist blasted from the bedrock of the island.

A fine layer of dust had settled down over the storefronts for several blocks in all directions. Secretaries on their lunch hours had for half a year now been ogled, yelped at, shown obscene gestures and spattered with mud by the excavating crew and the truck drivers.

The dynamite blasts, muffled under their blankets of woven steel cable, had rattled buildings up and down Lexington, had twice shorted out the IRT subway electrical system beneath the avenue, and had on one occasion caused an elderly passer-by to clutch at his heart and faint in the doorway of a prescription drugstore. A doctor who happened to be in the store at the moment returned the passerby to consciousness and hustled him to Lenox Hill Hospital for emergency outpatient treatment.

During the razing of the various buildings that once had stood along Lexington, shards of granite, chipped at tremendous force by the swinging wrecker's ball, had punched holes through the safety-glass windshields of parked cars.

A limestone pebble, dislodged and sent flying by a workman's sledge hammer, had rapped into the temple of a television time salesman named Geroge F. Hauser, who had been hurrying along Lexington at a quarter to five in the evening on his way to his mistress' apartment on 56th Street. Hauser had fallen, an angry welt had arisen on his temple and for several days thereafter he had suffered headaches and double vision. But he had been one of the few victims not to sue the demolition company and the building contractors, since he felt diffident about explaining his whereabouts at that time and in that place. After a while, normal vision returned.

During the several months of demolition and the several more excavation, normally four-lane traffic along Lexington had been pinched down to two and often one lane, partly by the constant coming and going of the trucks and partly by the dogged insistence of architects, engineers, inspectors and other highly skilled college graduates that they had every right to double- and triple-park their personal vehicles along the block.

Downtown-moving Manhattan traffic, particularly taxis, began to avoid this stretch of Lexington, further jamming up Park Avenue to the west and Second Avenue to the east, as well as the many crosstown streets connecting the various avenues. Additional police were assigned to intersections near the construction and to others at fairly distant points, where they helped handle increased traffic diverted from the Lexington Avenue congestion.

Someone in Harry Klaman's office, an assistant auditor or cost-control pencil jockey with a wry sense of propriety, had figured out that what with subway delays, added police, additional wear and tear to city pavements caused by the trucks, taxes lost during the interim period in which the property was technically unimproved, loss of revenue from vacationers at nearby hotels who cut short their New York holidays and from shoppers who refused to patronize nearby department stores during the melee, underground disruption of Con Edison cables, steam lines and sewage pipes, extra costs of cleaning walls and windows in nearby office buildings, plus the 117 large and small damage suits currently in litigation, this particular piece of construction would have to pay real estate taxes to the city of New York for 473 years before the public broke even.

"Fire the prick," Harry had said on being told this amusing anecdote.

On this particular Tuesday morning in the life of this particular construction job, things were not going too well. Harry stood across Lexington Avenue from the boarded-off area and watched an immense bucket of concrete being lowered on cables from a crane that towered twenty storeys in the air. On what would be the fifteenth storey of the construction, workmen eased the bucket into place over a set of plywood forms braced with two-by-fours. The foreman opened a valve in the bucket, and concrete sluiced down into the form, engulfing the tangle of heavy steel rods that ran down its core.

This was to be a thirty-storey office building, the first that tall to built in Manhattan without steel girder support, but by the relatively newer technique of reinforced concrete columns and floors. Harry's publicity man had kept the real estate pages of the newspapers filled for several months with the special construction features of the building – "the building without a rivet or a rivet hammer!" Because it rested on the tunnels of the IRT subway, the entire construction on the Lexington Avenue side was held up by only six piers which neatly delved between the subway passages to bedrock. Moreover, the publicity men pointed out, these piers were damped with alternating layers of lead – $60,000 worth – and concrete to avoid transmitting the vibration of subway trains to workers in the building. If one had never visited the site but had only read the quiet stories printed by the newspapers, one would have assumed that the rivetless, lead-damped construction had been carried on in a cathedral-like hush.

As Harry watched the concrete being sloshed into the form at the fifteenth-story level, he felt underfoot the rumble of a passing express train. His small eyes squinted upward into the morning sunshine. The cables holding the bucket had begun to vibrate. The bucket swayed faintly. But the men pouring the concrete were lucky. Enough of it had poured out of the bucket so that they could calm the movement with the strength of their own arms, leaning on the swaying bucket and holding it in line. Harry's forehead was damp.

He closed his eyes. He could picture the headlines if concrete had rained down all over pedestrians and cars along Lexington Avenue or if, God forbid, the bucket had jostled one or two men loose and sent them flying to meet the pavement. Harry sighed, opened his eyes and mopped his face.

Construction work in New York had to be carried on in what were, from Harry's viewpoint, such excruciatingly confined quarters that the effect of even a small error or accident became magnified by the great masses of people and expensive property close at hand.

Most of the accidents, fortunately, happened within the boarded-up confines of the construction itself. Even so, news of a few trickled out each day via passersby or through the families of injured men. Fortunately, the public catastrophe – the crane toppling off balance, the misjudged dynamite charge, the fallen workman – had become part of the folklore of Manhattan, along with the muggings in parks, the junkie holdups, the double parking, the male prostitutes, the poisoned air, the traffic jams and the losing baseball clubs. To live in New York was to live next to disaster every hour of the day. If Harry Klaman goofed spectacularly and killed a few people, so?

Harry crossed Lexington and plunged in among the underpinnings of the building, the trailers, shacks and Portosan toilets. A public-address and PBX telephone system had been rigged throughout the concrete floors and columns, and a girl at a switchboard paged men all day.

"Jesus Gallindo, day laborer. Jesus Gallindo, day laborer."

She spoke very slowly and as carefully as her New York accent would permit. She pronounced *Jesus* properly, and she always repeated everything at least once, often three and four times, to be certain that the man in question or a co-worker near him heard the summons. It also seemed to be part of protocol that each man's job description be included in his page.

"Luigi Gagliodotta, bricklayer. Luigi Gagliodotta, bricklayer."

"Ralph Perlmutter, ductwork. Ralph Perlmutter, ductwork."

"Jimmy Groark, electrician. Jimmy Groark, electrician."

The men being paged would get to the nearest PBX telephone and identify themselves to the switchboard down at the ground level. They would then be given a message, summoned to see someone or have an incoming telephone call switched to them.

Harry Klaman disapproved of the whole idea. He disapproved of anything that distracted the men or broke the self-hypnotic flow of their work. He disapproved of men getting personal calls on the job, no matter how urgent the message. He disapproved of their co-workers stopping to razz them about getting calls. He also disapproved of foremen and engineers summoning men to see them, rather than getting their asses up off their swivel chairs and humping up topside to the actual work.

He had reluctantly installed the paging system because the unions had told him he had to. In another few years, Harry felt certain, the foremen would insist on closed-circuit television systems to allow them to straw-boss a work gang on the fifteenth floor from a cozy cubby down below.

"Marvin Turtletaub, plumber. Marvin Turtletaub, plumber."

"Melchior Herrera, day laborer. Melchior Herrera, day laborer."

"Al Palazzolo, concrete. Al Palazzolo, concrete."

Harry walked inside the main trailer and watched the paging-system girl at her microphone. More payroll money wasted. Then he brushed past her into the rear of the trailer, where his own lieutenant on this particular job kept his offices.

Sal Geraci was nearly Harry's age, fifty-five, but in much

102

better physical shape. Although he had the usual job-inflicted ailments, among them bad hearing and the permanent cough that results from inhaling cigarette smoke and cement dust for thirty-five years, Sal was tall and rather spare, with powerful shoulder muscles and a deeply tanned skin. With his hairpiece on, as it was now, he resembled Harry Klaman's eldest son or kid brother, the one who taught basketball in the Y. Without his hairpiece, he merely demonstrated what a drastic diet, two weeks in Bermuda and 100 push-ups a day could do for Harry Klaman.

Neither of the men noted the resemblance between them, although it had been pointed out many times over the years. Sal Geraci had gone to work for Harry's father in the depths of the Depression, digging sewage ditches in Van Cortlandt Park. He and Harry had met on the same work gang, and even though he wasn't Lou Klaman's son, Sal had gone up in the organization about as fast as Harry had, but not as far.

Harry had taken over the business just before the war and made Sal his coordinator of big projects. It didn't matter whether the project were an immense office building like this one, a tract of 500 one-family houses in Ossinging or a shopping center in Atlantic City. If enough money had been sunk in the operation, Sal Geraci had to be the one to supervise it.

"Ramon Diosado, day laborer. Ramon Diosado, day laborer."

"Leo Connachy, boiler man. Leo Connachy, boiler man."

"*Wie gehts*, Sal?" Harry asked, sitting down across the desk from him.

"*Gurnischt.*" Sal rubbed his eyes and coughed. Then he put down the slide rule he had been holding and looked across at Harry. Pratt Institute night classes had taught Sal how to work the slide rule and those few other instruments he normally used, including a comptometer. Other than that, his schooling had stopped when he graduated from high school in 1918. But as he was fond of pointing out to Harry, who had never been to college either, what he had been taught in high school was now the first four years of the modern college curriculum.

"Stop playing with that thing and give me a straight answer," Harry demanded.

Sal frowned and tucked the slide rule away in the breast pocket of the white button-down shirt he habitually wore on the job, sleeves rolled up high on his thick-slabbed biceps. Now that he and Harry were frowning at each other, they gave the

103

effect of one man with a trick mirror that seemed to make him look bald.

"What questions?" Sal asked.

Harry made a disgusted face. "How many more weeks can we hold the line here?"

Sal shrugged. "As long as we can meet payroll, we can last till April. But—"

Harry waited. From his viewpoint, the mirror made him look as if he had hair. "But what?"

"But you know how these things go, Harry. Your masonry supplier stops your deliveries, you lay off the bricklayers and concrete men. Your payroll cash goes farther that way. You keep stiffing your suppliers, you can keep men working here into June. There won't be more than a handful of them around. But they'll be working."

"You're the funniest man I know," Harry said sourly.

Sal shrugged again. "What do you want me to tell you, Harry? You're the money guy. Do I have to draw a diagram?"

"Julius Pokorny, lathing. Julius Pokorny, lathing."

"Paco Menendez, day laborer. Paco Menendez, day laborer."

Sal coughed softly. "For a real laugh," he said somberly, "try this one. The Hertz people tell me either you pay the last six months' rental fees on the dozers or they pull out the crane. Now."

"The master crane?"

Sal nodded. "What's happened to your banks, Harry? You were always in so tight with your banks."

"Tight, shmight. You read the papers. Money's tight all over the country."

"But should we feel it this fast?" Sal's eyes widened slightly and got a pleading look. "Shouldn't a job this big be capitalized against financing that holds up?"

"Don't talk like a kid, Sal. Who finances a whole project in one loan?"

"But we should at least be financed through to topping out."

Harry flapped his hands reassuringly. "You'll top out. This I guarantee."

Sal looked reassured. Harry was usually able to do this for him. "Once we've topped out, you renegotiate and—"

"And leave it to me, Sal. Do I ever let you down?"

"Luis Ortega, day laborer. Luis Ortega, day laborer."

"Herman Stutz, welder. Herman Stutz, welder."

Sal smiled at Harry. "About as much as I let you down, sonny boy."

Harry grinned and got to his feet. "I wanted to look at the central ductwork at the fifteenth floor, where the switching control's going to be. I got a nut for an architect, Sal. Who ever heard of controls not being in the basement?"

The two men picked up hard yellow plastic helmets as they left the trailer and walked to the open-cage elevator. A Hertz truck was parked nearby as electrician's helpers unloaded lengths of conduit pipe. Harry frowned at the truck. "Six months' credit those Hertz *gonifs* give me? Six lousy months?"

"It's not a question of credit," Sal explained, coughing. "You're supposed to pay the rental every month. Just like your tenants pay you. What you are is five months in arrears."

"Don't worry, bubby," Harry said as he adjusted the helmet at a slightly rakish angle. "In a week or two we'll have money for everything."

"You're pulling money out of the Brookhaven job out on the island?"

"No."

"You're stopping the Piney Acres excavation in Armonk?"

"Are you kidding? How would that bring in money?"

"Then what?" Sal asked.

"Murray Krochmal, carpenter. Murray Krochmal, carpenter."

"Rocco Carfano, wireman. Rocco Carfano, wireman."

"Never mind," Harry said in his best reassuring tone. They stepped into the open cage of the elevator and held on as it started its sickening surge upward. Harry closed his eyes, nearly gagging. He had once begged Sal to slow up the engine hoist on all Klaman elevators. But Sal had pulled out his slide rule and computed the man hours per day lost thereby. So the elevators still ran at sickening speeds.

"All right, never mind," Sal said, calmly watching the open work floors of the building flick by. "But it's not as if I'm one of the workmen, Harry. I didn't ask because I'm nosy. I got thirty-five years of my life in this company."

Harry failed to answer, not because he didn't have any words but mostly because he was busy holding down his breakfast as the elevator car squealed to a fast stop at the fifteenth floor.

"One of the banks is getting up the new loan, huh?" Sal asked.

Harry swallowed gingerly. They stepped out of the elevator and stood stock still for a moment on the raw concrete floor.

"Innocencio Diaz, day laborer. Innocencio Diaz, day laborer."

"I'm through with banks," Harry said then, looking around him for the central ductwork core. "I'm going right to the source, Sal-baby, right to the mint itself."

"What?" Sal led the way to the ductwork. "Fort Knox, maybe?"

"Better. That big bond and mortgage company Gaetano Fischetti operates."

Sal frowned. The tanned skin around his nostrils wrinkled in deep creases. "What makes you think you can tap that one, Harry? That's *private* money." He emphasized the word strangely.

"Never mind. I got a way."

"Manuel Flores, day laborer. Manuel Flores, day laborer."

"They promised you?" Sal asked. His eyes had gotten big again, not with pleading but some other quality Harry couldn't read.

"What promise?" Harry asked. "To get money out of that drum, you have to hold a gun on them, right?"

"Harry!"

"Calm down. Relax."

"Harry –" Sal's face had frozen dead – "promise me you're kidding."

"What kidding?"

"Harry, you got to be kidding," Sal insisted.

"Javier Lopez, day laborer. Javier Lopez, day laborer."

Sal Geraci's face and body seemed to have frozen somehow to the floor on which he stood. He seemed unable to move, as if watching a catastrophe of proportions so great that one small human being was powerless to intervene.

"Harry."

"Stop Harrying me."

"You . . ." Sal ran out of words. He began to cough again. His right hand moved slowly, stiffly, upward.

"Francisco Munoz, day laborer. Francisco Munoz, day laborer."

Sal crossed himself.

Palmer had called in the two men whom he wanted to handle the take-over of People's Bank.

Bill Elston had more or less relegated himself to second place on the team, in Palmer's thinking, because he couldn't seem to reason above the level of a small-minded gossip-monger. Even if he'd been a genius, Palmer reflected now as he waited for the two men to enter his office, Elston was only an assistant secretary. The size of People's Bank was such that it behooved Ubco, in swallowing up the smaller institution, to assign someone just a bit higher in rank than an assistant secretary to officiate over the digestive process.

He had pretty well settled on Donny Elder for the job. Donnelly Elder was Harry Elder's boy, the son of Ubco's long-time executive vice-president who had retired a few years back. It had been Harry Elder's impending retirement that had led Ubco to bring Palmer in from Chicago as number two man. It had been Palmer's own idea, however, to become number one within the first year after he'd joined Ubco. He owed Harry Elder nothing. The other man had neither helped nor hindered Palmer's ascent to the presidency. But Harry had left Ubco a son who, in Palmer's opinion, was not the usual brain-less nonentity most nepotism-ridden banks inherited. Donny Elder had somebody else's brains, perhaps his mother's. In any event, he was an asset and an assistant vice-president, in that order.

Donny came into Palmer's office first, nodded, smiled and sat down. He opened a leather-bound portfolio across his knees and looked up attentively, all short-cropped hair and smile. "What can I tell you, Mr. Palmer?"

"This is just a little preluncheon-meeting briefing. Come in, Bill." Palmer watched Elston enter with that diffident sideways crab crawl of his, insinuate his skinny buttocks in a chair, open a thin manilla folder and spill its contents on the carpet.

"I just wanted to make sure we were all on the same wave-length before we met the People's people." Palmer paused and smiled at the repetition. "It's way past time they changed their name, at that. Ubco sounds much more efficient."

"A prison number across their shirt is more like it," Elston said. "The things I've been digging into, Mr. Palmer, make me wonder why we want to buy them at all."

Palmer glanced at Donny Elder, saw no sign he was as offended by the statement as Palmer had been. Palmer decided he had some kind of personal animus against Elston and would have to guard against rejecting every idea the man put forward.

"Nevertheless, Bill," Palmer began, "we plan to buy them. We made application. We argued the application. Our reasons for wanting the bank may have been more valid ten years ago, perhaps, than they are today. Perhaps, too, the bank isn't as well managed today as it was then. But when Ubco indicates its intentions before the world, Ubco goes through with its plans or has a damned good reason for altering them."

"We just don't have the right to change our mind in public," Donny put in.

"That's about it," Palmer agreed.

"Why not, when it's good business to change?" Elston's eyes bulged slightly.

"First," Palmer explained, "we don't yet know what's good or bad business in this situation. But second, and more important, a bank the size of Ubco can't move precipitously. It can't do things on impulse. It can't seem to veer off course. If it did, people would suspect us of poor management, of not being the omniscient, godlike institution they want to believe we are. The minute they lose faith in Ubco's all-knowing powers, they lose faith in a hell of a big chunk of the U.S. banking system. Do I have to go on with this?"

"The mind boggles," Donny murmured. "Look, as far as I can tell from reviewing their lending situation, People's is not much worse off than any other bank that's blown its wad in home-building credit and personal loans. They're simply over-extended. But they can recoup."

"They're worse than overextended," Palmer said. "They're extended over a cliff with one foot on the dear old banana peel."

Elston squinted at him. "I don't follow you, Mr. Palmer."

And never will, Palmer added silently. "It shouldn't come as news to anybody in this institution, I hope, that the housing industry is the sick man of the economy, at least for the moment. Any bank intimately linked to construction is like a Siamese twin: what's he do when his brother dies?"

Donny hefted the portfolio in his lap. "They've tightened up on credit to their main borrowers. This builder, Klaman Company, for example. They haven't gotten a nickel in some time. But if you shut off money tight enough, don't borrowers start to go bad on all their previous indebtedness?"

"That's the kind of tightrope these smaller banks are always walking," Palmer said. "Some big ones, too."

"Not Ubco," Elston put in.

"Not that I know of."

"Then why buy a bank that is?"

"Leave that part to me at lunch," Palmer said. "Watch how it works."

"I don't understand what lunch has to do—"

"He means he'll put Phelps Lassiter and his bunch through the hoops," Donny explained. "Let them tell us why we should buy them."

Elston made a derisive face. Palmer leaned back in his chair and let the two younger men argue. "That's poker playing," Elston said with a show of righteous disdain, "not banking."

"Oh, it's banking all right," Donny assured him.

Elston slapped his manilla folder. "This is banking. The facts. The research. The evaluations. Not a lot of bluffing around a lunch table." He shook his folder. "The facts are all in here." At this, the contents of the folder spilled out on the carpet again.

Palmer suppressed a smile. Elston was so damned awkward and ill-spoken. Donny Elder was so damned well-bred and knowledgeable. It was hard not to start rooting for Elston.

Palmer sat forward. "Everything is banking, and banking is everything. I have spoken."

He slapped his hand palm down on the top of his desk, not heavily, but with enough strength to put a full period to the argument between the younger men. "Let me talk for a few minutes so all three of us know the same things about this deal."

He got up and wandered aimlessly around the room within a few yards of the other men and his desk. "The key to the whole thing is cash," he began. "It all starts there. Cash. New money. The stuff wage earners get every week."

He paused and held up his hand. "Now I know the stuff is only paper smeared with green ink. That's not the point, however. The smeared-up paper signifies value. Someone produced something of value and got this paper in return. So he brings it in to us. Right?"

The two younger men nodded, both mystified by the kinder-

109

garten turn of events. Palmer returned to his chair but stood behind it for a moment. "We take in the cash and we promise to give it back whenever the people want it, and what's more, we pay them four or five percent just so we can have it in our vaults. But of course, it doesn't stay there. We immediately lend it out at six or seven percent, or nine or ten. Still with me?"

"Sir," Donny said, "I think both of us took those courses in school." He smiled when he said it.

"This is a refresher," Palmer said deadpan.

"Yes, sir."

"I'll be asking trick questions later," Palmer added in a flat voice.

"Yes, sir."

"Now, then." He sat down in his chair and watched the younger men. "As long as people earn more than they spend, there is a cash flow into the banks, new money we can lend to businessmen, builders, even back to the wage earners for some special goody like a car or a vacation or a color television set. Which of you can tell me what happens when people spend more than they earn?"

"They can't," Elston snapped. "They don't."

"They do," Palmer retorted.

Elston gestured vaguely. "Well, then our cash flow stops."

"Exactly. Of course, it hasn't stopped yet. But it's begun to slow up. And the minute we see it slowing, what do we do?"

Neither of his listeners spoke for a moment. Then Donny ventured a guess: "Curtail credit?"

"Not all credit," Palmer corrected him, "just the kind of loans that don't produce enough income for us, the six and seven percent mortgages and home-improvement loans. We aren't alone. The insurance companies operate in the same money market. Their cash flow is less erratic, of course, because their policyholders have signed a contract and must meet premium payments. But in this period, the insurance people have less cash to invest, too. Can you tell me why?"

Donny looked blankly at Elston. "He said they'd be trick questions," Donny murmured.

"B-borrowing!" Elston burst out. "Borrowing on policies!"

Palmer smiled. "The policyholder has first crack at the cash the insurance companies are looking to invest. He can tap the money merely by borrowing on the cash value of his policy, and the companies can only charge him about five percent.

So you can both now begin to see the way a vicious circle starts."

Elston frowned. "The policyholder needs cash because he's overspent and can't afford the high interest rate on personal loans caused by him being overspent. So he borrows on his insurance policy, cuts down their cash flow and forces them out of low-rate lending, too."

Donny grinned. "Glad we're not in the insurance business."

"But we're in the same kettle," Palmer reminded him. "Or, I suppose it's more proper to say the insurance companies are in our kettle with us. Neither of us can afford to make the low-rate loans the housing industry needs. So it's grinding to a standstill."

"And individual builders are going bad on their other loans," Donny said.

"Now," Palmer told him, "you're beginning to get the full, rich stench of it. What we have here, gentlemen, is two or three interlocking vicious circles rolling downhill together like hoop snakes in heat."

"How did we let that happen?" Elston wanted to know almost plaintively.

"Unlimited personal credit."

"We don't offer the public unlimited pesonal credit," Elston demurred in a shocked voice. "About the farthest we go is a one- or two-thousand-dollar personal loan, and then only to a risk who checks out as steady pay."

Palmer nodded. "That's all we do." There was a questioning note in the statement. "Right?"

"Right."

"Right."

Palmer nodded again. 'We're the biggest and the most reputable, so we don't do anything disreputable or picayune. Right? We don't contribute to the impoverishment of the wage-earning class. We don't let weak-willed people spend themselves into irretrievable debt. Right?"

"Right."

"Right."

Palmer got up and began pacing the carpet again. "Have you ever looked at a roster of our commercial customers?" he asked the younger men. "Aside from all the big manufacturing concerns, that is."

"Regular list of blue chips," Donny remarked.

"I'm talking about some of the retailing operations, the

service organizations, the credit-card systems, that sort of thing."

"Also blue chip," Donny assured him. "We don't mess with any of these fly-by-night outfits."

"But the outfits we do mess with," Palmer persisted. "What do we do for them? Basically we extend them a line of credit. I mean, if a department store is carrying several million dollars a month in customer debt as accounts receivable on thirty-day-pay charge accounts or ninety-day-deferred-pay charge accounts, or revolving-credit charge accounts, we extend them the credit, cover their receivables. And if a restaurant credit-card operation wants to offer several kinds of accounts, including thirty-per-day and revolving credit, we finance both types for them. And if a hotel credit card, an oil credit card, a travel credit card or any other what-have-you all-purpose, charge-now-pay-later plan wants a basic line of credit from us to finance its operations, we're happy to oblige. Isn't that so?"

"I suppose it is," Donny admitted.

"Furthermore," Palmer plunged on, "if a commercial credit group finances a lot of small retailers – television stores, clothing shops, appliance dealers and the like – so they can lure more customers with buy-now-pay-later deals, who does the commercial credit group come to for its foundation financing?"

"Yes," Elston said, "but we –"

"I just wanted to make it clear to both of you. You seem to have gotten the idea that Ubco is somehow in a different business from People's. That because we're big enough to lend money to governments and giant space-age corporations, we are in some mysterious way not involved in the systematic rape of the wage earners. But moneylending is moneylending. Directly or indirectly, we do every kind there is. The minute you start to get a smug feeling of intense superiority" – Palmer glanced at Elston – "because in your daily work you don't come across the human wreckage created by unlimited credit, fight the feeling."

"Forgive me," Donny said, "but you can hardly accuse us of wrecking human lives. We're only giving people what they want."

"So are the cigarette companies."

The look of shock on both their faces amused Palmer. He found it extremely interesting that for all the wide difference in their backgrounds, both Donny and Bill Elston took it as a

112

basic article of faith that nothing pertaining to the Ubco monolith could be questioned. By extension, nothing about banking could really be questioned, either.

"Are you inferring," Elston began, "that—"

"You're inferring," Palmer corrected him. "I'm implying."

"— that unlimited personal credit is a destructive force?"

The confused interchange reverberated in the air. Palmer was sorry he had corrected Elston, but he wasn't at all sure the younger man had heard or understood the correction. Palmer was also a little miffed at having worked himself up with this lecture to the point where he had taken to correcting their language as well as their thinking. But, in for a dime...

"I am straight-out telling you," he began, "so that you can spare yourself any inferences. There is nothing destructive or constructive about money, except in the way it's used. For five dollars you can buy a meal that will sustain your life and delight your sensibilities. Or you can buy a bag of heroin and kill yourself. In both cases you are using money to satisfy your inner need. So it's the need, not the money, that is either good or bad for you."

He paused. For some reason he didn't quite understand, he had their rapt attention. They were watching him as carefully as they would an actor on a stage or perhaps an animal in a cage. Palmer returned to his chair and sat down.

"For whatever the reasons, and each of us can argue for his own pet theory, the country has for some time now been in a period when the needs of a wage earner have far outstripped his financial ability to fulfil those needs. Maybe he and his wife have become consumption addicts. Maybe they have overwhelming desires to go out and buy, buy, buy. Maybe they're zombies, hypnotized by advertising. Maybe they're celebrants in a black mass of overconsumption trying to exorcise the shadow of the bomb. Maybe they're undereducated and have the need-satisfaction syndrome of a child. Maybe they're brainwashed. Self-indulgent. Unable to defer gratification. Unable to link cause and effect."

He stopped and eyed the two other men. Another minute, Palmer realized, and they would have him marked down as a nut of some kind.

"Lecture over." He stood up. "You both have things to do before our luncheon meeting. Be in the lobby at noon, and I'll pick you up."

"Wait, sir," Donny said. He showed no inclination to move

113

from his chair. "What if even half those theories you mention are true?"

"Yes," Elston chimed in. "Even a third of them."

"Why, people like that can't be trusted with a nickel, let alone unlimited personal credit," Donny began. "It's like giving a loaded revolver to a baby."

"And if there are as many of them as you inf – imply," Elston stumbled on, "we have no business financing any of these credit operations."

Palmer shook his head. He led the way to the door and swung it open. "If we have no business financing their credit, we have no business at all. This is where we make our money, the high-risk, high-yield end, not fully secured, low-yield credit. Often that kind of loan barely pays much more than what it costs us to service it. We loan money to manufacturers and builders because it's steady, low-risk business, and in our portfolio of investments it balances the more volatile personal-credit stuff. But it's the personal credit that makes big profits for us. And it's the big profits that end up in your profit-sharing bonuses. It's ironic, isn't it, that by pursuing the bigger profit we pinch off our own cash flow?"

"Then you're in favor of unlimited personal credit?" Elston asked. "Or are you?"

The two younger men were standing side by side in the immense doorway of Palmer's office. Both looked thoroughly confused.

"I'm in favor of Ubco showing a profit," Palmer said. "I don't think one should look too deeply into the social good or bad that leads to profit. But I don't think, either, that one can blithely float along, unaware of some of the depths over which Ubco is sailing. That's the reason for the lecture. Try to remember bits of it as we sit down with the People's people. And remember, they've been a lot closer to the firing line than we have. All of us have ivory-tower jobs, far from the foreclosures and bad debts and dunning letters and third notices and all the rest.

"These people have been down in the dung pits where the money grows," he said. "I don't want you to turn up your noses at how they may smell."

27

The morning started out quite routinely for Don Vincenzo Biglioto. He had awakened after ten and now stood at the third-floor window of his house on lower Fifth Avenue, one of the last of the private houses at this end of the thoroughfare. The plane trees by the Protestant church across the street were beginning to send out thin shoots of green, and Don Vincenzo saw no sacrilege in smiling at them, even though the sight of the church itself was abomination.

He flexed the muscles in his still-powerful arms and took in three deep breaths of fresh March air, or as fresh as air got in New York City. *Ah, un soffio di vento fresco.* His weekend home in New Jersey was the place for that.

He glanced at his wife, still asleep in the immense carved mahogany double bed. Her face was a small as a bird's. *Ah, una ragazzina piccolina.*

The bus and auto traffic along Fifth had died down a bit from its earlier roar, and the trucks had not yet started grinding through with deliveries. It was a pause in the morning's headlong dash toward lunch, and Don Vincenzo had long ago trained himself to sleep until this particular moment of the morning, when, with a burst of speed surprising in a man his age, he would dress, eat and be out of the house by ten thirty at the very latest. *Meraviglioso.*

Don Vincenzo was in particular good spirits this morning. He had no more reason on this than any other morning, but there was something about the alert, refreshed way he had awakened and the snap of his movements that pleased him tremendously. He felt young and tall and virile, a regular Ben Fischetti.

He smiled at the thought. Privately Don Vincenzo considered Ben a dolt, *un scemonito*, a blockhead with a handsome face and an athlete's figure. Publicly he praised the outward appearance of his son-in-law, but to himself Don Vincenzo admitted sadly that there was nothing much to the boy, no real drive, no ambition. He had had it all too easy, that was the trouble. And not only with Ben, but with the other young men of his age in the family.

There was Augie Limandri, the grandson of Don Enrico, and even his own nephew, Charley Notarbartolo. And for that matter his first wife's family, the Profacis, had spawned a few *zoticos* of their own.

There was something soft in the air these days. It wasn't just in the family, Don Vincenzo realized now as he stood at the window and looked down at the street.

There was a strain of softness, like a sustained violin note among the crash of brass. The young men in their twenties, and even in their thirties, these dunces were all soft between the ears. They had no *maschiezza*, no *virilità*, no balls.

Everything they had – and only someone in Don Vincenzo's position could really know how much money, how much property and how much power would eventually come to this newest breed of the family's men – had been handed to them on *una argenteria*. The silver platter had been loaded to over-flowing with everything he, Don Vincenzo, and the men of his generation of the family had had to fight for. It fell into the baby-soft hands of these – these *college* men without a struggle.

And of course, Don Vincenzo reminded himself, none of us has anybody to blame for this but our own stupid desires to raise American sons. Thank God, he told himself, for Rosalie and Celia. If he had had to raise sons, he would now be in the position Gaetano Fischetti and all the other fathers were in, of having overeducated, overbred and overprotected the generation that would soon fall heir to all that belonged to the family.

Don Vincenzo sighed and turned from the window. Moving softly so as not to awaken his wife, he stepped through a side door into the dressing room he used. Rocco stood there, smoking a cigarette. *"Buon giorno."* His voice, as always, sounded thin and dead.

"Spicciati, amico."

Rocco ground out the cigarette, reached a hand into the stall shower and turned the lever to a point halfway between medium and hot on the dial. Then he turned back to Don Vincenzo and received from him his robe and his pajamas. Squaring his shoulders and sucking in his gut, Don Vincenzo stepped naked into the shower. Rocco placed his pajamas in the laundry hamper and removed from a heated shelf a large huck towel.

Rocco Sgroi was now over fifty years old, some eight or nine years younger than Don Vincenzo. Neither looked his age. Whatever Don Vincenzo did to keep himself fit and active, Rocco also did. Wherever Don Vincenzo went, Rocco went. Whoever Don Vincenzo saw, with a few exceptions, Rocco

116

saw. It was true that Rocco went places and did things and saw people Don Vincenzo would not, but then, that was Rocco Sgroi's job.

He was Don Vincenzo's *cuscinetto*. It paid well. Don Vincenzo had once tried to explain *cuscinetto* to a young lady of the evening who had objected to submitting to Don Vincenzo with Rocco Sgroi sitting in an easy chair across the room, watching.

"I'll do anything, honey, you know that, but why does he have to watch? Or is that his kick?"

"He's my, ah – what's the word? – he's my *cuscinetto*. The pillow? The pin cushion?"

The young lady had been afraid of pins. A previous client had proved too handy with them. They had been his pleasure, and his pleasure had nearly given her blood poisoning. "No pins," she said, getting off the bed.

"No pins, no pins. *Cuscinetto* is ... *come si chiama?*"

Rocco had stirred in his easy chair and grunted a single word: "Buffer."

"*Si*, buffer. Buffer. He is my buffer so, *figuri*, he has to stay here."

Don Vincenzo, rinsing off the soap under the shower water, turned the handle to medium and then began to edge it toward cold. His doctor had warned him to give up cold showers but had said nothing about ending a regular shower with a blast of icy water. When Don Vincenzo had wheedled the handle halfway toward cold, he grunted, and shoved it all the way in one magnificent gesture.

"*Ai! Fa freddo!*" His fury voice went up an octave.

Teeth chattering, Don Vincenzo stepped into the warm huck towel and let Rocco rub him dry. Moving quickly now in a kind of straight-faced ballet, the two men took little steps forward, moved their arms this way and that, bent and turned as Rocco helped Don Vincenzo dress. When his white-on-white tie had been carefully eased into a firm knot, Don Vincenzo glanced at himself in the mirror. He saw that Rocco had clothed him today in a suit of the same dark green-brown that Rocco was wearing, with the same black shoes and black silk socks, the same white shirt with a white silk figure embroidered on it and a tie almost identical in whiteness and pattern.

"*Buono.*"

The two men moved rapidly, half trotting as they made their way down the stairs past the parlor floor to the ground floor, where the garage fronted the street. Don Vincenzo had been careful, many years ago when he had bought this house, to make certain the easement created by the stable that had been there would also cover a garage for an auto.

He and Rocco Sgroi entered the garage and sat in the front seat of the black Ford Galaxie. Earlier, about nine thirty, Rocco had checked the ignition, the braking system and a few other points of possible premature or deliberate wear and tear. Now he started the car. At the sound of the engine turning over, a younger man stepped out of the shadows near the back of the garage, gave a casual salute to the men in the car and walked around it to get to the garage doors.

Rocco touched a button on the dashboard. The doors rose about a foot and stopped. The car was facing out towards the street. But even before the doors had risen far enough for Rocco to see the sidewalk in front of the garage, the young man had dropped to the floor and was peering out through the foot-wide slit toward the morning sunlight. He stood up and nodded. Rocco pressed the button again and held it this time until the garage doors had swung up overhead and out of the way.

Then he gunned the motor and sent the car up over a slight incline and down into Fifth Avenue. As he swung the wheel right, he let go of the dashboard button. Behind the car, the overhead doors were swinging shut. The mechanism was pretty much the same as the one that protected Don Girolamo's modest apartment in the rear of the Amato nurseries. A crystal-regulated radio frequency triggered off the door mechanism. The quartz crystals in the car and the door were changed once a week. Only Rocco Sgroi was entrusted with this task for Don Vincenzo's garage door. Don Girolamo's door was under the supervision of a different man.

Don Vincenzo watched the way Rocco guided the unobtrusive Ford through the traffic at the foot of Fifth Avenue, then west on Waverly and Christopher and down Seventh to Bleecker.

A good man. *Un uomo massiccio* and solid in other ways, too. One of the best of them. Don Vincenzo watched Rocco's profile, the narrow nose and sharply cut mouth. This man, he thought, has what Ben Fischetti and Augie Limandri and Charley Notarbartolo and all the rest of the up-and-coming young punks will never have. *Coraggio, animo, cuore, spirito,* and on top of that, *l'onore stesso,* the very soul of honor.

118

If anybody knew what his own buffer did, it was Don Vincenzo. Valet, driver, bodyguard, these were what the world saw. But Rocco was also his confidant, friend, go-between, substitute and double. In Germany once, before the war, when Don Vincenzo and his father had taken a business trip to Hamburg to see about some ships he had heard himself described as his father's *Doppelgänger*. It had been explained as a shadow, something as close as that, but with mystical, spiritual overtones.

But there was more, Don Vincenzo knew. His buffer was also his, ah, his *pinza*, his pincers, his forceps, his tongs. Through Rocco, Don Vincenzo touched whatever he wished to touch, no matter how hot it was or how dirty, without soiling or burning his own fingers.

So Rocco was Don Vincenzo's *pinza* and his *Doppelgänger*. It was to men like him that the family power should be left, instead of to youngsters with no balls. Don Vincenzo sighed heavily at the thought that Rocco was almost as old as he was. There was small question of leaving him much. When Don Vincenzo went, his *Doppelgänger* could not be far behind.

28

Sean had spent most of the morning going over the books with Murray, his accountant. Despite the fact that Sean trusted his friend Augie and had found his advice generally good, he still could not bring himself to believe that the main purpose of Mod Modes was to lose money for Mr. Fischetti. Instinctively he knew enough not to broach the subject to Murray in just those words. But as their examination of the books drew to a close without revealing any clear-cut reasons for the slump in business, Sean found himself unable to resist a few questions he hoped would sound innocent enough.

"If nothing has changed from last year to this," he began slowly in a soft voice, staring at the black hairs sprouting from Murray's left ear, "if the line is just as good and the market is just as firm and the salesmen are trying just as hard and costs haven't gone up, then what makes the difference between the black ink last year and all this red ink we have now?"

Murray covered his breasts with hands that were themselves covered with black hairs. He then proceeded to shrug, throwing his shoulders not only up but forward. It was a total

119

gesture that conveyed the who-knows content of the normal or common shrug, with strong overtones of you-could-kill-me-and-I-wouldn't-know as well as this-is-a-crazy-world-we-live-in and what're-you-asking-a-schmendrick-like-me-such-tough-questions-for?

"In other words, luv, you won't talk."

"Did I say that?" Murray demanded, all hurt dignity.

"I've heard," Sean said, risking a desperate long shot, "that you've been through more than a few bankruptcies with Mr. Fischetti. What will this one make, the tenth?"

Murray started to do his complex shrug again, then apparently thought better of it. He worked his brown eyes for a moment, adjusting them to a more hurt expression, but gave that up, too. Finally, with a disgusted look, he said: "Seventeenth, but who counts?"

"Well, I don't suppose it matters, actually. You get paid regardless of what happens to the firm."

"So do you." Murray's voice became suddenly defensive. "Let's not give only half the picture. You'll do all right out of this, too."

Sean sighed. "You're right, of course. I don't know what the bloody hell I'm making such a fuss over."

"So just leave it lay."

"Except –" Sean stopped, thought, then went on quickly. "Of course, it's different for you. You're a native. Making it big here isn't important to you. New York is your home, not some fabled treasure chest across the sea. But in England, of course, we think and scheme and intrigue to get over here, because we dream about making it big and New York's the town to do it in. If you're born and brought up here, of course, this town doesn't mean any of that. It's just a ... a place. Rather ordinary, really."

Murray, who at first had been avoiding a conversation, now seemed unable to stop. "Don't sell us so short, will you?"

"Yes, but, I mean..." Sean gestured as if to indicate a total poverty of dream stuff.

Murray's tone had gone huffy. "Just because I'm an accountant instead of a designer doesn't mean I don't have feelings. I know about dreams like that. You never hear the saying, 'Show me a dentist, and I show you a medical school dropout'?" Murray nodded fiercely. "Show me an accountant, and I'll show you a kid who never made the grade in law school. You follow me?"

"Yes, I'm sure you —"

"So about dreams I know plenty. Because it's my hometown makes no difference at all, buddy. Just remember that."

"I didn't mean to —"

"To make it big in this world, let me tell you, isn't any easier for me, pushing a pencil, than you for you, pushing a pencil. Follow me?"

"Of course. It's just that —"

Murray cut him short with a peremptory wave of his hand. "Don't tell me. I know the book by heart. Business." Murray emitted a sound somewhere between a snort and a derisive laugh. "Business. Success in business. What does it take? Let me tell you something, buddy. I come here once a week, right?"

"Right."

"Ever wonder where I am the other four working days?" Murray rubbed his face with his hairy-backed hand. "I have other accounts. I got another right in this building, better frocks. I got a supermarket chain in Queens. I got three restaurants. I got a check-cashing operation in Brooklyn. I got a meat wholesaler. I got an electric-supply company down on Chambers Street. On Saturday I do tax work for private clients. On the seventh day I rest."

"All Mr. Fischetti's companies?"

"Nah. Just this one and the supermarket chain. And the restaurants. But that's not the point." Murray slapped the ledger book shut with a small bang. He stood up and reached for his ratty tan raincoat. "The point is, I know what makes success in business. You're not talking to some kid fresh out of CCNY's Baruch School. You're talking to a man who's seen an awful lot of the business world, buddy, maybe too much. Follow me?"

"All right," Sean said. "What does it take to be a success?"

"Take my word. You haven't got it."

In the silence that followed, Murray buckled the tan belt tightly around his thick waist. "I'm sorry, buddy, but you wouldn't want me to lie to you. Not this late in the game."

"What does it take?" Sean asked.

"Only a few things." Murray tucked two Number 3 pencils and two ball-point pens in the breast pocket of his suit jacket. "It takes connections. That you have. It takes a few brains, not as many as you'd think. And that you've also got."

"Crikey, thanks."

121

"It takes some luck, not too much." Murray squinted at the middle distance. "And then it takes a certain kind of" – he squeezed the air, trying to wring a word from it – "a sort of instinct, a killer instinct almost. What I mean is –" He stopped again. His face grew almost pale from the effort of his thinking.

"It's a way you have to be," he said at last. "You have to take yourself very seriously. You can joke about a few things, but whatever you do yourself, that's got to be the only important thing in the world. About that you can't even have a teeny sense of humor. It'd kill you. You have to wear, like, blinders. You have to look straight ahead only at what you are and what you're doing, and about none of it do you joke. It is the most serious thing God ever made. It's more serious than women or food or fun or life itself. It's beyond. It's everything. It's the end. That you ain't got, Sean, buddy. Me, neither."

"Mr. Fischetti has it," Sean pounced.

"Nah. Him, neither."

"Ben?"

Murray laughed that snort of his. "Him least of all."

"Then who?"

"Who?" Murray made the syllable sound mysterious, as if uttered at midnight by a lurking owl. "Who?"

"Vinnie Big?" Sean guessed.

Murray gave him a disgusted look. "What would you know, buddy? You're off on a wild goose chase. I told you you'd do all right out of this. Stop pushing."

"Nobody gets hurt."

"Correct. All us little people make out fine."

"Us little people who don't take it seriously enough," Sean added.

"I should have my head examined, talking to you."

"Maybe if we took it more seriously, we'd do better than just not getting hurt."

"Take it seriously enough," Murray said, "and you'll get hurt dead."

"Really?"

Murray walked to the office door. "There's only room enough in this world for a few very serious people, buddy. Don't tangle with them. Let them tangle with each other. Follow me?"

"Dig."

"See you next Tuesday."

29

Jimmy hustled the long Lincoln through the heavy noontime pedestrian traffic along Broad Street and eased the car to the curb at the other main office of United Bank and Trust Company.

The new Ubco logotype, with the B, C, and O held inside the U like grapes in a compote dish, had been affixed to every one of the bank's nearly 250 branches throughout the metropolitan area in the new brushed-stainless-steel-and-gold color combination. But here, on the facade of what had once been the bank's only main office, the original logotype remained intact and unchanged, its spidery Roman capitals with their fanciful art nouveau serifs intertwined in a design of greenish bronze against limestone.

As Palmer got out of the Lincoln, he stared for a moment at the almost frenzied twist of the letters. He mentally assigned their date of creation at about 1890. Being now the height of camp, they were much newer in feeling than the austere block Gothic letter of the new logotype designed for Ubco by a concern that specialized almost entirely in "corporate imagery." This translated, Palmer had decided, mainly into redesigning client trademarks and writing several reams of presentation copy to justify the change which, in Ubco's case, had cost about $50,000 in fees to the design firm and nearly $1,000,000 more to manufacture and install and changed logos all over town, on the letterhead, the statements, the envelopes, the passbooks, the various contract forms, withdrawal and deposit slips, business cards, advertising giveaways and premiums, wallpaper, floor tiles and last, but damned well not least, the patented water-marked paper used in Ubco checkbooks.

The whole con job by the design company had centered on upgrading and modernizing Ubco's "image" with this space-age steel-and-gold futuristic design. If, instead, he reflected now, Ubco had merely reverted to the art nouveau logo on the Broad Street main office, it would now be so in, so modern and so "with it" that its female tellers would be wearing pop art miniskirts, its officers would have shoulder-length hair and Palmer himself would he wearing a button that said "Legalize Pot."

"Coming, sir?" Donny Elder asked.

Palmer's glance shifted to the two younger men who had gotten out of the car with him. He realized he had been standing at the kerb, lost in reverie, for nearly a minute.

"Right." Stepping off briskly, he led the way through the lobby ("Morning, Mr. Palmer; hello, Mr. Palmer; afternoon, Mr. Palmer.") and up the broad, curving flight of stairs to the conference-diningroom on the second floor. Having told Jimmy to get them here at precisely twenty after twelve, Palmer relied on being able to organize the luncheon arrangements in the ten minutes before Phelps Lassiter's party arrived. Because the guests had come down all the way from Westchester, they would have allowed too much time for the trip and would, he felt sure, have spent the last half hour shopping in some of the hunting, fishing, marine and hardware stores that lay somewhat uptown and to the west of the area. ("But for God's sake, be sure to get back to Ubco by twelve-five. I can't have you straggling in one by one like lost souls.")

Palmer checked the bar, the menu and the table arrangement. He found them all in order, much more so than they had been a few years ago, when these events were catered and stage-managed by a staff of four ancient Ubco employees, a cook, two waiters and a cleanup man. The food had been abominable, the service slow. Palmer had pensioned them all off and made an arrangement with a nearby dining club, one of the many private ones in the financial district that had earned a good reputation for its kitchen and service.

"Donny, you sit down at the end over there. Bill, you take the other end of the table. I'll sit here in the middle, or wherever Phelps decides to sit, unless he sits next to one of you. In which case, I'll sit next to Ralph Fenger or Charley Kornbluth. Is there anybody else we have to worry about?"

Bill Elston produced his old maid's knitted-brow frown. "Not that I know of."

"Donny?"

"Those are the only three," Donny said with smooth certainty.

"Um." Palmer glanced at his watch. Twelve twenty-six. He touched the buzzer button and summoned a waiter. "Will you be good enough to set the three of us up with drinks? Take your time making them."

The waiter took their orders. Elston's frown deepened. "Don't fret so, Bill," Palmer assured him. "We want to look like three jolly boozers when they arrive. Li'l drinky-winky sort of thing."

"Is that the sort of impression you want them to have?"

"I thought I just said so."

"I —" Elston stopped, thought for a moment and quickly took his drink from the waiter.

"I told you this was a poker game," Donny reminded him somewhat smugly.

Palmer almost laughed at the look of intense discomfort on Elston's face. "You do drink?"

"Oh, yes." Elston took a tremendous gulp of his rye and ginger ale.

"Woods, you old rummy." Palmer turned to see Phelps Lassiter in the doorway. If there was such a condition as puberty praecox, in which children looked far older than their years, Phelps must once have suffered from senility praecox. Although he could not now be more than sixty, the very design of the man's face, narrow and fleshless, together with the sparse white hair and unhealthy blotched yellow skin, made him look a cadaverous eighty.

"Just in time, Phelps." Palmer's voice lost its precise, hard-voweled Chicago edge. 'We're way ahead of you. Tell the man your pleasure."

"Hee." Lassiter's laugh escaped from his constricted throat like the first faint peep of steam from a whistling kettle. "Ralph you know, and Charley."

Palmer shook their hands and introduced them to his own lieutenants, noting that by picking men in their thirties to match Lassiter's fifty-year-olds he had preserved exactly the right careless air of let's-have-a-go-at-it-chaps that would put the People's crowd off guard.

"And this is my veepee for new Business, Ben Fischetti. Ben, say hello to Woods Palmer."

Palmer took the younger man's big, firm hand and pumped it twice. He stared into the ripe-olive eyes with their long lashes and wondered who the pretty boy was. Then he remembered.

"Good grief, you don't look a day older than when you ran that ball thirty-seven yards against Navy," he said.

Ben's dark, wary face split in half with a wide, white grin. He seemed to grow several inches in height. "I had no idea anybody remembered that far back."

"I don't usually follow Army," Palmer said. "It's just that
125

we happened to come East, and someone gave us seats for that particular game. Normally we follow Northwestern. Still do."

"You're from Chicago?"

Palmer nodded. He had no idea why he was spending this much time with the newcomer. But something about the way he had effortlessly dredged up that long-forgotten touchdown run of almost a decade ago made Palmer realize that his own subconscious was telling him to learn as much as he could about Ben Fischetti. Not yet knowing why, Palmer decided to obey the signposts his subconscious was showing him.

"Of course, after the Point I did my graduate work at the U of C, which meant no football at all," Ben was saying.

"Graduate School of Business Admin?" Palmer probed.

"Yes."

"What'd you do your thesis on?"

"Consumer credit."

"Very good. And what're you drinking?" Palmer grinned at Ben and turned his grin on Phelps Lassiter. He almost noticeably backed away from Ben Fischetti now, to make certain the younger man didn't begin to feel he was being given the third degree. Palmer knew, however, that having set up Fischetti with the thirty-seven yard run, he could now do no wrong with this good-looking young man.

It was not until most of the way through the meal that Palmer turned his attention back to Ben Fischetti again. The conversation had been glib and totally superficial during the drinks and the food. Palmer and Lassiter had discussed the fact – as Palmer had guessed – that Lassiter had arrived early and spent a few dollars in a marine-supply store on a dozen three-inch Monel screws. This had steered the talk to boats and sailing, which took Fenger into the conversation with them.

The younger men, as far as Palmer could recall, had all looked faintly uncomfortable as they sat in silence, apparently not yet able to master the art of inconsequential chitchat on the brink of important business palaver. Even Donny Elder, who, of them all, would have the best background in time-passing conversation, seemed to be too isolated at the far end of the table to slip in a few words with any ease.

"I don't suppose you sail?" Palmer asked Ben as the dessert plates were being cleared.

"I crew about, oh, four times a year, if that often. But I just do what I'm told. I have no idea what I'm doing."

"Great sport. Get yourself a dinghy and learn the ropes. Do

126

you have any sons?"

"One. He's not quite old enough yet. Only seven."

"That's old enough. Make sure he can swim and then, you know, strap him in a life jacket and take him along. He'll be begging for a sail after a while."

"I'm sure of that."

"It's a matter of forcing the wind to take you where you want to go. You sort of trick the wind," Palmer explained. "You can even go against it by tacking. Just as long as there's any kind of breeze, it's your motive power. It's not like a bank, in that respect. With a bank, when you run out of cash, you've had it."

There was a horribly long silence. Bill Elston dropped his spoon into the saucer of his coffee cup, and the sound seemed to rattle around the big room like a loose ping-pong ball.

"You folks," Palmer went on then in the deadly hush, "seem to have run out of motive power. I mean, there's no cash flow. There's heavy loan delinquencies, and as far as I can tell" – he wheeled on Lassiter and fixed him with a glance – "you're in really big trouble."

"Hee." Lassiter's skull-like face seemed to twitch in several places simultaneously. "I think we can pretty well stop worrying about that," he said then, the grin on his face stark denture white.

"I'm happy to hear it."

"Yes. We've just about dried up those chancy lines of credit completely," Lassiter continued. "And it will be only a matter of weeks, probably, before –"

"Before they default on their other indebtedness.'

Lassiter frowned at Palmer as if to remind him, first, that he was considerably older than Palmer, and second, that there were subordinates present. "I, ah, don't, ah, believe that..." Lassiter's voice died away, and he turned to Ralph Fenger.

"What Phelps means," Fenger began slowly, his little moustache bristling, "is that we, ah, have instituted some, ah, rather hopeful promotional efforts in the thrift field. We've upped our interest rate a quarter of one percent," he hurried on, surer of himself now, "and we have every reason to expect that –"

"That your local savings bank competitor will raise his a quarter over yours."

Fenger looked hurt by Palmer's remark. He turned to Charley Kornbluth, whose eyes widened with the effort of having to think of something to say. "Well," he began, "you

127

mustn't overlook the very favorable conversion deal we've worked out on repossessed properties. So far we've been able to unload seventeen one-family homes and eleven two-family semi-attached houses, with integral garages, at only seventy percent off list. That may not be a profit we're taking, but it sure as hell isn't a beating, either."

He seemed proud of the accomplishment. Palmer let him gloat for a moment. "Which generous institution took them off your hands?"

Kornbluth's eyes widened again. The movement worried Palmer. He recognized it as the way some people prefaced a lie. Kornbluth had done it twice, as if clearing his face of everything but innocence. Palmer felt sure his story was mostly true, which was why the eye movement seemed out of place.

"Uh, Downtown Bond and Mortgage," Kornbluth said very fast. "You know."

Palmer nodded. The name was vaguely familiar, but it actually meant little to him. "What makes them so willing," he asked, "aside from being able to pick up good properties at a thirty percent discount?"

Kornbluth's eyes widened again, but before he could speak, Donny Elder cut in. "Why Downtown Bond and Mortgage?" he wanted to know. "Do you know who you're dealing with there?"

Kornbluth shrugged. "Couldn't care less," he said somewhat huffily. "All I'm interested in is recouping the bank's investment, or as much of it as we can."

"Did you ever," Palmer asked, "think of listing your foreclosed properties with realtors and sweetening your mortgage offer to a prospective buyer?"

"Huh?"

"Look," Palmer explained, "you're giving away thirty percent of valuation this way. What if you put the properties on the open market and let it be known you'd write a six percent mortgage on them? Not on everything, just these special properties, just the ones you owned by foreclosure. Isn't that a hell of a lot better than taking a thirty percent beating?"

"But you're forgetting," Ralph Fenger cut in, "that when the prime rate jumps over six, we lose money on a six percent mortgage because it costs us more than six of the money, plus the servicing costs."

Palmer closed his eyes. When he opened them, they were on Ben Fischetti. "Tell your colleague," he said slowly, "that it

doesn't matter what money costs. He isn't buying the properties, he already owns them."

As Ben's mouth opened, Palmer swung back to stare at
Phelps Lassiter's bony face. "Phelps, I can see you all did a lot
of deep thinking on this one."

Lassiter's face twitched, and he restored to his hissing peep
of nervous glee. "Hee."

Palmer wheeled on Ben Fischetti. "Is this what the U of C's
Graduate School of Business Administration taught you?"

"I don't think you're being quite –"

"Forgiving?" Palmer suggested. "Willing to overlook small
trifles?" He stood up from the table and began walking, his
long, skinny legs covering carpet at a tremendous rate. "I've
looked at the dossier," he said then. "Ten years ago, when we
first offered to buy this bank of yours, you were fairly solvent.
You had a good cash flow and a balanced portfolio. You
weren't going to set the world on fire, either in rapid volume
increases or higher profits. But we didn't care, apparently.
What we wanted were your locations in Westchester, that and
a well-run bank. All you've got now are the offices. The rest is
a mess."

He stopped at the door and turned back on the rest of the
ruined luncheon. He noticed that even his own men were ill at
ease now. Good.

"It would appear," he continued thoughtfully, "that you
went all out for volume, writing any kind of loan on any kind
of collateral that was even remotely acceptable. Probably a lot
wasn't even that. There's a name for going all out that way.
It's called going for broke. I'm damned if I don't think you've
done it."

Lassiter's mouth moved soundlessly for a moment. "Woods,
you're not –"

"Most of this I blame on you, Phelps," Palmer continued.
"It's easy enough to say, well, it's all the fault of your new-
business man. He brought in all this crap. It's his fault the
portfolio is full of junk. But Ben can't be blamed for doing
what he was supposed to do, bringing in new business. The rest
of you, the seniors, you're to blame for not evaluating what he
brought you, for not weeding out the crap and for not teaching
him to stop wasting his time bringing in any more of it. Instead, you apparently wrote up whatever deal he brought you,
and that's how a bank goes for broke. All the way."

A look passed between Fenger and Ben Fischetti. Palmer

129

tried to read the look, but got only a guarded now-we're-in-for-it feeling about it. It did, however, tell him whose boy Fischetti was, not Phelps' and not Charley's. Ralph Fenger had sponsored him.

"Well" – Palmer swung open the door – "I imagine I've pretty well ruined everybody's lunch. Suppose we all go back home and sharpen up our wits and see what we can do to that portfolio of yours. The way it is now, I can't justify buying you to my board of directors. The stockholders would hang me from the nearest traffic light. You've got a little while still. I suggest you start by holding onto properties you have to repossess. Dumping them at a fat discount is not my idea of cutting losses. It merely deepens losses. Do you agree, Phelps?"

"I, ah, certainly." Lassiter stood up. His eyes roamed around the room somewhat aimlessly, as if unable to focus properly on anything concrete. His skull-like head bobbed twice in silent agreement. Then he walked out of the room without saying even good-bye. The rest, murmuring farewells, followed him.

Palmer closed the door behind them, went to the large cedar cigar box on the luncheon table and took out one of the very thin panatelas the bank bought from "21". He lighted it and sent a plume of white smoke into the air. "That wasn't poker," he said then, "it was mayhem."

"Blood all over," Donny agreed.

"I had no idea they were really in such bad shape," Palmer mused.

"You know what I told you," Elston reminded him.

"Yes. But all any of us had were suspicions. Their defense was so weak today, our suspicions are now confirmed. So we no longer suspect, we know." Palmer examined the pencil-thin cigar and tipped off its ash.

"And that business with Downtown Bond and Mortgage," Donny said. "That really smelled pretty damned high."

"What's that about?"

Donny gave him a you-mean-you-don't-know look. "That's a rough outfit, sir. Being from Chicago, I thought you'd know all about them."

Palmer's eyebrows went up. "Rough? Rough how?"

Donny gestured confidently. "You know. Nothing anybody can fault. Just who owns the outfit. Ever hear of a gentleman named Vinnie Big?"

"The state won't let anybody like that own a bank."

"He doesn't show as the owner. And come to think of it, Downtown isn't a bank. It's just a, uh, you know, a financial institution. Sort of."

Palmer grinned. "What's a, uh, you know, financial institution?"

"I mean..." This time Donny's gesture was less confident.

"You mean commercial bank, savings bank, savings and loan association, credit union, what?"

"What he means," Elston said, trying hard to keep the smug note out of his voice, "is that Downtown does a little bit of everything. They make personal loans. They make auto loans. They factor a lot of garment-center manufacturers. They finance receivables. They handle bond issues. They write mortgages. I mean, you can do all that and not be a bank."

"Certainly," Palmer agreed. "Anybody can do any of those things as a private citizen or company. But he's got to have the same thing a bank does."

"What's that?" Donny asked.

"Cash flow."

Palmer watched their faces. It hit him, about ten seconds before it hit the young men, that with Vinnie Big in the picture, Downtown never had to worry about a cash flow.

30

The storefront looked deserted at first glance. A cardboard sign in the window said "Operation Boost". The store lay in the middle of a block along upper Madison Avenue north of 116th Street in that no-man's-land of Harlem where the Puerto Rican population shades off into the Negro population and barrio merges into slum.

Edith Palmer got out of the second car in the motorcade. The first, preceded by a lone police motorcyclist with a silent siren, contained the mayor's wife, a Senator's wife, a well-known Negro contralto, two photographers and a harassed driver.

The second car contained, in addition to Edith, the white wife of a prominent Negro entertainer, a woman poet from the Caribbean and the wife of the chairman of the board of a large insurance company.

The women had been chosen by advisers to the mayor's wife, and the selection, Edith saw, had been done with a sharp eye to

131

equal representation. Not only were there just about as many Negroes as Puerto Ricans but, after Edith and her insurance company confrere, the white Anglo-Saxon Protestant roll call ended and the Catholic-Jewish delegations began. Days later, when she recounted the afternoon's procession to Woods, he worked out the formula for her, so many Jews to so many Irish to so many Italians to so many Negroes to so many Puerto Ricans to so many Wasps.

"It's called Instant Melting Pot," Woods said. "The formula elects anything from councilmen and mayors to governors and Senators. There's also a business-to-show-business ratio, so many symphony conductors to so many garment manufacturers, so many songwriters to so many corporation attorneys. But, what the hell, Edith, you're not running for office. Yet."

What she was running for this afternoon, Edith could not quite figure out. She had gotten the invitation, on the mayor's wife's personal notepaper, two weeks before, one of many such invitations the wife of Ubco's president got every day. But this one had been so noncommittal as to be positively mysterious.

Edith watched the insurance lady remake her mouth in her handbag mirror as the photographers unloaded their equipment and began looking for neighborhood children to pose. Edith glanced at herself in the storefront and saw that she needed lipstick but otherwise looked pretty much all right. She could not fail to note her resemblance to Woods. Both were tall and thin and fair, to begin with. And, Edith supposed, after nearly two decades of marriage, people began to resemble each other if only in the fact that they had shared the same environment of deterioration.

Horrible word. Neither of them showed any real signs of deterioration, did they? Neigher had gained weight. Both managed to keep their muscle tone, despite lives grown rather more sedentary each year. They dressed quite correctly and in the current style for their age and position. It was just that in recent years people had taken to saying of their three children how much they resembled both parents. From there, it took even the dullest observer only a second to realize how much the parents resembled each other.

Edith watched three uniformed policemen begin shooing small, dark-skinned children toward the storefront where the photographers waited, lenses poised.

She supposed she had been chosen not only because the Palmers had money and Ubco carried prestige, but also as a

132

physical type dying out in big cities except where politics was concerned. The type had already gone out of style in fashion models, film stars and pop singers. Being tall and thin was all right. Being blonde and blue-eyed was all right. But being all these things and having the narrow, short nose, the high cheekbones, the high forehead and the scattering of freckles, together with the very slightly buck teeth, made for a type absolutely exotic in today's scheme of things. Edith had the feeling that she had perhaps been invited as an example of yet another kind of minority problem.

The storefront door opened, and a tall, dark man in narrow chino slacks, loafers and a knitted sports shirt came out into the pale March sunlight. He blinked at the ladies and smiled uncertainly, then spotted the mayor's wife and went to her.

"They told me three o'clock," he said. "I don't think we're quite ready yet."

Edith listened to his intense voice. It had the head tones of a very good Eastern college, although the man himself looked like a Negro. He carried himself with the kind of assurance that made him seem even taller than his six feet. Edith was particularly sensitive to people's height since she herself stood five-ten in her stockinged feet.

Ready or not, the storefront was now being besieged by ladies, photographers and small children propelled by policemen. Edith found herself edged through the doorway and into the store itself.

Long tables had been set up, reaching far into the rear of the store. Dozens of folding chairs lined both sides of the tables. Great quantities of paint pots made from old mayonnaise jars, coils of sisal and bunches of wicker lay on the tables. The smell of turpentine-thinned varnish hung in the air, giving the rather too lived-in store a faint woodsy quality.

Several children between eight and twelve years of age wandered about the store examining the arts and crafts supplies. The idea of the project was fairly simple, perhaps, Edith thought, too simple for big-city kids like these. Operation Boost was a throwback to William Morris and his cottage-industry counterrevolt against the industrial revolution.

It sounded plain enough when Edith had first red about it in the *Times*. Negro and Puerto Rican children too young to take out working papers would be taught a craft and would earn money while learning it. Operation Boost would teach them to produce a variety of marginally useful artifacts of the sort

133

usually associated with primitive societies, blind people or hill folk in the South – pot holders, fireplace brooms, shoehorns, front-door mats, boot scrapers, felt slippers, bread baskets, cutting boards, coasters, and all the other sad lopsided crudities used to camouflage a charity and make it look like a business.

Joshua Kimberley, the tall, dark man who had greeted the mayor's wife, was the creator of Operation Boost, it's chief organizer and publicist and, to date, Operation Boost's only crafts instructor available to teach the few children who had forsaken the exciting, melodramatic streets of Harlem for this dull oasis of safety and boredom.

Edith walked slowly around the long room, pausing to examine some of the things the children had made. In front, just inside the door, the photographers had shoved two frightened Puerto Rican girls against a table while the mayor's wife stooped over them and paid extravagant attention to some raffia socks meant to fit around the bottoms of squat old-fashioned glasses. Flashguns flared and flared again. Edith wondered if either child had ever seen an old-fashioned.

Edith found herself in a small ell off the main room. A foldup cot stretched along one wall, covered by an olive-drab Army blanket. On a table beside the cot sat a wooden fruit box. It contained a large, mismatched collection of old chisels and gouges used by sculptors. On the floor next to the cot stood an unfinished statue about as high as Edith's eyes. She stood for a long time examining the sculpture.

The basic shape had been assembled from pieces of scrap lumber, mostly two-by-fours, glued to each other to make a central plinth about a foot thick. Although Edith's knowledge of wood was limited to polished furniture, she could recognize scrap bits and chunks of fine walnut, maple and oak. The sculptor had added projections where arms and legs might be on a body. He had then begun the job of chiseling out of this make-shift core material what was destined, it seemed to Edith, to be a woman with extremely large breasts. Square chunks of six-by-six had been cemented to the upper trunk, and the sculptor had already gouged out an extremely provocative walnut nipple, erect as a penis, surrounded by a pebbled areola that began to curve back into a rounding breast.

Edith stood without moving for much longer than she realized. She had never before seen a piece of unfinished art. The statues and paintings and prints she had seen had all been in galleries, museums, or people's homes. Even when she and

134

Woods had acquired the rather expensive paintings for their own home, it had never occurred to Edith that at some point prior to her first view of these works they had been blank canvas and oil colors in tubes. Nor did it occur to her that many of them had been built up on the canvas from something that only faintly resembled, in its early stages, what the final result would be. To Edith, works of graphic art were identical, in a way, with the plays she saw on Broadway or the concerts she heard at Lincoln Center. They were finished, polished examples of their art form. They had no other existence for her than in their final state.

For Edith to come upon this lusty body only just beginning to emerge from the wood, shoving up and out of the squared-off core of the sculpture like a butterfly from its cocoon, was a distinct shock.

"You're not supposed to see it just yet," a voice said behind her.

She turned and looked up into the dark gray eyes on Joshua Kimberley. At close range he did not look at all like a Negro, Edith noted. His nose, for one thing, was narrow and faintly beaked, and his cheekbones were high and broad. If it weren't for the gray-brown hue of his skin, without a touch of red, she would have thought him an Indian of the Southwest or of Mexico.

"I'm sorry. Is it yours?"

He nodded and picked up the Army blanket, draping it over the wooden form with a quickly executed flick, like a matador with a cape. "I haven't worked on her in days. Maybe a week. Maybe a month." The thought seemed to depress him.

His voice sounded faintly nasal, with the accented drawl of a good Ivy League prep school.

"Is this what you do when you're not organizing Operation Boost?"

"This is what I used to do, yes." He paused. "I'm sorry, but in all that hassle up front, no one introduced me to you. I'm –"

"Yes, I know. I'm Edith Palmer."

The vague look in his eyes prompted Edith to continue. "My husband is the president of Ubco – United Bank and Trust – Woods Palmer."

Recognition sharpened his glance. "You own a Hannah Kurd."

"We do. Woods had it in his office. Then he let it go on one of those State Department rotating exhibitions a year ago. I

135

believe, at the moment, the sculpture is in Kobe."

Kimberley shook his head. "Melbourne, Australia. It was in Japan last month."

"I suppose, as a sculptor, you keep track of these things."

"I have a piece in the show. In fact, the Hannah Kurd you loaned them is the only other sculpture on the tour besides mine." He thought for a moment. Then he twitched off the blanket and let the wooden piece stand naked again. "I don't usually let anyone see unfinished work. But you and your husband are collectors."

Edith shook her head. "It's the only sculpture we own. I don't even like it. It never did resemble our children, even at the age they posed for it, so I really don't at all mind the State Department kidnapping it more or less permanently."

Kimberley's dark forehead creased. "That particular Kurd is probably valued at fifty thousand dollars."

"Oh, as an investment, of course, yes."

The moment Edith said this, she regretted it. She knew enough about the New York art scene to know there were two kinds of artists. The very successful dressed like hippies, sold work composed of neon tubing for fantastic sums and were generally made fun of in serious circles; the much less successful ones dressed neatly, like Kimberley, taught slum children in return for a place to sleep and were usually beatified by serious critics within ten years of their untimely deaths from malnutrition.

She also knew that while the successful artists would do almost anything for money, including pornography, the less successful ones like Kimberley took their honesty very seriously and didn't like to hear works of art referred to as investments. Investments in our national cultural heritage, perhaps, Edith amended, but not for the purpose of making money.

"As the wife of a banker," Kimberley said in his precise, slightly nasal voice, "you'd naturally think of the Kurd that way. And it's true. Her work has appreciated tremendously in recent years since her arthritis."

The last was said about as bitterly as Edith had ever heard anyone speak. The words had a terrifying wry twist, as if human lips could not utter them in any calm, straight fashion.

"You mean she can't ...?"

Kimberley nodded. "She hasn't worked in over a year and won't ever again. She can't hold a chisel. She can't even squeeze clay. Too painful."

136

"Do you know her?"

"She taught me for three years. That was long ago. Recently I took over her classes when she could no longer get to and from the university. It all came a full circle."

He sat down on the edge of the cot and stared at the unfinished wood figure, all angular planes and abruptly shifting textures. "It gave me a very odd feeling," he said, more to himself than to Edith. His slate-colored eyes unfocused. "It was as if I were pushing my mother around in a wheelchair. As a child, she had pushed me in my stroller. Now ..."

"I had no idea she –"

"Of course not." Kimberley's eyes snapped up to stare at Edith in a rather cold way. Then, seeing the bewilderment in her face, his glance softened. "You didn't really come here for a lecture, did you?" He relaxed.

"I'm not sure why I came here. I suppose because the mayor's wife –"

"Because your conscience itched," Kimberley finished. "It's nice somebody's conscience itches from time to time." He stood up, all business now. "Do you think you could make a contribution to Operation Boost?" He gestured toward the main part of the store. Edith walked out of the alcove and looked at the deserted room. Everyone had left, children, ladies, photographers, cops.

"We need materials, paints, tools, everything. Even boxes to ship things in. Even string to tie the boxes."

Edith turned to Kimberley. Although he was smiling, his face seemed melancholy. "Do you live here," she asked, "or just work here?"

"Well" – he seemed to think for a long time about the answer – "I share an apartment with some other people on Bedford Street in the Village. But I haven't lived there much since Operation Boost got started last fall. We need a watchman up here. Otherwise, at night, people break in and steal the handicrafts material. So I'm the watchman. I commute to NYU from here. It's a big pain in the neck."

"You teach at NYU?"

He nodded. "Otherwise, I could never afford Operation Boost."

"You mean –"

'Did you think somebody was paying me to do this?" When she didn't answer, Kimberley nodded silently. Then: "It's an approved nonprofit organization, Mrs. Palmer. Your

137

contribution is a legitimate tax deduction."

The air between them had gotten very chilly. Edith tried smiling, but it failed to warm things up. She dug in her hand-bag and brought out her checkbook. Kimberley's eyes surveyed her coolly.

"How much does it cost to run this place for a week?" she asked.

"I have the store rent-free. In summer our expenses are about forty dollars a week, more in winter, because we buy coal for the stove. Say they average fifty dollars a week. Two hundred a month."

Edith scribbled in her checkbook, ripped out the check and handed it to Kimberley. He glanced at it, at the same time saying, almost automatically. "Thank you."

Then he read the amount. "Twenty-five hundred?" he asked.

"That's enough for a year," Edith explained.

His dark gray eyes widened. The corners of his mouth tightened. He moistened his lips and then, without any warning, began to sob uncontrollably.

Edith's lip trembled. "Please," she heard herself saying. "Please." Her voice echoed oddly in the huge, empty room. "Please."

31

Tippy slit open the letter. "Dear Billy Beanbag," it began. "Why don't you send your fans pictures of yourself, the way other 'disk' jokies do? I think you are not as big and fat as you sound. I think you just put that 'on.' I would love to come to town and visit you at the statin and watch you broadcast. I would like to see how you 'spin' those platers and do your 'chater.' See, I'm a poet, to. And while you on the 'air' I culd maybe sit next to you and help you do you show. I culd give you the next 'plater' and rub you back and put sugar in you coffee and rub you any other place you 'like.' There isn't any-thing I wuldn't do for you, Billy, no mater how crazy or dirty it might be. You wuld never 'regret' it ether, because I am considered real 'good,' a real pro with smooth, soft lips and very gentle hands and, believe me, Billy, I 'know' what to do and none of the boys ever complained but allways come back for more. I culd do 'it' rigt wile you on the air and nobody wuld ever know becase you on radio, not TV. But even if you on TV I wuldn't mind doing 'anything' for you, Billy, becase you real goovy and you send me so I get all wet down there when I listen to you and all you groovy chater. It wuld be the bigest thing that ever 'hapened' in my life, Billy, even if you on TV and the whole world was watching I wouldn't care but only do it to make them all 'jealous' of you, Billy."

The letter was signed "Georgette," but a P.S. indicated that the picture should be sent to a George.

Tippy filed the letter in a bulging folder labeled "obscene" and slit another envelope open.

"Dear Billy Beanbag. I dare you to read this one on the air, Beanbag. I wrote in very early Friday night for your genuine free offer of a cup of hair, and it's been two weeks and no cup of hair. I suppose you've got some cockamamie excuse about going bald, or something. If you don't read this on the air, you and I are finished, Windbag."

It was signed with a man's name and a dormitory room number at Columbia University.

Tippy rolled a sheet of letterhead into the typewriter. "You didn't hear the whole offer," she typed. "It was a cup of hair to the first five people who promised to drink it. Your move."

She signed the letter with a "Billy Beanbag" scrawl and slit open another envelope.

"Dear Billy Beanbag. My husband must never know I'm writing this. He hates you. He says you're nothing but a fat slob who's stealing money for gabbing over radio when you should be out on the street digging ditches. I told my husband to shut up. I never answer him back, Billy, but where you are concerned, I get very emotional.

"To tell you the truth, I don't know what I would do during the long, dark nights without your voice in my ear. I put my transistor under my pillow and plug the earphone into my ear to drown out the horrible racket my husband makes when he sleeps, snoring and mumbling and groaning and thrashing around.

"I even leave it plugged into my ear so I can listen to you while I submit to my husband. I'm sure you wouldn't approve of that, but then neither would he. Fortunately, I have very long hair, and he's never noticed. Now you and I are the only ones who know, and I am relying on your discretion.

"If I couldn't have the sweet sound of your voice and your music in my ear at such a moment, I think my whole marriage would have foundered on the rocks long ago. As it is, you are single-handedly responsible for keeping us together. Bless you, Billy."

Tippy wrote a fast answer. "Madam, your secret is safe with me. I shall try to adjust my programming accordingly."

She picked up the letter knife and was about to open another envelope. The deck rocked. She felt her body slew sideways. She lifted her right hand and drove the letter knife point down into the desk with such force that the dull tip buried itself almost half an inch in the wood.

A fierce pain angled across her skull from back to front. She stared fixedly at the quivering knife and then blacked out.

When she came to, only a few seconds had gone by. Her face was damp with tiny beads of sweat hardly bigger than the pores through which they had come. Her heart had slowed to a draggy thud.

She got to her feet and shoved an immense stack of letters into her wastebasket. Several hundred of them landed inside, and a few fell to the floor. Carefully she retrieved these and added them to the rest in the wastebasket. Then she dumped another load on top of them and covered them with a few sheets of crumpled typing paper so that a casual passerby wouldn't see the jettisoned letters.

She grabbed the letter knife and tried to pull it out of the desk top. It refused to budge. She was frightened now, mostly at the realization that she somehow had found the strength to drive the knife in that far, and also at the dawning knowledge that this had been a temporary strength far beyond her normal abilities. Desperately she worked the blade back and forth, trying to free it. After a few moments she was able, by pulling it with two hands, to yank it out. She stared down into the deep gash in the wood.

At first it looked like a mouth, a pursy-lipped mouth not much given to blabbing confidences. Then it resembled a fish, slipping like silent silver through water. It was a vulva, tense, resisting an imminent entry. It was a lidded eye, watching every thought she had ever had. It was a dart, aimed at her heart.

The telephone on her desk rang. It rang again.

On the fifth ring, Tippy blinked and looked at the instrument. She picked it up. "Tippy?" Ben asked. "Hello?"

"Where the fuck have you been?" Tippy asked.

"Delayed. Aftermath of the meeting."

"I'm leaving for Sean's now."

"See you in twen—"

Ben's voice died as Tippy hung up on him. She made her way unsteadily – only a bit unsteadily now – to the closed door of her room. She lifted her coat from the hanger on the back of the door. Muscular coordination returned to her in a sudden rush. She was able to function. She shrugged into her coat while opening the door.

Tippy dashed out into the corridor, past the small black formica rectangle in which white letters had been incised reading "Dorcas Tipton."

She was in too much of a rush to make a note of the man in the lobby of the building at the cigar counter who watched her departure and followed her in a second cab. That is, she saw the man and knew she had seen him before. But that fact did not, at the moment, arrest her attention.

It would later.

32

Ben listened to the dead telephone for a while, then replaced it in its cradle. He glanced hurriedly around the small office set aside by Downtown Bond and Mortgage Company, Inc., for visiting customers. Like the rest of the offices in the suite, this one was a perfectly anonymous room, featureless, containing standard furniture, with a window that provided a typically New York view of a brick wall twenty feet across an air shaft.

Ben looked at his watch. She would beat him to Sean's apartment, and by the time he got there she would be in a complete fury.

He found her anger exciting, since its chief ingredient was sexual hunger. He had never had a woman whose central need was so naked to even the most casual observation. She had never pretended, even from their first meeting, that she had any other motives than orgasm.

This goal she pursued with techniques Ben found bewildering at first, almost frightening in the way they ravished the privacy of his body. Later – the affair was now in its second week – he could accept what she did to him and eventually want it. She had so totally taken the initiative, first of arousing and re-arousing him, then of consummating the act in whatever way pleased her at the moment, that Ben had come to enjoy his passive role.

Once she had established herself in this manner, Ben realized, some of the original kick had gone out of it for Tippy. Her techniques had grown rougher. He was coming home to Rosalie the last few nights with scratches and bite marks that could not be explained. Tippy's appetites had begun to veer slightly off the core of orgasm, Ben realized, and were beginning to be attracted by the powerful lure of physical domination.

Ben knew quite a bit about this particular state. A year ago, with another leggy blonde of Sean's, this one known as Elfi, he had found himself in the reverse situation.

Elfi had been in the country less than a year, having originally come over as an exchange student from Stuttgart. Apparently she had always enjoyed subservience in her sexual relationships. Her extreme passivity, her greedy enjoyment of whatever was done to her, stirred needs in Ben he had never before suspected were there.

At first it had been a game, a teasing kind of test in which he sought to see how much he could humiliate her before she complained. But she never complained. He began to feel irritated, enough to change his intentions. He was no longer testing. He wanted simply to enjoy her pain.

He pushed her far beyond the limits of prudence. There were days when she couldn't go to any of her classes because of what he had done to her. She took it all. When they broke up finally, she let him know why. "You're such a baby, Ben. You're still playing. You're not yet serious."

It stunned Ben to think that before him, back home in Germany, there were men who had been able to convince Elfi they weren't playing. He had the feeling Tippy wasn't playing, either.

At the thought, the hairs across the back of his shoulders and neck prickled coldly. His throat thickened. He put on his coat and walked past the open door of his father's office without saying good-bye. He was late already, and there was no way of knowing how furious Tippy might be.

33

They were sitting on the edge of Kimberley's cot in the little alcove at the back of the store. Edith was sitting bolt upright, hands folded in her lap, one inside the other, palms up, lying tensely on her tweed skirt as she examined their lines and whorls like some gypsy palm reader. You will meet an interesting man.

Kimberley sat as far from her as the cot would allow, far up at the head, his gaze on the unfinished statue, his short, squat, powerful hands playing with a torn fringe of olive-drab wool on the edge of the Army blanket.

His eyes were dry. After that first outburst, he had run from Edith, as if to hide himself. She had followed him into the alcove, but only after she had heard the sobbing stop. Kimberley had composed himself by slow degrees. First he had stopped the tears. Then he had somehow quelled the sobs rising like vomit from deep inside him. Finally he had managed to smooth his face into a mask empty of expression.

But he still, Edith saw, was unable to look at her or speak in anything like a normal voice. She assumed he was not in the habit of tears. Most men were that way, she knew, but many were probably secret weepers to whom a rare public outburst was never as shocking as it had been to Kimberley. He seemed more upset by the fact of his own tears than by the gift that had occasioned it.

"Well," Edith heard him say then. She waited. His brown face was still slightly turned from her. "Well, anyway," he said then, bringing the words out fairly smoothly, "thanks for the money."

They both began to laugh, Edith first, then Kimberley slowly joining in. He turned to her, his eyes searching her face for clues to the emotional climate.

Edith was strongly reminded of her younger son, Tommy, as he had been at the age of anywhere up to ten. Woody had never cried much at all, but Tommy had been a softer child, the youngest, whose whims had been much more humored. After such an outburst he would scan her face as if reading a barometer for signs of continued storms or fair weather.

It bothered Edith, for a moment, to think of this man, who was probably only ten years her junior, in the same terms as one of her own children. Somewhere she had read that the typical modern American male lived almost solely for the approval of females, which was what was killing him off. From his earliest days, she recalled reading, he learned to please his mother first and later the girls of his acquaintance, ending in the one he married. He was, in a sense, programmed to provide behavior pleasing to females and it was only natural,

143

Edith decided now, that from time to time he would send out small glances of reconnaissance, testing his effect on the female of the moment.

"In a year's time," Kimberley said then, some self-confidence entering his voice, "we should know if Operation Boost is a success or a dud. If you hand't made it possible, I think we'd never know. It would have folded by July."

"Why July?"

"In Harlem, any activity that provides a warm, dry place is going to capture a few children in winter. But as soon as the streets get warm, we'd have lost them."

"Don't they know how dangerous the streets are?"

Kimberley's face twisted wryly. He made a slight shrugging gesture, and Edith realized with his next words that he no longer considered her an outsider to shut away coldly. "Dangerous for you, yes. Even for me, with my Whitey accent and clothes. But no more dangerous for these kids than the ocean is for the fish that swim in it."

"Fish get eaten in the ocean."

Kimberley stood up and began rummaging in one corner of the table. He dislodged a few slips of paper that fell to the floor at Edith's feet. Then he found what he was looking for, a liter bottle of tequila, nearly full.

He showed it to Edith. "Wine of my childhood," he said, grinning. "I'm a New Mexico boy still, you know, one-quarter Hopi, one-quarter Irish, one-half African. How about some with a little lime?"

The last thing she needed, Edith felt, at this hour of the afternoon was a shot of tequila in a Harlem storefront with a half-breed colored sculptor. "Why, yes," she said.

While Kimberley went about the business of remaining a lime and mixing it with powdered sugar and tequila, Edith picked up one of the slips of paper from the floor. It turned out to be a single sheet of 8½-by-11 paper mimeographed on both sides and folded in thirds.

"Discipline for Peace Demonstrations," it read. One corner of of Edith's mouth quirked downward disapprovingly. "Public demonstrations for peace can achieve the following objectives, among others," the pamphlet read. "A. Ideas can be communicated to many people through signs, slogans, leaflets, coverage of demonstrations in the mass media, and conversations with persons who see the demonstrations. B. Demonstrators are given an opportunity to take a public stand on

144

issues about which they are deeply moved, and by –"

"Here." Kimberley handed her a jelly glass rimmed with salt crystals and filled with a liquid of the faintest, most delicate pale green. "It's room temperature. I have no ice. Salud."

Edith touched the rim of her glass to the one Kimberley was holding. Instead of a ringing sound, she heard the salted rims grate on each oher. "Cheers."

The first sip of the Margarita was entirely confusing to Edith. The liquid itself had a tart, sweet taste, faintly musky with tequila overtones. The shock of the pure salt on the rim of the glass sent pangs through Edith's tongue and seemed to blast open her taste buds. For one moment, she could sort out each individual taste. Then with the second sip, they blended together again.

Kimberley picked up the peace demonstration handbook. "You interested in this sort of thing?"

"No."

"I am." He scanned the pamphlet for a moment. "Why aren't you?"

"I ... well ..."

"You're for the war, then?"

"Unfair question."

Kimberley nodded. "You have children. Any sons?"

"Two." She paused. "One is of draft age."

"Then ...?"

Edith slipped. "His father fought in World War II. I ... we ... we have all just naturally assumed that ..." She stopped, realizing none of them had assumed anything at all. "Of course, we keep chivvying Woody on his grades. That's terribly important these days, isn't it? I mean, if you don't get into a college, you're more or less instantly drafted."

"Yes. Even the son of the president of United Bank and Trust." Kimberley grinned mockingly at her. "If he couldn't matriculate at a college, that is. So many millions of young-sters can't and don't. Especially the black ones up here. But I'm sure that somewhere, somehow, there's a college that'll accept the son of the president of United Bank and Trust Company, no matter what his prep-school grades were."

Edith found herself grinning back at him. "Mr. Kimberley," she said, "are you some kind of Communist?"

"If you're going to ask questions like that," he said, "you'd better start calling me Josh."

34

Gaetano Fischetti saw, through the half-closed door of his office, the wide-shouldered form of his son rush past. From a distance he heard the receptionist murmur something as Ben left the suite of offices.

Gaetano wondered why Ben hadn't said good-bye to him. He looked down at the desk for a moment and the up into the flat blue eyes of his cousin, Don Vincenzo Biglioto. In that instant he knew why Ben hadn't stopped. He hadn't wanted to talk to Don Vincenzo, his father-in-law. He almost never did, Gaetano reflected, except when forced to by circumstances or family protocol.

In a life of more than fifty years now, Gaetano Fischetti had learned the immense, the all-surmounting, the nearly supernatural power of protocol. The order of things and of people, the order of respect and responsibility, the order imposed by tradition and family, these elements of protocol were everything. The rest was nothing.

Who lives and who dies was nothing before the inexorable majesty of family protocol. Who prospered and who grew poor, who was happy and who sad, none of these questions amounted to anything because all of them were contained within the body of family protocol, which contained everything and thus was itself the all-in-one, the single entity that was everything.

Naturally, thinking as he did, Gaetano had never gotten too far in the family. His total lack of imagination or daring was not in itself a bad quality. But his complete inability to generate an idea had severely limited his usefulness.

In fact, one of the few positive things Gaetano Fischetti had ever done to improve his standing and his chances was the clever act of having a handsome son of intellectual accomplishment who could make a suitable husband for Vinnie Big's older daughter. That marriage alone was keeping Gaetano gainfully occupied, that and his single talent for losing money.

As he stared across his desk at Vinnie Big, Gaetano wondered if the older man had heard Ben's sudden departure. A moment later he no longer needed to wonder.

"He don't even say good-bye anymore?" Vinnie asked.

Gaetano shrugged. *"Chi lo sa?"*

Vinnie's eyes flared like Bunsen burners, and Gaetano winced. "Whadya mean, who knows?" he asked harshly. " better know, Tony Fish, that's who. One of these days I'm gonna knock you and him together and talk real hard, you understand? Real hard. I don't like anything the two of you are doing lately. Is that right, Rocco?"

Rocco Sgroi, his glance fixed on something in the middle distance, seemed to ponder the question for a moment. Then slowly he nodded his head, as if giving a considered opinion of some substance. "'At's right," he said, by way of reinforcing the gesture.

Tony Fish's mouth did a small dance, alternately assuming the faintest outline of a smile and the briefest sketch of a thoughtful frown. Failing to make up his mind which better suited the moment, he broke into speech. "How was anybody to know, Vinnie? Tell me that. Tell me how this *pezzo grosso*, this whadyacallit, this Palmer, could grab on so fast. So fast nobody could know. Tell me, how I could know that?"

"I'll tell you how, *cretino*!" Vinnie Big got to his feet and began pacing the long, carpeted space in front of Gaetano's desk. "By doing what I told you all along. By pinching off Klaman a year ago, eight months ago. Even six months ago. Before the merger, before everybody started poking into everything. If you do it then, you and that *scioccone* son of yours, I would have Klaman *con tutt'e due le mani* and nobody in the world would know. This way, because the two of you are stupid, first this Palmer knows and soon the whole world."

Tony Fish bunched four fingers of each hand against their opposing thumbs, as if rolling small balls of bread. "Vinnie, be reasonable. You still got Klaman. You got him right now, only he don't know it. This Palmer, what does he care who or what you got? He doesn't even know who you are."

Vinnie Big's open hand flashed upward in the air to demonstrate the obvious idiocy of his cousin's thinking. "You hear, Rocco? This Palmer, he's not only stupid, he's deaf, dumb and blind."

Sgroi made a huffing sound deep in his throat that signified laughter. After a while he subsided and looked placidly first at Tony Fish, then at Vinnie Big. "One thing," he said then in a low-keyed voice. "This Palmer probably knows all about you. But when Tony says he don't care who or what you have, I think he's right. It figures. Why the hell should he care what you have as long as it isn't something he wants?"

147

"Maybe he wants Klaman," Vinnie muttered, not yet placated.

"He's got him, on paper. When he takes over Klaman's bank, he takes over Klaman's paper. Those loans Klaman has to pay, no matter what, right?" Rocco's eyebrows lifted twice. "So Palmer has Klaman's paper, and you got the real Klaman. You both get what you want, right?"

Without giving any obvious outward sign of agreement, Vinnie Big continued talking along an entirely new line which gave tacit approval to Rocco's thinking. "Tony, this is one operation you do right, you hear? Klaman is getting himself all ready to tap us for money. I see all the signs. I know what bad shape he's in. Any day now he falls into our hands. When that happens" – he stopped and pointed his finger at his cousin, aiming it at his right eye – "you do this right or you never do nothing again, ever."

"*Si*, Vincenzo."

"The papers have to be drawn up exactly so."

"*Si*."

"The agreement has to be our paper, not his."

"*Si*."

"Our lawyers."

"*Si*."

"And when it's all over, everything is ours."

"*Si*, everything."

"We step on Klaman like a fat grape, and we squeeze all the juice out from beneath our heel. *Capite?*"

"*Si*, Vincenzo."

"And then we feed the pulp to the pigs."

The three men chuckled softly, in a careful, not too ostentatious, way.

35

The slanting afternoon sun cut through the grimy side windows of the greenhouses, sharpening the green of the leaves with a bright wash of yellow. The air was heavy with moisture, and to Don Girolamo it smelled rich with oxygen, the life-giver.

He shut off the motor of his golf cart and sat in the silence, breathing deeply. The plants were always good to him in the daytime. A man of eighty-six years, he knew, was fortunate to be able to spend his days in these greenhouses like some rare plant, almost but not quite sinking roots into the rich loam. Ten years ago, when he had given over the active, day-to-day control of the family to Don Vincenzo, his son, he had retreated to his prepared position like a wise general deploying his troops. Here he was safe, at least during the daylight hours, and here he would stay while the world came to him.

An emissary of the outside world had already arrived. That was why Don Girolamo was heading the golf cart back to his sealed-off sanctuary. But a man of his age could be allowed a moments pause for reflection. A man who commanded as much respect as he could was more or less expected to keep visitors waiting. Not long, for that was needlessly rude. But a few minutes of waiting was necessary for form's sake.

So thinking, Don Girolamo switched on the motor and guided the cart along a corridor of green leaves and black shadows. Changing odors came to him as he drove through drafts of air, one from potted mimosas, the afternoon sun igniting their yellow bursts, one from waxy-leaved English ivy, one carrying the family rotting spice of small palms. He pulled to a stop before the sectional overhead steel door and touched the radio-control button.

Don Girolamo's reflexes were not those of a man of eighty-six. As the door started to rise, he already had the cart in motion toward it. As he passed under, he activated the mechanism that shut the door again. When he left the cart and walked, stiff-legged, to the inner room with its fireplace, he saw that his visitor looked a good deal thinner than the last time he had seen him, scarcely a year before. He sniffed.

"How thin," he exclaimed, advancing toward the visitor.

The younger man jumped to his feet. "*Si, padrone*, and it makes me look older. But you, you look ten years younger than the last time." Humbly he reached for Don Girolamo's hand and, when it was given to him, gratefully kissed it. Then he remained standing, head reverently bent, until the older man had gotten into his easy chair next to the fire. A chunk of cannel coal glowed red, filling the small room with heat.

"Sit down, Charley. What is the news?" Don Girolamo now spoke in Italian.

Charley's mouth tightened in a line of intense compression, as if, having come here solely to report news, he nevertheless had the greatest reluctance to do so.

"Speak."

"*Si, padrone.* I have information from someone who is useful to us." At *servizievole*, his word for "useful," Charley's hands made a mixing-up motion, as if tossing salad by hand in a great bowl. "He is a licensed investigator. What the Americans call a 'private eye.' You understand me?"

Don Girolamo nodded. He had a premonition that he would not like Charley's news. There was something in the set of the younger man's face, and something even more about his inability to get to the point, that told Don Girolamo the news would be unpleasant.

"Is this not something for Don Vincenzo?" the old man parried. "It is to him that most of this information now goes."

"There is a ... ah ... a reason why I tell it to you," Charley assured him. "It involves Don Vincenzo's son-in-law, Benedetto Fischetti."

Don Girolamo's eyes narrowed. "The f-football player?" He spat out the "football" scornfully in English.

He had his own private feelings about the entire Fischetti clan. It had been bad judgment on Don Vincenzo's part to marry his daughter to the son of an underling, and a stupid one at that.

Moreover, the son-in-law had grown far away from the family – if, indeed, anyone ever could – in spirit if not in fact and could not be relied on for any but the most camouflaged of activities.

In fact, the whole subject of the Fischettis was a sore spot to Don Girolamo. They were weak links in the chain, both of them, and both were situated much too close to Don Vincenzo for comfort. It all came of marrying that skinny Torinese bitch. If Don Vincenzo had not yielded to the sin of pride after the death of his true wife, if he hadn't been tempted by the thought of being seen with a flashy piece of trash on his arm, there would be no daughters and no Benedetto Fischetti.

"Charley," Don Girolamo snapped, "are you to tell me this or not?"

"Yes, yes, of course. I was saying it involved the son-in-law. It also involves one of Don Vincenzo's business associates, the Jew, Harry Klaman."

The old man's eyes widened slowly, like one of his flowers beneath the rays of the sun. "I see," he said slowly. "Go on."

36

Edith found the Margaritas insidious. She thought so after Kimberley had made a second round. She had been staring at the half-empty liter bottle of tequila, her glance focused first on its top.

Surely that was not a United States revenue stamp, Edith had thought. She had stared for a very long time at the narrow white paper stamps with the light blue printed pattern and the olive green printing: "Imp. Fed. $1.20." Then her glance had moved slowly, studiously, to a second stamp on the neck of the oddly shaped bottle. The other label had read "Texas State Tax Paid. Liquor. Qt. 42 Cents." Then, because the label of the bottle was turned away from her, she had read the back of the label through the glass. A fancifully drawn picture of a mescal plant had been printed in light green ink and above it the legend "*Destilado Puro*."

It was at that point that Edith had decided the Margaritas were insidious. The salt caked on the rim of the glass gave her a burning thirst that the tart liquid almost, but not quite, quenched. When she accepted a third drink, it was with a certain fatalism.

"It's too late to try getting me drunk," she told Kimberley. "I've already made out the check."

The remark went virtually unheard. Kimberley had stopped talking to her at least one drink back and was now talking aloud to himself. It was not, Edith saw, that he believed himself to be alone. It was simply that he felt like enjoying a monologue, and by God, he wasn't to be frustrated.

In keeping with the catch-as-catch-can nature of Kimberley's talk, Edith sometimes listened and sometimes forgot to. It had started off as a why-I-am-for-peace statement, but it had somehow gotten derailed, first, by his reminiscences of the Korean War and second, by his struggle to "pop," as he put it.

"You can know you're great," he was saying, "and you can have a piece traveling around the world in a State Department show, but that cuts no ice. Back home you plug along on nickels and dimes from teaching. You hustle around, doing almost anything that lets you keep your integrity. And you keep doing your work, hoping, well, maybe, this piece or the next, or the next show or whatever, you'll pop. Pop! You explode from the great unknown out there into the instant now of success and fame. Pop! One day it's anonymity. The next day it's glory. Pop! Well, it isn't easy. A lot of people never do. I probably won't, either."

He stopped on this note and fell to watching the unfinished statue, giving the nude as much attention as if she were another guest at what by now Edith had begun to think of as a party. Kimberley's slate-gray eyes grew darker with some unvoiced emotion having to do with the losing struggle against anonymity.

"A life in art," he murmured unhappily. "Big deal."

"I do like this one, though," Edith heard herself say, indicating the other guest. "I wouldn't do too much more to her. I haven't any idea what you were planning to do, but she's almost ready to show."

Kimberley's glance swung around to Edith. His eyes widened slightly. "You're putting me on."

"Maybe some more face?" Edith asked. "Just an eye?"

Kimberley squinted at the statue. "It's hardly even started, and you want me to call it finished?"

"But it's more than started. I mean, look at the way you have all the wood attached."

"That's just blocked in. It isn't meant to be final."

"I like the way it looks," Edith persisted doggedly.

"It's just cemented together that way because I can't afford one big piece of wood."

"So much the better."

"It's mostly scrap."

"Wonderful," Edith said.

Kimberley jumped angrily to his feet. He walked around the statue and then retired to a corner of the little alcove to stare disgustedly, first at the statue and then at Edith.

"You know," he said finally, his voice starting to lose its sharp Ivy League nasality as the tequila began working on his centers of speech, "the arrogance of the ruling class is absolutely beyond belief."

"Don't, then," Edith remarked somewhat sulkily.

Kimberley's dark skin had a faint powdery bloom on it, she saw, somewhat like the natural dust of a grape. His beaky nose seemed to thin at the bridge as he grimaced. "I'm not knocking it," he said. "I'm beginning to see what arrogance can do for somebody who doesn't come naturally to it. It's a psychedelic drug. Leave the statue alone and say it's finished. Pop! Spit in your audience's eye and make them cheer. Pop! You know something, baby, it just might work!"

"I'm old enough to b—" Edith stopped herself in mid-thought. The room grew silent. Kimberley sat down on the cot next to her and continued staring at the statue. His thigh next to hers felt as hard as wood. He seemed to be breathing hard.

Edith felt absolutely sober. Or more or less so, she decided. She knew she wasn't drunk. It usually took several more than she had had. But she did have the usual sense of warm well-being that came, for her, with the second drink.

It was more than the alcohol this time, she knew. She had in some way she still didn't understand shaken Kimberley profoundly. The check had pushed him off balance, and her casual remark about leaving the statue unfinished had somehow finished knocking him for a loop. But even if she failed to understand exactly what she had done, she knew enough of it to feel an added sense of well-being. It was almost, she told herself now, as if she had in some strange way participated in a creative act.

She watched Kimberley's dark hand pat her knee. "It just," he was musing aloud, "might work."

She patted his hand. He turned and looked at her. After a moment, he took his hand from her knee, slid it around her and pulled her to him. His tongue tasted salty at first. Then she tasted the sweet musk of the tequila. She relaxed and lay back on the cot, wondering simultaneously whether Mrs. Gage would think to give the children dinner and whether Kimberley had locked the front door of the store.

37

The modest, featureless room was silent for a long moment after Gaetano Fischetti left. Vinnie Big stared across his desk at his buffer, Rocco Sgroi. The two men, so similar in size and appearance, seemed to be listening to silent reverberations in the air, their ears jointly attuned to immensities of meaning in the soundless room.

Finally Vinnie got to his feet. The movement was quick and smooth for a man his age. He padded silently across the room in his small, pointed shoes and gently eased the door shut. As he started to do so, Rocco began to get out of his chair in a silent offer of help, but the older man shook his head without speaking.

Once he had shut the door, Vinnie moved quietly back to his chair and sat down again. He stared for a moment at the plain black-linoleum top of his desk. Then his startling blue eyes lifted slowly to glare at Rocco.

"How long has that miserable little *blatta* been that way?"

Rocco avoided Vinnie Big's stare. He knew from too many years of experience how disturbing those eyes could be, even if their wrath or scorn or hatred were directed not against Rocco, but a third party.

"Quite a while," Rocco said. Then quickly, to ward off the lightning from his own head: "Not anything really bad, you understand. Just stupid." A thoughtful pause. "Not stupid, you understand, *padrone*, more like, ah, what could you call it?"

"I call it stupid. And anybody who didn't report how stupid he was is as stupid as him. You get what I'm saying?"

Rocco Sgroi's hands flew out sideways, palms up, as if releasing a beautiful white dove of truth into the tense air. "*Padrone*, think what you saying. A Fischetti? Your cousin? Your daughter's father-in-law?"

Vinnie Big's eyes hooded slightly in his dark-skinned face. "That's one big trouble with the family," he said then, more to himself than to Rocco. "It gives *scemoniti* like Tony Fish a little hole to hole up in. They can't fight their way out or think their way up. But they can crawl into their little hole and sit it out like a roach in the wall. And the wall protects them. That's the part that hurts. Goddamn it, *I'm* the wall. He's a little termite inside me, and he's gonna eat my insides out rotten."

Rocco's hands, outstretched, began a new pantomime of gentle rejection. Palms facing Vinnie Big now, the hands made small shushing gestures, as if heaping together a mound of rich whipped cream.

"That bad he ain't, *padrone*. That bad nobody is. I mean, give the poor bastard a little credit. He's done what he was told to do, right? Nobody can set up a patsy corporation prettier than Tony Fish. Am I right?"

"Any idiot can set up a patsy corporation. Did you ever hear what happened the first time I gave Tony Fish a contract to scam?"

Rocco nodded. "I heard something."

"You musta heard nothing, goombar, or else you wouldn't

stand up for him." Vinnie Big settled back in his chair and turned the fury of his stare at the neutral ceiling.

"This was right after the war, World War II," he recalled. "My father and I worked out the whole scam. In the old country it used to go through like shit through a goose. We just gave it a few touches to kind of Americanize it." Vinnie's mouth widened in a sharklike grin.

"The two of you dreamed up the first scam?" Rocco said. "I didn't know that."

Vinnie shook his head modestly. "We didn't dream it up, Rocco. We *imported* it." The shark's smile faded slowly. "About two months before Christmas, just the right time. We had this little electrical-supply company in Queens all picked out for the scam. These people made bombsight parts during the war, and now they made lamps and sockets and switches. They had good lines of credit with every big metal company. I had Tony Fish all set up. He was supposed to be a jobber out of Cleveland."

"What kinda jobber?"

"Electrical goods, what else?" Vinnie Big stared at the ceiling, as if at a movie screen on which these reminiscences were unreeling. "He hit this outfit in Queens with a fifty-thousand-buck order on a check payable to a Cleveland account I set up there out of Downtown funds. They delivered, we transshipped to one of our Chicago outlets. No real profit, but we knew we at least made back our fifty Gs, right?"

"Right. And now you got this Queens outfit eating outta Tony's hand."

"That's the idea. So Tony hits 'em for two small orders on credit, like twenty Gs apiece. He pays in ten days, net, and that makes him very kosher with these idiots in Queens. So then he really bangs it into them with a two-hundred thousand-buck order for sockets and switches, with a rush on it and a premium for delivery before December first. At the same time—" Vinnie broke off and considered the ceiling in silence.

"At the same time," Rocco supplied, "the owner of the company is in to one of your gambling boys for at least the same amount, right?"

Vinnie Big shook his head impatiently. "We didn't use anything *tanto grezzo*." He glanced down at Rocco. "*Grezzo?*"

Rocco's mouth moved silently for a moment, framing and rejecting translations. "Crude?"

"*Sì.* Nothing so crude on these Queens boys. We had a little

155

wiring company in the Bronx they were after. That's how I first got wind of them for a scam. And they wanted to buy the company for a piece of their own. They only wanted the wire company so bad they could taste it. But we don't sell for stock, only cash."

"Which they don't have."

"Not without a little liquidation here and there." The shark's grin returned for a moment, fleetingly, as if Vinnie Big were tasting an unusually pleasant morsel. "But we priced the wire company low enough to start them thinking about getting up cash. It was a nice squeeze. They wanted our little company, and it's too cheap to pass up. That's when we hit them over the head with a sockful of shit. They had just shipped Tony Fish's two-hundred-G order when he put in an order for a hundred thousand bucks' worth of lamp fittings."

Rocco chuckled. "This stretches their cash out of sight, right? They have to hit their suppliers for credit, right?"

"While also trying to find the cash to buy this little bargain in the Bronx."

"The rest is automatic, *padrone*."

Vinnie's Indian face darkened appreciably. "Automatic is right. Only it ain't automatic if you got Tony Fish working for you."

"How could he fuck it up? It's a foolproof scam."

Vinnie shrugged, almost philosophically. "I got my boy Umberto up in the Bronx, Umberto Notarbartolo, Charley's father. He's the guy running the wire company, see? He's supposed to send these Queens people to see me at Downtown for a cash loan. It's all cut and dried. I'm gonna factor their accounts receivable, including three hundred thousand bucks' worth of phony orders from Tony Fish. I got 'em by the nuts, right?"

"Right."

"Out in Cleveland we got a month-to-month rental on an old warehouse. We're using it for an address and to transship loot to Chicago. This is Tony Fish's responsibility. Now, get this. The day these Queens people have a date to see me about a loan, the day I'm getting my hooks in their heart, what happens?"

Rocco shrugged. "Tony blows the game?"

"Nothing that simple, Rocco. Nothing like that for Tony Fish." Vinnie's eyes blazed out at Rocco. The younger man blinked and tried to look away. "Can you feel how close we were? If I'd factored their accounts receivable and Tony's orders went bad, they'd default on their loan, giving me a piece of their business, a controlling goddamned interest, for Christ's sake."

Vinnie Big's voice had started to rise slowly from a furry rumble to something as close to a shout as he ever got. "It's so close, I can almost reach out and touch the thing. Control of the Queens company. The perfect scam, Rocco. Gut their lines of credit. Hit up their suppliers for two million bucks in wire and metal orders, transship to a dozen different cover names, cash in the goods and let the Queens company go bankrupt. The perfect scam. Two million in loot, Rocco, because their lines of credit are solid."

"Is there anything to get excited over, *padrone*?"

"A two-million scam? In those days? It was something to get excited over, goombar, believe me."

"But, I mean ..." Rocco gestured largely. "I mean, like today, *padrone*, today a scam like that ain't worth your time."

Don Vincenzo Biglioto's thin-lipped mouth turned down at the corners. "I still would give a two-million scam a few minutes' thought. I wouldn't kick it outta the bed, Rocco. And there's always a few soldiers down the line in the family who can use good clean loot like that. Button men gotta eat, too."

"Two million feeds a lotta button men."

Vinnie shrugged. 'I'm a liar, Rocco. Two million in shipments from the suppliers to me. But we couldn't of got more than a million in cash on it. We'd get more today. We're better organized now than we were then." Vinnie fell silent, a faint smile on his knifelike lips.

"So what happened with Tony Fish?"

"Tony Fish!" Vinnie stood up and began pacing the carpeted room. "The day these Queens people are supposed to step in my office and get their balls cut off, the very same day that first big shipment of two thousand Gs' worth of sockets and switches gets returned from Cleveland marked 'No Such Consignee.' You understand, Rocco?"

"No."

"The warehouse in Cleveland. Tony Fish missed a month's payment on the rental. So they close it up and take down our sign and refuse to accept any shipments. One lousy month's rent he forgets to pay in advance, my big money man cousin, and he blows a two-million-dollar scam."

"No chance to patch it up with the people in Queens?"

157

"You kiddin', Rocco? The minute that shipment bounces, they smell a rat. They pull in their horns, and we never lay eyes on any of them again." The room reverberated into long, full silence.

"So that's the story of Tony Fish."

"That's the story." Vinnie Big had stopped pacing. He stared down at the floor. "That's why I never let him near another scam. He's okay for setting up patsies. Any idiot can do it, and he's as good an idiot as anybody. But a scam takes brains and speed, and this Tony Fish never had and never will."

"The son . . ." Rocco Sgroi let the idea fall gently in the room.

"The father is way too dumb," Vinnie said in a curiously flat, dead voice. "And the son is just too smart." He laughed without joy.

38

It was dark in the back room of the store. The window over the bed was set high in the wall and overlooked an alleyway in which garbage had been thrown for many years now, silting down into a kind of mulch of neglect. The window itself had been washed rather thoroughly a few months before, when Kimberley had opened the Operation Boost headquarters. Since then no one had had time or the inclination to wipe it clean of the soot and ash collected on it.

Edith lay on her back and stared hard at the faintly lighter oblong that was the window. In the gathering dark she had a sensation of floating, as if both she and the window were free objects in space. The window, she felt, wasn't attached to the wall. And her body was certainly not bound down by gravity to the rough blanket and hard mattress under her.

They hadn't spoke at all for some time. After they had kissed for a while, he had taken off her blouse and freed her rather small breasts from the minimal brassiere she wore. He had spent some time making her nipples grow hard and out-jutting by biting them gently and sucking on them.

Now he had removed her skirt and was slowly freeing the hem of her stockings from the garter belt snaps. He took an inordinately long time with this, and Edith got the sudden feeling that perhaps he was trying not to run her nylons.

In any event, she thought, none of this has any reality because we are all free-floating objects in space.

She had begun to feel a faint stirring of desire for him when her nipples had grown so hard. But now, as he seemed to fiddle about endlessly with her garter snaps, she began to wonder if anything would happen at all except this endless preamble that wasted her with waiting.

"Let me," she said at last, reaching in under her slip and deftly freeing the last of the snaps.

She rolled sideways to get clear of him and quickly pulled off her stockings. As she started to roll back, she felt his strong harsh-skinned sculptor's fingers run quickly up and down her thigh. A faint tremor quickened in the pit of her stomach.

He pulled off her panties and began to finger her clitoris with long, slow upward strokes, pressing it from two sides with a roughness that excited her. She let her legs part until her feet stretched to each corner of the bed.

She could no longer see the window or Kimberley. It had been this way on her honeymoon, too, she recalled. Utter blackness in the huge bedroom of the bridal suite and Woods groping about in the darkness, first for her breasts and then for her vagina. He had grown so excited so quickly that he had reached his climax long before she had begun to feel anything at all.

It was often to be this way, and she had always been reluctant to discuss it with him. As she lay there now, feeling the long, sure stroke of Kimberley's fingers, she realized how seldom she had reached her own climax with her husband. The last time seemed shrouded in the mists of antiquity. Probably, she thought now, on some night when he'd drunk too much to come fast. She could hardly recall the feeling.

None of the books she had read on the subject could even begin to give her more than the vaguest idea of what she was supposed to feel. None of her friends discussed the matter.

Kimberley lifted her buttocks up off the cot and pulled her slip over her head. She lay naked on the blanket now.

She wondered for a moment what kind of man Kimberley was. It couldn't be that he was timid or inexperienced. That seemed clear now. Nor could he possibly have guessed how timid and inexperienced she really was. Not by anything said or done had Edith for a moment betrayed the fact that this was her first extramarital relationship. She was absolutely certain of this. She wasn't at all sure how one did act if one were experienced and brazen, but she felt certain she was accounting herself rather well.

He had been kissing her abdomen and navel, his hands beneath her, each clamped around one cheek of her buttocks. Now she felt something soft stroke upward through the lips of her vagina, and she realized he was licking her. She started to struggle free, then lay absolutely still.

A terrible sense of shame flooded over her. Had she been particularly careful washing herself this morning? What did he get out of this? It was hard to understand. Her mind couldn't seem to . . .

Sudden, sharp, jolting waves seemed to attack her from inside. Her clitoris twitched as if electrified. She felt as though something alien had taken possession of her groin.

"Now?" she heard him ask.

"Yes. Yes."

She felt his penis thrust in and up with terrible heat and power. She reached into the darkness and held his long, thin body, pulling him down on her, crushing his chest into her breasts. Her legs wrapped around his. She could feel his hard-muscled torso bunch and thrust. She rubbed the palms of her hands up and down his back.

She could hear his breath surging in and out of his mouth. She heard another's breathing and realized she, too, was gasping with the mounting intensity of the act.

She could hear herself moaning. It was almost as if she were listening to another woman, to one of the women in the delivery room as she lay waiting for one of her own children to be born. She was saying something now to Kimberley, but she couldn't make out the words, only the urgency with which they were uttered.

Hot wheels of light exploded behind her eyelids. She felt a gigantic cave open inside her, a bottomless immensity through which stars shone and the wind howled. Her whole lower trunk seemed to flare up in a spasm of orange heat. She heard an animal growl with blood lust. Her teeth sank into Kimberley's shoulder. His skin tasted faintly sweet and salty, like tequila.

39

The Lincoln threaded its way through the usual heavy pedestrian traffic that begins to clog the streets of the financial section of New York after the market closes.

The last of the March sunshine shone in faint horizontal rays along one of the narrow east-west side streets, shone briefly and disappeared for good as the dark gray limousine plowed northward toward the start of the East River Drive.

Woods Palmer sat in the back seat of his car on the far left. There was plenty of room for both Bill Elston and Donnelly Elder to sit beside him. But Bill had elected to pull up one of the jump seats and straddle it, more or less backward, to face to the rear, while Donny had chosen the far right corner. It was, Palmer noted to himself, as if neither of them wanted to be too close to him after the display of dirty fighting he had given them at lunch.

"Well," he said then, in a perfectly level conversational tone, as if the subject had been discussed continuously for the last week and he were merely adding a late thought to it, "I suppose this does pull down our offering price to People's Bank."

Four young eyes swiveled toward Palmer. "We've made a firm offer," Donny Elder said in a quiet tone.

Palmer let the words die away slowly in the muddled traffic noise. "A firm offer," he repeated then.

The phrase had a faintly British air to it, as if uttered by a stuffy, plump old man with a ruffle about his neck, seated in a coffeehouse smoking a long clay pipe. "Demme, sir, a firm offer."

"What is a firm offer?" Palmer asked aloud.

Donny, usually so poised, seemed to struggle for a definition, and Palmer almost expected to hear something along the lines of, "By God, Palmer, if you don't know what a firm offer is by now, then you'll never understand."

Instead Donny composed himself and slowly, almost gravely, as if responding to a solemn catechism, said: "A firm offer is any offer United Bank and Trust makes."

Palmer grinned, but not with happiness. "That it can't get out of if it wants to," he amended.

"I shouldn't like to think that," Donny said quickly.

But not, Palmer noted, so quickly that he had forgotten to

use the subjunctive. "I should," Palmer said then. "In fact, I do. I believe that the first and almost only duty of a business-man is to buy low and sell high. If I can find a way of cutting the price at which I buy, I take that way. Because as a banker I am, above all else, a compleat businessman, the archetype thereof. Clear?"

Donny fell silent, still not aware of how he had betrayed himself or, rather, how his background and training had be-trayed him.

"Are you suggesting we withdraw our original tender to People's?" Bill Elston asked.

"It's damaged goods," Palmer said. "It was represented as flawless, and it's not."

Elston shrugged slightly. "What is? These little suburban banks all have skeletons in their closets. Otherwise, why would they be so willing to sell out?"

"You may have a point there," Palmer agreed. He watched the big Lincoln slip between several cars and take the lefthand lane, moving swiftly northward. He looked at the array of hospital buildings that began shortly after Peter Cooper Vil-lage, old, new, dirty, swank. He tried to think of what was hidden away inside, from delirious winos to terminal cancer cases, but his mind would not leave the problem at hand.

He wasn't quite sure which problem he was attacking, the purchase of People's Bank or the education of two mis-educated young men who, for entirely different reasons, lacked all it took to be good bankers.

"The real point is not how many small banks are hiding something," he said then. "It's whether or nor we should stick to our original offer in this one case. I have a feeling, for example, that Phelps is shaken enough to listen to any reason-able price, even a million lower than our first tender. But the longer we let him alone, the longer we delay hitting him hard, the more courage he'll absorb from his confreres. Especially from that young Fischetti fellow. He seems to be the link, doesn't he?"

Elston frowned. "I thought you and he got along awfully well. He fell apart just at the mention of that Army-Navy game. Incidentally, who fed you that info? It wasn't in our dossier."

"Nobody fed me anything. I happened to see him make that run."

Donny had been staring out the window. "Funny, him playing for Army. Funny, him playing a contact sport at all. He looks too pretty to get messed up, and his background's too greaseball for Army to accept him."

Palmer made a tsck-tsck noise. "I warned you, Donny."

"About what?"

"I told you those people had been on the firing line, working hard to impoverish the laboring classes. I warned you not to turn up your nose at how they smell. Now you find out one of them has, shall we say, less than impeccable connections. And suddenly you're reverting to pure Wasp hatred syndromes. Bankers can't afford such luxuries, Donny."

The younger man grinned slowly, aware he was being made fun of. "All right," he said then. "We are all brothers under God, and I am Ben Fischetti's keeper. But that doesn't make his connections smell any sweeter."

Palmer shook his head. "I don't care about any of that. I wish the two of you could get that straight. It doesn't matter if Ben Fischetti's father is a card-carrying Communist and his sister pushes heroin and, to top it off, he's surly to his mother. The only meaning these horrid secrets may have is the leverage they can give me in dealing with Fischetti and his bank. Can I use them to advantage? If not, forget them."

Both younger men paused for a moment to absorb this, to them a rather revolutionary concept. Palmer watched them take the idea in, each in his own way, not liking it but forced to do so because it was the boss's.

"Bill?" Palmer prodded.

Elton rubbed the lower part of his face with the palm of his hand. "I think Ben Fischetti's connection is a two-edged sword. I think it can cut him badly if we swing it right. But it can slice us up pretty good, too."

"How?" Donny Elder asked.

"Lots of ways. We have no idea how many lines Downtown Bond and Mortgage has out around town. Tangling with a partially concealed operation like that is a little like a fly trying to march up a web to the spider's lair. You just never know when you trigger the spider and he pounces."

"Poetic," Donny snapped. "But what the hell does Ubco have to fear from a bunch of shysters like that?"

"Good point," Palmer put in.

Bill Elston paused for a moment. Palmer leaned forward and directed the driver up the ramp onto 42nd Street. He intended to drive Donny Elder to Grand Central Station and then take Bill Elston home to his apartment in the east fifties.

"I'm not arguing from actual facts," Elston confessed. "I'm arguing from feel, from suspicion, from what I've heard and read without any of it being what a court would call hard evidence. Maybe a little out of ignorance and fear. I'll admit that, too. But I know that what we see as a typical business transaction, cut and dried, dollars and cents, a matter of negotiation and contract, these people see differently. They see it so differently that once in a while people get shot to death in barbers' chairs. I don't call that playing the game our way."

"Another good point." Palmer thought for a moment. "Donny?"

"I don't think we have to be frightened by a bunch of Sunday-supplement boogiemen. These men exist, but I'm damned if I can see that they're more powerful than any other sneak thief. It's the romantic newspaper writers who've puffed them up out of all proportion to reality. They can be rough as hell on their own kind, but show me a case of them stepping outside their charmed circle to take on an adversary from the rest of society. From our own level, for example."

"Here's Grand Central. Is there a train you can make?"

Donny glanced at his watch. "In ten minutes. Many thanks. Discuss it tomorrow?"

"First thing."

Palmer and Elston watched Donny stride across the kerb and disappear inside the terminal building. The driver steered the limousine west on 42nd and waited for the light to turn up Madison.

"Think he's got a point?" Palmer asked Elston, still trying to strike sparks by rapping one man against the other.

"Not much of one. It might have been true before the war. It might have been true after the war for a few years, too. But it isn't true anymore. These people aren't the sneak thieves Donny remembers from his childhood."

"How do you know that?"

"I don't know. I hear the same things you do."

Palmer nodded thoughtfully. "I'm still a freshman in this town, Bill, still very much the country boy. Maybe we don't hear the same things."

"And you from Chicago? I would have thought –"

"Chicago's not New York."

"But where organized crime is concerned, Chicago wrote the book."

"Not as much as you think. Chicago's an anachronism. Bill. It's the last purely crooked big city in the country. It's the absolute last stronghold of the gigantic, all-inclusive fix. In no other city does the mob so completely own the police, coerce the politicians and trammel the public prosecutors. It's a straight money deal. You can't tell me New York's that way."

"Not as openly, but—"

"That's my point, Bill. A child of ten can understand how Chicago operates because it's all out in the open. But New York corruption is so far underground it takes a very astute man with a great deal of information to make heads or tails of it."

"I'm not that man," Elston said with some sorrow. He fell silent as the limousine turned east in the fifties and headed for his block. "But I suspect New York corruption is as thick as Chicago's," he added then with an almost chauvinistic tone of gloomy pride.

"Maybe thicker." Palmer brushed at the air between them, as if cobwebs had drifted down from the car's ceiling. "It's not important to know that as much as it is to know how far we can push the People's deal in our favor. How unseemly is the Fischetti connection? How terrible would it be if exposed? Is it horrid enough to let us cut our offer by a million or even two million? And if so, can we enforce the new bargain?"

The younger man turned with a slight air of wonder to stare at Palmer. "You know," he said then, "when you first came to the bank in such a high position, a lot of people wondered why you'd been picked over any of the eligible ones already at Ubco."

"Yes."

"Now I know why."

"Yes?"

"You've got a ... a kind of — meaning no disrespect — killer instinct. I guess Ubco needs that."

"Me?" Palmer waved off the dubious compliment. "A plain old country boy like me?"

Elston's face grew red, and he stopped talking again. The limousine crawled slowly east through thickening traffic. "Your wife expect you home this early?" Palmer asked suddenly.

"She won't be home yet."

"Oh?"

"She works. We haven't any kids yet, and until we do..."

The younger man's voice trailed away. "Works for the savings banks, as a matter of fact."

"Does she? Our mortal enemies?"

The two men laughed silently. The fierce feud between the savings banks and commercial banks like Ubco had died down in the last year as the result of legislation neither side liked but which gave both slightly broader powers to set up new branches.

"What does she do for them?"

"Public relations. She used to be a newspaper girl back in Cleveland."

The skin across the back of Palmer's neck prickled coldly. "Oh? Ah ... let's see, you've been married how long?"

"It'll be five years soon."

Palmer realized he had been sitting bolt upright in the seat, as if tensed to receive a blow. He consciously slumped back into the seat. "I believe one of our Ubco girls is working over there," he said very casually.

"Ginnie Clary? She's my wife's boss."

"How is she doing?" Palmer watched the younger man's face with the same hooded intensity with which he had watched suspects being grilled during the old days of the war. There was a kind of masked concentration one perfected, an outward look of indifference that concealed the almost fanatic concern with which one awaited answers.

"Ginnie? Great, from what I hear."

Palmer's eyes raked Elston's face for a moment. He could find no sign of any but routine interest. A lot of people who shouldn't have knew about Palmer's affair with Virginia Clary two years ago. But he'd been lucky enough to keep it from spreading around Ubco, even though both of them had worked there, Ginnie had bowed out — what was it, a year and a half ago? Had it been that long? Had it been that short a time?

"Sorry we lost her," Palmer heard himself saying. He tried to pump some fairly neutral feeling into the words, but they came out totally dead, like four bricks squeezed from a brick-making machine.

"They like her work over there," Elton said, staring up the street. "Pay her very well, too. Here's my block."

"Yes. Good. See you first thing tomorrow. Try to get your thoughts all straightened out in a row."

The younger man grinned as he stepped past Palmer's knees in leaving the Lincoln. "So you can shoot them all down?"

166

"Ha. Good night."

He directed the driver to take him home. A picture of Edith came to him, grayed out as to details. Which role was he seeing her in, mother or wife? Neither appealed to him.

He felt a very slight twist inside him, at about where he believed his sternum to be. His insides had given a faint but very real swerve at the thought first of Virginia and then of Edith. He had made the wrong decision for all the right reasons. And he was stuck with it.

He hadn't thought of Virginia in some time, having schooled himself to avoid it. Thinking of her pained him; she had left an ache inside him like the kind he imagined he might feel after his leg were removed. And now, he thought, the first time I think of her again, I get that same wrench inside, that same pain of loss.

The limousine pulled up in front of his house. Palmer tried to arrange his thoughts so that he could get through his evening with Edith.

40

Now it was completely dark in the back room of the store. The narrow cot had forced Kimberley and Edith to lie on their sides. They faced each other without being able to see each other and, for a while, Edith felt a sense of deprivation. She had forgotten what he looked like for a moment.

She heard him sigh comfortably and stir, as if he had been asleep for a few minutes. Then his rough-skinned hand stroked downward from her breast to her buttock and lingered there, fondling.

"Do you have to go?" he asked then.

"I'm not even sure what time it is."

He stirred and began to climb over her. The skin of his body was as smooth as hers, she realized, and not at all the rough skin of his hands. A match flared in the darkness and he held it to his wristwatch.

"Only a little after five. It gets very dark back here. There's probably still a little light in the front of the store."

"But no one clamoring to get in."

He laughed softly and blew out the match. "Not likely. Operation Boost's pretty much of a flop. Until now."

"Do you have a very tiny light back here?"

"No."

"A candle?"

"Um." She felt him get off the bed and heard him padding around in his bare feet. He bumped into the wooden statue and cursed quietly.

Edith began to feel chilly. "Never mind. Come back to bed and keep me warm."

"Second." She heard him fumbling in a drawer. A moment later he struck another match and held it to a short length of fat, white plumber's candle. The dimensions of the room reasserted themselves in the orange-yellow light. She could see him clearly now, his face intent as he shielded the candle from a slight draft by propping an open book partway around it.

He was terribly thin, she noted, even thinner than she was. The two of them, lying on the narrow cot, were ideally suited for cramped lovemaking, long and narrow. If either gained weight, Edith thought, the whole affair was off.

She smiled lazily, and the thought struck her that surely they had no affair as yet. What they had between them was a rather large check and some real gratitude and a lot of tequila. Edith had no illusion that, as yet, there could be more to the relationship. She shuddered as a draft blew across her naked body.

"Cold."

"Yes," Kimberley said. He turned to face her and looked a little less emaciated. While the skin of his face had a brownish-bluish cast to it, his body was lighter in color, enough to show her that he had a faint covering of tightly coiled hair between his nipples that ran in a funny thin line down to the matted black tangle of pubic hair.

"How did you ever escape circumcision?" she asked then. She felt so odd, asking the question, that she began to giggle almost helplessly.

"Just lucky, I guess."

The two of them were laughing uncontrollably now without knowing exactly why. She began to fondle his penis, rolling back the foreskin gently as he stood over her. "Does that hurt?"

He shook his head. "New plaything for you?"

She thought for a moment. "Actually ... yes. My husband and both my boys are circumcised and..." Her voice died away.

"And this is the only other cock you've ever seen," he fin-

168

ished for her.

"Cock." She stroked him. "I like that word."

He knelt down on the edge of the cot. "You like the whole thing, don't you, baby?"

"I'm beginning to realize how much I do."

"Late-blooming flower." He grinned at her, and they began to laugh again. "Slow, but beautiful."

"And a lot of wasted time to make up for."

He covered her with his body, and her skin began to warm. Only then did she realize how cold she had been. The warmth seeped into her as their bodies rubbed against each other. It made her catch her breath with the simple fact that she needed it so badly. To need it and then to have it. What else was there?

PART THREE
Friday

41

Rosalie had left all four children in the care of Mrs. Traficanti, who could give them lunch and dinner. This was to be a very full day, as Rosalie's days went. Lunch in town with Mamma and her sister Celia, an afternoon all alone and dinner with Ben. Somehow, Rosalie had vowed, she was going to lose a little weight. Rosalie fitted halfway between her slender mother and her fat sister. The three of them, short and dark-haired, looked like photographs of the same woman taken over a period of time as an advertisement for reducing pills.

They sat in the small midtown restaurant Rosalie had insisted on choosing – a steak house where she could find food that wasn't as fattening as the usual run of pasta and sauces – and slowly sipped their espresso.

"You see?" Mamma said, inclining her small head like a tiny bird in Rosalie's direction. "You see, Celia? She's doing it. She's gonna be skinny yet, you wait."

"Oh, Mamma." Celia's glance locked with her older sister's for a moment. The girls were a year apart in age and had often, when younger, been mistaken for twins. There was no mistaking the differences between them now that Rosalie had started doing something about her weight.

"It isn't fair to tease Celia," Rosalie put in. "Living at home with you and Papa, what kind of chance does she have to watch her weight?"

"What you eat today?" her mother asked challengingly. "Steak, *si? Insalata verde, con aceto e olio*. What's so hard about that? I give that to Celia at home any time she want."

"Plus pasta," Rosalie said in a bored voice, this being an old discussion, "plus *gnòcchi*, plus tons of bread, the white and that whole wheat from Zito's, plus butter, plus potatoes and green peppers and onions fried together." She glanced at her watch. "I'm late."

She got to her feet, feeling terribly guilty. She had invented for her mother and sister a mythical date with a neighbor from Scarsdale who was taking her to a shop "uptown". For a girl born and raised in Greenwich Village, "uptown" meant anything north of 14th Street, and Rosalie used the word on purpose, knowing how vague it would be.

The waiter arrived a second after she had gotten up. Because these were Don Vincenzo's wife and daughters, there had been two waiters assigned to the table throughout the meal. Only the elderly one with the Irish brogue showed up now. "Yes, miss?"

"No, nothing." Rosalie waved him away. She started to shrug into her cloth coat, a new one in faintly military olive color, with epaulets and brass buttons. The waiter scrambled to be of some help. Rosalie smiled at him, then pecked her mother and sister in turn, both on the left cheek. "You'll be home tonight?" she asked.

"Si, come no?"

Rosalie gestured vaguely. "Ben and I will probably have dinner in the Village. It might be nice for him if we dropped in for a drink before we head back up to Scarsdale. He doesn't see Papa that much, you know."

Rosalie dashed out of the steak house and immediately hailed a passing cab, feeling guilty at keeping up the pretense of being rushed. She actually had no clear-cut idea of where she would go now. Perhaps that place near Papa's house, the New School. Perhaps NYU itself?

She got out of the cab at the bottom of Fifth Avenue and stood for a moment, staring at Washington Square Arch. Its fussy upper area was as confusing to her as it had been all her life, even as a baby in a carriage, being wheeled past the arch or lying under it, trying to puzzle out the scenes from Washington's career.

But the bottom of both pillars had been fairly well scribbled over with inscriptions whose meanings were impossible to misunderstand. Rosalie passed one of the pillars slowly, her face red with shame, but unwilling to seem shocked. "Fuck war." She blinked. "Fuck war up the nose."

She moved away from the arch past a group of high-school-age children, mingling with the hard-core hippies and older loafers. She wondered how many of the kids were playing hooky from St. Joseph's or Our Lady of Pompeii, and how many would get the palms of their hands swatted till the tears came to their eyes, when one of the sisters or fathers found out how they were spending their time.

Two boys detached themselves from a crowd surrounding a boy playing a guitar very badly and a girl rattling a tambourine. The two boys fell in step with Rosalie as she walked around the curve of the center fountain.

"Quarter, baby? Half a buck, huh?"

"Rap me some bread, baby, and I'll blow your mind."

"Nah," one of them said, "she's cherry, man."

"Bust your cherry for a quarter, baby?"

"We got a pad east of here, baby," one boy said, quickening his step to catch up with Rosalie. "Real boss grass, turn you on and ball you forever, baby. How much bread you holding?"

One of the boys fell back, winded, but the other persisted, trailing Rosalie along the path that led east out of the park. Later, thinking about it, she couldn't decide if he had been deadly serious or only teasing. But at the time she was too frightened to make the distinction.

"Cool boo, baby. What say we fire up a joint, huh?"

"Leave me alone."

"You wanna ball?"

"Go away."

"Ball you any way you dig it, baby. My buddy and me, we make it front and back. You so cool, but you blow hard when I munch your snatch and he bugger you. Buck apiece?"

"No. Leave me alone."

"How far out you dig, baby? I had a chick once blow her mind when I peed on her. You dig that scene, baby? Huh?"

"Please."

"What's your bag, baby? Acid? Speed? You a down-head, baby? I get any shit you want, even the hard stuff."

Rosalie's heels rapped sharply up a flight of stone steps. She pushed blindly through a large glass door and found herself in some NYU building. She stared back through the glass in time to see the boy, smirking with a certain amount of self-satisfaction, turn and slouch back to the fountain again. He seemed to be about seventeen years old.

"Yes, miss?"

Rosalie turned on one heel. A small, elderly lady sitting behind a desk had spoken. "N-nothing. That boy."

"They get terribly fresh these days."

"This wasn't fresh. It was..."

The receptionist's steel-rimmed glasses glinted blindly as they reflected the light of Washington Square back into Rosalie's eyes. "Some of them have terribly foul mouths," she agreed in an almost complacent voice.

"You have to see them every day, I guess."

The elderly lady nodded with a faintly smug air. "There have always been young loafers in Washington Square Park. I
175

have seen them come and go. While I've only been in this building since the war. I've been in other university buildings since 1931. The boys have always been foul-mouthed." She nodded twice, as if confirming both the depravity of male youth and her own hegemony over whatever filth was going in the area.

Rosalie stared into the blind spots of light reflected off the steel-rimmed glasses. "What building is this?"

"Mostly fine arts. Partly business administration. Which did you wish?" The receptionist's dentures fitted in such a way that, together with a touch of lateral emission, the question came out "Wish dishu wish?"

"Uh ... fine arts?"

"Up the stairs, first door to the right on the second floor." The sightless moons disappeared as the elderly lady dropped her glance to the book she was reading on her desk. She seemed to have lost interest in Rosalie, foul boys and the rest of the entire world.

Rosalie sped up the stairs, somehow mingling in her mind the boy's menace with the blind glare of the old lady. This wasn't the right place for her at all, but now that she had blundered into it, she would have to give the appearance of bringing it to a conclusion. She had begun to hate her series of deceptions, first to her mother, now to the old lady. Was this what the world was like, away from Scarsdale and the children? Was everyone dirty and uninterested?

She paused on the stairs, out of sight of the lobby, and wondered how long she would have to wait until that boy left the park.

42

Woods Palmer cut his lunch short and returned to his desk to finish reading through a series of portfolios Donny Elder had left for him. They proved to be a group of dossiers on some small businesses throughout the Midwest and West. None was terribly interesting, Palmer thought as he finished the last of them. They had a common thread to them – mismanagement due to stupidity, rather than to greed. He buzzed Donny to summon him.

"Why have these reached my desk?" he asked, trying to sound pleasant, although he resented having his time wasted.

The younger man flushed. "I don't believe I can act on these alone."

"Possibly not. But one of the senior vice-presidents can help make the decision with you."

"I thought, in view of the special situation..." Donny's voice faded away.

Palmer frowned. His mind raced backward over the dossiers, trying to recall something special he hadn't noticed. "I don't believe I –" He stopped short. "Surely you're not referring to the fact that" – he stopped again – "that the original financing was made by my father's bank?"

"Well, uh, yes."

Palmer's face, blank with disbelief, broke into a wry smile. "I had no idea you were that much of a young gentleman, Donny. Good God."

"But these were originally investments by your old bank, sir."

"Years ago. I even recall working on one of them. But why on earth should that make it special? If Ubco's holding the paper now, it's strictly an Ubco matter and –" Palmer stopped himself a third time, finding it hard to credit the boy's old-fashioned air of innocence.

"Look here," he began again. "Sit down. Listen for a second. This ... this goes beyond belief. How could you think I would have some sort of sentimental attachment to money invested by my father's bank? The old fellow's dead. I sold the bank more than two years ago to come east with Ubco. In some manner that is totally without interest to me, Ubco now holds the paper on these investments, and they're going bad. Well, they're going bad. Money is an impersonal thing at any time and even more so when it's a bank's money. Do I get through to you?"

The younger man nodded. "My mistake, sir. Uh, but as long as I've bothered you with the matter, could you give me a steer on its disposition?"

Palmer's eyes narrowed. Donny Elder might be a hopeless gentleman, in the worst sense of the word, but he could recover fast enough. He spread open one of the portfolios. "This steel-fabrication plant. Its orders are running twelve percent under last year, and its profit is eighteen percent under last year. The management is overage." He slapped the portfolio shut with a soft but final sound and opened another. "This petrochemical company is amazing. It's the only one to lose money consistently over the past decade." Another folder. "This milk-processing plant has been in trouble with the health authorities five times in three years and in trouble with us every quarter when its notes come due."

He looked up at Donny Elder. "We're dealing with wholesale incompetence. We're dealing mainly with privately owned concerns answerable to nobody but themselves, family institutions kept going to give idiot sons and nephews a place to hang their hats. We're dealing with the remnants of nineteenth-century capitalism in the heyday of laissez-faire. But it just won't go anymore. The best we can do for these anachronisms is wipe them out."

"Foreclosure?"

Palmer shrugged. "Then you have the damned things on your hands while you look for buyers. Check our account lists. Find me a big, bustling steel-fabrication company, a petro-chemical works and a dairy-food processor. Let's open the jar and let the merger bugs loose. Let them bite a few people and see what happens."

The younger man made a face. "Some of these companies aren't worth buying, even for a tax loss."

"Sweeten the offer. Renegotiate the notes. Tell anybody interested in buying that we'll lengthen the term and lower the rate."

"In other words, cut the ground out from under these little companies and sell them off, even at a loss."

"It's no loss to us. We'll still hold their paper, and in the end we'll still make as much on the loans. A short term at high interest yields about the same as a long term at low interest. Or didn't you listen to that part of the lecture back in school?"

Donny flushed again. "It seems a little hard, though. Oughtn't we to give these people a crack at rehabilitating themselves? Maybe if we tell them what we'll be forced to do, it might goad them into getting straightened out on their own."

"Donny" – Palmer let the word hang in the air for a moment – "if I give you a free hand in this, your sentiment will trip you up. I know what will inevitably happen if you let these people try to get back on their feet. They'll stumble and fall again, and it'll have been your decision that cost the bank six months or a year of arrears when we could have been off to a new start, making new money from these accounts."

"Is there something personal here, some personal information you have that isn't in the portfolios?"

Palmer shook his head. "Everything we need to know is in these dossiers. Whoever compiled them did a good job."

Donny smiled uncertainly. "I did."

"Good. Now learn to evaluate what you've collected."

"I just don't see," the younger man went on with a dogged air, "that these companies are all that ineffective. You make them sound doomed, like a ... like a hero in Greek tragedy."

"Very apt."

"Sir?"

"A very apt figure of speech. They are doomed, and for the same reason as a Greek hero. They have a fatal flaw, each of them. It's the flaw of failure to move with the times. I suppose one could call it pride. Or perhaps *hubris*, since we're being classical today. It's sheer *hubris* of these little tin-whistle outfits to think they can slouch along against the financial, distributive and managerial systems of the second half of the twentieth century. There is no room for shoddy little anachronisms in the ferocious world of free enterprise. And we do them no favor by playing generous uncle and letting them flounder around, wasting their substance – and ours, too, damn it – to resolve a dilemma we already know to be resolved."

Neither of them spoke for a long moment. "Very well, sir." Donny said then. "Of course, with the big outfits like Ubco, bigness becomes a recognizable virtue. But there are small banks who might carry these companies because they recognize smallness as a virtue. Why can't we just unload their paper on a small local bank in their area?"

"None of them would touch it." Palmer stood up impatiently and began to walk toward the window wall at the far end of his immense office. The ceiling curved upward as he neared the window, so that he seemed to be inside the horn of some immense old phonograph. He stared out the giant panes at the street below.

"These so-called little banks," he said then, more to himself than to the other man. "Have you ever studied the correspondent system of banking in these United States? Can you honestly say that a small bank would do anything that might be frowned on by the big bank that handles its business? Is there, in fact, a small bank anywhere that doesn't have a bank the size of Ubco breathing over its shoulder? It's the only thing that keeps these little banks from going under, in the same way and for pretty much the same reason that other little companies go under."

"That's some future you're painting, sir. Giant banks, giant companies, merger upon merger until there's nothing left but one conglomerate business enterprise and one bloated bank to finance it."

"That day will come."

"You're not serious?"

Palmer turned to face Donny Elder. They were now more than thirty feet apart, but the singular acoustics of the room made it possible for each of them to hear the other's faintest whisper.

"Oh, but I am," Palmer said quietly. "And you know, of course, what they'll call that company and that bank?"

Donny shook his head. "No."

"Why, the U.S. Government. That's what they'll call it."

The two men watched each other for a long moment. "And that," the younger one said in a soft voice, "will be the end of the whole silly thing."

Palmer nodded. "All the scurrying will be over. Capitalism will be dead." He grinned suddenly. "So let's not stand in its way, Donny. Let's merge these little nincompoops and get them the hell off our books."

He walked back and sat down at his desk. When the younger man failed to respond, he looked up. "All right?"

"Yes, of course. Except that I can't help feeling a little funny about it. When you think of all the sweat and tears somebody put into these companies once, somewhere in the past."

"You're sentimentalizing," Palmer said. "You remind me of –" He stopped himself. "Of those," he finished lamely, "who confuse the morality ordinary people can cultivate and the morality of the banking world, if you will."

"Double standard?"

Palmer handed back the portfolio folders. "Get these straightened out in the next ten days, will you?"

"Right."

Palmer watched him leave the room. God, that had been peculiar. He'd almost mentioned her name. It was as if, having surfaced in conversation earlier in the week, she continued to bob around his lifeboat. But Ginnie Clary was buried too deeply for that.

43

The social club storefront on Bleecker Street seemed deserted. A block or two along the street, where the seafood and fruit stores had set up their goods on the sidewalk, housewives dawdled over the *calamari*, overripe from having sat there in the sun all day and now, toward closing time, a possible bargain. The tiny rubbery squid lay in odorous clumps, seemingly on the very edge of putrefaction, while housewives and fish sellers enjoyed a little leisurely screaming down of prices.

From time to time cars arrived in front of or near the social club. Two or three men would disembark and enter the dimly lighted storefront. They would leave after fifteen minutes or half an hour. Some moved with alacrity as they left, but some seemed drained of energy, listless to the point of somnambulism.

Inside the social club, in the small but adequate office where Don Vincenzo Biglioto did business – the business he could not transact at Downtown Bond and Mortgage – the room had grown stuffy, but neither Vinnie nor his buffer, Rocco Sgroi, seemed to notice the staleness of the air. A certain odor filled the room as definitely as the stink of dead squid rose in almost visible waves from the trays in front of the seafood store. But this odor was a more subtle smell, part perfume, part sweat, part fear.

Two rather solemn men had just been ushered into Vinnie Big's presence. He nodded, and they bobbed their heads ceremoniously. "Good to see you again, Don Vincenzo," said one.

"A very, very great pleasure, Don Vincenzo," murmured the other. They stood before Vinnie, waiting to be invited to sit.

Vinnie's glance brushed sideways against Rocco's face. Rocco grinned slightly from a vantage point behind the two arrivals. "*Padrone*, you remember Jimmy and Augie Calandri?"

Vinnie's flat blue eyes sucked in the news and grew calm with thought. "Could I ever forget these two goombars?" he asked rhetorically, stalling for time until his mind sorted out their particular affairs from among the literally thousands he kept filed in his head. Something about gravel and asphalt, he thought. Something about road building in Nassau and Suffolk counties out on Long Island. Something –

"You settle the price on those trucks?" Vinnie Big asked,

his brain coming up with precisely the issue in question.

"*Si*, Don Vincenzo, but..." The one called Jimmy placed the palms of his hands together in front of him in a position of prayer and rocked them up and down several times.

Vinnie frowned. "Sit down."

The brothers quickly took seats. "Those are pretty old trucks, Don Vincenzo," Jimmy continued. "I know they're good trucks, but they're old trucks. And what I mean is, that old they shouldn't cost that much."

"What's much?" Vinnie pounced.

"Scafolani wants four thousand apiece. That's eight trucks. Don Vincenzo. That's thirty-two-thousand simoleons."

"And," the brother called Augie cut in, "those trucks are ten years old. I mean, we always do what's right, Don Vincenzo. You know that. You never have no trouble with us. But ten years old. And the titles aren't good on half of them. And one I recognize, Don Vincenzo. I mean, I hate to say this, but that one truck, she's stolen from us last year. Now Scafolani wants we should buy it back. We do what's right, but is that right?"

Vinnie's narrow lips twisted in a grin, and he began to laugh. "My God," he gasped, "that's the funniest thing I heard all week." Eyes brimming with tears, he turned to Rocco. "Is that the limit, Rocco?"

Rocco shook his head. "That Scafolani's got balls the size of tombstones."

Vinnie's flat eyes went suddenly dry. He leaned forward. "Okay," he said, "you made your point. Here's what I suggest." Vinnie raised one hand, palm out, fingers curling back. "It's a suggestion, you hear? Take the trucks. Pay the thirty-two thousand."

"But –"

"But, but, but, what?" The light blue eyes flashed with terrible heat. "You come to Vinnie Big for help and advice? You listen to all of it or you're not welcome here no more."

"*Si, si, padrone*."

"So. Buy the trucks. Pay the price. I talk to Scafolani, that thief. I tell him the next trucks he sells you, you get a bargain. You get the family price. And what's more, you also get that road-building contract out near Riverhead. It's a government thing out there, some kind of an atom reactor thing. Miles and miles of two-lane concrete. You ought to bring it in with money for everybody. You see? I tell you to pay for the trucks, and then I make you the money to buy them." His eyes

182

grew moist again as he laughed good-naturedly. "Okay. *Arrivederch'*."

The brothers Calandri left the room quickly, eyes straight ahead, unable to determine exactly whether they had won or lost. Behind them, some of their indecision and fear remained in the air to mingle with the scent of the shaving lotion they had rubbed on their moist jowls.

Vinnie Big eyed his watch. "Two more and then it's *finito*, Rocco."

"*Si, padrone*." He ushered in a small man in a worn winter overcoat doing double duty as a spring topcoat. Vinnie stood up as the newcomer entered. He walked forward a pace to grasp his hand. "*Buona sera*," he said, pumping the man's arm. "My God, nobody told me you wanted to see me."

The other man sat down in a chair and shrugged almost irritably. He looked older than Vinnie by several years, but it was a trick of his clothes and the fact that he paid no attention to his appearance. A day's growth of whitish beard frosted his cheeks and chin. His eyes, set in papery folds of skin, swept quickly about the room and settled on Vinnie.

"The Paramus store," he said then.

Vinnie sat down in a leaning-forward position and made an I'm-trying-to-understand-you face. "*Si*, the Paramus store."

"Stealage up eight percent." The visitor spat out the words quickly and then stopped to wait for their effect. When he got no response, he went on speaking in a jerky, offbeat rhythm.

"The Teaneck store, okay. Tenafly, okay. Newark, Weehawken, Jersey City, all okay. But stealage, she's up eight percent in Paramus. I think, yes. I think maybe some of the younger boys, yes. I think they going in business for themselves. Is what I think."

Vinnie's well-manicured hands shot out into the air between them, gently soothing sideways the cruel words that had been uttered. "On the grave of my mother, it's not true." His visitor failed to respond by so much as a flicker to this avowal.

"Listen to me," Vinnie continued, "to a man of your respect and standing, I don't lie. From a man so important to the family, I don't hide things. You understand me?"

The visitor regarded him impassively for a moment. "Okay, Vinnie. You I believe. So tell me, yes. Tell me what it is, yes. That's pushing up the stealage in Paramus only?"

"I got no idea. I'll find out and let you know."

The newcomer got to his feet. "That last shipment of

183

assorted hardware," he said then. "The grading was sloppy. Took my boys three nights to sort it out for retailing. That's time and a half."

Vinnie Big nodded.

"And two weeks ago, these folding chairs. Where did we get them, yes? Half of them were assembled without hinge pins."

Vinnie shrugged. "The boys don't always check every shipment they, uh, take over."

"You're telling me?" The visitor turned to leave. "Okay. You know what's on my mind. See you." He left the room.

Vinnie Big let a full minute pass until he heard the front door of the social club open and close. Then he said softly, for Rocco's ear alone: "How long's he been going around that way?"

"Few months. Six?"

"Looks like a crazy man. He's got better clothes, hasn't he? How does it look, the owner of a chain of big, fine discount stores dresses like a tramp?"

"Want me to mention it to him?"

"Get it mentioned," Vinnie corrected. "Give him a month to shape up. If he keeps going his own way, out he goes."

Rocco's eyebrows went up a fraction of an inch. "All the way?"

Vinnie looked pained. "What all the way?"

"I mean, like, final?"

Vinnie thought for a moment. "What I wanna say is no," he confided. "In my heart I know he's getting old and he's going a little, ah, eccentric. It's time he went down to Miami and got lost in the sun for the rest of his life. But that's only what my heart tells me. Understand?"

Rocco nodded. "What your heart don't say is that from eccentric he'll end up a real troublemaker."

"'At's it, Rocco. 'At's the truth of it. So." Vinnie thought again, taking more time. "So feel out the situation. If we gotta put out a hit, we gotta. I'd like not to, you understand. He's a first cousin on my mother's side."

Rocco nodded again. "Time for one more? It's those three bastards from Staten Island."

Vinnie grimaced, as if in pain. "This business isn't easy, Rocco. You should know better than anybody. Those two Calandri brothers, putting them in a box was a pleasure because they're stupid and they deserve what they get. And it ain't as if I'm leaving them without a dime. But Paramus. This

184

man is gonna be trouble unless he's stopped cold. And stopping him can go against a man's heart, believe me. Send in the Staten Island bastards."

Rocco ushered in three youngish men, two in customary dark suits, the other wearing a zippered jacket and a sports cap modeled after those worn by the Afrika Korps.

"I only talk to one of you bastards at a time," Vinnie began without preamble. "Which one of you does the talking?"

The bastard in the middle, taller than the rest and a few years older, cleared his throat. "We didn't come here to get insulted, Don Vincenzo."

"What then? What gives you the idea you can keep hijacking my trucks and get away with it?"

The older man cleared his throat again. "Who says we hijacked anybody's trucks? We ain't in that business."

"No?" Vinnie barked in his furry, hoarse voice. "Good. Then you live a little longer."

"We came about a shipment." The man in the middle seemed about to go on, but stopped short and waited.

"What shipment?"

"It's, ah..." The man's glance crawled in the direction of Rocco. "It's kind of –"

"Get them outta here!" Vinnie yelled. "Out!"

Rocco jerked his head toward the door. "Move."

"Listen, we came here with a legit proposition. You can't –"

"Move."

Rocco returned ten minutes later. "All set," he announced.

"What's the idea letting them monkeys in here? I don't associate with shit peddlers, and you know it."

"Sorry, *padrone*. I didn't know what they were peddling. But it turns out to be two kilos of pure. We're brokering it through Eddie Getz in Brooklyn."

"I don't want to hear about it." Vinnie closed his flat eyes and sank back in his chair for a long moment. He sighed. "Anybody waiting?"

"That guy Elfbein with the storm-window company up in Westchester."

Eyes still closed, Vinnie sighed again. "Tell him he's finished. Tell him we're liquidating him and his inventory. Tell him we'll find him a spot with, uh, with the meat company in the Bronx. Anybody else?"

"The Schimmel people from the paint factory."

Vinnie grunted softly. Then: "Tell them to dice. We'll let

them merge next year. Right now they're overextended in accounts receivable."

"The juke box guy. He just dropped in to say hello. No problems."

"Good." Vinnie opened his eyes. "Anybody else?"

"Indrisano from the Teamsters called about dinner."

"Cancel."

"Piggott, the guy with the fuel oil outlets?"

"Tomorrow."

"That's it, *padrone.*"

Vinnie got to his feet and nodded toward the rack on which his overcoat was hung. "I gotta bellyful of business for one day. Let's have a drink at Mamma Lorenzi's and maybe a little of that cannelloni with the ricotta that floats right up off the plate."

"We may run into Indrisano there. It'll look funny, you canceling and all."

Vinnie Big sighed heavily. "My God, Rocco. People think this job is fun or something. Come on outta here, will you? It stinks in this place."

Shaking their heads in unison, the two men left by a back entrance.

44

Kimberley stood at the door of the second-floor studio-classroom and surveyed the room before he left it. The two-hour session had been endless, time crawling slowly as he went through the motions of teaching an unteachable talent to untalented students. The girl from Boston hadn't done too bad a job with the assignment of the day, but then she didn't do too badly at any time. She had the knack; in time Kimberley would know if she had the talent. But one student out of eighteen?

His glance swept slowly across the room, making certain none of the students had left his work out. All the clay pieces had to be swathed in wet cloth and put carefully away for the next session. Finding everything in order, Kimberley locked the door and dashed off along the hall toward the stairway.

He had been afraid to give Edith a key to his apartment on Bedford Street because at the moment he wasn't sure if he shared it with one or two other instructors of NYU. He was afraid if she let herself in she might run across one of them and be unable to lie her way out.

She was very innocent in so many ways, Kimberley thought, rounding a corner of the stairs at full speed and nearly knocking over a small, plump, pretty girl with dark hair and an expression of terror.

"Sorry."

When she didn't answer, Kimberley checked himself in midstep. "Anything wrong?"

Rosalie blinked. "No-no."

Kimberley nodded and, being in a hurry to meet Edith, dashed down the rest of the stairs and out the door into Washington Square. The pale spring sunlight tinted leafless trees a faint yellow. He strode rapidly across the park on a bisecting course, heading west toward Washington Street.

A young boy broke loose from the knot of young people at the fountain and veered on a slanting path that would intersect with Kimberley's a few yards farther along.

"Any action, man?" the boy asked, pulling up beside Kimberley.

"Bug off, kid."

"Suck your flopper for a half-pound note?"

Kimberley's grin looked as if it had been gouged out of pale walnut with one of his own chisels. "Suck this," he said and spat on the pavement in front of the boy.

"Man, you evil." The boy was running out of breath as he tried to keep abreast of Kimberley. "You dig the whip bit, man? Wanna flog Whitey for a sawbuck? It's double if you draw blood, man."

Kimberley had reached the western edge of the park, where the street ran south into MacDougal. He stopped before crossing the street and shook his head at the boy. "This is your bad day, Chico," he said. "Can't you make the price of a bundle any other way?"

The white boy looked disgusted. "Shit, man, I ain't hooked. Users is losers, man."

"What's your bag? Speed? Acid?"

"What's yours, baby, Narco Squad?"

Kimberley gave him a mirthless grin and let him extract whatever meaning he could out of it. The boy seemed to fade away into the yellowish tree trunks, and Kimberley continued westward toward Bedford Street.

He lived in a house that had been designated as an official landmark. It lay between Christopher on the north and

187

Morton on the south, along the odd stretch of Bedford Street that includes little frame houses that seem to have survived since Colonial days, airy art nouveau constructions reminiscent of Europe, a prisonlike school for "troubled" students from other public schools, stolid, blank-faced apartment houses from the 1920s and a few certifiable landmarks in which long-forgotten linen merchants or ship chandlers had lived in the early days of New York's busy life.

He hurried along Washington Street now, as it angled with West Fourth into Sheridan Square, and continued west along Christopher to the little walk-down delicatessen where he had suggested Edith meet him.

He had spent a while picking the place. Not knowing that much about her, he imagined her acquaintances might well include some of the artier faggots around town. This would preclude any of the fancier drinking or eating places in the West Village. He had chosen the delicatessen because instead of being a place where one came to be seen, all it did was sell good food.

He dashed down the steps, threw open the door and failed to find her among the crowded tables for two and four in the small town. He closed his eyes for a moment, feeling faintly sick. He hadn't arrived too late, he knew that. Nor was he too early. He opened his eyes and saw her, seated at the farthest table in back, unwilling to wave at him but watching him very closely.

At a distance, she looked like one of his students, young, gawky, still not capable of handling herself in the relatively new role of woman. When she saw that he had seen her and was making his way to her table, she smiled. At once, Kimberley realized she was the prettiest woman in the room.

"I'm sorry I'm late," he said, taking her hand as he sat down. He noticed a girl at the next table glance at the two of them, then carefully ignore them. Reverse racism.

"You're not late." She couldn't seem to stop smiling. She handed him the menu. "What would you like to...?" Her voice died away as he took the menu from her and laid it face-down on the table.

"Not hungry." He found himself grinning back at her. "For food."

They got to their feet. He picked up her check and paid it on their way out. The afternoon sun poured along Christopher as they headed west, past Bleecker, to Bedford. He kept turning to her to see the way the wind from the Hudson River blew at her short hair. Then they turned left onto Bedford, and the wind died away. He pulled her into a doorway and kissed her for a few moments. Neither of them spoke. They stepped out of the doorway and continued walking along Bedford.

"I'm terribly out of place in the Village with these clothes," she said after a moment.

He turned to stare at her, not having noticed what she was wearing. It seemed like a perfectly good tweed suit, the narrow skirt worn not as short as was the case at the moment, a kind of brownish tweed with flecks of yellow and gray. A pale green scarf protected her rather long neck. She wore dark brown, matte-finish pumps with two-inch heels.

"You look a little out of uniform for this place," he agreed then. "All these rebels down here, they conform to a pretty strict uniform."

Both of them laughed as they turned in the door of Kimberley's apartment house. He unlocked the downstairs door and pushed the bell button three times. When no one answered, he nodded to her and led the way upstairs.

"I could buy some bell-bottom slacks and one of those pea jackets," she suggested at the door of his apartment.

Kimberley opened the door with a different key. "That's last year's threads, baby. Maybe it's even what they wore three years ago." He led her inside the entry hall and closed the door behind her. She watched him bolt the door and put the burglar chain in its slot.

"What do they wear now?"

"Nothing you'd want to wear," he said, laughing again. "God, I don't normally laugh this much."

"Nor do I."

"How much time have you got before you have to be home?"

Edith walked into the apartment. It seemed to consist of a rather large living room with a big fireplace and a mantel that ran most of the length of the wall to two rear bedrooms. At some previous time, perhaps when it had first been built, dark brown Tudor-style half-timbering had been set into the creamy white stucco at various angles and levels.

The mantel and the horizontal half-timbering produced a tremendous amount of narrow shelf-space on which had been placed a seemingly inexhaustible collection of the kind of very good color postcards to be bought in European museums. The reproductions of paintings and statues had been laminated to pieces of thin fiberboard. Edith rubbed her hand over the face of a Renaissance nobleman seen in profile, with a nose so wildly hooked as to suggest caricature. Some kind of protective coating had been laminated to the face of the postcard, making it washable. She picked up the reproduction and turned to Kimberley. "Did his nose really look like that?"

"Federigo, Duke of Montefeltro?" Kimberley took it from her and held it up to the light. The nobleman faced left, clad in a red tunic with a plain red hat clamped over his short-cropped, curly black hair. "That's probably the town of Urbino behind him there in the painting. Della Francesca usually made a point of that sort of thing."

"That nose."

"It's his. He was quite a man, Federigo. Supported dozens of poets, sculptors, writers, painters. You're not in his league. You've only got one miserable sculptor on your payroll. I bought that reproduction in the Galleria Nazionale delle Marche. It used to be Federigo's palazzo, had it built about the middle of the fifteenth century. Great man."

"Did you put up all these plaques?"

He shook his head. "A lot of people made their contribution over the years. This apartment's never vacant, you see. It's too good and too cheap ever to get out of the hands of people who can appreciate it. So it's always been in the hands of nuts like me." He began laughing again. He started to replace the Duke of Montefeltro, and this led to a wholesale shifting around of prints and portraits until a new grouping had been made on part of the wall near the front windows. "There."

"Much better." Edith's arm went around his waist. "Infinitely better."

"You can't even tell the difference," he said, starting to laugh again, "and neither can I."

He turned to her and took off her jacket. She removed his and hung both of them rather carefully over the back of a chair. She unhooked her skirt and stepped out of it, folding it over the arm of the chair. "I have until about five thirty," she said then. "Or five, if you want to take me to a local shop to buy some local clothes."

"Or earlier, if one of my roommates arrives and finds the chain on the door."

"Won't he be a gentleman about it and go away?"

"Gentleman?" He took off his trousers and laid them care-

190

fully on the opposite arm of the chair from her skirt. "One's a painter and the other produces sixteen-millimeter movies. About the best we can hope for is that neither jimmies open the door and starts sketching or filming us."

"Very unorthodox behavior," Edith said. She had unbuttoned her rather plain, pale yellow blouse and was now looking for a likely spot to leave it.

"They'll give us a few minutes to get dressed and then they'll be back, pounding on the door. Let me." He took the blouse from her and folded it carefully before placing it on the seat of the chair. Then he knelt in front of her and removed her stockings and shoes. He began to kiss her thighs.

"So we have only about an hour?"

Kimberley looked up. "What?"

"There's no two ways about it," she said, removing her garter belt. "I'll have to get a little place down here."

45

"Dear Billy Beanbag," the letter began.

Tippy saw that the writer used almost no slant and paid careful attention to dotting i's and crossing t's. The notepaper was thick, creamy stock with horizontal laid marks. She brushed her fingertips over the printed address and confirmed that it was raised. Then she turned the sheet over to see if it had been engraved or merely thermographed. The indentations told her she was holding a fairly expensive piece of engraved stationery.

"Dear Billy Beanbag," the letter began. "Is it possible that radio emanations from programs – not yours, I hasten to assert! – can cause bodily harm? I am aware that radar operators work under shielded conditions to avoid excess contact with electromagnetic emissions.

"I realize this sounds like a crank letter, but the fact is that a neighbor in this rather old apartment house plays one program as constantly as I play yours. I have remonstrated with her to no avail. I have recently begun to note slight shooting pains in the lower limbs, of faint reddish discoloration in the urine and extreme loss of sexual powers.

"I know this may sound like a crank letter, but–"

Tippy pulled open a file drawer and dropped the letter in a folder marked "Crank." At that moment the door to her office

191

burst open, and her boss arrived.

It would not be fair to Billy Beanbag, or his image of himself, to call one of his arrivals a mere entrance. Tippy had once tried to find words that more adequately described his arrivals. He gave her the feeling that he was, in fact, disembarking from some intergalactic saucer. His entrances thus were events, phenomena, in fact, that made of a simple arrival an adventure in coming into being.

"Who is Baxter Barfbag?" her boss croaked.

Tippy examined him casually. He seemed about as he always did, short, fat and sweaty, with small blue eyes set too close together in a suety face that lacked even the adornment of hair at its upper border. His lips, the mouth of a ruined cupid, pursed wetly like two slugs making love.

"I don't know," Tippy said, feeling like the interlocutor at a minstrel show. "Who is Baxter Barfbag?"

"Doan chew handle my fan mail?" Billy Beanbag inquired. "You know I do, love."

"This fucking Baxter Barfbag somehow eludes your net. He spurns the U.S. Mule. He employs private messenger services, process-server types who seek me out and lay on me his missives. Take a squint at this one."

He made a slight underhand gesture, as of scattering coins to the poor, and chucked a vomit bag from American Airlines onto the center of Tippy's desk. It landed with a thump. "*Ouvrez, s'il vous plaît*," Beanbag barked.

Tippy fingered the folded-over mouth of the bag. "Must I?"

"Why not? Do you glean some inkling in my demeanor of the contents of this container? Do you intuit some faint mephitic whiff of coprophagy?"

Tippy opened the bag and stared down into it at the small curled turd that lay within. Her nose twitched and she quickly sealed the bag. "Thanks. I needed that."

"Last week he sent me a United Airlines bag with the heart and lungs of a chicken in it. Or perhaps a turkey. Fowl play, one might say." Beanbag extracted a card from his flaming orange vest pocket and flicked it onto Tippy's desk. His little pig eyes regarded her unblinkingly. "Read it."

She picked up the card. "I love everyone, Billy Beanbag," the child's scrawl began in blue ink. "I love you, and I love all things of God and man." It was signed "Baxter Barfbag" in red ink.

"I see," Tippy said then.

"I don't." Beanbag paced in front of her desk, making tight movements that shook the glass wall of her room. "I don't see what I'm paying you for if this Barfbag bastard can reach me with his little love mementos whenever the mood hits him."

"Maybe it isn't a him."

"I thought of that. One of these days she'll have a miscarriage and send that to me – in two barfbags." He delved into a pocket of his giant-check tweed hunting jacket and threw a folded slip of paper at Tippy. It hit her mouth and fell to the desk.

"Make sure the librarian clears those discs for tonight's show," Beanbag said, and walked out.

Tippy's lip twitched where the slip of paper had hit her. She watched her right hand go out to pick up and unfold the paper. On it someone had typed ten record titles by about six different recording groups. None of the titles sounded familiar to her, but she recognized the groups as being Billy Beanbag favorites, groups he plugged so steadily and so relentlessly that she was sure he was being paid off double by whatever record company had perpetrated these discs. She had even, in fact, checked the name of the company, only to find that more than a dozen concerns were involved.

She felt her lip twitch again where the slip of paper had touched it. She picked up her telephone and buzzed Beanbag's secretary. "Is himself there yet?" she asked.

Billy Beanbag required that all masculine pronouns referring to him be rejected in favor of such locutions as "himself," "Billy-Baby," "The Magnificent Bean," "El Beano" and in his less modest moments, "The Largest Beanstalking, Bag-Blowing, Billy-Boy Baby-Doll South of the Pole." Although he used all these titles rather freely, sometimes mixing them up deliberately or unconsciously (one night, Tippy heard him call himself, on the air, "The Bean-Teen-Weinie-Bag-Blowing Mother Himself"), most of his associates settled for "himself."

"Himself just arrived," the secretary announced, "in a large economy-size tizz. Somebody sent him for a sack of shit."

"I know. He stopped on his way in to let me delve around inside it. Is he there?"

"Momentito por El Beanerinoracho himself."

There was a click, a buzz and two clicks. "So?" Beanbag asked.

"Just checking," Tippy said. "You're using Stacy Nova and the Joint Ventures three times tonight."

193

"So?"

"And you're using the Flesh Colored Bandand twice tonight."

"So?"

"And you're using a year-old disc by Little Grabber and the Sister-Lovers, backed up by one of his newest discs."

"So?"

"Well, I mean, you know." Tippy gestured helplessly. "I mean, you've used them all this week and all last week. What I mean is . . ."

"Yes?"

Tippy's mind wandered slightly, moving sideways from the subject. "I mean there are . . . uh . . . other groups." She had lost interest in the matter, her glance fixed at the third number on the list, "Country Boy," by Big Big Liz and the Clit-Clats.

"You still there?" Billy Beanbag demanded.

"I just thought . . ." Her voice died away again. She heard her boss hang up.

Tippy got slowly to her feet and wandered back toward the record library of the station, carrying the slip of paper with her. She felt floating, as if her body had no weight. The walls of the corridor contracted slightly as she moved along. After they drew nearer to her, they expanded into a hallway as wide as an avenue. Tippy could feel her teeth gritting against each other so tightly they squeaked. She pushed open the door to the library.

"Beanbag for tonight," she said, handing the slip to the teenager who helped the librarian. She examined a small rash of acne pimples below his left eye as he read the list.

"Have you got them all?"

"Sure," he said.

"Let me monitor number three?"

"Sure."

He pawed through a pile of 45 r.p.m. records until he found the disc, slipped it onto a nearby turntable, flicked on the amplifier and cued the pickup head with the professional aplomb of the engineers he had been watching in his spare time. Holding the record slightly off the turntable, he switched on the motor and then let go of the record. The song started at once with an insistent bump-thwang that reminded Tippy of stripper music.

"Country boy from Holland," a thick, heavy, deep voice began. For a moment Tippy thought it was a voice belonging

194

to a man. Then she decided Big Liz had to be a woman, but with a head cold.

"Country boy from Holland
Came to town one day
Saw the hole was leaking
Hollered hey-hey-hey!
Shoved his finger in it,
Shoved it out of sight.
Shoved it till it hurt him;
Shoved it in a dike. Singing ...
Count ... tree boy. Singing ...
Count ... tree boy. Singing ...
Count ... count ... country boy.
Hey, country boy, will you tell me what's it like?
Hey, country boy, with your finger in a dike. Singing ...
Count ... tree boy. Singing ..."

Tippy closed the door of the library behind her and walked back along the corridor. It had stopped swaying in and out now, but there were ripples in the tiled floor. It seemed to be set in roller-coaster waves that twisted as she walked along. Her lip twitched where the paper had brushed against it.

She banged against the door of her office, opening it by shoving blindly into it with her breasts. She leaned back on the edge of her desk and watched the floor curve up around her ankles. Then she sat in her chair and opened another letter.

"Dear Billy Beanbag," it began in straggly writing. "I love you, sweetheart. I adore you, my darling, my own. I worship night and day at your shrine and I –"

The ink swelled into a huge blot. Everything was dark. She heard a faint thump as her chin hit the top of the desk. There was a rushing noise, as of blood through the dead heart of a chicken or some other fowl. Then everything was silent and black.

46

Outside the immense mullioned windows of Palmer's office, dusk had come quickly to Fifth Avenue. He stood for a moment, watching the traffic snarl and untangle, spurt forward with a spastic lurch, then slot into immobility again while the whistles and horns shredded the peace of evening.

He walked back slowly to his desk. The room was a long one, and he had once decided that if he were careful about not lurking behind his desk and instead made it a point to hop up and pace throughout the day, he might walk the equivalent of ten miles from nine to five.

He glanced at the pile of papers in his "out" box. They represented the afternoon's budget of paperwork, to be collected in a few minutes, as the morning's had been at lunchtime. His "in" box was absolutely empty, an unusual condition.

At that moment, Miss Czermat entered his room, the way she usually did, rear end first, backing in with her hands full of whatever new beadwork she was bringing him. He must remember to try to locate that fellow Spitzer, the one with the beadwork theory.

"It's long after five, Miss Czermat." He watched with dismay as she carried a hefty packet of papers toward his desk. "I hope none of those are urgent."

"Routine, mostly, Mr. Palmer."

He watched her dump the papers in his "in" box, remove the load from the "out" box and leave the room, seemingly unaware of the effect of her act on him.

Palmer sat down behind his desk. He was not going to examine the new papers. They were for tomorrow morning. Instead he was going to go home, have dinner, talk to Edith and the children, spend a pleasant evening reading a book, go to bed early and enjoy a good night's sleep.

But there was something terribly depressing about the fact that the beads he was supposed to weave together into some kind of meaningful pattern tomorrow had already been delivered and were waiting. They would be waiting here all night long. It was, he decided, chilling to the heart to realize that the flow of beadwork had a momentum of its own, that it piled up at an inexorable tempo which took no account of human fatigue or boredom.

Sitting there, staring at the "in" box, Palmer suddenly picked up the entire bundle of loose papers and with a red marking pen made a line down the side of the packet, leaving a tiny red mark on the very edge of each sheet in the pile. Then he got up and moved swiftly along the nearly deserted floor, splitting the bundle of papers into five unequal piles and adding a pile to each of the "in" baskets in the other offices.

He returned to his office without having been seen. He stood in the doorway for a moment, listening for anyone to call his name, any witness to this cruel and deliberate short-circuiting of Ubco's intricate chain of command.

In exactly twenty-four hours, Palmer knew, all of those papers would either have been disposed of about as well as he could have done himself, or they would have found their way back to his desk. The telltale red mark would help him spot those. But he had a hunch few would return. The absolutely random way in which he had redistributed the paperwork was probably as efficient a method of coping with it as any.

He caught sight of one piece of paper he had dropped from the bundle, stooped and picked it up. It was a large, rather stiff off-white envelope containing an engraved invitation to a dinner given by some of the savings banks to honor a retiring president. The invitation was a mere empty formality. Few of the savings bankers had any reason to like Palmer or his bank. More likely, they feared him and Ubco.

He had returned to his desk and started to chuck the invitation into the wastebasket when he saw that it was marked with an R.S.V.P. He sat down at his desk and stared at the off-white card.

Ginnie Clary, since she worked for the saving banks, would probably be at the dinner. Not probably, he amended, absolutely.

He flipped open his appointment book to see what he had on for the date of the dinner. He found the evening was free.

47

Harry Klaman's Thunderbird sat motionless at the curb in front of the building where the radio station kept its offices. The afternoon had grown somewhat cold for that time of year, but there was a fine dew of sweat on Harry's forehead and cheeks. A little of it collected into drops and gathered under his lower lip in the indentation where his chin began. He touched his handkerchief to it now, his eyes darting from face to face as people walked past.

When the private detective arrived, it was he who spotted Harry first. He opened the door of the Thunderbird on the passenger's side and slid in on the front seat next to Harry.

"Right on time," he murmured.

Harry glanced almost fearfully at the man. He'd been recommended highly by several people as a discreet operator who handled almost any kind of job. He looked it, Harry thought now. The man was short and chunky, like a line blocker and, also like a lineman, had long, looping, apelike arms. His flat face looked like a bruised slab of bacon under a tightly clipped rug of dark blond hair. At some time in the past, Harry felt sure, this *gonif* had run full blast into a steel door.

"So?" he asked.

The detective smiled slightly, hardly a parting of his pale, flat lips. "I got the cunt nailed in solid with the ginzo," he began. "Everything but photos, and I can get you those, too."

"When you say nailed in," Harry countered, "what does that mean?" He mopped his forehead slowly.

"I got them going and coming together, day in, day out. I got phone conversations on tape. I got a paid third-party witness. What else do you need?"

Harry waited before he spoke. He hadn't actually thought it out to the point of trying to determine what kind of proof would convince Vinnie Big, first, that Harry really could prove his case and second, that what he had was worth paying to keep quiet.

"Photos might be a nice touch," he said then. He felt his forehead go damp again in an instant. "Photos don't need no explanations, right?"

"A photo is worth ten thousand words," the detective stated solemnly. "Only in this case it's five Gs. Yes or no."

"What's the photos show?"

"What d'you want them to show?"

Harry gestured meaninglessly, hoping to convey a feeling of substantiality. "They should show, you know, something more than holding hands."

"Whatever them two lovebirds do, I can grab a shot of it," the detective said. "But this could blow the whole bit, you understand. They might wise to the action. Once they're hip, we blow the tail and everything."

"That's all right. You get me prints of the photos fast enough and I don't care if they know you snapped them."

"I dig."

"But they should be doing something," Harry cautioned, "that there can't be no mistake about what they're doing."

"These two cats do everything." The detective winked.

"So make me a picture."

"Check."

"When?" Harry persisted.

The detective paused for a moment. "Give me three days."

"Too long."

"I need that long to get set. Besides, they may not meet for a day or so."

The whole business was beginning to get to Harry. It seemed to take so long to get anything usable. All he had had for the first week were oral reports which only confirmed what he already suspected without giving him what a court might call evidence. Now he was facing more delays.

If Downtown Bank and Trust was to bail him out in the nick of time, the nick was getting too close. Harry had begun to lay off men on the Lexington Avenue job, and it would only be a matter of time before a few sharp-eyed passersby, insiders who knew what to look for, would spot the fact that the Klaman Company had slowed the job almost to a standstill. Explain that one to the creditors.

And once a crack that wide showed in his armor, Harry knew, it was like a thread of blood to a shark. The rest of his creditors would taste it miles away and come swimming in for the kill.

He moistened his lips. At that moment the car telephone rang. He answered it and found himself talking to Gaetano Fischetti. For a moment he had the queer feeling he was in a trap and that the father of the man he was having shadowed had somehow heard about it. "Yeah, Tony." He glanced sideways at the detective, who continued to stare straight ahead.

"Harry, my good friend," Tony Fish began ingratiatingly. "I gotta see you very soon, Harry."

"Here she is," the detective muttered, indicating Tippy as she walked out of the building entrance. She moved in a slow, dazed way.

Harry started the Thunderbird and let Tippy get to the corner, where she stopped and tried to hail a cab. "Okay, Tony," he said into the telephone. "You name a place. But not today."

"How about my Irish steak joint, Harry? I treat you to a real good chopped liver appetizer."

"Lunch tomorrow."

"Thank you, my very good friend."

Harry hung up the phone, wondering what Tony had in mind. At that moment Tippy got into a cab. Harry let the

199

Thunderbird creep into motion behind the cab as both cars waited for the light to turn green.

"Funny," Harry mused aloud. "What the hell would he want?"

The detective smiled again, a faint upward twist of the bloodless lips. But Harry, concentrating on the cab ahead, did not see him smile.

48

Edith sighed contentedly. She turned to watch Kimberley's dark, hooded face, so blank of emotion in sleep. Then she felt about on the top of the small table next to the bed. She was searching for her watch, but what her fingertips encountered were first, the telephone, and an ashtray choked with butts, then a few loose coins, and finally, a folding travel alarm. Once she identified this object, she picked it up and held it to her eyes in the half-dark of the room. Four forty-five.

She replaced the clock and resumed her examination of Kimberley. If anyone had told her a few weeks ago that she was about to have an affair, Edith would have been both insulted and badly disturbed. If they had predicted that it would be with a Negro, she would probably have fainted dead away.

And if they had told her the man would be some kind of artistic hippie type, radical and unpatriotic, penniless and not at all concerned about it, touchy and overproud and insane about her body – her poor, breastless, bony body – Edith would have died in an access of shame and grief.

She leaned over Kimberley now and licked at his earlobe. Then she tightened her tongue into a hard cone and sank it into the inner recesses of his ear, tasting the faintly salty wax. She moved her head back and forth a fraction of an inch, working her tongue like a piston until she heard him come half awake.

"Baby?" A plaintive murmur.

"You can sleep tonight, when I'm not here," Edith said. "Right now I'm here."

Kimberley sighed in mock resignation. "You chicks only want one thing."

He rolled on his back and stared at the dark wood beams in the high, whitewashed ceiling. "Are we going to know each other ten years from now?"

200

Edith blinked. "I ... is that a fair question?"

Kimberley grinned at the ceiling. "I have to know. 'Cause if you're going to want it this bad ten years from now, I'm going to have to hire a boy to fill in."

Edith laughed softly. "I was thinking about that, in a way. I was thinking that I've changed a lot in the last few weeks."

"Have you, now?"

"I don't know whether it's you or me." Edith stopped and thought for a moment. "Do you know which it is?"

Kimberley reached for her and pulled her over on top of him so that he was staring up into her face. Lying head to toe this way, his feet extended slightly farther than hers. "How can something in you be the work of anybody else?" he asked. "It was there all along. I happened to come by and unlock the door or something. But don't think it wasn't always there."

Edith shook her head. "It couldn't have been there. I would have known about it."

"You did. You just pretended not to."

She smiled down at him. "You're really not as smart as you look," she said. "It's just your manner. You come out with something in that supremely self-confident way, as if there could possibly be any doubt about it."

"That's a description of you, baby, not me."

"No, it's a trick some men have. You and Woods both have it."

"Woods?"

"My husband. He –"

The doorbell rang insistently. Edith jumped to her knees, straddling Kimberley's body. "Good God."

He laughed up at her. "That isn't him."

"What a start it gave me."

"That's a roommate." Kimberley glanced at the travel clock. "We have fifteen minutes' grace." He reached his hand in, palm up, between her legs and rubbed the patch of hair with long, fierce strokes. "Fifteen minutes in this state of grace."

"You're going to set me on fire."

"Boy Scout style. I have a stick all ready to rub." He began to play with the folds of skin at the front of the vagina. She sank down on her haunches, trapping his hand beneath her as she rolled her pelvis back and forth.

"I feel exactly like an animal," she said.

"That's exactly what you are, baby."

She felt his penis move inside her slowly, working from side

201

to side to gather lubrication, then in and out in small strokes. She brimmed over with wetness, and suddenly she felt him thrust in and up with such force that she seemed to feel him in her throat.

She rocked forward, her fingers grasping him by the shoulders. With the change of angle, she realized she was more in control of the act in this position than he. She grinned down at him and began to rise and fall with a slow, insistent pulling movement.

"You learn fast," he grunted. His breath was short now, and his eyes looked glazed as they seemed to concentrate on some immense vision above them, some cataclysm scrawled across the ceiling.

"Christ," he moaned.

"Um." She contracted her vagina slightly as she rose, and she could see the blood drain from his face. His eyes went wide.

"Baby?"

"Yes."

"Baby?"

"Yes."

A strangled cry rocketed out of his throat. His eyes rolled back in his head, unable to watch whatever was happening on the ceiling. His back arched convulsively, and then he lay absolutely still.

She watched the color of his face darken slightly. The lines around the outside corners of his eyes seemed to smooth away. His mouth settled in a peaceful curve, and he looked suddenly like a young boy.

Edith sat on him for a long while, trying to understand what she had done. All the other times he had worked carefully on her, to the point where she had experienced what she now could recognize as a full orgasm. In the process he, too, would come. But the act had always seemed to be mainly for her benefit and, thinking about it now, Edith realized that she had accepted this condition without question.

For decades, sex had been less than nothing for her. She had been a soft vessel in which men – Woods – could masturbate without becoming involved in her own body's needs. What Kimberley had been doing for her, since the beginning on that little cot in the back room of the Harlem store, was to repay the male sex's debt to her by concentrating almost completely on what she needed.

Now there was something new. Edith leaned down and kissed Kimberleys mouth softly. "Ten minutes of grace."

"Pure grace."

He opened his eyes, and they watched each other calmly. Edith realized she had not reached a climax this time at all, but had set out deliberately to cause as complete an orgasm in Kimberley as she possibly could. She wondered if this were love.

49

When Ben Fischetti arrived at Sean's apartment on Ninth Street, he fully expected to find Tippy in the bedroom, where she usually lay in wait, clothed in something that gave him a clue to the game she had planned for them.

This afternoon instead he found her dressed in what she had worn to the office, sitting on the long, low couch in Sean's fussy living room and spearing a group of cigarette butts in a large ashtray with the glowing tip of another cigarette she was ostensibly smoking.

'Hi.'

She failed to look up. Ben hung his topcoat in the hall closet and then, as an afterthought, hung his suit jacket away, too. "Good afternoon, Miss Tipton," he said then.

She nodded and continued poking around in the ashtray with a live cigarette. "What's up?" Ben asked then.

Tippy made a disgusted face, took a drag on the cigarette and then made a face of infinitely deeper disgust. She ground out the cigarette and turned away both from the ashtray and from Ben.

"Moody today?"

Ben watched himself in the hall mirror as he stood waiting for a response. He smoothed down the sides of his hair with backward movements of both hands, working in unison. "Tippy?"

He turned his attention to her, or rather to her back trying to guess if this were their game for today. She had grown pretty inventive in an obscene way, using long black vinyl boots and the black vinyl belt of her raincoat as a whip. Sometimes she cast Ben in the role of a slave, other times as a pet dog, occasionally as a beast of burden. Ben had grown accustomed to the games and was storing up some of Tippy's better ideas for the time when he would reverse their roles and dominate her. Perhaps today was the day.

He came up behind her and put an arm around her neck, tucking it under her throat and pulling up slightly to block her windpipe. "This is how we do it in Central Park after dark," he muttered. "Don't scream, lady, or I break your throat."

He felt her head loll limply to one side. He released his hold. "S'matter, lady, you don't dig mugging?"

She sank back on the couch. "Listen," she said then.

There was a long moment of silence as Ben strained his ears to hear something, perhaps someone at the door or in the hall or some disturbance on the street outside. "I don't hear anyth –"

"Listen," Tippy said then, "what does it feel like when you're going crazy?"

Ben's eyes widened slightly. "Crazy?" He sat down on the edge of the couch. "Like who? You?"

"Yeah, right. I think I'm having a nervous breakdown." Ben saw that her nails were dirty and broken in several places. "I'm sure I'm having a nervous breakdown."

"How can you be s –?"

"A man is following me," she said then. "For days now, I see this man following me. He has a flat, nothing face. He doesn't exist, but I see him. He's something I dreamed up. And then today..." Her voice died away.

"That's crazy, right?" she asked then.

"What happened today?"

"I fainted at the desk. Oh" – she nodded vigorously – "it's happened before. Last week I stabbed the goddamned letter opener so deep into the goddamned desk that I could hardly pull it out. Crazy, right?"

When Ben failed to speak, she nodded. "Yeah, right."

His eyes swiveled to watch him more closely. He had said nothing for some time now. "Scary," she said. "Better run for cover, right?"

When he remained silent, Tippy jumped to his feet. "I'm imagining other things, too. A record today. Big Liz and the Clit-Clats? What is that? Is that a name? Is that a record, some kid with his finger in a dike? Is that going out on the air? I mean, it's got to be a nervous breakdown. Right?"

Ben watched her face, pale beneath her makeup, her heavily mascaraed eyes staring out of her skin like cartoons of eyes scribbled on unsized paper. "Big Liz and the Clit-Clats?" he repeated slowly. "What?"

"It's all part of the same thing, Ben. I'm losing my mind."

"Come here." He pulled her onto his lap and kissed her hard on the mouth, bruising her lower lip with his teeth. Her lip tasted salty. She drew back and touched the lip, then stared at the tiny smear of blood on her finger.

"You bastard."

"Today's the day, sweetheart." He grabbed hold of her blouse front and pulled, making the row of buttons slide out of their buttonholes, all but one which popped off and spun across the room, clattering to the floor. Tippy looked down at her brassiere.

"You bastard."

"Today's the day," he repeated. He could hardly recognize his own voice. He felt his penis swelling inside his trousers. Today he would be the master. "On your knees," he told her.

"Ben, I told you I don't f –"

He slapped her across her left cheek, not hard. "On your knees."

"Ben, please."

"All right." He shoved her off his lap. She landed on the floor. They stared at each other for a moment. He started to unzip his fly.

Tippy burst into tears. "Ben, p-please. I tried to tell you I –" A sob cut her short.

Ben watched her. Wasn't this the game? It reminded him of a time at the Point when he'd been a freshman, running slave errands for upperclassmen. One of them had ordered him to clean up his room, and while Ben was kneeling on the floor with the scrub brush, the upperclassman and his roommate had pulled down Ben's pants and underwear and ordered him to fart. He had thought this was some kind of traditional hazing routine, and being ordered in that way tightened his sphincter still further. It was only after they had taken his broom and shoved the handle two inches up his rectum that he realized no one was playing a game. The pain was agonizing. He had been forced to crawl down the hall on his hands and knees, the broom wagging behind him until it finally pulled free. Feeling like the lowest scum on earth, Ben had snatched at the broom, pulled up his pants and scuttled off to his room while the long corridor echoed with the hoots of upperclassmen. The commanding officer had stared blankly at him the next day when he requested permission to report the atrocity. Ben had seen in that instant that his future at the Point depended as much on not reporting the atrocity as on anything else he did in the four years. He got out of the confrontation with some sheepish lie or other, spent the next two weeks nursing his rear end with carbolated Vaseline and finished the four years as one of the more popular cadets there.

But there had been that horrible moment of painful uncertainty as he had knelt there with his pants down, wondering if this were really a game. He watched Tippy now and wondered perversely how she would react to an ungreased broom handle up her ass. It was all a game anyway, wasn't it? The two upperclassmen hadn't been fooling, but it was just that he'd failed to recognize what the game really was. It was pinch-the-Guinea-bastard-and-see-if-he-screams.

And what was Tippy's game today?

"What is it?" Ben heard himself ask. "I'm beginning to think you really are going off your chump." He zipped up his fly and moved away from her. He wondered how early he could get to the restaurant before Rosalie and have a few fast martinis.

"Do you listen to Billy Beanbag?" she asked then.

"Never. Oh, maybe in the car if I'm out late driving." He frowned. "What's that got to do w–?"

"Does he play songs like that? Or am I imagining it, or what?"

"Songs like what?"

"It's a dike singing about somebody with their fingers in a dike and her name is Big Liz and the Clit-Clats. Ben," she sobbed, "I didn't make that up. There is such a record. I swear there is."

He shrugged. "So what? Is it the end of the world?"

"But I have to be wrong," Tippy insisted. She tried to brush away the tears that were rolling down her cheeks. "He's the crazy one, right? Billy Beanbag is the crazy one. And all of his moron fans. They're crazy, right?" She nodded vehemently. "Yeah, right."

"I think..." Ben paused. He tried to say something that would calm her and let him get out of this place before she blew up. "I think he plays a few songs like that. But you can't really hear the words too well, not on a little radio."

"This was on a studio amplifier. I could hear every syllable." She stared forlornly at him. Her mascara had started to streak, and she looked ludicrous. "Tell me I'm right, Ben."

"You may be right," he admitted grudgingly. "But I told you, I'm not a big fan of his, or any of those crazy-talk record shows. To tell you the truth, I don't think he plays anything much different from the station on the dial to the left or right of him." He stood up. "They all play these whiny, draggy, twangy things where nobody's singing. They're either shouting or complaining. They could be singing about almost anything they please. They get away with it because nobody can understand them." He began to walk toward the hall closet where he had hung his jacket.

"Ben, you're walking out."

"I don't like your whole mood today."

"Don't walk out on me."

"I'll be back tomorrow."

"That's Saturday."

"I'll be back Monday."

"I need you now, not Monday."

"You're in a real crazy mood, Tippy."

"What other way should I be? I'm going crazy. The walls don't work right." She crawled toward him. "The floor doesn't work right. But I know they're crazy, not me. Isn't that right, Ben?" Her words echoed hollowly in his head. He stared down at her. "Please, Ben?"

The mascara had smeared around her eyes and down her cheeks, giving her the look of a cheap clown doll left out too long in the rain.

He felt himself sit down on the floor next to her. He had to be crazy, too, he told himself. This dizzy bitch had a mind as warped as his. But she had that look on her face that he couldn't stop seeing, that look of shock that the game being played was not the game being played. Postponed, due to circumstances beyond our control.

He realized he had cradled her head in his lap, and he was crying, too.

50

The entire executive floor of the bank was dark now, including Palmer's office.

In a few minutes the night guard would begin his rounds. Although he knew by checking out his departure list that Palmer was still in the building, to find his boss sitting alone in the dark would give him enough of a fright to make him reach for his gun.

Palmer reached inside the top left drawer of his desk and counted the switches there until he reached the seventh of nine. He clicked it, and a 100-watt spotlight concealed overhead sent a beam of light down on the desktop in front of him.

The lightning made him feel as if he were on a stage. There was always something terribly theatrical about a spotlight, with its lenses of cylindrical snout. The fact that it lighted only what it was focused on, and in so doing isolated it from the surrounding blackness, seemed to Palmer much too obvious and stagy a device for a banker's office.

He had remarked on it once to Ginnie, in the days when they had been intimate. She had agreed.

"You bankers don't need theatrical devices," she had pointed out. "You hold your audience without any gimmicks, just the simple death grip you have on their money."

Palmer grinned at the darkness around him. He and Ginnie had been such entirely different types. He had known it then, and the intervening year and a half or so had only re-emphasized their differences. He had always been just about what he was now – quite cold in the brain, quite unemotional and, like that kind of person, very suspicious of emotion.

He had always known this about himself and this, too, was part of his character, being able to see himself a little bit clearer than most people saw themselves. Or at any rate, to admit the truth of what he saw.

"It's you who resemble your father," Ginnie had said once. "You've always said it was your older brother who followed in his footsteps while you were the classic rebel. But that isn't it at all, is it?"

Palmer had never bothered to explain to Ginnie the truth of the matter. Hanley had been killed in a training plane crash at the very start of the war. As the only Palmer to return alive, Palmer had been forced to be both sons to his father. Or so it seemed at the time. Perhaps, he thought now, Ginnie was right after all.

Perhaps he was his father all over again, the same nay-saying, joyless, ice-blooded, petty little man. Ginnie had been certain that all bankers like Palmer and his father battened on the poor. As a girl who had grown up in a lower-middle-class New York Irish family, she had certain twists of thought that

Palmer could never quite follow, certain illogical loyalties and deep-planted hatreds.

And so, when she had left Palmer, Ginnie had seen to it that he did not believe her reasons were entirely personal for breaking up their affair. It was true that she was going nowhere with him. It was true that he had revealed how brutal he could be in business when pressed to it. It was probably true that she would in time have fallen out of love with him. But to all this she had added the differences in the way they felt about people.

As exemplified in the kind of banking they espoused, Palmer added. He grinned again at the thought that there was anything personal about the practice of banking. Ginnie hadn't been in it long enough to understand that.

He, who had been in it all his life, understood very well the terrible impersonality of handling money. But he could never convince her of this.

"That's the philosophy of a man who's always had money," she had told him once. "Naturally, money hasn't the meaning to you it does to the poor."

There was a bit of uncomfortable truth in that, too, of course. He admitted it now.

He stood up and left the small pool of light on his desk. He moved toward the far end of the room with its immense mullioned windows. He stood there, looking down at the going-home traffic on Fifth Avenue, the glut of taxis, the trail of buses, the nose of one tucked into the rear of the one ahead, a parade of moles feeling their way blindly.

He wondered why he could admit now that some of what Ginnie believed was true. Was that the way it was in such affairs? Did the whole physical thing tend to keep one from understanding the rest of it? Or did one bask in such a self-satisfying glow of sexual accomplishment and relief from tension that one's mind was unable to cope with reality?

There had been no doubt that with Ginnie he had been a different man. She had brought out in him a level of interest and performance and insight he had never achieved before.

Or since, he added.

Behind him in the silent building, he heard the elevator start up. In a moment the night man would start his rounds. It wouldn't do for him to find the chief executive officer mooning at the window.

When a bank got as big as Ubco, Palmer told himself, it had a right to total devotion from its highest officers. He returned

209

to his desk and got his coat out of the hidden closet behind his chair.

It wouldn't do for such an officer to stand around reminiscing in the dark, a sad solo scene, simply because he'd received an invitation to a dinner he knew his former mistress would attend.

Instead, it was required of such a man that he put on his coat and go home to his family. Wasn't the family the cornerstone of everything? Hadn't it been designed solely for that? And hadn't it been fortified by interwoven strands of guilt and frustrated lust into a powerful shield against the onslaughts of a hostile world?

Yea, Palmer told himself, verily.

He heard the night guard approaching along the corridor. "Henry?" he called.

"I thought I'd still find you here, Mr. Palmer, sir."

"I'm on my way out."

"A lesson for all of us," Henry said, coming to the doorway. He was a sixty-year-old former cop who had fallen quite easily into the servile attitude he assumed Ubco required of him.

"Yes, sir, Mr. Palmer," he added, nearly tugging his forelock. "A lesson you are to us all."

51

The clothing store on Greenwich Avenue was crowded with teenagers of varying degrees of cleanliness when Kimberley brought Edith there. The two of them stood for a moment, trying to concentrate on the clothing rather than on the extreme types who were shopping for clothing.

Edith knew that teenagers – other than her own – had declared their independence of soap and water, to say nothing of comb and brush. She knew this not only from pictures of them in newspapers and magazines but also from a few of her children's friends who came home on occasion, grubby little girls Gerri had befriended or lanky, wispy-bearded young men in Woody's class at school.

Edith had assumed, out of total ignorance, that the grimy young people couldn't afford soap or came from families where personal hygiene received little parental stress. It came as a shock to learn that many, if not most, of the unkempt teenagers were in revolt against middle-class families where

210

the virtues of hygiene, credit cards and authenticated tax deductions were not merely stressed but a living part of everyday existence.

"How can that poor girl see?" she whispered to Kimberley.

She indicated with a sideways sweep of her glance a sixteen-year-old in a horse-blanket poncho and bare feet. A pair of gold-rimmed spectacles perched on her nose. The lenses were made of the facet-cut red glass normally found on auto tail-lights.

Kimberley smiled slightly. "Maybe," he murmured in Edith's ear, "she's seeing just what she wants to see. Or better yet, not seeing what she wants to blot out."

"Um." Edith picked a pair of wide-wale oyster-tan corduroy slacks off a rack and held them against her as she looked in a mirror. "Yes?"

"Lower." Kimberley pushed the belt line down till it hung across the points of Edith's pelvic arch. "Them's hip-huggers, baby."

She shook her head, put back the corduroys and picked up some artificially faded blue jeans with artificially ragged cuffs and artificial patches in strategic areas. "Early Salvation Army," she murmured, checking the size and disappearing into a changing booth. She emerged later, wearing the jeans and her blouse. "Yes?"

"Square ... but, yes."

Before they left, Edith also bought a long scarf of horizontal violet and olive stripes, an imitation Army surplus campaign hat of Spanish–American War vintage, artificially scuffed and frayed off-white sneakers and two men's shirts cut to resemble, respectively, the suntan chino shirt of an Army officer and the dark blue work shirt of a Navy enlisted man.

"Isn't it fascinating," she said as they walked west toward the river, "that the young people's peace revolt is outfitted in imitations of military uniforms?"

"There's big money in revolt, for clothing manufacturers anyway."

"I think it's very, uh, American," Edith said.

"In what way?" They were walking down Bedford Street again toward Kimberley's apartment.

"I mean, our economy is based on consumption."

"I keep forgetting you're a banker's wife."

Edith grinned at him. He was carrying all the parcels, and she could hardly see his face behind them. "What I mean is, it's very American that when these girls and boys revolt against

America they continue as prime consumers. The economy simply couldn't spare them."

"The fake hippies you see in stores like that are not what it's all about."

"Fake?"

"What you saw there were some middle-class kids playing let's-pretend with their allowance money. But there are real dropouts from society who've simply stopped being everything society wants them to be. They've stopped being consumers, soldiers, taxpayers — you name it."

"They'll end in jail."

Kimberley nodded, or seemed to, behind the packages. "But meanwhile they had the courage to see it as is and tell everybody."

They stopped in front of his house. "Well," Edith began.

He shook his head. "Wait here a second." He dashed inside and returned a few minutes later without the bundles. "I put them away for your next visit." He took her arm. "Let me show you something. You've got five minutes to spare, haven't you?"

They headed down to the intersection of Bedford, Seventh Avenue and Morton Street, then turned west on Morton along a block whose tall trees had just begun to show green. The street curved in midblock, and when they reached the curve, Edith could see that Morton led directly to the river. They walked along another block, this one of warehouse buildings, and passed a truck lot before they crossed under the elevated West Side Highway and began walking out on a pier that jutted into the Hudson River.

The sun was already touching the peaks of buildings across the water in New Jersey. A wide yellow-orange path shimmered on the river, reaching to the water that lapped at the Morton Street pier. Several people with bicycles or dogs had paused to watch the sunset. Kimberley and Edith sat down. Their legs dangled over the water.

"But what is so desperately bad about everything that they are in such desperate revolt?" Edith was asking.

"I couldn't expect you to see it, not all at once."

"Try me."

"You haven't had my disadvantages," Kimberley said, putting his arm around her waist.

"If they were that bad, I'm glad I didn't."

"The middle class is the dominant class, as in most Western

212

lands. And the morality of the middle class, that mixture of mealy-mouthed piety and secret horror, is the governing morality. Look at you."

"Leave me out of it."

"I can't. You're a perfect example. On the outside, devoted mother and wife. Fulfilled. On the inside, unfulfilled and badly in need of everything that makes life worthwhile."

"It strikes me that your remarks are in dubious taste," Edith said, "considering that this is my first lapse and you are the cause of it."

They both burst into laughter so loud that a woman reading a book nearby glanced venomously at them, got up and walked away. Edith studied the Jersey side of the river for a moment. The wide swath of sunlit ripples on the water had constricted into a narrow line of pale fire from the tiny bit of sun that remained, peeking around a high-rise apartment building.

"Everything is changing," she said then. "I know that. I've only to read the papers to know it. But it's hard to know why so many people want to change so much so fast."

"Let me show you a few things from time to time. This city is very instructive."

"For instance," she went on, seemingly not hearing him, "these riots. What can they be thinking of? What can a Negro be thinking of when he burns down the neighborhood in which he lives?"

"He wants to destroy it."

"But it's the roof over his head, over his family."

"It's a rotten roof. It's a roof over rats and roaches and disease."

"Burning it won't get him a better roof."

"He thinks it might." Kimberley watched the last bit of sun disappear from the sky. "But even if it won't, it does his heart good knowing he's burned the old one down."

"But that way, he might some day burn them all down."

"And white roofs with them."

"Yes."

Kimberley nodded. "That really doesn't bother him one bit."

"Does it bother you?"

He shrugged. "I'm too much in hock to Whitey. I owe him my schooling, my accent, my profession, my livelihood. How many Negroes buy sculpture? I'm the wrong man to ask, honey. I am what they would call Mr. Charley's lapdog. If you want to find out how much violence the black man wants to hurl

213

at the white man, go ask one of the street youngsters I'm working with at Operation Boost. His stake in the white establishment is nil. Worse, he actually has a stake in the overthrow of the white establishment. He only benefits when it dies. So when he says 'Burn, baby, burn,' it's not rhetoric."

With the death of the sun, the color seemed to fade out of the scene. The river turned to ripples of lead. Edith shivered. "Why can't he believe that we want to help him?"

"Because you don't. And he knows it."

"But we do," she insisted. "I've never thought of myself as one of these liberals, but I know we have to help the Negro get up out of his present condition."

Kimberley's arm tightened slightly around her waist. "The liberal ethic is dead, honey. Black people haven't believed in white liberals for several decades now. Most of them don't believe in anything white anymore. When I see that in one of the kids I work with, I think, can the whole thing ever be undone peacefully? And the answer is, it can't. Some of those kids will die for it, one way or another. Either they'll die in a riot or they'll be sent to Vietnam to die over there. And why not? They've been dying on the barricades for years. Their death rate is higher than the whites', and they die sooner, too. Not because they're physically weaker but because they live in an environment that grinds them up faster. So it's no good telling them to wait for help."

"But other minorities have –"

His arm dropped away from her waist. When he spoke, his voice shook very slightly. "That's another of those white liberal lies. They tell us the Irish and the Jews and the Italians were all discriminated against but made it. That's a lot of shit. You can't compare any white minority with any colored one. The real analogy is between the American Negro and the American Indian."

"I'm afraid I'd –"

He got to his feet in the fast-gathering darkness. "I wouldn't expect you to," he cut in. He started to speak again, then stopped. For a long moment he stared down at her in silence, his face growing harder to see.

"Ah, forget it," he said then. "You do me the honor of believing in Operation Boost, and I spit in your face."

Edith stood up. "No, really, if that's the way you feel, perhaps Operation Boost is a hopeless dream."

"Pretty hopeless. But it will help a few kids. And even a few

214

are better than none."

They started walking west to find her a cab. "Do you often get to feeling things are that hopeless?" she asked after a while.

"Quite often."

"But Operation Boost was your idea."

"Born of desperation. Just my way of trying to help my people. I don't have anything else they can use."

"I had no idea it was so hard to be a Negro."

He laughed softly. "You gittin' hip, baby," he said, dropping the Ivy League accent.

"You're making fun of me."

"Yes."

"I don't mind that. I always used to." They stopped at Hudson Street and looked for a cab. "When I was a girl in school, I got teased a lot for my height and my skinniness. But I don't mind when you tease me."

Kimberley waved at an approaching cab. "You ain't dat skinny, baby," he growled in mock lust. The cabdriver veered toward them, hesitated when he saw Kimberley, then took heart from the color of Edith's skin and stopped.

"Monday," Edith murmured as she kissed Kimberley's ear. She got into the cab.

"Right, miss," Kimberley said in a loud clear voice.

The cab drove off.

52

The place was one of twelve gay bars Tony Fish had started, or had caused to be started, in the last year. The operation was a simple one. After one of his regular bar locations went bankrupt, he would get a faggot decorator to do it over and help him through the first few weeks of business by inviting his friends. All a gay bar really needed, Tony Fish had learned, was that little starting push. Then it ran on its own momentum.

He sat at the last stool near the cash register, seemingly one of the customers, and waited for Sean and Augie to show up.

Personally, Tony Fish knew, he didn't mind faggots at all. They were mostly neat and well-spoken and nicely dressed, and God knew they were friendly enough. Most of their jokes went right over his head, and he knew it. But they made excellent customers. They didn't at all mind paying one thirty-five for a ninety cent highball as long as they could have the records they liked on the jukebox and some reasonable assurance that the fix was in as far as police raids were concerned.

Tony had opened the twelve bars in three precincts where the captains were friendly. There was a basic peasant economy to the move that was typical of the way Tony Fish's mind operated. Pay off only three captains to keep a dozen bars raid free ... beautiful. His cousin, Ettore Profaci, who served as his bagman, had complained once that the bars should have been spread over more of Manhattan.

"Maybe you gotta juice a few more cops that way," he said, "but it don't call as much attention to itself."

This elementary thought failed to make a dent in Tony Fish's peasant logic: less juice equaled more profit. And once he saw how well the gay bars did without any real effort on his part, he knew he could count on them as money-makers, not money-losers.

Sean came in first, looking tired from a long day in the garment center. He nodded coolly, Tony felt, and stood at the bar rather than occupying the next stool.

"What's the caper, Mr. Fischetti?" he asked in his broad Cockney accent. The *caper* was a proper enough *capah*, but the Fischetti had the accent on the first syllable, *Fish*etty, and it made Tony nervous, as always, to hear his name wrenched about that callously.

"Where's Augie?"

"Here in half a tick."

That was another thing Tony Fish liked about his gay-bar operations. The faggots rarely started fights on the basis of race. They were pretty broad-minded that way. Tony had once had a bar wrecked by a riot between some tough Irish kids and three black boys who strolled in to order a beer. As a matter of fact, the entire foyer of one of his posh restaurants had burned to the bare walls when a visiting couple from West Texas had gotten into an altercation with some Negro diners and candelabrum with three real candles – lighted, unfortunately – had set fire to the flocked wall covering.

Augie came in at that point and said hello to a few of the customers before joining Tony Fish and Sean. "Let's find a booth in back," he muttered. "This place is crawling with designers."

They ended up eventually in the manager's office, a room about eight feet square which doubled as a storeroom for light

216

bulbs, bland menus, fake flowers and the like. Tony Fish sat down at the minuscule desk upon which Sean sat in cross-legged style, like an old-country tailor. Augie stood playing with an extremely large fake anemone made of gentian and fuchsia velours.

"What's all this about you leaving Mod Modes?" Tony began. "Mod Modes has been good to you, Sean. Don't tell me it ain't. I been good to you, too."

Sean nodded. The air in the room had grown stuffy almost at once. "It's not a question of who's being good to whom. It's simply that I tear my bleeding heart out doing simply super designs, and none of the line sells. So, there being no real contract, I've decided to sever the dear old relationship."

Tony Fish shook his head slowly, wagging his big but well-shaped nose from side to side. People said Ben Fischetti resembled him, handsome Ben with his hero's profile. But Tony knew the boy resembled his mother. He was better-looking, Tony told himself, and smarter and better dressed than either of these two faggots in here with him, and that was a fact. And Ben was as straight as they came.

"I treated you like a son," he told Sean. His eyes swung to Augie's dark face. "Did I ever do anything but the right thing by Sean?"

Augie looked very grave. "It's not what you did, Mr. Fischetti. It's what your salesmen aren't doing. A designer's only as good as his last line. Sean's line is a good one, but it's dying on the racks. And it isn't his fault."

Tony Fish turned his hands palms up and held them tightly to his chest, little fingers touching his rib cage. Then in a motion from the wrist only, he swung his hands out like semaphores of despair and gently wiggled the tips of his fingers in a pleading gesture. "Come on, boys," he said in a begging tone. "Whose fault is it? Mine?"

Augie nodded. "The time came to pull the plug on Mod Modes, Mr. Fischetti. You and I have been through that scene before, haven't we? I mean, half the designers in the market have had the plug pulled on them at one time or another, and chances are it was you doing the pulling."

He held up his hand to dam the flood of outraged emotion Tony Fish was about to unleash. "Nothing personal, Mr. Fischetti," he said then. "No hard feelings. It's just that Sean's too hot a property to waste a year watching Mod Modes swirl down the toilet bowl. He can be as big as he ever was if he gets the right promotion and the right distribution and the right salesmanship. We think we have a way of doing it."

Tony Fish's face went dead as his peasant's brain tried to sort out the information. The air in the room reeked of nervous sweat. Augie opened the door a discreet two inches.

"Boy's," Tony said at last, "I can't hold a man against his will. And especially if he's a close personal friend like Sean. But at the very least, if he's gonna be such a heavy money-maker, why shut Tony Fish out of the action?"

Sean's eyes watered as he yawned. He started to say something, but Augie's glance stopped him. "Don't worry, Mr. Fischetti," Augie said. "We're using the right fabrics from the right companies. You don't mind sharing the action that way, do you?"

"Not much of a share."

Tony Fish sat there, shifting uncomfortably in the tiny chair. He didn't like the smell of this at all. Not that he minded losing Sean. Mod Modes was finished. All that remained was sliding it quickly into bankruptcy and spreading its loss situation back through various owners to various other enterprises. The operation was cut and dried.

It wasn't that that worried Tony Fish. This was a nickel-and-dime chicken-shit outfit the two faggots were getting together. He didn't need any part of it, but the black one telling him he was getting the fabric was almost an insult.

It was the *ripulsa, il rifiuto*, the rebuff. It wasn't right for these two little *effeminatos* to rebuff him. It wasn't fitting. There was no respect, no honor. If they could do it to Gaetano Fischetti, anyone could. And if Don Vincenzo heard of it . . .

Tony Fish rubbed his forehead and right eye. His skin was paper dry. It worried him that he couldn't seem to sweat anymore. It was healthy to sweat. He glared at Augie for a moment, trying to see in him the source of all his troubles. But he knew in his heart that Augie was merely the most recent in a long line of troubles.

Still and all, he told himself doggedly, if he could get a little more of the faggots' action, something to show besides the fabric, he wouldn't feel he'd been so badly put down. There were a lot of ways, Tony Fish knew, for his various interests to help themselves to a piece of Sean's new business. He could supply everything from wire hangers and cardboard boxes to trucking and wholesaling. There was literally no part of the manufacturing and distributing processes that he couldn't supply, but the fastest return and the easiest was on the financing end.

"Who's bankrolling you?" he asked abruptly.

"A group of people," Augie said quickly. "You probably don't know them. They're around. They all kicked in a little. It's a kind of co-op."

"A syndicate never works. You got too many bosses to please." Tony Fish thought for a moment. "You need help with your contracts?" He watched Augie's impassive face for a clue to the truth. Even union negotiating, Tony knew, was a good way for him to get a slice of the action.

"All signed."

"Funny I didn't hear nothing about it, boys."

"We're not that big, Mr. Fischetti. We're small potatoes with a small line, but we can concentrate on it and sell like hell."

Tony Fish continued to study Augie's face. He knew the truth when he heard it, and he could pretty well imagine that Augie and Sean would sell their numbers very nice to faggot buyers in the big-city stores. In fact, it wouldn't surprise Tony if some of the buyers weren't helping bankroll the operation. It was all one big happy family.

"Why the frown, Mr. Fischetti?"

"Nothing. I was thinking about families."

"Families?"

"Yours," Tony Fish said with a heavy sigh, "and mine."

53

Woods Palmer was home by six. The Lincoln pulled to the kerb and he bade Jimmy good night, crossing the sidewalk and passing under the pierced concrete entry facade to the front door in three long strides. He was feeling very odd, very physical, not at all cerebral.

He opened the front door and had his topcoat off by the time he swung it shut behind him. The long, curving, open stairway stretched upward before him, thick oak planks spiraling skyward on a massive skeleton of black steel.

"Gerri?" He chucked the coat at one of the wall pegs and was pleased to see it settle down properly, its collar engaged. "Woody? Tom? Edith?"

He walked into the great living room and seemed to be greeted by echoes of his own voice, still reverberating in the long stretches of space. Someone had carefully laid a fire on the broad grate of the hearth. He supposed it had been Mrs. Gage.

"It was me," Gerri said, coming up behind him and, as usual, reading his mind. "And if you're going to light it, don't. I've been saving it for myself."

"It's not really cold enough for a fire," Palmer said, pulling her head against his chest. Her hair was so fine it floated away from her head at the touch of his hands, bearing static electricity.

"This fire isn't for heat. It's an aesthetic fire."

"I see."

She knelt before the hearth, her wheat-colored jeans pulled tight across her boyish rump, and touched a match to the kindling in three places. "One-match fire," she commented smugly.

"You hope."

"Nothing to it." She stood up and checked the damper lever. "Works every time. Did Mom come home with you?"

"Isn't she home yet?"

"No."

They stood side by side, watching the flame move with furious speed from the balled-up bits of newspaper to the thin splinters and from there spreading out sideways through the narrow sticks of wood until the fire lapped ferociously at the bark of the three big logs.

"You did a great job," Palmer said.

"Do I ever," Gerri asked in a mocking tone, "perform in any manner except utter perfection?"

"It's been known to slip a bit to merely superior."

She hugged him and put her face up for a kiss. This was the last of his children he could kiss, Palmer reflected, and he had better make the most of it. Of course, he'd always be able to kiss Gerri, but he missed being able to kiss all three of them when they were much smaller. Imagine kissing the great oaf Woody now?

Imagine hugging him, or even Tom? And, Palmer realized as he hugged Gerri, he apparently suffered from a lack of hugging. He wondered if there was a medical name for the condition.

Obviously Edith didn't suffer from the same need.

At the thought, he loosened his hold on Gerri. It wasn't right, he knew, to force his daughter to provide the affection his wife couldn't or wouldn't or, in any event, didn't give him.

"We held a debate in Soc class today," Gerri announced, "and I won it."

Palmer tried to remember whether Soc – pronounced with an *sh* on the end – were Sociology or Social Studies or Societal Relations or one of the other newteach labels for Civics.

He wondered why it was necessary to cloak the thinned-out curriculum in resounding jargon titles, as if by calling it more one could ever hide the fact that it was less. Thus, instead of learning grammer and composition and vocabularly and penmanship and punctuation and spelling and logic and rhetoric and research and literature and drama and all the other things one once learned in four years of high school baldly labeled "English," the child today learned about half of these subjects badly in classes with the self-congratulatory title of "Language Arts."

"Good," he heard himself say. "What was the topic?"

"*Resolved.* It is always best to tell the truth."

"And which side did you take? Pro?"

"Con. I made them realize how bad it was sometimes to tell the truth. How it hurt people."

"Good point."

"I nearly got it bad, though. The pro side was losing, and the teacher stepped in to help them."

"Hardly fair."

"Oh, she'd helped our side, too. Anyway, she threw a real hairy one at me. She said: 'Who's to judge when the truth should be withheld?' Did I set myself up as a competent judge of that, at all times, everywhere? Well, he almost had me."

"How'd you wiggle out?"

"I used the if-not-me who gimmick."

Palmer frowned. "What?"

"If I am not competent to judge, who is? I am the only one leading my life. Who is better to judge than me? If I judge wrongly, I pay for it. It killed the people, let me tell you."

"It's not logical, Gerri."

"Not everything in life is logical."

His frown deepened. "I know it's very fashionable these days to give extra weight to the irrational element in life. But more of life has logic than lacks it."

She eyed him for a moment. The firelight seemed to burn in the curves of her hair. "Do you believe it's always best to tell the truth?" she asked.

221

"N-no."

"Well, thanks for the honest answer, anyway."

"What does that mean?"

"You know." She gestured gropingly. "So many parents do that holier-than-thou, do-as-I-say-not-as-I-do bit. I mean, kids see through all that. You saw through Grandpa's guff, and I see through yours. Except you don't give me too much. Which is what I thank you for."

"Amazing," he said drily. "What other truths may one receive from your lips?"

"Don't get me started."

"Is that a threat?"

"You once told me a banker was a kind of superbusinessman. That makes you pretty vulnerable."

"To what?"

"Suppose I take the pro side?" she pounced. "Suppose I say the trouble with the world today is too many lies. If people told the truth more, there'd be less crime and poverty and mental illness."

"Great. Let's start telling the truth, then. Let's start by saying you have a big smudge of soot on your cheek."

"No diversions," Gerri persisted. "Do businessmen tell the truth? Isn't it a fact that they often lie? About what they sell, its value, its freshness, its usefulness?"

"Most of the time, yes," he admitted.

"How is the average businessman different from the average crook? He lies, too."

Palmer laughed. "So do statesmen and diplomats ... and parents."

"But isn't it the business of the businessman to buy cheap and sell dear? Doesn't he buy his help cheap, too, and sell what they make? Doesn't he make all these shady deals, price fixing, cartels, monopolies, rigged bids? Doesn't he steal ideas and men from his competitors? Doesn't he connive to put them out of business? Isn't his lying just for money?"

Palmer took her by her narrow shoulders and spun her around so that she stood in front of him with her back to the fire. 'What kind of Soc teacher have you got there? Carlotta Marx?"

"She didn't tell me any of that."

"All your own idea?"

"My Soc term paper is on ethics."

"When I was your age, we did papers on the rise of the

222

protective tariff or the significance of the cotton gin in the economy of the South. We didn't go around bad-naming our daddies."

"I'm not bad-naming you. Although I did run across a story about you in *Time* a year ago."

Palmer felt his cheeks growing red. The fire evidently had heated up his face. "Nobody believes anything they read in *Time*, honey. It's written to entertain, not to inform."

"Still and all."

"Still and all, that article was nothing but misquotation, conjecture and plain old-fashioned ax grinding, all tricked out to look like hard news."

"Still and all."

He grinned down at her. "Where there's smoke there's fire? So now you know how your dear old dad pulled a few close ones to keep the bank from being snatched out from under him."

"Couldn't care less." She stared up at him. "I'm not in business with you. I'm your dear old daughter."

"Getting older all the time."

"I just threw that *Time* bit in there to shake you up. To show you that business ethics aren't any different from the crooks' code."

"I am beginning to get bored with this, Gerri."

"Okay." She shrugged out of his grasp and, stepping sideways, let the full heat of the fire reach him. "Will you read my paper when I finish the first draft?"

"Before you mail it off to the *Daily Worker*? Yes."

"Yech." She did her imitation vomit. They watched the fire for a while. The flames from the kindling had fully ignited the two bottom logs and were spurting wild waves of yellow up over the bark of the top log.

Palmer felt a quaking in the floor. He turned to see his elder son coming down the last of the stairs. "Hi," Woody said. "Mom home yet?"

"No. How are you?"

"Fine." He stepped back and bellowed up the stairwell: "She isn't home yet, Mrs. Gage."

Palmer walked to the bar refrigerator and, removing the plastic pan under the icemaker, poured a cascade of frozen half-moons into the ice bucket. He put ice in three glasses.

"Coke?"

"Yes."

"No, thanks," Gerri said.

Palmer poured Coca-Cola in Woody's glass and Scotch in his own. They ceremoniously touched glasses. "To the ladies," Palmer said. "God bless 'em."

Woody looked pained. "God, how cornball can you get?"

"Mom home yet?" Tom asked from the doorway. "No fair, he's got Coke."

"No. Here," Palmer said, pouring some for his younger son. "Gerri?"

"No, thanks. I'm trying to keep down my sugar intake."

"Why?" Tom asked artlessly. "You're too skinny already."

"The family diplomat," Gerri said. "Mr. Tact. He gets it from his brother."

"*Resolved*," Palmer intoned, "it is always best to tell the truth."

"Good evening," Edith called from the doorway.

The three children and Palmer wheeled around to stare at her for a silent moment.

54

Kimberley had reached the Village square at five forty-five. The idea of the vigil was to have men and women with placards standing along the triangular perimeter of the little traffic island formed where Sixth and Greenwich avenues, Christopher, Eighth and Ninth streets ran together under the tall red-brown brick of the Women's House of Detention.

The vigil had been schedule to begin promptly at five thirty, when the first of the people coming home from work would be climbing up out of the immense Independent Subway complex beneath the intersection. Kimberley usually arrived on time or even a little early for these protest events. But he had wanted Edith in a cab and well out of the area before tonight's vigil began.

Not, he told himself now as he stood on the kerb holding a placard, because she shouldn't be exposed to this kind of event, but only because she couldn't be exposed so quickly, before she'd made any kind of full commitment to him.

He made a face of his own inanity. Here he was, holding a sign he hadn't even read yet, worrying about a woman with whom he was, after all only having a casual affair, right?

He glanced up at the sign and read: "FREE ELLEN GORDON!"

For a moment, so much had his affair occupied his mind, he couldn't remember who Edith Gordon was. Ellen Gordon. Then he recalled that she was a senior at NYU.

She had handcuffed herself and a boyfriend to the door of the induction center at Whitehall Street yesterday morning before it opened for the day. It had taken the cops three hours with hacksaws to cut them loose, and even then the two students had wriggled about so much the cops had had to saw the handle off the door rather than cut the cuffs.

The male student, whose name escaped Kimberley now, had been booked and released on bail when his father's lawyer had entered the case. But Ellen Gordon was being held in the Women's House here on the square in a tank with the usual catch of wino harridans, syphilitic whores and bull-dike lesbians on an open charge that nobody's lawyer had been able to do anything about, at least not all yesterday or today.

A woman reporter from the *Post* had gotten in to see Ellen earlier in the day and had run a story in the paper's last edition saying that Ellen had been sexually assaulted by one of the Dikes.

A veteran of these affairs, Kimberley knew the *Post* story would have Ellen sprung by about six or seven tonight. Too many girls without records, picked on antiwar or civil rights charges, had been mauled and worked over by the ladies on the tenth floor for the city prison officials to risk any further bad publicity. The superpatriotism of the whores was notorious.

Kimberley felt his heavy-lidded eyes start to close. He straightened up at his post. There were about twenty protesters on each side of the traffic island, all with slighly different placards. Since this was a silent vigil, there were no chants or songs to keep Kimberley fully awake.

He smiled at his own behavior. This wasn't at all like him. None of it, neither the sleepy indifference to a particularly hot cause right here at hand, involving a student at his school, nor his own engrossment with an affair. Edith was neither his first white woman nor his first married one. She wasn't the best he'd had, by a long shot. But she seemed the most interested in learning.

Kimberley felt rather than saw someone watching him. He knew all the protesters were being watched. He was well aware that some among the protesters themselves were professional or amateur stoolies, while from office windows nearby telephoto lenses were being used to get film close-ups of everyone in the vigil. Kimberley also knew that both the F.B.I. and the police were keeping a street-level surveillance. In a little while, with any luck, television trucks and crews with their flaring lights would wheel up to await Ellen Gordon's release. But this sensation was different, as of someone in particular singling Kimberley out for special attention.

He found her finally, the short, cute, dark-haired girl he had run into right after lunch, when she had been standing on the stairway of his college building looking lost. Now she was standing against the brightly lighted windows of the drugstore on the corner of Sixth Avenue and Eighth Street, her great eyes staring widely and directly at Kimberley as if in a trance.

He was not unused to this kind of scrutiny, either. There was a certain kind of girl – middle-class and in full rebellion, or on the verge of it – who dug spade cats and especially fairly white-looking ones like Kimberley.

It wasn't that he was light, Kimberley knew, because he wasn't that light. It was the un-Negro cast of his face, the slightly beaky Indian nose and of course the fact that he dressed in a manner these girls were familiar with, not the far-out hippie style of the Afrophile caftan and fez of the black nationalists.

So here was another of them, panting after a way of telling her parents to go to hell that didn't hang her up with real trouble.

Kimberley bared his teeth at the girl and gave her a wink. He had no intention of following up. For one thing, he was committed to this vigil until morning, if need be, unless they released Ellen Gordon sooner. For another, when they released her there would be such a melee that he would never be able to connect with this chick. And for a third, he was just about completely played out after his matinee with Edith. For a late bloomer and a slow learner, she really let you know what you'd been up to with her.

Kimberley turned away from the girl. She hadn't responded to the wink, anyway. Obviously he had misjudged her.

After a moment, she seemed to break out of her trance and hurry on up the street. Kimberley watched her enter a fairly expensive restaurant farther along on Sixth Avenue.

So much for my appeal with women, he thought. I'm not only slipping, but my mind is, too.

He grinned wryly at his own foolishness and, shifting from

226

foot to foot, thought about Edith in bed and wondered why he couldn't stop thinking about her.

55

At seven thirty, when Ben hadn't arrived, Rosalie got up from the restaurant table, her stomach knotted with hunger and fear, paid the check for the two glasses of white wine she'd drunk, and left the place.

The night air cooled her burning face. She felt the breeze drying the moistness in her eyes. Ben had never before stood her up, neither as a husband nor during their brief courtship. Either he was lying dead somewhere, or he was with someone else.

The second thought was so painful that Rosalie blinked and turned away, intending to go back down to the corner of Eighth Street and get a cab for Grand Central Station, where she could catch a train for Scarsdale.

She watched the people standing so silently in the little square there, each with a sign. She hadn't the slightest idea what the signs meant except the ones against the war and the draft. The name Ellen Gordon meant nothing to her. The fresh, good-looking colored man who had winked at her was standing just where he had been an hour and a half before. He looked tired, but so did all the other people with signs.

Rosalie thought they must be very serious people to stage such a – what did the sign say? – a vigil. Usually people held vigils in church. She liked what they were doing. It showed they were serious and felt they had right on their side.

They weren't like some of the nuts she had seen as a girl in the Village, with their wild clothes and crazy looks, shouting and milling around and trying to get arrested. These people were breaking no laws. There were police all around, and Rosalie knew if the people didn't have a permit for the vigil the police would have gotten them away from there.

As she watched, a truck rolled up with a tripod and TV camera mounted on the roof. Two men got out of the truck and climbed onto the roof. They donned headphones and swung the camera toward a door on Greenwich Avenue. The truck inched forward, and the camera's long black lens pointed unerringly at the door as a cluster of lights went on. Rosalie squinted into the glare.

Nearby, a police car edged across the intersection with a faint growl of its siren, like an animal waking up and lapsing into sleep again. Another squad car joined it, moving in from the direction of Tenth Street.

Rosalie noticed that a crowd of younger people, boys in jackets and girls with beehive hairdos, had gathered where the TV truck stood, shouting at the cameraman and waving into the lens. The people holding the vigil had not stirred. They continued silently to hold their signs.

"Hey, baby!" one of the neighborhood kids yelled. "Taka pitchuh!" He jumped high into the air so that the cameraman couldn't avoid him.

"Hello, Ma!" another boy shouted.

They were bobbing up and down like monkeys now, Rosalie thought. Another squad car arrived from a third direction, its roof light radiating a yellow beam.

"Looka, pitchuh, looka!"

"Hey, TV man, ovuh hee-uh."

Another TV truck was stalled on Sixth Avenue, trying to turn left into Greenwich Avenue, but the standstill traffic and squad cars kept it trapped.

Horns started to blare. Rosalie saw that cars were backed up to the east along Ninth Street as far as she could see. As she looked, she saw Ben dash out of one of the brownstones and run west toward where she was standing. She crossed Ninth and ducked into a doorway to avoid being seen.

At that instant the kids and girls horsing around the TV trucks began to scream rhythmically. A woman police officer and a man were escorting a girl about nineteen out of the Greenwich Avenue door of the Women's House of Detention.

"Hey, Commie!"

The lights of the second TV truck blazed brilliantly. The three people coming out the side door paused as the sudden noise and glare hit them. They glanced around in confusion.

"Get the commie cunt!"

A wave of neighborhood teenagers broke ranks and swarmed across the stalled traffic, trying to reach the girl, the man and the uniformed policewoman. At that moment uniformed cops appeared out of the surrounding darkness and ringed the trio, moving them east toward Sixth Avenue as quickly as possible.

"Die!" a girl with a puffed-up hairdo was shouting. "Drop dead and die!"

Rosalie watched the police shove their way to a waiting

228

squad car. They hustled the girl and the man into the car and slammed the door shut. A dozen boys began to shake the squad car on its springs, making it rock violently from side to side. They were wrenching at the door handles.

One of them managed to pull open a door. He reached in for the girl. A few yards away, the ranks of the vigil broke. Protesters dashed diagonally across the square toward the squad car.

A wedge of uniformed cops moved in on the car from the other side, hauling the teenage boy away by his heels and throwing him against a passing car. The boy's eyes rolled up in his head as his back slammed into the fender. He slumped, unconscious, under the wheels of the car.

Rosalie's ears began to ache with the constant blare of horns and the screams of the neighborhood kids. A girl howled hysterically as she tried to pull the fallen boy from under the car. A young cop who seemed not much older than the girl shoved her aside. She clawed at his eyes. His cheek started to bleed. He brought his nightstick down on her temple. He felt himself being shoved from behind, whirled and slammed his stick horizontally across the nose of an elderly man carrying a sign that read: "NO MORE WAR."

The man's nose spurted crimson. At the sight of so much blood, another young cop slashed his stick in a wide arc, trying to clear the area. There were cries of pain. The crowd closed in on the two police, and around the edges behind them, older cops began clubbing their way through to rescue the two in the center.

They clubbed methodically, laying out protesters and local teenagers alike, without favoritism. Rosalie could see Officer Cutrone, who had walked her to school every morning as a favor to her father. He was a sergeant now, but he was in there clubbing along with his men.

As she watched him work, his nightstick slamming down in long, easy strokes, like a man hammering nails, Rosalie felt her throat pulse. She turned sideways against the lighted window and vomited. Then she ran across Eighth Street and down into the subway complex below the street. Suddenly all was peaceful.

She walked for what seemed like blocks. Here under the city, there was no sign that upstairs her friend, Sergeant Cutrone, was killing people. She could hear trains roaring in and rushing out in the jagged tempo of the city beneath the city, aloof, peaceful, inhuman.

She felt as if she were in another country. She bought a token and started to put it in the slot, not knowing where she was going but wanting to get away from this crazy place where people were killing each other.

Eyes blinded with blood, a young boy stumbled halfway down a stairway and stood hanging there on the railing, afraid to go any farther until he could see. "Marty?" he called. "Linda?"

Rosalie ran up the stairs. "Here. Sit down," she said.

"You're not Linda." His mouth worked convulsively. "Where's everybody?"

"Please sit down."

She helped him sit on the filthy stairs. Then she dug in her handbag and found a clean paper tissue. She could smell his acrid, fear-born sweat. She began dabbing at his eyes. "I can't see," he was mumbling. "I'm blind."

"You're not blind. You have a bad cut right between your eyebrows."

"Who are you with?"

Rosalie frowned, trying to work one eye clear of blood. "I'm not with anybody," she heard herself say. Upstairs, a faint howl of sirens filtered down to her. "Stick out your tongue."

"What?"

When he stuck it out, she dabbed a clean bit of tissue on his tongue and rubbed the eye clear. "There."

He blinked and stared at her. "You're right. I'm okay." He started to get to his feet. Rosalie pushed him back down. "I gotta get up there with my group," he explained.

"You sit for a while. That other eye needs cleaning out, too."

He continued to stare at her with his good eye while she worked on the other. "Listen," he said then, "who are you with?"

"Does it matter? I'm with you."

The skin around his good eye wrinkled in thought. "You don't even know which side I'm with." His words had a faintly accusatory ring to them.

"Is that important?"

"Is that important?" he echoed. "My God."

"There." She stood up. "You're okay now." She tucked her arm under his and helped him to his feet, then guided him up the stairs. As she had thought, the riot was over. The Village

230

square was empty of squad cars. The TV trucks had moved off to scavenge other violence to feed the eleven o'clock news addicts. Even the vigil had disbanded.

Rosalie glanced around the square. Hadn't she seen Ben in all that mess for a split second, coming out of a brownstone on Ninth? The noise had probably reminded him of his date with her. It seemed like years ago. She let go of the boy's arm. "Can you walk all right?"

"Yeah. Where is everybody?"

"Arrested, or maybe they just ran away. How far is home?"

"Bronx. I'm okay."

"A doctor has to see that cut."

His hand went to his forehead, and he winced. "First my mother has to see it. And then you'll hear some hollering." He grinned at her, ducked down into the subway again, and was gone.

Rosalie walked east to Fifth. Her mouth tasted sour with knowledge. She was heading for her parents' home, too. She would call Mrs. Traficanti from there and ask her to baby-sit the children. Maybe she would stay over in town. Maybe she would just have a cup of coffee and talk about the riot and go home to Scarsdale. Maybe she would tell them about seeing Ben.

Maybe she would talk about that boy in the park. Maybe she would tell her sister Celia about the strange, hot pictures he had put in her head. Maybe she would talk about Sergeant Cutrone. Maybe she wouldn't tell them a damned thing.

She wasn't sure yet what she would or wouldn't say.

56

By ten o'clock, after a telephone call to Scarsdale, Ben had figured it out and gone to Don Vincenzo Biglioto's house on lower Fifth Avenue. The man who answered his ring at the door was a stranger to Ben. He had expected Rocco Sgroi to answer.

"It's Ben Fischetti," he said impatiently. "Let me in."

"Hold it." The man firmly closed the door in his face. Ben toyed with the idea of leaving. Of the scenes he liked least, the sight of himself pleading for entrance to his in-laws' castle keep was least pleasant. Before he made up his mind to leave, however, the door opened again. Behind the soldier at the threshold he could see Rosalie's small, round face and glossy black bangs.

"Tell this ape it's all right."

"It's all right." The words echoed Ben's in a tinny way, as if produced by an agency other than the human voice.

The guard, showing not the slightest sign of remorse, grudgingly allowed Ben to enter. Rosalie walked ahead of him through an entrance foyer and along a hall toward the rear stairway, past old mahogany sideboards and chairs, each with its own crocheted antimacassar. Rosalie headed up the back stairs to the second floor and led the way into the room Ben remembered as the one she had had as a girl.

"Everybody's asleep," she whispered. "Or at least, they're nice enough to pretend they are. Mamma went to bed half an hour ago, and Celia's reading in her room."

"And *il pèzzo novanta*?"

Ben sat down on the edge of Rosalie's bed and watched her struggle with the Italian phrase. He knew that having heard only Sicilian as a girl, and having never learned to read or write the language, she found most of the lesser-known conversational phrases incomprehensible.

"Speak English, Ben."

"*Ma*, shu'." – He gestured in an exaggerated manner, like an Italian pushcart vendor. "*Il pèzzo novanta*. How you call him ina Inglesa? The biga shot?"

Rosalie grimaced. "If you think you're being funny . . ."

"Not me, baby. Just the sight of *una bella ragazza* like you not knowing the mother tongue."

Rosalie sat down in a chair beside her desk. "If you're referring to my father, he's away on business."

"Beautiful business."

"What's your excuse for standing me up at the restaurant?"

Ben's mouth tightened for a moment, then produced a thin smile. "There was all that trouble at the corner. Police. Everything couldn't get through. And after I did, you weren't at the restaurant."

Rosalie shook her head. "Wrong. The trouble started more than an hour after we were supposed to meet."

Ben repeated the pushcart gesture, a complex series of movements involving a shrug, an outward throwing of the hands and a down-dropping of the mouth emphasized by rising eyebrows. "Okay, lady."

Rosalie nodded. "Why did you come here?"

"To find you. Take you home."

"This is my home, too. I'm always welcome."

"Which is more," Ben said, getting up, "than I can say for me." He yanked open his tie and collar. The rooms in this place were always kept too warm.

"You're welcome. But not to stay here tonight."

"That's fine with me." Ben took off his jacket and hung it over the back of the other chair in the room. He lighted a cigarette and was about to put away the pack when he remembered to offer it to Rosalie. Then he remembered it was Tippy, not Rosalie, who smoked. He pocketed the cigarettes.

"It's me, Rosalie," she said then. "Get with it, Ben."

"Right." He blew out a long plume of smoke and then opened the window. He stared out at the broad expanse of Fifth Avenue, where even at this hour cars, buses and cabs were at a standstill, waiting for a minor jam to unsnarl itself.

"This place makes you nervous, doesn't it?" she asked.

"Yes."

"Why?"

"I always think there's somebody across the street in an upstairs window taking movies of everybody who goes in and out."

"That's possible."

"That's nervous-making, too."

"But it isn't what makes you nervous," Rosalie said.

"Why not?"

"You're nervous about—" She stopped and seemed to think for a moment. "You're nervous about being who you are," she said then. "I think you don't like who you are."

"But you," he said, turning on her, "simply adore who you are."

"No."

"Then what?"

"I accept who I am," Rosalie said. "I accept who my father is. You keep fighting who you are and who you come from."

Ben started to speak but thought better of it. Lately, he noticed, Rosalie had stopped chattering aimlessly, the way she used to do. She had apparently forgotten they had a television set at home. Instead she could usually be found reading. As a result, he found a new and unpleasant trait in her personality: her conversation made sense. He had been able to cope with her quite well in the old days when her mind hopped about without any pattern, the way the thoughts and images on the

233

television tube did. Lately, however, she had seemed to learn or re-learn the knack of thinking in a sequence. It was disconcerting, to say the least.

"Nothing to say about that?" she asked then.

"Just standing here wondering what gives you the right to suggest things like that."

"Don't pretend you're angry with me, Ben." She laughed softly. "I don't think you're enough interested in me to get angry about anything I do any more. But I'm still a little interested in you, because if I see signs in my children of the way you are, I'll have to take steps."

Ben shook his head. "You're fantastic. They're my kids, too."

"I can't have them growing up to hate who they are."

"Stop with that stupid women's magazine crap."

"It's not."

"It's the cheap crap they pump into you in these idiot magazines to make you dissatisfied with everything, so you go out and buy another rug or another lipstick or something else they advertise."

Rosalie looked hurt, Ben thought, but not very. "That's the most cynical thing I ever heard anybody say," she said then. "Don't you believe in anything at all?"

"Not in that kind of crap."

"There were people out in the square tonight getting beat up for what they believed in. I don't know if they were right or wrong. But at least they have something to believe in. You don't."

Ben took a long, calming drag on the cigarette and started looking for an ashtray. There being none, he tapped the ash in the metal wastebacket next to the desk. Then he turned away from Rosalie and resumed his inspection of the traffic jam on the street below.

"Ben?"

"What?"

"Aren't you going to talk to me?"

Still looking out of the window, he said: "This isn't one of your *Reader's Digest* dialogues, Rosa. This is a real person you're talking to, with real hang-ups and problems, not the cardboard crap they yak about in magazines. You say I don't like who I am? That's for me to think about. You say I don't like who I come from. We come from the same stock, so maybe we can talk about that tonight if we have to talk at all.

234

But for Christ's sake, spare me the self-help shit."

"Ben!"

"Sorry."

Behind him, he could hear Rosalie stir slightly in her chair. He had the feeling she couldn't sustain for too much longer the vaguely philosophical level of the conversation.

"You don't think it was easy," she began, "for Celia and me in school? To know that behind our backs all the girls were making fun of us. To our faces they were always sweet as sugar because Papa could buy and sell their families. Behind our backs they were cruel and nasty and spiteful. But that didn't make us hate what we were."

"It's different for a girl." Ben sat down on the edge of the bed again. "Nobody expects a nice Italian girl to do anything but get married and have kids. Which you did. You're a success. I mean it." He sighed and put out the cigarette in the waste-basket.

"But for an Italian boy it's very different," he continued. "First, he has to be the man his father was. In my case, that was easy. But then he has to surpass the old man. That wasn't too hard, either. Okay. Now, what has he done lately? Everything is questioned, analyzed. Did he go to the right school? Did he get the right job? Is he paying back the big investment made in him? Will he continue to pay off like a slot machine till he takes his last dying breath? Does he look suave doing it? Does he dress right, move right? Can he express himself? Can he move around in society? Is he upward mobile? Can he handle booze? Does he speak properly? No accent? Good grammar? Can he tell a joke? Does he treat his wife and kids right? How is he to his parents? His in-laws? His uncles and his cousins and his aunts? Does he show respect? Does he know his protocol? Does he have the right opinions? Does he make the right decisions? It's all decisions, and you stand or fall with each new decision. Never mind if you were a hero yesterday. You can be a bum today. It's a shitty way to live, Rosa."

"That word."

Ben started to laugh. He felt for a moment that he couldn't control the odd bubble of amusement in his throat.

"Beautiful, Rosa," he said then, slightly out of breath. "You ask me a real question and I, like a jerk give you a real answer. But you're not interested in real answers, just in proper language, right? Right?"

235

"I don't like gutter talk in my parents' house."

Ben stood up. "Fine. I'll leave."

She got to her feet. "I'm not driving you out, Ben. It's just that I can't take that kind of talk."

"Fine."

They eyed each other for a moment. "I'm sorry you feel you've had such a rough life," she said. "You might compare it with somebody else's, one of the kids in the street whose father has no money at all and who couldn't care less what his son does as long as he brings in a little money."

"You mean the kids that grow up to work for your father?" He noticed that Rosalie's eyes looked unusually shiny. "All right," she said. "They work for my father and your father."

"You mean the kids that grow up to be button men? Who learn to make clean hits? Who make a living doing what neither your father nor mine would do for himself?"

"Never mind about my father!"

The words came out of Rosalie with such force that Ben blinked. He stared into her moist eyes with their big black pupils surrounded by dark brown irises. "Touched a nerve, huh?"

Her hand moved so quickly he felt the slap before he saw the movement. She had launched the blow with little premeditation, so that it stung but didn't really hurt. Ben stepped back out of her range.

"Just because you think you're too good for the rest of us," Rosalie said, her breasts moving up and down with the effort of her breathing, "don't think you can stand here in my father's house and say bad things about him."

"Too good for you?" Ben reached for his jacket. "Is that it?"

"Everybody knows Ben Fischetti thinks he's too good for the rest of the family. Everybody knows he thinks he married beneath him. The big football hero? The big graduate student? The big brain? How could he ever have come from a bunch of dirty Sicilians with funny accents?"

Ben buttoned his collar and tightened his tie. Then he put on his jacket and buttoned it, moving all the while with a slow precision he hoped would irk Rosalie. Then: "I notice someone's been using my big dictionary at home. Mrs. Traficanti doesn't read, and the kids are just starting. Have you been looking up words?"

"And if I have?"

236

"Here's another one to look up: *deracinate.*"

"I haven't got time to play your games, Ben."

He walked to the door of her room. "It has two meanings. To tear up by the roots. You had enough Latin to know that."

"And the second meaning?"

"To wipe out."

The silence between them grew long enough to be embarrassing to Ben. He had no idea why he had said that. The word had popped into his mind, and he had found himself talking when he knew he shouldn't even try. Not that the idea was beyond Rosalie. He realized now that she was perfectly capable of handling the whole thing, perhaps even better than he. But the word gave away too much of his own fears to hand it over to her.

He wondered as he watched her now where she had found the strength to handle these things. There was a lot to his idea that fewer demands were made on girls. And then, too, they always had their little magazine homilies to see them through. Women lived in an unreal world at best, Ben knew. They had no idea of what happened in the real world, nor did they care to know. In some ways, they had a point.

Finally Rosalie nodded and turned away. She sat down at her desk again. "If you tear up your roots," she said then in a toneless voice, "you wipe yourself out. Is that it?"

"That's not at all what I said."

"I know." she sighed softly. "It's what I said."

He closed the door behind him as he left.

57

At a little before eleven o'clock, Palmer finished the work he was doing in his study. He had said good night to the older children a few minutes before. Mrs. Gage, who normally slept in, had left after the dinner dishes were finished to spend the weekend with friends in Connecticut. Edith was in her sitting room. The house was ready for sleep.

Palmer filed away the packet of personal checks that had cleared through his Ubco account. Miss Czermat had run a tape for him, as she always did, and posted the results. Everything was in order. As usual, most of his checks were to Cash, and most of the family's expenses were paid for by the checks Edith wrote on the account. Although he could have had as many different checking accounts as he wished, Palmer had long ago decided to make life easy on himself and whatever bank had his account. He kept one common joint account on which both he and Edith drew.

He made his way across the third floor to Edith's sitting room and found her there, switching on the small black and white television set, the only one in the entire house. Complaining loudly, his children would monopolize the set during the early evening, commenting freely on how much better a particular scene might have been if they'd been lucky enough to have color and a decent-sized screen instead of the small portable that represented the Palmer family's entire stake in a modern mass communications.

"A bigger screen means bigger balderdash," Palmer had stated flatly. "And a color set means not only more, but gaudier, garbage."

Palmer realized as he stood there watching Edith turn to the channel she favored for news that in some ways he played the heavy father as heavily as his own father had done. But, he hoped, with more justification.

Edith glanced up at him without speaking. "Ready for bed?" he asked, simply to fill the vacant air with noncommittal sound.

"After the news."

"Um." He sat down on the edge of her desk and waited in silence through half a commercial on borrowing money from one of Ubco's competitors.

"Easy monthly payments over a period of..."

"Stop conning the public," Palmer advised the screen.

"Your own ads do the very same thing," Edith said.

"For any worthwhile household or family expense, including..."

"Taking a flyer on the market," Palmer interpolated, "paying your psychiatrist or getting your credit card out of hock."

"The very same thing."

"Troops occupied an advance position on Lonesome Ridge in the Vietcong's central stronghold," the announcer said, "at a cost of twenty-three U.S. dead and reported five hundred and seventeenth Communist casualties. Here's a platoon moving up along the south ridge under heavy Communist mortar and rocket fire with..."

"They're all Communists," Palmer told the announcer. "All these peasants are card-carrying members of the party."

238

"Woods, can you possibly stop talking back to the set?"

"It gripes me to hear inaccurate nonsense like that."

"Field hospital behind the lines. This was the same ridge, you will recall, that U.S. and South Vietnam troops originally took three months ago and retook last week. It has now been retaken for good. Meanwhile, in Washington ..."

"Lunacy is king," Palmer slipped in. "Lunacy Bird is queen."

"Woods!"

"Here in Manhattan, demonstrators touched off a fist- and club-swinging melee outside the Women's House of detention earlier this evening when Ellen Gordon, a nineteen-year-old ..."

"What the hell is this?" Palmer demanded. He watched a close-up of Kimberley, standing almost at attention, holding his sign, while on the sound track Palmer could hear strange outcries and yowling. The film cut to a view of teenagers rocking the squad car. Then there was a brief interview with a police sergeant.

"Just local neighborhood kids. High-spirited and patriotic."

"But you were –"

"Sergeant," another off-screen announcer called.

"Isn't it true," the original announcer began.

"Sergeant, just a word about –"

The film then cut to another close-up of Kimberley, without his placard.

"Tell us how this started?"

"Ellen Gordon was arrested and placed with known female criminals in the House here, and they –"

"Could you speak a little lou –"

"Sexually molested while in police custody by –"

The studio announcer, a tiny frown between his eyes, stared directly in Palmer's eyes and said: "In Fargo, North Dakota, today the second set of quintuplets to be born on ..."

"What was that all about?" Palmer asked Edith.

She seemed to have some difficulty answering right away. "I mean," Palmer said, "they are supposed to be covering a news event, and I'm damned if I can make out who, why or what. Can you?"

"No."

"What?"

"No."

"Is something wrong?" he asked, watching her more closely now.

"No."

"Sure?"

She nodded and started to get up. Palmer switched off the set. "If this stuff upsets you," he said, "you shouldn't watch it."

Edith turned toward him. She was dressed for sleep in a nightgown and a rather plain robe with a thin ruffle along the collar. Palmer tried to read in her face what was wrong tonight.

"You sure you're all right?"

She nodded and, instead of leaving the room, sank back in her chair and seemed unable to move. Her breathing seemed heavy to Palmer. He frowned, watching her. "Sure?"

"Yes."

"Somehow I get a different idea. Well, anyway, what I came in for...." He paused. "I ran across this two-thousand-five-hundred-dollar check to whatever it is. Operation Boost. Is that some charity?"

He waited for a reply. "Or what?"

PART FOUR

Wednesday

58

It was a weekday, but the construction site on Lexington Avenue stood almost silent. For weeks the concrete, reinforced with rod, had been cast as high as the thirtieth storey, all columns and floors aligned but bare of any of the trappings of electrical conduits and wires, air-conditioning ducts, sewage pipes and the like. At the moment the building was no more than a layered shell of rough-cast concrete spotted by brownish-red rust where reinforcing iron peeked through.

To casual passersby, and there were hundreds of thousands of them on a typical day along Lexington Avenue, the building seemed to have reached one of those mysterious hiatuses that New York City construction often underwent, an unexplained pause that, if they thought about it at all, passersby might vaguely attribute to distant trouble, some faraway strike or shortage.

The practiced eye of the builder, developer, general contractor or architect, and there were hundreds of them moving about the midtown area, saw something different. There is a tempo to the construction of anything as sizeable as an office building that takes up most of a square block. The stoppage to the city's normal traffic patterns alone requires speedy completion. The budget of any major builder also requires speed. During construction, the building produces only deficits. The sooner these can be written off against income, the better.

"Klaman's in trouble," was the offhand analysis of the more knowledgeable passersby. Under normal conditions, wiring, ductwork and pipes would have kept pace with concrete pouring, moving skyward a few floors behind. Now the great shell lay silent, like a burned-out wreck. No laborers were paged on its immense intercom system. No trucks arrived or left. The gigantic cranes had been removed a week before. The site lay in curious silence, so unlike the clamor of the past months.

A few watchmen prowled the lower levels, expelling derelicts in the morning from their temporary beds, ignoring them at night when the frail, unshaven men, the lucky ones with pints of muscatel or Sneaky Pete in brown paper bags, would take refuge under anything that promised to keep off the rain and block the wind.

On this Wednesday morning Sal Geraci sat alone in the

office trailer and stared out the window at the four portable green outhouses next door. Some workmen of the throngs who had scurried over this site in the past months, stringing iron and pouring mix, had scribbled various clever titles for the toilet sheds.

"Irish Steak House," Sal read for the hundredth time. "Italian Consulate." He squinted at a third epithet, trying to make it out. Someone had chalked it there last night, probably one of the watchmen. "Birthplace of Harry Klaman," he finally read.

Sal grinned, despite himself. He picked up the telephone and dialed the headquarters office of the Klaman Company. Harry had promised to be at the site no later than nine, and it was now nine thirty. As he waited for Harry's line to answer, Sal watched two secretaries late for work stop and stare at the privy graffiti. Their little knees looked cold in the brisk March wind.

"Harry, Sal."

"I said I'd be there. Stop bugging me."

Sal noted that Harry was using his tycoon-of-industry-plagued-by-the-world voice. But there was a haunted note beneath it that Sal also heard. "You okay, Heshie?"

"Why wouldn't I be? Everything's absolutely perfect. Works at a standstill on Lexington. I had to stop that foundation excavation up in Yonkers. I can't top out in Paramus, and what's more, I got ghosts."

Sal frowned. "You got what? Where?"

"Not in my friggin' TV set, boychick. I call my bank, all they do is take messages. Nobody returns them. Tony Fish calls me and makes dates. He don't keep 'em. I call him, he don't return the call. Finally he makes new dates and never shows. It's like I'm surrounded by ghosts."

"This is getting kind of spooky down here, too, Harry. I'm gonna stop showing up in the mornings. I mean, you promised to be here."

"I know," Klaman sighed. "But the worst is our friend on Bleecker."

"Who?"

"Vinnie. It's like he dropped off the face of the earth. At least if I call the bank or Tony Fish, somebody answers and takes a message. Fine. They never get back to me, but at least I'm connected to a human being. I call Vinnie, and the minute somebody picks up the call and I say hello, the line goes dead.

They know my voice, Sal, and the bastards hang up on me. That whatshisname, Rocco, hangs up on Harry Klaman."

Sal nodded slowly, knowing Harry couldn't see the movement. "Okay, buddy," he said then. "I get the picture. Let me come to see you. It's too goddamned depressing around here."

"Right." The line went dead.

Sal locked up the officer trailer, said good-bye to one of the watchmen and started walking along Lexington toward the garage in the forties where he parked his car.

The time was now nine forty-five. The streets seemed to Sal to be choked with people. It wasn't, he told himself, the pedestrian jam-up caused by his own construction. He had already walked two blocks south of the building. Nor was it any immediate proximity to a subway station. He was well above Grand Central at this point, so incoming commuters couldn't be creating the jam. And anyway, most of them were at their offices already. No major holiday was coming up, with throngs of gift buyers clogging the streets as they did before Christmas.

He lifted his glance from the faces of the people on the sidewalk and took one of his rare glances at the immediate skyline. His face moved slowly from north to south, taking in the dozens of high-rise office buildings and hotels along the avenue and those he could see beyond them, to the east, of the buildings along Third Avenue. He recognized at least three Klaman buildings he had supervised.

Few of the buildings he saw were smaller than twenty storeys. Most were a great deal taller and took up anywhere from a third to a half block's street frontage. With the latest of efficient floor plan manipulation, Sal knew, most of the companies that rented this exceedingly expensive space were determined to cram as many desks and offices as possible into the least space they could get away with. At ten or fifteen dollars a square foot in monthly rental cost, every inch counted.

Sal started to reach for the thin slide rule he kept in his shirt pocket, then stopped and continued walking. He knew he could figure out approximately how many people worked in and visited these buildings. He also knew the figure would depress him even more than he already was.

He wondered, as he waited on a corner for the light to change, why there had to be such congestion in the city, in all the cities. Someone shoved him from behind, and he whirled to see two young men in Ivy League suits dash diagonally across the street through the temporarily stalled traffic, dodging be-

245

tween cabs and trucks and buses like quarterbacks on a crowded gridiron.

Sal watched several other people follow, crisscrossing the intersection and scattering in all directions. One truck driver, confused by the movement and temporarily unsure of which direction the lights indicated, began to give small, sharp beeps on his horn, sounding exactly like a nervous calf.

When the light finally did change, too many pedestrians were tangled up along the vehicles to allow for a fast getaway. Forgetting his own need to cross, Sal stood and watched the traffic back up Lexington for six blocks as the particular interesection at which he stood remained clogged with indecision.

Sal noted that part of the problem, as always, was double-parked cars and trucks on both sides of the avenue. Normally quite a broad thoroughfare, Lexington was in many places pinched down to two lanes by double-parked vehicles, construction like Sal's own building, street-repair crews, utility trucks and the like. Farther south, near the post office, trucks trying to turn west into 45th Street were backed around onto Lexington in a double curve that further snarled the flow of traffic. And cabs slowing as they passed Grand Central Station, either to drop passengers or in the hope of finding some, more or less totally throttled free movement along the avenue.

A woman's narrow heel came down hard on the little toe of Sal's right foot. He doubled over in pain and inadvertently butted another woman in the behind.

Her eyes glared hatred. "Filth," she fizzed.

Sal's face colored as he straightened up. Someone trying to jump the changing light and cross the street knocked him sideways. He was not a small man by any means, and when he ricocheted off the stone side of a bank building his shoulder throbbed with pain. He stared after the unknown, unseen assailant, wondering which of the dozens, the hundreds of retreating backs belonged to the person who had caused him this pain.

He stood there, rubbing his shoulder until the pain went away. Most of the time, Sal realized now, he was insulated from this kind of thing. He drove his car directly to the site at about seven thirty or eight in the morning, when the streets were fairly empty. A foreman would take the car from him and either park it on the site or at a nearby garage. The same foreman would get the car at quitting time, and Sal would drive off through thick traffic, of course, but alone in his car with the windows shut, the radio on and the air conditioning providing his own supply of fresh air.

His face set in an expression somewhere between a grimace of disgust and a wince of pain, Sal began walking south again, threading his way through the crowd, shoving and being shoved.

He wondered that Harry could tell him when he got to the office. That there would be new financing? Not in a million years. Worse yet, what could Sal Geraci tell Harry? That the silent treatment he was getting meant good news? Never.

Sal knew the way Vinnie Big operated. Everyone knew, but Sal, being in construction, had a certain closer familiarity with some of Don Vincenzo's tricks. And Tony Fish did whatever Vinnie Big told him to do. He had no mind of his own, Tony Fish. Everyone knew that, too. It pained Sal to realize how poor a reputation Tony had because there was a family connection, of course. Tony had married a Limandri girl whose brother, Bruno, had married Constanza Geraci, Sal's aunt, long dead. So what did that make it? Cousins twice removed? Something like that. Which meant, of course, in a way, that Sal was a third-removed cousin of Vinnie Big.

He entered the parking garage and surrendered his slip of pink cardboard. The clerk accepted it silently, almost grudgingly. Sal took his place at the end of a line of people waiting for their cars. At ten a.m., he reminded himself.

Standing there, shifting impatiently from foot to foot as cars were driven up and people got into them, Sal tried to trace the connection back to Vinnie Big. It had been a Fischetti who had married a Biglioto back in the middle of the last century in Sicily. That Biglioto had been the father of Don G. and grandfather of Vinnie Big. His Fischetti wife had been Tony Fish's great-grandmother, which made him ...

One of the cars edging out of the driveway stopped in front of Sal, and its horn blasted deafeningly in the enclosed space. Sal jumped back and glared at the driver, who with no seeming sarcasm gave Sal a small salute and drove out of the garage. It hadn't seemed to have occurred to him, Sal realized, that blasting a horn in a man's face was disrespectful or, as in this case, painful.

There seemed to be more pain than usual lately, Sal decided. He had been first in line for the past three cars now, but for some infuriating reason the cars of people behind him had been delivered ahead of his. The city seemed to be more filled with pain than it had ever been before, he thought.

The noises were louder and the air stank worse and the people pushed harder and they acted crazier and more in a hurry and there were more of them and they hated each other more and, all in all, the city seemed capable of giving more pain than it ever had in Sal's memory.

That was in addition, he reminded himself, to the pain people could set out deliberately to give to other people. Look at Harry. If he felt nervous and haunted now, wait till they really started tightening the screws. Everyone knew how Vinnie Big did it. The only wonder was that he could get the bank up in Westchester to play ball, too. Between them, they were squashing Harry like a louse between two thumbnails.

Sal's car arrived. He got in, slammed the door and wrapped himself in the blessed insulation of his own radio and his own cleaner air. Feeling a little better about the city, he touched his toe to the accelerator pedal and eased the car out into the center of a complete traffic standstill.

And it's only ten fifteen, he thought.

59

At ten thirty Woods Palmer, Jr., called the meeting to order. Like most meetings since he had become chief executive officer of Ubco, this one was being held in an informal atmosphere. This influence, which Palmer had brought to the bank, he knew was considered "Midwest" or even "country" by the immensely conservative New York staff, young and old.

He glanced around the room at the executive committee of his board of directors. It gave him no great feeling of achievement or status to know that at the age of forty-six he was probably the youngest man at the long, narrow boardroom table.

To his right at one end of the table sat Harry Elder, Donny's father, retired as a senior vice-president but still on the board of directors. A small, chubby, white-haired man, Harry Elder's hands and face had begun to show the brownish liver spots of encroaching old age. He had an all-weather voice, like a man with a permanent sore throat, that made everyone strain to hear his words. Because what he said was usually worth hearing, Palmer always sat him close by.

To his left was one of the board's twelve outside members,

men who had no executive position with the bank and in fact were not connected with banking. The burly man was Barney Kinch, president of a large holding company known as Jet-Tech International. Two years before, Palmer had beaten off Jet-Tech's bid to grab control of Ubco's board in order to improve its borrowing position with the bank. So decisively had he defeated Jet-Tech that he could afford to relent a year ago when, after several mergers, spin-offs and refinancings with other banks, Jet-Tech had shown itself more tractable. Barney Kinch had started in life as an engineer. He was still much more a technical man than an administrator or moneyman. Palmer found him easy to work with.

Among the other outside board members at the executive committee meeting today was Tim Carewe, a thin, balding man slightly older than Palmer who had recently left Washington after more than ten years in space-missile administration work to head a large investment trust. He had two claims on Palmer, neither of them strong; he was the third or fourth husband of Edith's Aunt Jane, which made him, Palmer believed, something of an uncle twice removed. His other claim was that Palmer had used him unmercifully during a tight place in his scuffle with Jet-Tech. Palmer recognized that the two things gave Tim a kind of hate-loyalty to Palmer that was more reliable than most other kinds of relationships.

Another outside member of the board, Eddie Hagen, sat at the far end of the board table, painstakingly reading the minutes of the previous executive committee meeting. Eddie had been one of Billy Mitchell's young protégés in the 1920s. His Army career had suffered somewhat because of his allegiance to the unlucky general, but by the end of World War II, Edward Everett Hagen had risen to brigadier general in the Air Force and had retired to head one of the many technical manufacturing companies in the Boston area that had proliferated in the shadow of M.I.T. He had been Palmer's superior officer in Mediterranean Theater Intelligence, the guiding genius behind the Sicily mission and others Palmer could now recall with only fading accuracy as the years passed.

The rest of the men at today's meeting were staff officers at Ubco of the rank of senior vice-president. As was typical in organizations like Ubco, where rank was paramount, the two men who knew most about the main topic on the agenda were not present.

The topic was the forthcoming merger with People's of

Westchester, but neither Bill Elston nor Danny Elder enjoyed enough rank to be present. Bill's research was tucked into Palmer's folder, which was about all that could be expected.

The executive committee had gone through nearly all the other items Palmer had caused to be placed early on the agenda and voted to increase the line of credit they had extended a new government in Central America, cut back the financing presently enjoyed by a rather large credit-card company, crack down on the lax payment schedule of a major television-manufacturing concern in the Midwest, liquidate two debtor companies whose loans were going bad, back the purchase by a friendly brokerage house of a new issue of municipal debentures, undertake the rental to any taker on a yearly basis of certain factories and capital equipment of the rolling-mill class, remove the props from a dubious bond issue being unsuccessfully promoted by an airport authority in Minnesota, underwrite a new low-grade-shale exploratory venture in west Texas, extend the term of a 25-million-dollar housing project and shopping center development near Baltimore, break off relations with a small Middle East nation, shift major arbitrage operations in gold from Geneva to the Brussels market for the month of April, finance a new supersonic bomber-passenger plane sales approach being made by a manufacturer's lobbyist in Washington and bolster a Benelux sterling bloc softening to help hold off further devaluation of the pound.

"Now this Westchester merger," Palmer began. "Small potatoes but deep waters, if you follow the mangled metaphor."

Harry Elder squinted at him. "How's that, Woods?"

Palmer shook his head. "Sorry. No, I simply meant that there seem to be wheels within wheels on this one."

"That's never stopped us," another Ubco officer said.

"Damn the torpedoes," Eddie Hagen intoned from the far end of the table. "What's the trouble, Woods?"

Palmer sat back in his chair. The boardroom was exactly the size of his own office. Hagen sat fully thirty feet away from Palmer. Palmer had no need to raise his voice to reach the man, even though there were twenty more feet of empty space behind each of them, as if they were table tennis champions.

"You might remember this one, Eddie," he began. The use of first names was part of the "Midwest" informality Palmer had brought to Ubco. Prior to his arrival at the peak of power, board members had addressed each other by last names, like stuffy clubmen characters in a Peter Arno cartoon. "Dammit, Carruthers, you've gone too far this time."

"Remember Don G?" Palmer asked Hagen.

The former general's eyes crinkled at the outer corners in a good imitation of the traditional steely-blue squint of the airplane pilot. "Don G." He rubbed his chin. "Sicily, 1943. Roger?"

"Wilco. Over and Out." Palmer glanced around the room. "You'll excuse the Air Force chatter, gentlemen. This People's situation seems to be all tangled up with Sicilian gentlemen."

Harry Elder sat forward suddenly. "Mafia?"

Palmer made a negligent gesture with one hand. "I don't believe that's an accurate label. But you're on the right wavelength."

"I'll be damned," a senior vice-president named Phipps said. "This is the second case this month of these people infiltrating a bank. At the ABA convention a fellow from San Francisco was telling me about a take-over in Denver or Salt Lake City, I can't remember which."

"It has to be more than the second case," Palmer said. "I think it's been going on for a decade or so. It's simply the second case you've heard of in the last month."

"I'll be damned," Phipps repeated.

"Well," another senior vice-president said, "that washes out the merger."

"Does it?" Palmer asked.

"Woods," Tim Carewe began in his prim, almost effeminate New England accent, "you shew-uh-ly cahn't go through with it."

"Can't I?"

"What's the point of it?" Harry Elder demanded. "We had a commitment, true enough. But this cancels any good faith in the deal. It leaves us clear to renege."

"Should we?"

"Is there any doubt?" Edde Hagen asked. "What is there about this bank that makes it worth the kind of headache we'll buy?"

Palmer was silent for a moment, listening to various members of the committee murmuring to each other. Then he cleared his throat. "You forget that what I believe to be the case about this bank can't be proved, not even in court, presuming we'd be foolish enough to want to take it into court. So there's no case of broken faith if we can't prove broken faith. Secondly, we do have a commitment, and I believe we will cause more harm than we avoid if we renege on it. Unless someone here can show me a way to renege without seeming to."

"You're not really suggesting we go through with it?" Hagen asked.

"I'm flatly stating that unless we have a graceful way of bowing out, we must go through with it."

"Find something wrong with the bank's audit," Tim Carewe suggested.

Palmer shook his head. "That would surely start a run on the People's Bank. We can't be responsible for that."

"Refuse to give them representation on the board," Phipps offered.

"They hardly merit it now," Palmer countered. "I don't think they're expecting a seat to begin with. So not getting it wouldn't put their nose out of joint."

"Refuse to take most of their loan portfolio," Harry Elder said. "Claim it's too marginal a packet of paper to accept."

"Won't work. We've served as their correspondent bank for some time. Why do we suddenly pretend to turn up our noses at loans we used to accept?"

The men around the table were silent now. Finally Eddie Hagen sighed unhappily. "How can we guarantee these Sicilian gentlemen don't gum up the works once People's Bank is part of Ubco?"

"Eternal vigilance?" Palmer suggested.

"Shit on that," Hagen said, grinning. Phipps and Tim Carewe winced. "We have enough trouble running this outfit as it is."

"I wonder," Palmer began, then stopped. "Can anyone tell me something?" He stopped again, struck by the idea and unable to put it into words for a moment. "Let me put it to you this way," he began again. "What exactly are we afraid of here?"

Tim Carewe's face wrinkled with disdain. "Really, Woods, I'd hardly expect to hear such a question in this room. These men are crooks. It's as simple as that."

"More than that," Phipps said, "they are known to resort to violence. Even in their legitimate enterprises – and we know how many thousands of those they've gotten into – they are never far removed from the blackjack or the pistol."

Palmer glanced at the rest of the executive committee. "Gentlemen, can I hear from a few more of you? The question is: What are we afraid of here?" No one volunteered. "Eddie?" Palmer prodded.

Hagen shrugged. "Skip me while I think about it. Come back to me after a few more people have had their say."

"Nobody seems willing to talk. Harry?"

Elder cleared his hoarse throat. "It's one of your trick questions, Woods. I don't know what the trick is, but I smell the style of it. Anyway, for what it's worth, I'll be the first to admit I don't really know what we're afraid of here. These people have a bad reputation, but we do business with people just as bad. We all know that. We've financed many a stock grab in a proxy fight. We've had many a personal note go bad from people who belonged to the right clubs and went to the right schools. I don't have to tell you what business is these days. And these Sicilian gentlemen, as you call them, play the game as well as anybody else."

"So you're saying we should ignore the issue and expedite the merger?"

"I did not say that." Harry Elder's voice went raspy in its lower registers. "The minutes are not going to show that Harry Elder said we should let the Mafia into Ubco. But I'm admitting that I just don't know what there is to be afraid of. Maybe one of you could tell me. Until you do, I'm running only on intuition. Woods here," he added with broad sarcasm, "would call my intuition plain, ordinary prejudice. Maybe it is. And maybe it isn't."

"A firm, forthright stand," Palmer commented. "Barney?"

Kinch sniffed abruptly, as if Palmer had pinched him. "Woods, what I know about these things you could put in your eye. I may have dealt with this type of person now and then. There's never any way of knowing. Out in our radar-assembly plant in Colorado we had a hell of a union problem till I met with a man somebody said could help me. For fifty thousand in cash, he cured my union trouble. And you remember that metal-tubing shortage we had all up and down the Eastern seaboard last fall? My missile plants were hurting. Even my office-machine factories needed bar and sheeting. Well, a man came to me and asked me if I cared where I got it as long as it was up to standard. I said 'Hell, no,' and he delivered within seventy-two hours. It was standard stuff with all the labels off. I assumed it was hijacked goods, of course, like the Christmas booze we get at half price. I mean, my metallurgy and electronics divisions alone buy anywhere from three to five hundred cases of gift-wrapped booze in December. And my vehicle and ground support firms do, too. You never saw such thirsty Congressmen and mayors and union business agents and what have you. At half price, can you picture what we save on holiday booze? The stuff is the real thing, original bottles and labels, even original gift wrapping. And when it comes to entertaining, we support half the hotels in Las Vegas and the Bahamas. So what I mean is, I may have dealt with these folks now and then, but I have nothing much to add in the way of an opinion. They're just businessmen doing business, as far as I can see. They supply what we want. Just the way we supply what others want."

Palmer let the words die away for a long moment. "For a nonexpert, Barney, you're a lot more knowledgeable than any of us, Eddie, have you stopped mulling it over?"

Hagan looked unhappy. "I had no idea Barney's people were as involved as all that. I suppose my people are, too, since we're in similar lines of work. But that shouldn't decide it for us. I mean, it's like screwing a nymph. Everybody does it, but that doesn't mean it's smart to marry her."

"You're making a distinction, then."

"Whatever that means, yes." Hagen stared belligerently across the length of the table at Palmer. "I am making a distinction, if you will, between the way I do business and the way the Syndicate does business. Barney may not see the difference, but I do."

"Bravo." Palmer smiled at his old commander. "Tell us, Eddie, what is the distinction?"

"Well," Hagen stopped and rubbed the crew-cut gray hair over his right ear. "Woods, you're going to force me to use words like *class* and *breeding*. But I don't at all mind using them, even at the risk of sounding like a real reactionary. The fact is, these people are low-end product. They're at the low end of the breeding process, damn it, with ideas just one remove from the zoo or the swamp. I hate to sound like a man who hates Italians. God knows I employ plenty of them. Two of my research V.P.s are Italian boys. But they're the high-end product. Why, they don't even speak Italian."

Palmer nodded. "There's a V.P. for new business at People's Bank. He's a West Point graduate, and he holds an M.B.A. from the University of Chicago. I personally saw him run that pigskin thirty-seven yards against the Middies and win the game for Army. He's tall, good-looking, well-spoken and bright as hell. And he's married to the daughter of the biggest Mafioso in the East. Or the second biggest. The first is his wife's grandfather. Don G.," he added, nodding at Hagen.

"Christ."

"Yes, indeed."

"To think," Hagen mused, "you could have wiped out that little old wop the way you'd step on a cockroach."

"These weren't my orders."

Harry Elder cleared his rasping throat again. "Is this a private nostalgia session or will you let the rest of us in on it?"

Hagen's face had gone scarlet. "Those weren't my orders either, Woods. I was only a chicken colonel in those days, and I took my orders the same as you did."

"I know." Palmer got to his feet. "It's getting late, and we all have work to attend to before lunch. I suppose we can table this till the next committee meeting, but I'd like to get your okay to refer it to the action panel, in case we have to move fast before the next regular meeting."

There was a murmur of agreement. Palmer knew that anything this thorny the board would be happier passing to the action panel, a group of three men empowered to act between board meetings on any matter specifically entrusted to it by the board. It was a way, Palmer knew, of the board passing the buck. As such, they welcomed it.

"So move," Eddie Hagen said.

He most of all Palmer thought, was willing to unload the responsibility. The action board was made up entirely of inside directors – Palmer himself, Harry Elder and Walker Phipps.

"Second," Tim Carewe said.

"I favor?" Palmer asked and listened to the chorus of ayes. "Opposed?" He let a long moment of silence pass. "Passed. Now a move for adjournment?"

"So move," Eddie Hagen said, getting to his feet. He seemed, to Palmer, to want to get out of there and forget the whole thing as quickly as possible.

"Second," Harry Elder said in his husky voice.

As everyone rose, Palmer muttered "Meeting adjourned." Then to Eddie Hagen, "Got a second?"

But Brigadier General Hagen had left the room.

60

Tony Fish felt a little better today. He knew from his informants within the Klaman Company that he was beginning to succeed.

He sat in his plain, anonymous office at Downtown Bond and Mortgage and checked through a packet of three-by-five-inch file cards. His son, Ben, had taught him the value of file cards. As Ben had explained it, "A person can have good ideas but organize them badly." Or something. But if you put one idea on each card, you could keep shuffling the ideas until they worked into a sequence that made some kind of sense.

For the past weeks, Tony Fish had been working on Harry Klaman's unfinished Lexington Avenue site the way a boxer works on the bleeding eye of an opponent. Tony's single aim was to make Harry bleed a little more profusely on Lexington than almost anywhere else in the tristate area where he did business, because it was at the Lexington Avenue showcase that all the world could see the upcoming downfall of Harry Klaman.

Tony sorted the cards, removing from the packet the dozen or so having to do with Harry's suppliers.

He laid aside immediately the masonry suppliers and the companies that sold Harry conduit and wiring, receptacles, switches, sockets, boxes and the rest of his electrical gear. All were owned by Vinnie Big one way or another and had, of course, cut off Harry's credit weeks before.

Finito. Tony Fish laid on top of these sure-shot cards several more that had always proved cooperative. These included cards for some of the craft unions on which Harry very much depended at all stages of construction. Tony Fish had talked to one local's business agent a few days before, and the business agent had invoked a little-known clause in the bylaws calling for a "quorum shop." A certain number of his union members had to be employed on a job, or all walked off. This effectively prevented Sal Geraci from using skeleton crews to keep even a little of the work going. Tony Fish laid these cards on the sure-shot pile.

He then picked up and thought about a card on which he had written the name of Ben's bank up in Westchester. He knew the lifeline of cash on which Harry Klaman depended had been cut off at the source weeks before. But as he placed this card with the other certainties, he reminded himself to telephone Ben and make certain no one at the bank had gone suddenly crazy enough to let Klaman take out any more cash.

The rest of the cards in the packet represented to Tony Fish what nuclear devices must mean to the Chiefs of Staff. They were ultimate weapons in the sense that if used, Harry would never fully recover from their effects.

A group of four cards were clipped together, each bearing the name of a friendly deputy in a city building department. This group alone could bring any construction to a total standstill within a week's time by finding imperfections in surveys, permits, titles, easements, deeds, clearances and the like.

A second pile of cards represented cooperative officials in charge of water supply, gas and electricity whose inspectors, properly briefed, could find enough violations to fill several citation books. To these groups Tony Fish now added one more card listing the name of a friend in the Fire Department who could close down any construction – or any completed building – in a matter of hours.

Tony frowned as he fanned out this subpacket of devoted municipal servants. If left to his own devices, Tony would always choose to kill a fly by smashing it with a Mack truck. But he knew how finicky Vinnie Big could be with what he considered thoughtless, unnecessary overkill.

Vinnie usually tried, if possible, to send just a little less pressure to do the job than prudence dictated. Vinnie would say: "You ever keep a dog or a cat? Underfeed them a little, just a little, and they obey real good. And they look better for it, too. That's the way it is with people. If you move them with a little less muscle than you figured to need, it's all gravy. Next time you can economize a little more on the pressure. One day, you don't even need muscle. You just wink, and they get down and lick. So, why overpressure? It gets people mad at you. And besides, it's bad business."

Tony Fish unfanned the cards and set them to one side. Only two cards were left, the kind Vinnie almost never let him use. One was the best take-out team in the East, a torch, a driver and a blanket man who could take out anything, even an unfinished concrete pile that didn't look as if it had anything on it to burn.

The other was what Tony's father used to call a pineapple man. He made everything himself out of untraceable ingredients – nitric acid from a marble works in Vermont, commercial glycerin from a dozen drugstores scattered over New York State, fuller's earth he dug himself in Tennessee and carried up north in gunnysacks in the trunk of his car. He could wire up a dollar-ninety-eight drugstore alarm clock, two D-cell batteries and his own home-poured dynamite, each stick wrapped in the Sunday roto section of the *Daily News*, take out the ground floor of Grand Central Station at high noon and be three states away when it went.

Tony Fish sighed nostalgically. The real artists weren't appreciated anymore. Vinnie Big had no use for these old-time *artigianos*. Him, with all his complaints about young kids like Ben being too much Americanized, even Vinnie Big himself had no use for the old ways anymore.

It was all business now, Tony lamented, all pressure, all a lot of frigging around with lines of credit and union contracts and trucking agreements and the like. Everybody had to be a lawyer or an accountant these days. And a good pineapple man was worth shit.

He shuffled together the arsonist, the demolition man and the covey of City Hall quail and put them to one side. Harry Klaman was starting to bend with just the steady business-type pressure currently being applied. In a day or two, no more, Tony would report to Vinnie that Klaman was ready for reaping.

He tore the cards into little pieces, dumped them in a large ashtray and set them afire.

61

The house on Morton Street was around the corner from the apartment on Bedford where Kimberley lived. Edith had been on her way to Kimberley's when she had seen the moving truck pulled up in front of the Morton Street location.

The block itself, she felt, was charming. Like St. Luke's below it and Commerce above, it was a block with a kink in it. On its way from Seventh Avenue to Hudson, it took a 40-degree turn in the middle that made it impossible to see one end of the block from the other.

And it had trees, great tall ones, five storeys high, bursting with the pale green buds and leaflets of late March.

In all her life, Edith Edison Palmer had never before barged

258

into a strange apartment house. Now she pushed past the moving men to accost the squat, gray-haired building superintendent.

No, there was no apartment available. No, the one being vacated was already spoken for. Well (business of twenties being folded twice in Edith's hand), that is, he believed it was spoken for. He wasn't completely (more business) certain. Finally Edith was allowed to inspect it.

The super had called it a two-and-a-half. It had in fact, a small living room and an infinitesimal bedroom, barely big enough for a double bed. But it also had a wood-burning fireplace and a view south through the topmost tree branches. The super gave her a day to make up her mind.

"What do you mean, move in?" Kimberley asked at noon. She had invited him to walk on Morton Street and was now showing him through the apartment while she unwrapped sandwiches and handed him a can of beer. They sat down on the floor and smiled at each other.

"You know. I can't be down here all the time," she explained. "Certainly not at night, or not too often, that is. You could be sort of caretaker."

"Batcrap." His pale gray eyes grew wary, and she realized that caretaker was the wrong word.

"I don't mean that way. I mean, well, you can't do any of your own work in that Bedford Street place. There's no room there, and you certainly don't work in that Harlem storefront. Not the times I've visited you there. So consider it the loan of a studio not too far from NYU."

"With hot and cold running bankers' wives."

"I seem to run more hot than cold."

He stretched out his leg. They were sitting side by side on the floor with their backs supported by a wall. Now he ran the toe of his loafer up her bare leg. "You seem to want to own me body and soul, don't you?"

"Nonsense."

He shook his head, and the noon sunlight sparkled slightly in his tightly curled hair. "No. First you buy me Operation Boost for a year. Now you buy me a Village studio. And you don't ask anything in return except regular servicing. It's too much. It's a puberty fantasy. Tell me the truth: aren't you too much, baby?"

He failed to smile, and Edith realized that she had somehow pushed too far into his life, farther than he was ready to let her

259

go now, perhaps farther than he would permit anyone ever to advance.

But surely, she thought, he had to understand how she felt in all this, how uncalculating she was, how inexperienced. "Don't treat me that way," she said then. "I'm not a nympho, and you're not my gigolo."

He nodded. "Okay. That's what we're not. What is it we are?"

Edith sighed. "Two people attracted to each other. Old enough to cut out the courtship dance. Clearheaded enough to know that money means something, even in matters of the heart. And God knows, I have money."

"Matters of the heart." He spoke the words dully, and they seemed to sink into the uncarpeted floor with a faint clatter, as of juggling slabs of lead.

Edith was horrified to feel her eyes grow moist. "Yes, of the heart. Of my heart, anyway."

He glanced sideways at her, then examined his loafers at great length. "What about yours?" she asked then.

He shrugged. "I've had no news from that quarter in years. The only message I get is that this is too good to last. Don't you hear that from your heart?"

"N-no." Edith tried to keep her voice firm. A dangerous bubble of emotion was shaking it from inside. "My God," she said then, the words starting to boil over, "if you th –"

She cut herself short with some effort and waited until she could control her voice. Finally, in a lower, slower tone: "It isn't as if we're getting married. This isn't anything more than two people doing what they have found it pleasant to do. Why can't it last?"

"If that's all it was, I'd agree."

He stood up and went to the window. It opened onto a fire-escape landing. Kimberley shoved the window wide open and sat on the sill, one leg outside the apartment. Several times Edith started to say something, but each time she was able to control herself until eventually Kimberley began to talk about it again.

"It's the unlikely combination that's one thing against longevity. It's the type of person you are and the type I am, for another bad thing. I mean you, of all people, are not the roll-in-the-hay type. And I am very much a play-the-field guy. And for a third thing, we're politically as unsuited to each other as it's possible to be. If we argued about nothing else, we'd fight all the time about that."

"Politics?" she asked, her voice sounding faintly derisive.

"Politics. The war. Everything. I mean" – he turned toward her and gestured in short jabs, as if hacking away clay from a statue – "it's bad enough that a devoted wife and mother betrays her whole family for a black cocksman who, God forbid, teaches art. But to betray her class, too? To turn her back on the very forces in society that have nurtured her?"

"God, that is such ... such batcrap!" Edith exploded.

Kimberley laughed delightedly. "Learning, learning."

"But it is. What have I got to do with these vague forces of yours, these antagonists in the class struggle? I've told you I've changed about the war. You know I'm against it now."

"But you don't know why, honey, and you never will. Whereas I have it in my bones and couldn't escape knowing if I wanted to."

"That's nothing but reverse snobbery."

He laughed again. "You're right." Then his face went dead. "So what?"

"What has any of this to do with you living here?"

He shook his head slowly for a long time. "Nobody keeps me. It's fine for you to pay Operation Boost's way. Considering how that money was accumulated, it's fitting that you support a dozen Operation Boosts. But not J. Kimberley, Esq. I support myself in the mangy little ways I know. A lousy living, but it's honest."

Edith watched him for a moment, realizing they had reached an impasse that might not be completely impassable if she changed subjects for a while. "What was that about my not knowing why I was against the war? About my never knowing?"

"Maybe I came on too strong there, but it's mostly so."

"I'm against the war because you are."

He nodded. "Beautiful."

"But it's not as idiotic as it seems. Whatever you support is worth supporting and whatever you hate is worth hating. What's bad ab–?"

"Protect me from the liberal ethic," Kimberley cut in. He got to his feet and walked to the fireplace. He stood without speaking for a moment, gently nudging into line some half-burned logs left by the previous tenant.

"Let me ask you something, baby. You read the newspapers, right?"

261

"Yes."

"Okay." He turned to face her again. "You remember about, oh, a few months ago when college kids were rioting against recruiting on campus by chemical companies?"

"Yes."

"These were companies that made anticivilian horror novelties we use in Vietnam. Remember?"

"Yes."

"It got so bad after a while that the government issued some kind of commendation to these companies to bolster their prestige."

"I remember something of the sort."

"Okay." Kimberley squatted on his hams to bring his face down more on a level with Edith's. "Now this is the part I hope you also remember. One of the companies, after all the fuss was over, popped up in the news with its own statement about everything. Remember? The president of the chairman of the company issued a statement?"

"Ye-es."

"Try to remember. He said something about not feeling any one way or the other, but simply following orders, of providing the materials the government required and therefore of not feeling any guilt whatsoever. For this, the government issued a commendation. Does that ring any bell?"

"Vaguely."

Kimberley hunched forward across the room until he was squatting directly in front of Edith. Their faces were inches apart. "Now for a real feat of memory, baby. Think back twenty years."

"To what?"

"To Nuremburg. To the war-crimes trials. To what we did to fat-cat Kraut industrialists like Krupp. You remember his defense? That he was only providing what the government required, only doing his duty?"

"And we accepted that?"

"Hell, no. We slammed his ass in the pokey. Didn't spring him till Korea, when we needed his help again."

Edith frowned. "So when a company supports somebody else's government, it's a crime. But not if it supports our own government?"

Kimberley shook his head. "You got it backward, Baby. How does a woman as bright as you get life so ass-backward?"

Edith's mouth flattened in a tight line. "You are the sole

custodian of what is right, I take it."

"Easy, now." He rubbed the tip of his nose across hers. "You mean you don't get the idea?"

"If you let me think about it, instead of browbeating me." She smiled at him. "Save me from true believers. They're all the same, left or right."

"Um." Kimberly looked glum for a moment. "You free tonight?"

"Till when?"

"We're picketing a hotel, midtown. From, say, eight to eleven."

"What for?"

"If you're free, I'll explain."

"And if I can't make it, you won't waste time explaining."

'Shee-it! You mighty feisty today, baby," he said in his mock-watermelon accent.

"If I knew what that meant, I'd take umbrage."

"Umbrage?" He got to his feet in a long, smooth movement, went to the spread-out waxed paper and picked up another half sandwich. "I 'splain *feisty*, baby, if you 'splain *umbrage*."

"First you have to explain about Krupp."

He shrugged monumentally. The wind outside the windows made the tiny, pale green leaves shiver slightly, a steady vibration that seemed to make the trees pulsate as Edith watched them.

"Look at it this way," Kimberley said, swallowing a bite of the sandwich. "If we called it a crime for Krupp, how can we issue a commendation for doing the same thing today?"

"But did Krupp do the same thing these chemical companies are doing?"

"No. Krupp made guns and tanks and ammo. Conventional weapons. These chemical companies make jellied gasoline you dump in flaming globs on little kids."

Edith watched the leaves behind his head shudder. "You're not being too objective."

"You're so right. I'm not."

Neither of them spoke for a long moment. He started to take another bite of the sandwich. He stopped suddenly. "What about tonight?"

62

They met by appointment at one of the less run-of-the-mill luncheon places on the periphery of the garment center where some of the younger people gathered. Sean had gotten there first and, being well known to the owner, was able to sit down at a corner banquette for six and monopolize it until Tippy arrived.

Unlike the usual garment-center eating places, which tended to be dull in their decor and old-line Jewish in their cooking, this place had been decorated, Sean knew, by a friend of Augie's, an absolutely darling little fruit who did amusing things with old daguerreotype pictures blown up to mural size.

The menu was more or less the creation of the designer, tending toward the typical faggot food expected in these places campy juxtapositions of ingredients that failed to go together (duckling stuffed with anchovies was one speciality, while another popular entrée was candied bacon rind crumbled over a peanut butter mousse), *outré* methods of serving dishes (steaks broiled in horseradish sauce were cut into square and overlapped in an old-fashioned banana-split boat) and, of course, the divinely mad nomenclature of the menu (string-bean salad with whipped cream was called "Urgent Virgin," while a coffee ice-cream sundae with chocolate sauce was known as a "Big Black Mother").

Sean had nodded to half a dozen refugees from the market, as all of them tended to call the garment center, and had finished one extra-dry martini (listed as a "Miss-ter Sphincter") when he saw Tippy enter and stop cold just inside the doorway as if unable to take another step.

He waved to her and then realized she was not really looking for him. She seemed literally unable to do whatever it was one did after coming inside a place. Finally her glance lifted from the floor in front of her and wavered for a moment before landing on Sean. Her mouth creased in what seemed to be a smile, and she started for the corner banquette.

Sean squinted in the half light, trying to make out what she had done to her face. She was wearing an out-of-date tent dress he had given her, that yellow number she seemed to be attached to. He noticed that it not only looked dated but grimy as well. It seemed to have needed dry cleaning for several months now.

Sean stood up and tried to embrace her, but Tippy side-stepped and gave him a cursory peck on the cheek before she sat down. Her movements were erratic, Sean noticed, seemingly unplanned, as if each gesture or direction had been improvised on the spur of the moment.

"Are you all right, luv?" he asked.

She nodded. "Can I have one of those?"

He gestured to the waiter and ordered two of the martinis. "You look rotten, darling," he said then. "I know it's extremely helpful to tell you this right now, but I mean, after all, what are friends for if not to make you completely miserable?" He took her hand and squeezed it slightly above the table, the way Augie sometimes squeezed his below.

"But I mean, you do look a fright, ducks. What is that dress? And don't tell me you brushed your hair this morning. And whoever put on those lashes for you is a mortal enemy. And—"

"Ah, God, Sean, fuck off, will you?"

He blinked, not so much at the words, but at the vehemence. The Tippy he knew had always had that magnificent throwaway quality with hard words that Sean was quite sure was the exclusive property of the American rich.

He knew Tippy's family had quite a lot of money, although he had never been sure how much of it would eventually come to Tippy, assuming she kept from publicly disgracing herself in the interim. But her casual way with strong language, the way she would tell a person what to do in the most utterly bored way, Sean had always taken as the true sign of an affluent background, a sort of acid test quite like the princess kept awake by a pea.

"I'm telling it like it is, baby," he quoted now, lapsing into some of Augie's jargon. "I'm calling them as I see them, what?"

"I don't need your candor, darling," Tippy said then in a tight voice, as if monitoring every word before she let it out.

"You are in a state."

"Yeah, right." She began to pick at the nail of her left index finger, and before Sean could tell her to stop, she had ripped the nail in a jagged tear that ran diagonally back into the quick.

"Christ," Sean said. He accepted the drinks and shooed away the waiter, then lifted her glass to Tippy's lips and tilted

265

it slightly. "Take long, healing sips."

Tippy yanked her head back. Her teeth rattled on the rim of the glass. "Hands off," she hissed.

Sean put down her drink and looked away. If there was anything he hated more than a scene it was a scene over which he seemed to have little control.

"When I want a drink, I'll pick it up for myself," Tippy went on. "I am not quite yet a basket case, thank you."

"I see."

Sean hoped he had iced the words sufficiently to chill Tippy's bitchy little soul. This girl owed everything to him and seemed to have forgotten all of it. One thing you could say about the faggots, they understood the meaning of friendship and gratitude, at least the ones he knew.

"It's that horrible job," Tippy said then. "Working for that horrible man, answering all those horrible letters from all the mean, nasty, twisted, sick people who listen to him."

"Oh, is that it?" Sean said in a gelid tone. "Funny, the girl who had the job before you seemed quite able to cope with the letters. Only quit to get married. Never a word of how it got her down. You must bring something to those letters, some little thing of your own, luv, some extra little touch of sickliness, eh?"

"Drop dead." Her voice sounded morose and draggy.

"Thank you, ducks. It's about the intellectual level I might have expected. Tell me, pet, how's Ben? The two of you haven't been mucking up my bedsheets for the last few weeks. Gone celibate, have you?"

"He comes to my apartment," she said. "Sean, please stop picking at me, will you? I thought this was going to be a happy lunch."

"I'm not the one who started using foul language."

"No. But you're the one who couldn't wait till I sat down to start telling me how rotten I look. As if I don't know. As if I care."

"I'm sorry." Sean patted her hand. "How is Ben?"

"Jumpy."

"Wifey catching wise?"

Tippy shook her head. "We know someone's shadowing us, both of us. He's outside my apartment when I leave in the morning. Ben's seen someone parked across the street from his bank. There seem to be different people, and it's got Ben jumpy as hell."

"Why doesn't he –" Sean stopped.

"Do what?"

"Nothing. It was a stupid idea."

"What?" she persisted.

"Oh," he gestured embarrassedly, "I thought maybe he could get his father or his father-in-law to take these people off your back, so to speak. But, of course, that's out of the question."

"Any other bright ideas?"

"The wife?"

Tippy thought for a moment. "That was my first thought, but he said no. He said she didn't suspect and even if she did, good Italian girls don't make that kind of trouble for their husbands."

"No, but their fathers might."

"Yeah, right. That was my second thought," Tippy admitted. "But Ben said absolutely not. It wasn't Vinnie Big's style. And it wasn't his wife style to go crying to her father."

"He's probably right. Then who?"

"I had the idea it might be somebody who's after Billy Beanbag."

"What?" Sean turned to stare at her.

"He has enemies. And even his friends are pretty scary. There's one who sends him absolutely revolting little love gifts."

Sean patted her hand again. "Forget Beanbag. What about an ex-boyfriend of yours?"

"Or one of Ben's ex-girlfriends? I understand you used to find plenty for him."

"That was before you, luv."

She picked up her drink and sipped it. Sean noticed that half of it was gone within less than a minute.

"I sometimes wonder," Tippy said then in a low, faraway tone, as if speaking neither to Sean nor to herself but to someone unseen in another room or at the end of an imaginary telephone line. "I wonder whether it's not something we're imagining. It's been so wild between us. I've never gone as far with a man as I have with Ben. I don't think I ever will. But there's something we do to each other. We bring out the absolute bottom worst and it's ... like a ... it's like a purge. All the rottenness comes out. We act it out against each other, and afterward there's such peace."

Sean waited for her to continue. He had no fully accurate idea of what she was talking about, but on several occasions he

267

had found streaks of blood or excrement on the sheets. He had been disgusted and terribly aroused by what he had found. He had an idea of what Tippy's apartment must look like at this point.

When she failed to go on, he looked at her more closely. The skin under her eyes had gone faintly brownish in places, and there seemed to be too much white around her irises.

"You know, ducks," he said then, "if I'd thought it was going to get this serious, I'd've warned both of you long ago. You're the wrong people for a deep affair."

She turned to him. Her eyes had gone moist, and now her eye shadow was beginning to streak very faintly. "How would you know that?" she asked. "Have you ever had a deep relationship in your entire life?"

"Except with myself? No."

She smiled slightly, unwillingly. "Is that supposed to be profound?"

"Sweetheart," Sean began, "we are living in extremely rotten times. Everything's much worse than it used to be. Ask anyone. Ask anyone at all. And it's got so bad, you know, that it's a major feat just to understand and relate to your own sweet, sick self. I don't even try to go beyond that, except as tentatively as one can."

"Augie would adore hearing that."

"We're about to be partners, did I tell you?" Sean perked up for a moment, and his reddish-blond elf locks seemed to radiate electricity. "I don't mind relating that way. I don't even mind Augie thinking we have an affair going. It makes him feel more secure to think that. But I never fool myself about it, luv, and neither should people like you or Ben."

Tippy watched him for a long moment. "God, Sean, you know, you're right. It's no fun feeling like this. I never felt this way with any of the others. Yeah, right. But everybody can't be the way we are, can they?"

"I think we're the thin edge of the wedge," he said. "I think we're today what everyone will be in the next generation. And their only hope is to see it clearly and accept it. That was one thing Dr. Apfelshpein did for me. I hate the old fart for his middle-class Hebraic values. But talking to him absolutely crystallized my feelings about it all. That's why I haven't gone to him in weeks now. I don't need the guilts he was trying to make me feel. I don't need any guilts at all."

"Maybe I ought to see him. Or someone like him."

Sean shook his head so violently his elf locks were disarranged. Feeling them out of place, he soothed them back with his fingertips as he talked. "Can you imagine what a shrink would do with that whole SM bag you and Ben have?"

"What's SM?"

"Sadomasochistic. About as in as one can get these days." Tippy's cheeks reddened very slightly, Sean saw, but not enough to qualify as a true blush. "I shouldn't have told you that."

"Why not? We all have these absolutely foul needs. You've simply had the courage to do something about them. I think it's very brave and very – oh, what shall I say?" His hands cupped around air, trying to trap the word. "So very pure, if you take my meaning. Classically pure. And the way you express yourself. I mean, to say you feel purged. Simply smashing."

"But that's just the way I feel afterward."

"Quite so. And then?"

She frowned. "And then?"

"And afterward," Sean prompted her, "after these foul needs are purged. Then what?"

She sighed. "Then..." Her voice died away.

"Then you purge them all over again next time," Sean supplied. "Only each time you have to go a bit farther to get the same effect?"

She sipped her drink and said nothing.

63

Casa Coppola was always crowded for lunch. It's flocked red wallpaper reflected a healthy glow of pride and satiety onto the faces of those seated at its many tables. Despite their forlorn expressions of deprivation, even those waiting in line for tables seemed in the ruddy glow of the place to have found a modicum of happiness.

When Ben Fischetti arrived at one fifteen, about half a dozen couples stood beside the velvet rope, while a few single men sat at the bar, waiting for the captain to signal them that a table had become available.

At the prices Casa Coppola charged, it had no need to cram tables too closely together. Nevertheless, the restaurant was a big place with ample room for at least fifty tables. Forty-nine had been occupied since half past twelve. Some of those forty-nine were now emptying. The fiftieth table, a corner one at the back of the room, had been empty all along. The captain ushered Ben directly there, and two waiters materialized at once.

"*Si, signore*, a cocktail?"

Ben waved the captain away, but the man refused to leave. "Il Don Vincenzo arrives soon?"

"I'm early," Ben explained. "He'll be here."

"How about a cocktail?"

Ben found the man's accent irritating. He knew this particular captain to be a nephew of the owner. The captain had lived nearly all his life in the United States. Yet he persisted in calling it a "coke tel."

This might be the stuff to impress the squares, who required broken English with their pasta. But it was insulting to use it on Vinnie Big's son-in-law.

Ben succeeded in getting the captain and both waiters not only to quit the immediate area but to stop darting back to him at his slightest move, proffering matches, water, bread, butter, wine and inevitable coke-tel.

It amused Ben to know that most of the diners were mystified by the performance. That meant they would be downright flabbergasted at the show his father-in-law and Rocco Sgroi would trigger off when they arrived. It tickled Ben to be able to pooh-pooh the pompous old bastard and at the same time warm himself in the fierce glow he generated wherever he went. Captains, bartenders, waiters, busboys, cops, clerks in the posher stores, newspaper people of a certain kind, in fact nearly anyone who recognized Vinnie Big immediately paid him the servile respect usually reserved in the old days for Morgans, Mellons and Rockefellers.

Ben reflected now that these early robber barons had nothing on old Vinnie and his mysterious, will-o'-the-wisp father, Don Girolamo. The key to everything was family, wasn't it?

The Goulds, Astors, Vanderbilts and all the rest looted and raped the country and set up immense dynastic networks of interlocking family responsibility. As the old hard-skinned founding fathers, the original thieves, died out, their sons and grandsons took over the business of whitewashing the family escutcheon. And there was all the money anyone needed for the job. By the time the grandsons assumed control, the old

270

thieves had been safely ensconced in the pantheon of national heroes.

Well, Ben thought, *autres temps, autres moeurs*. And other families, too. It was about time new thieves set up some new dynasties.

He sensed rather than saw the arrival of his father-in-law. There was a flurry of activity around the doorway, as of a fox in a henhouse. A few of the hard-eyed loungers at the bar straightened up and looked more presentable. Some of the diners – not too many in this predominantly expense-account advertising-man crowd – recognized the old gent from the few dated photos the newspapers used.

Ben smiled slightly. The newspapers' approach to the family's affairs was always historical, rather than journalistic. Since virtually nothing new had been uncovered in many years and what had rarely fit into place with what had gone on before, newspaper accounts of a major slaying, narcotics, roundup or exposé of municipal corruption tended to rehash the same bits of information in their usual nonlinear relationships. The same photographs were printed, the same names tentatively linked with the same "reputedly" and "allegedly" verbiage. One started reading these accounts, tricked by the headlines into expecting something substantial and new. One finished the articles feeling like a dog snapping at a fly in mid-air and missing it.

"*Buon giorno*," Ben said, getting to his feet.

Vinnie and Rocco took seats on either side of Ben.

"Rocky," Ben said, nodding.

"Benny." They shook hands, and it was understood that the handshake took the place of Ben's more formal greeting of his father-in-law. By protocol he would have had to kiss his hand, but it was understood that in this place at this time, such a move would have been ill-advised.

Ben sat down. He often wondered what kind of tail his dear father-in-law carried around with him, whether indeed an army of F.B.I. and local police, to say nothing of T-men, were not at this moment standing unobtrusively around in the foyer or outside the entrance, waiting, waiting.

No one had ever told him in so many words, nor would they ever, but Ben had long suspected that his father-in-law's fairly innocuous police record, his open manner of being seen all over town, his availability to virtually anyone, meant that he was some kind of figurehead or front man. The real movers

271

and doers in the family, Ben suspected, were much shyer and more retiring. Some led hermitlike existences in nurseries. Other moved from place to place. But open, obvious ones like Don Vincenzo could not, he felt, be entirely for real.

Ben wondered how much of the slim record the authorities had on Vinnie Big was available to someone like this Woods Palmer, who ran Ubco. It was one thing to be known to the police, not for anything criminal but simply on the strength of family association. It was another for this association to get noised about in Wasp circles like those in which Palmer and the rest of the Ubco crew circulated.

It was well known, Ben realized, that like the founding thieves, the banking community was largely white Anglo-Saxon Protestant, at least among the biggest banks. They had their Irish and Italian officers, their occasional Jew and even a Negro or two on the lower officer echelons. But the directors and the top executives were mostly pure Wasp. Ben wondered what a Wasp like Palmer would make of the man who had married Vinnie Big's daughter.

"You always sit there like a dummy?" Vinnie Big asked.

"Sorry."

"Is that all they teach you in those fancy schools? How to say 'Sorry' and how to stall around and sit there like a dummy?"

Ben turned to Rocco. "What brought this on?"

"Your father-in-law, he's getting impatient, Benny." Rocco's eyes, nowhere as flat or as awesome as Vinnie Big's, tried to indicate impatience with a flash of indignation. "This merger, it's dragging on too long."

"It's gone sour," Vinnie Big said.

The waiters arrived with an immense platter of red and green peppers, laced with anchovies and swimming in oil and vinegar. They quickly transferred quantities of this appetizer to each man's plate. When one ate with Vinnie Big, Ben reflected, one had no choice of food. Casa Coppola and a half dozen similar places in the tristate area knew exactly what Don Vincenzo liked and how he wanted it prepared. As he entered a place, whether they were expecting him or not, Rocco had only to whisper a word to the owner or captain and the proper dishes were forthcoming.

"It's gone sour because you and your Westchester friends've been dogging it," Vinnie Big went on. Ben watched a tiny tip of anchovy flutter between his lips, as if struggling to get out of

272

his mouth. The big, square, white teeth bit down and ended the struggle.

"It's the other way around," Ben explained. "We're like the bride at the church. These Ubco people are keeping us waiting on the steps."

"Yes?" Vinnie Big's flat blue eyes flashed disgust.

"Your father-in-law," Rocco Sgroi began in a slow, patient voice, "he's got a lot of plans for you. They depend on the merger going through."

"They depend on my being an officer of Ubco," Ben translated.

"You wanna put it that way, yes."

"And if the merger doesn't go through?"

"Then," Vinnie Big interrupted heavily, "your father-in-law has no plans for you at all. Get it?"

Ben watched Don Vincenzo summon the waiters with a wave of his left hand and then, with both hands, indicate that the antipasto be made to disappear. The instant the platter and individual plates were removed, the captain arrived, pushing a small serving cart on which a chafing-dish stand waited, its blue alcohol flame flickering.

"Fettucini Biglioto," the captain announced with a flunky's ingratiating smile, his eyes darting to Don Vincenzo Biglioto's face some sign of approval.

As he had several times before, Ben silently watched the ritual of making his father-in-law's own personal fettucini. The tin-lined copper pan on the blue flame had grown hot enough so that when the captain dropped six pats of butter into it, they sizzled and melted at once. He spooned a quantity of fresh white ricotta cheese into the pan and gave it a stir to start its melting.

Holding his hands over the pan, palms pressed together in an attitude of prayer, he rubbed back and forth, sending a brownish shower of crisp bacon crumbs into the pan, quickly followed by oregano chafed into shreds the same way. The ricotta was already beginning to bubble as he stirred in a heaping tablespoon of Parmesan cheese.

Suddenly with a great flourish, he lifted the sauce and poured it into a larger copper pan, which then replaced it over the flame. This pan contained fettucini fresh from a kitchen pot, boiled *al dénte* european style, twice as chewy as *al dénte* American style.

The captain swirled the sauce and noodles together for

another brief moment and then quickly transferred the Fettucini Biglioto to three dishes, which the waiters placed before Don Vincenzo, Rocco and Ben.

Once the three of them began eating, there was an end to talk. People at nearby tables who had watched the entire performance – a rarity at Casa Coppola, since almost all dishes were brought prepared from the kitchen – now returned to eating their own mundane and undramatic victuals.

"Just what do you have in mind for me as an Ubco officer?" Ben asked then.

"Eat," Vinnie Big commanded.

"It's important for me to know."

"When it's important for me to tell you, you'll know."

They ate on, Ben using a spoon to help twirl the fettucini firmly on his fork, Don Vincenzo and Rocco preferring the old country method, using the fork alone.

"I'm going to see Palmer tonight," Ben said then.

Rocco eyed him with veiled distaste. "You're talking. You're not eating."

"We're both going to be at the same savings-bank dinner tonight."

"Eat," Ben's father-in-law growled.

64

The executive dining room on the top floor of Ubco's Fifth Avenue headquarters was deserted at two o'clock, when Palmer entered the room.

He had deliberately postponed his lunch so that any of the officers who normally ate there would have left. He reckoned without Harry Elder, however, who apparently had stayed on at the bank after the director's meeting.

"Harry," Palmer's voice was pitched at a civil level, but only barely.

"Woods." Elder's husky voice had the same damn-I-thought-I'd-be-alone note to it.

The young waitress in the all-white nurse's uniform was an employee of a nearby restaurant which catered the daily lunches. It was Palmer's secretary, Miss Czermat, who at about half past eleven each day made a quick telephone canvass of the two dozen men who had high enough rank to use the executive dining room. She would then inform the restaurant how many lunches to prepare.

Since neither Palmer nor Elder had told Miss Czermat they were using the dining room on this day, the only food the waitress could find for them was the extra lunch her management required her to bring for such emergencies. Instead of explaining the problem, she silently divided the steak in two, put half the baked potato on each plate, juggled the salad into two bowls and threw together a heaping bowl of leftover rolls and bread as a kind of makeweight.

It was symptomatic of the way both men felt that they wearily accepted this obvious improvisation. They sat without speaking – the chief executive officer of one of the largest private banks in the world and one of his directors – and slowly munched their scant, lukewarm, leftover food.

"Christ, Woods," Elder said at last, "the food was never this bad when I worked here full time."

Palmer nodded. "They're very big on bread, though."

Elder's wheezy laugh sounded like the noise a toy dog makes when its belly is squeezed. He pushed his plate away and sipped coffee. "At least the coffee's hot. Remind me not to hang around after director's meetings anymore. I could get a better launch at the Automat."

"Much better." Palmer sipped his coffee. "Why did you hang around?"

Elder shrugged. "No reason. I get kind of lonesome for this place. I've been hanging around this corner of Fifth Avenue for nearly forty years now. Started in the big boom after World War I, when the old building was still here. I ... well, you know what it's like. I mean, you're not a man for hobbies, either. The job's the thing. And when you retire, it's ... a hell of an adjustment."

"Hobbies?" Palmer watched him closely, guardedly over the rim of his cup. "Who says I'm not a man for hobbies? My biggest hobby is trying to figure out what my own board wants me to do."

"That was a pretty crappy meeting, wasn't it?"

"We'd still be at it, getting nowhere if I hadn't bucked the merger along to the action committee."

Elder shook his head slowly. "You were asking too many tough questions in there, Woods. And what was that private little flare-up between you and General Hagen?"

"A bit of ancient history that got stuck in my craw." Palmer put down his coffee and stared aimlessly around the empty

275

room. The Chagall on the far wall showed a sinister gentleman with long sideburns about to apply a curved knife to the throat of a goat.

"It didn't help matters, hearing the two of you squabble that way."

"You knew Eddie was my commanding officer during the war?"

"No."

"We had special jobs in Intelligence. He would send me on what they called T-Force missions, tactical sweeps. usually ahead of or up with the advancing main force. We'd sweep into somewhere, pull off whatever we were supposed to do – mainly snatch secret documents or V.I.P.s – and lam out fast. This one mission was in Sicily. Do you remember the situation there?"

"You're asking too much of my memory."

Palmer signaled the waitress for more coffee and waited till she had left the room. "Chaos. The Germans were losing, and we were looking for local help. Mussolini had been down on the Mafia, you know. He hated any secret societies. They impaired the monolithic quality of the Fascist state. He had almost wiped out the last of the Mafiosi, all except Mr. Big and his group."

Elder nodded. "I remember. We threw in with the Mafia figuring them to be anti-Fascist."

"We saved them from extinction, put them back on their feet, and in a few years they had Sicily by the jugular again." Palmer swallowed his coffee and stood up. "And you're looking at the man who saved Mr. Big from being killed by the partisans. And Hagen was the man who sent me on that mission. Neat?"

"This Mr. Big . . ." Elder's rough voice died away.

"Now an ancient gentleman named Don Girolamo Biglioto. It's his son, Vincenzo, who's known as Vinnie Big in these parts."

Elder nodded. "And it's Big's son-in-law you were talking about, the kid at People's Bank."

Palmer began pacing. He stopped for a moment in front of the Chagall, then moved on to a giant Manet of the Water Lilies period. "What I think about constantly now, but never once gave a thought to in all these years until we started this merger, is why Hagen gave those orders."

"He said he didn't know."

Palmer resumed walking. He had covered two sides of the room and was passing the door to the kitchen. "I believe him. Or rather, I believe he's never bothered to find out why. It's not important to him. And now, when he's faced here at Ubco with a kind of spin-off of his original orders, he gets huffy and walks out before I can question him."

Elder laughed again. "There I can't blame him. You have the goddamnedest method of boring in on a man with the goddamnedest questions."

"Harry, listen."

Palmer had stopped his pacing at almost the dead center of the room. He stood near the big table where Harry Elder sat, and his eyes were turned on Elder with sudden intensity.

"Yes, Woods."

"Listen to me a moment." Palmer's mouth pressed into a tight line as he tried to formulate his thoughts more carefully. "There are certain questions I have to ask. I don't like them any more than you or Hagen do. But the nature of this merger, the echoes of it, the nuances or some damned thing, seem to make it necessary for me to know certain answers. And the opener is still the same as I asked this morning. What are we afraid of in dealing with these people?" He caught sight of himself in the sideboard mirror.

Elder gestured vaguely. "Well, nothing really, except –"

"You're missing my point. I'm not expressing it properly." Palmer saw that his own face seemed drained of blood. The hollows under his cheeks looked vaguely gray, and his light eyes seemed surrounded by darkness.

"Let me put it another way," he went on. "We fear the unknown. We fear the hostile. But what is there about these people to fear? Are they so unknown? Barney Kinch seems to know all about them and use them to good advantage at that. Are they hostile to us? No one's come up with that kind of evidence. But Harry, it all boils down to a basic question."

The older man got to his feet heavily, as if carrying a lot more weight than he normally did. He eyed Palmer across the table and his round head, with its crew-cut white fuzz, bobbed slowly up and down.

"I know, Woods." He sighed and nodded once more, vehemently. "It all boils down to the question of whether there's any real difference between them and us."

Palmer's glance seemed hooded. He turned away from Elder. "And don't think the rest of them at the meeting didn't

277

see it just as clearly as you do."

"Woods, we're a money-making body, not a philosophy debating society."

"Right." He started out of the room. "We've all got our orders, haven't we?"

"Hey, don't go away mad."

Palmer stopped in midstride and turned back. "Banking's changed a lot in forty years, hasn't it?" He smiled slightly. "It used to be a gentleman's game."

Harry Elder's small mouth drew downward at the corners in a self-deprecatory movement. "Everything was different then, Woods. But I don't think you'd ever find more than a handful of people who could be counted on to swear that bankers were gentlemen. Oh, we thought we were. Your father undoubtedly brainwashed you, pretty much as I've brainwashed Donny. But in our hearts we always knew we were moneylenders, the same breed that got chased from the temple."

Palmer's right hand made a brushing-away gesture, as if rubbing Elder's remarks from a blackboard. "Yes," he said impatiently, "*gentleman* was the wrong word. I meant it in the American sense, a man with a lot of money who can afford all the outward trappings of a real gentleman, the whole life style lifted verbatim from Victorian England. In this country, we pay attention only to the outward trappings. Clothes do make the man, clothes and town houses and cars and all the rest. We never ask what's underneath, as long as the facade remains in once piece."

He stopped short and stood there, as if listening to the echoes of his own voice. There were none in that carefully soundproofed room. "As long as he speaks properly and says the right things and looks right doing them," Palmer said then in a hushed voice, "we never ask what's underneath, never."

Elder frowned at him and took a step or two around the edge of the gable in his direction. "Are you all right, Woods?"

Palmer nodded slowly, as if in answer to something else. Then he shook his head. "No," he said in a reluctant tone. "This damned thing has me a lot more concerned than it has any right to."

"This merger?"

Palmer nodded again. "Why does it bother me at all? It's yes or it's no, and that's it. Why the soul searching?"

"It's not that simple." Elder said. "This Mafia thing complicates it."

"Why?"

The single syllable shot out into the room between them with such force that both men blinked. "Why?" Palmer persisted. "That's what's worked its way under my skin, Harry. Why?"

Elder took another step toward Palmer, who turned half away, as if ashamed of needing any kind of advice or help. "Woods," the older man said then in his husky voice, "I think you're having a little touch of male menopause. Ever hear of it?"

Palmer made the same erasing motion he had before. "That's old stuff, Harry. What worries me is something that never before entered my mind, not once in forty-six years of living. It's this whole business of differences and similarities. Or whatever it is that's gotten its teeth into me."

"Male menopause. I know."

"Differences and similarities. You know that old joke? If it walks like a skunk and talks like a skunk and looks like a skunk and smells like a skunk, it's a skunk."

"What the hell is that supposed to mean?" Elder asked.

"Very profound, Harry. Differences and similarities. Under the outward trappings."

"I beg your pardon?"

Palmer shook his head slowly, thoughtfully. "When you start asking those kind of questions, Harry, you end up with very bad answers, bad for your own ego. Who am I under my outward trappings? You ask. Who are they, under theirs? Are we different or the same underneath?"

"Goddamnedest case of male menopause I ever saw. It's almost as pronounced as the female kind."

"That's a handy evasion."

Elder sat down abruptly against the edge of the table and stared hard at Palmer. "Don't force me to play father, Woods, I'm not that much older than you. For Christ's sake, don't you think other people ask themselves these kind of questions? It happens to all of us. But you learn to ignore the questions. You grow a hard shell the questions bounce off of. Otherwise the questions destroy you."

"You mean the answers."

"All right."

"You mean the truth destroys you," Palmer persisted.

"Yes, goddamn it, yes. All right. Yes."

Palmer eyed the older man, then started for the door again. "I don't intend to be destroyed by any truth," he said, stopping

279

in the doorway for a moment. "That's a hell of a poor bargain for a man my age, hiding from the truth like some kind of crook."

The older man's face had gone red under the shock of close-cropped white hair. "When you decide what the truth is, Woods, do me a favor?"

"Don't tell you?"

"Exactly." Harry Elder's voice had grown so hoarse he was hard to understand. "And don't tell Ubco, either."

Neither man spoke for a long moment. Then Palmer nodded and left the room.

65

Driving his own car, because he no longer trusted anyone in anything, Harry Klaman followed the three men as they left Casa Coppola. He watched Ben hop into a small German convertible illegally parked on a side street and drive away. He decided to stay with the big shots, not the small fry.

Don Vincenzo and Rocco Sgroi moved slowly, ponderously, along the same side street. The fettucini loaded them down like ballast. Behind Harry, a line of stalled cars honked their horns. Harry pulled over to let them pass but kept edging his Thunderbird slowly forward so as not to lose sight of Vinnie Big and his shadow.

He was aware that one other person had an interest equal to his in the two, a younger man who stood across the street in a doorway, one of Vinnie's own button men who at any moment could notice the creeping Thunderbird and wonder about it. Harry braked to a halt, double-parked on the narrow street, and watched the two men enter a plain Ford with the driver waiting behind the wheel. He had been waiting there patiently during the entire lunch, as had the button man across the street, who now joined the driver on the front seat. Loaded with all four men in the party, the Ford slipped out into traffic, and Harry accelerated to keep a block or two behind it.

Moving west, the Ford swung south on Park Avenue, and Harry trailed it all the way to Fourteenth without, he was certain, being spotted. It was now well after three o'clock, and if Vinnie kept to his usual schedule he would return to the Bleecker Street club to take care of any callers who had arrived since the morning session.

280

When the Ford turned west on Fourteenth and then signaled a turn south on Seventh Avenue, Harry stopped following it and made plans for his surprise entrance. He slipped through several side streets, and by dint of racing through yellow lights and actually running one red, he had reached Bleecker, parked his car and jumped out of it by the time the fettucini-laden Ford arrived on the block.

"Goombar!" Harry exclaimed, opening the rear door of the Ford and extending his hand inside to Vinnie Big.

The button man on the front seat whirled, his right hand dipping inside his coat, his eyes wide with apprehension. Then he recognized Harry Klaman and relaxed. At about the same instant, Vinnie Big recognized him and grew tense.

"*Si camerata?*" His flat blue eyes swiveled sideways to Rocco, who reached across him and took Klaman's moist, fat hand. Under the pretense of shaking it, Rocco climbed across Vinnie Big's knees and got out of the car, still easing Klaman away from it.

"I was just coming to see you," Klaman said. He found it impossible to let go of Rocco's hand without appearing to be rude.

Vinnie Big was standing on the sidewalk a prudent yard or two away. "What about, *amico caro?*"

"Business. Things."

Klaman's forehead began to drip moisture as he stood there in the warmth of the March afternoon, withstanding the scrutiny of the chilling blue Biglioto eyes. Finally Vinnie Big seemed satisfied. He gestured to Rocco, who dropped Klaman's hand, and all three men marched in silence the half block to the social club.

They pushed inside, Rocco in the lead. Vinnie Big nodded to several of the men sitting there and swept on past to the inside room. The door closed behind Klaman. Everything from confrontation to door closing had taken barely a minute. The even rhythm of Bleecker Street had been undisturbed. Nothing had happened to attract attention or excite interest. No one, Harry Klaman realized as he sat down and mopped his face, would be found anywhere among the throngs of schoolchildren or shopkeepers who could remember the incident.

He smiled broadly at Vinnie Big. "Are we brothers?" he asked then.

Don Vincenzo's two hands went straight out in front of him, wrists together as if manacled, elbows pumping back and forth.

"Is that a question, goombar? I'm ashamed you ask."

"Brothers have to tell each other the truth, right, Vinnie?" Klaman continued. He felt the sweat trickling down inside his shirt.

"Absolutely. Positively."

"Okay." Harry hunched himself forward with a short, fast motion that caused Rocco Sgroi to flinch. Harry realized suddenly that he was under a great deal closer scrutiny than normally. Were they expecting trouble from him?

"Okay, buddy," he continued. "I need money. I need the men back on the job. I need cash, and I need my lines of credit from suppliers."

Vinnie Big's eyes flared wide in his dark face. "I don't understand, goombar. Are you in some kind of trouble?"

"Don't try to shit—" Harry bit off the word hard. He had promised himself again and again that he would not let himself be needled. He held the trumps, not Vinnie, and it was time the guinea bastard realized it.

"Not trouble, exactly," Harry went on more calmly. "Just a few rough spots on the Lexington Avenue job and here and there. Nothing money won't cure. About half a million cash, to start with."

Vinnie's broad, thin-lipped mouth widened in silent amusement. His throat pulsed with unvoiced laughter. "You're crazy, *bambino*. I got no half a million cash."

"People's Bank does."

"Whadda I got to do with People's?" Vinnie Big asked.

Klaman let a moment pass. Then: "Okay, let's pretend that's so. Then I want the cash from Downtown Bond and Mortgage. Don't tell me you got nothing to do with Downtown."

"A little." Vinnie Big sat back in his swivel chair. "Tony Fish runs it, though. And he couldn't give you half a million cockroaches, let alone dollars." The thought seemed to amuse Rocco more than it did Don Vincenzo. The buffer chuckled softly deep down in his throat.

"I'm glad you mentioned Tony Fish. He ought to be here," Klaman said. He heard his voice waver slightly and swallowed to smooth it again. His heart had begun to throb almost painfully.

"He's due any second," Rocco announced, "and when he gets here, we all gotta leave. We gotta date across the river. You got something to tell him, too, Harry?"

"I got something to tell all of you." Harry shifted in his chair to ease the pressure of his clothes on his chest and heart. The skin under his armpits was rank with sweat. "But first I want to hear about the half million."

"Just that?" Vinnie Big asked with heavy sarcasm. "What about what you started off asking? The men on the job and the suppliers' credit and all that."

"All that," Klaman said firmly, his voice under control, "comes after we settle the cash."

Vinnie Big's large hands flew out sideways, palms up, then closed together in prayer and rocked up and down. "It's settled, goombar. Nobody's got that kind of cash." He glanced over Klaman's head to the doorway. "Right, Tony?"

Tony Fish eased his way sideways through the half-open door, like a party crasher. His glance shifted quickly, almost fearfully, from Vinnie Big to Harry Klaman to Rocco Sgroi and back to Vinnie again. "What kind of cash?" he asked softly, closing the door behind him.

"Here's *cugino* Harry, asking for half a million cash."

"*Marone!*"

"First he wants it from your boy's bank up in Westchester. Then he wants it from you. I mean, you got to hand him one thing, he's pretty sure *il tribù Fischetti* has half a million cash to give him."

In the silence that followed, Tony Fish's glance settled down. It seemed to Klaman that Tony had been afraid he was somehow at fault. When he realized the joke was supposed to be on Klaman, he relaxed slightly. Typical flunky, Klaman thought.

"In other words," he said, "the answer is no?"

Vinnie Big's shoulders did a small dance of regret. "In other words, *si*. The answer is no." He smiled a perfect smile of friendship and peace.

Harry Klaman took a deep, soothing breath. His heart was pounding so hard he felt sure everyone in the room could hear it. "In other words," he repeated, "you leave me no choice?"

Vinnie Big's eyes narrowed in their network of wrinkled skin. "How's that, goombar?"

"I made a straight business proposition, a half-million loan in cash, and got turned down. So in other words, I tried to do this like a gentleman and you wouldn't let me. Right?"

The silence appalled Harry. Not even the honk of a passing

auto broke the quiet in the room. The impact of three pairs of eyes fixed on him made him suddenly aware of what he was going to do with a clarity he had not had before now. He mopped his face again and, as he put away his handkerchief with his right hand, delved inside the breast pocket of his jacket with his left. Rocco sprang halfway out from the chair, then settled back as Klaman removed a fat white envelope.

Harry Klaman grinned maliciously at Rocco and then at Vinnie Big. Over his shoulder he called to Tony Fish. "Better step up, Tony. This concerns you even more than it does Vinnie."

He could feel his heart hammering wildly at the inside of his rib cage, as if trying to get out. His grin narrowed slightly to a smug smile as he opened the envelope.

66

Ben got home early that day, not much after 4 P.M., and Rosalie thought for a moment he had come early to see her. She saw the little Karmann-Ghia pull up in the driveway, its top down on the sunny March day. Ben jumped out and slammed the door shut, moving with that same grace that had once made her throat tighten. Now she watched him walk up the path to the house with no more emotion than she watched the postman.

By the time he had let himself in, said hello to the children and hung away his coat, Rosalie had left her vantage point in the window – a dead giveaway, she realized – and had gone up the back stairs to her room, where she was seated, reading a textbook from N.Y.U., when Ben poked his head in the door.

"Rosa, baby?"

She looked up slowly, as if awareness of his existence on earth, much less in this house, was slow in coming. "Oh, Ben." Just that. She congratulated herself on the tone.

"I'm sorry to surprise you, getting home early, but..." The absolutely blank look in her eyes stopped him, and his voice died away.

"Are you early?" she asked.

He eyed her for a moment and then his head disappeared as he kept talking. "Got to shower and shave and change for that savings-bank dinner tonight."

"Dinner?"

He poked his head back inside the room, his hands unknotting his tie. "I told you to put it down in your book, honey."

"You mean I'm supposed to go with you?"

"Sure." He paused just long enough to fire up her suspicion. "If you want to, that is."

"Some stuffy old dinner with a lot of politicians and bankers?" She laughed scornfully.

"You used to love to get out nights."

Rosalie let the silence remain undisturbed. She heard him walk down the hall to his room and kick off his shoes, then return a moment later without his shirt. "So what are you saying, you'll come or you won't?"

"I'm thinking about it. When would we have to leave?"

"Five thirty. The reception starts at six, and we wouldn't want to be more than half an hour late for it."

Rosalie made a face. "I hate receptions."

He stared at her for a moment, then walked back to his own room again. "When would we get home?" Rosalie called.

"Midnight."

She waited until he padded back into the room, this time wearing only his underwear shorts. She watched the play of muscles across his shoulders and upper arms. "Well?" he asked.

She wrinkled her nose. "I don't think it sounds like anything I'd like to attend. Or bother Mrs Traficanti for at this hour. She's too old to have her evening suddenly broken up for a baby-sitting job."

"In other words?"

"Ben, I'm speaking as plainly as I can. The answer's no."

He stared at her for a long time, trying to make her say something more. Then he turned and walked quickly out of the room. Rosalie saw the way his muscles shifted in the backs of his legs and his buttocks. There had been a time, before they were married, when she had had all kinds of schoolgirl fantasies about Ben's body. She had tried her best to forget these secrets, these sins too embarrassing even to speak of at confession. Now she knew that everybody had them, or at least that was what some of the books and magazines said. And in those fantasies, she had done all kinds of lascivious things to Ben's body and he to hers.

Once it became both legal and expected of them, none of these things happened. In fact, after the wedding, it turned out

285

that marriage entitled Ben to hurt her rather cruelly, she thought. He had an insistent way of behaving in bed that took no account of what she liked, or how she happened to feel, or any little problems or sore spots or anything. If she were to complain about her back, for instance, he would go out of his way that night in bed to hurt her back, lying on top of her for what seemed like hours, his powerful football player's muscles making his hard body thud up and down on her.

She welcomed the four quick pregnancies. During them he tended to leave her alone for fear of hurting the fetus.

Now, she realized from the books and magazine articles she was reading, this kind of behavior was rather common among American husbands of a certain kind, and less dangerous certainly than the other kind, in which they tended to ignore their wives completely. Rosalie often wondered why it was that no American men were able really to satisfy their wives. They erred on the side of either aggression or depression, it seemed from her readings, and everything was left to the wife to understand, solve and put right.

Rosalie was pretty sure she had lost the urge to put things right with Ben. They would simply have a bad marriage like other couples, and since divorce was out, that was that.

She listened to the noisy way he took his shower, spluttering and blustering under the immense sheet of icy water he usually turned on. The bathroom was always awash when he left, as if he expected life to supply him with an unbroken succession of locker rooms in which to cavort.

As she had known he would, Ben now returned partly draped in a towel. There would be wet footprints on the parquetry floor. She looked at him for a moment without speaking. This farce had been acted out often enough in the past – the imaginary dinner, the standard appeal for her company, her own reasoned refusal and finally, his one last plea before throwing on fresh clothes and dashing out of the house an hour early for the mythical appointment. He had reached the final plea now, she noted, and it came tonight as it nearly always did, after the shower. The only change in the script, it seemed to her, was that she now knew what role she had played all these years. And she was playing it again but deliberately.

"You absolutely sure you don't want to come?" he asked.

Rosalie pretended to think about it. "Would I have fun?"

"Fun? This is one of those deadly banking dinners, Rosa."

286

He stressed the word *banking* as if it had some other meaning, like typhoid. She seemed to consider this a long time. "Maybe I should come," she mused aloud, tormenting him. "Maybe it's wrong of me to stay away."

"Then hurry up and call Mrs. Traficanti. Let's move."

He did that rather well, Rosalie thought. Nobody ever said her Ben didn't run a great bluff. "Okay," she said, jumping up and going to the telephone.

Instead of reversing himself, Ben surprised her by padding out of the room. Rosalie sat by the telephone for a while, wondering if perhaps she had misjudged him. He returned shortly, combing his hair. "Okay with Mrs. Traficanti?" he asked.

"I didn't call. I changed my mind."

He stared at her. "You okay tonight, Rosa?"

"Sure." She got up, confused, and returned to the easy chair where she had left her book. Ben stood in front of the long mirror, studying the way his muscles shifted as he flexed his arms, hands above his head, comb flicking locks of hair in place. Ripples of muscle flickered across his chest and between his shoulder blades as he combed in long, hard strokes.

It came to Rosalie abruptly why her bluff hadn't worked. It wasn't that he had been telling the truth all these years. Tonight happened to be for real. Perhaps there had been another real dinner on a night or two in the past also. That must be it.

Feeling less confused, she studied the way Ben worked on his hair. The combing was finished. Now he was working with the two silver-backed brushes he'd had since his West Point days. He worked them in unison, left and right, and then began alternating them like a boy shining a boot.

Rosalie took off her reading glasses to see more clearly the effects of all this industry. Ben's shining black hair came into sharp focus at once, and so did two long red lines on his back. One ran from his left shoulder across to his right, the other lay across it at a slight downward angle.

"What happened to your back?" she asked from across the room.

Ben stopped his brushing and turned slightly to see his back in the mirror. "I don't see anything."

"Two lines or scars or something." She got up and started toward him.

Ben shrugged and moved quickly, but without too much

haste, out of the room. Rosalie stood where he had been standing and looked at herself in the mirror. She wasn't all that bad,
she thought. If she could lose another ten pounds, she'd be a
size nine again. The boys who hung around Washington
Square had stopped trying to hustle her for money now that
they knew her. Instead they whistled and made remarks
equally as obscene, but without a money motive. Some of the
things they had offered to do for her if she paid they were now
volunteering free.

Rosalie pulled in her stomach, which had the effect of
emphasizing her breasts. She turned slightly sideways to check
her profile. Not all that bad.

In the mirror she could see Ben returning to the bedroom,
wearing his undershirt and a dress white shirt with a ruffled
front, all buttoned up. He stood just behind her and over her
shoulder began tying his bow tie.

"What was that on your back?" Rosalie asked.

"I didn't feel anything there. What'd it look like?"

"Scars, or scabs. Welts. As if you'd fallen against something
with a sharp edge."

"Nonsense, baby." He tugged the tie and left the room
again.

She thought about the two lines on his back for a second or
two longer, but the sight of herself in three-quarters view
proved too engrossing. Forgetting all about Ben and his back
and his dinner and all the rest, Rosalie took a deep breath and
sucked in her stomach again.

67

Edith had no need to look in the long mirror of her dressing
room. She had already changed into what she considered was
correct for the evening, a brownish tweed skirt, walking shoes
and a deep blue long-sleeved cardigan. She called down to Mrs.
Gage on the second floor.

"Only four for dinner, you remember."

Palmer came out of the bathroom in his silk robe. He stared
at himself in the long mirror of his own dressing room. Edith
could see him frown at his unkempt hair, fresh from the
shower, and disappear from view. She glanced at her watch. It
was five thirty. Woods seemed to be too far along in his preparations she noted. He had miscalculated and would be

forced to spend time with them while they ate dinner without him.

Edith went down to the second-floor dining room and turned the wall dimmer switch up halfway. The room looked best in this diminished light. The pictures on the walls, most of them having to do with food, looked very impressive and unusual in this light. So, she felt, did her children and she herself.

Gerri was the first into the dining room, carrying a basket of bread from the kitchen and a butter dish. "Soup's on," she remarked.

"Not till your brothers get down here."

"Yech." Gerri went to the central stairway and called up: "Come ay-und git it!"

Edith winced. "Do you always shout that loudly?"

"Only to the deaf," Gerri stated. She walked back into the kitchen, her narrow model's figure held perfectly erect, her nearly unbulging buttocks shifting very slightly. She seemed to be balancing an invisible book on her head. Even as a little girl, Edith recalled, Gerri had had the knack of pretending all sorts of fanciful things and getting other people to fit in with her fantasies. A born leader, like her father.

The floor shook slightly as Woody thumped into the room and sat down at the table. Tom followed quickly behind him, a slight wisp of a child, even thinner than Gerri. Edith wondered where Woody got his immense bulk. It wasn't that he was fat. There was just too much of him, it seemed. She watched him slap an inch-thick pat of butter into a slice of bread, fold it over and cause it to disappear in two bites.

"Woody!"

Gerri returned with a huge enameled iron casserole, carrying it with hot-pot holders and laying it carefully on the wrought iron trivet. Then she sat down and with one of the holders, picked up the heavy iron lid. A delicious aroma billowed up. Edith sat down in her chair and gave the minimal directions it took to get dinner moving. "You can begin serving. Gerri."

They chatted about almost nothing at all, Edith felt as she picked at her *boeuf bourguignon*. It had taken her several years to cure Mrs. Gage of using too much paprika and too little wine. Now she seemed to turn it out perfectly and effortlessly. There was no need for the vast numbers of servants they had employed when the children were babies. Now Mrs. Gage and a cleaning woman sufficed, with hired help for parties. Edith thought how easy her life had become, now that her children were growing up.

She watched Gerri arguing a point with her older brother, and although she was not listening to the words, Edith could recognize that the two of them no longer argued as children but as nearly adult people, keeping their voices down and choosing not to use the deliberately inflammatory words that all brothers and sisters know have the power to madden their siblings and put an end to any pretense of rationality.

Edith thought for a moment about Woody in uniform. Kimberley seemed to think she should worry about this, and of course she did in a general way. It didn't seem right for Woody to have to go to war, but it hadn't seemed right for Woods to, either, in 1942.

She knew Kimberley was right. No war made sense. Nothing justified murder. But she couldn't help wondering how he might have felt if he were closer to her age and had lived through the business with the Nazis and the Japanese. She also wondered at times how he felt about the Apache war against the U.S. Cavalry and any street warfare that exploded betweeen the Negro and the police or national guard.

Among the other troubles with someone more than ten years younger than oneself, she knew, at least in Kimberley's case, was touchiness. This was always true of the young and, especially of Kimberley, where money was concerned. He seemed to hate the fact that he needed money and that she was perfectly prepared to give him whatever he needed. He seemed to think it might stultify his creativity, or something equally silly.

"I wish I were eating that instead of what's in store for me."

All of them, Edith included, looked up to see Palmer in the doorway, washed and brushed and dressed in the older of his two dinner jackets. He looked terribly thin, Edith thought. There was something about the half-light in the dining room that made the hollows under his cheeks look cavernous.

"What's for your dinner tonight," Gerri wanted to know, "chicken, roasted potatoes and green peas?"

"Or beef, baked potato and broccoli," Palmer said.

"Don't forget the *consommé printanier*," Gerri added, her accent strongly nasal.

Palmer sat down at the far end of the table from Edith. "What's happening to all of you?" he asked, not singling out anyone in particular.

Woody, his elder son, shrugged massively, causing one of his wrists to knock his water glass over. Palmer's reflexes were still good enough for him to reach out and save the glass at the last possible instant. "All right," he said with mock calm, "that's Woody's story. What about you, Tom?"

Tom gave one of his high, piping laughs. He resembled Gerri and his parents much more than he resembled Woody, whose features were rather too broad to seem really part of the same family. With four of them so narrow and long, Woody's blocky look set him apart.

"I have a spring project for Unicef," Tom told his father. "We're collecting money and cans of food."

"What' happening with your schoolwork?"

Tom thought this over for a while. "Not too much," he announced at last. "Most of our kids are pretty dumb, you know."

Palmer laughed, perhaps more than this deserved. He seemed, to Edith, too determined to get with it. "Gerri?" he asked.

"The usual. I don't have the same problem Tom does. The kids in my class are too smart. And the teacher marks on a curve. And if you think it's easy to get a good grade that way, I –"

"What's a curve?" Tom interrupted.

"Normal probability curve." Gerri sketched a parabola in the air. "A few A's at one end and a few F's at the other. A few more B's and D's at each end. Then a peak in the middle where the majority sits with its C's."

Tom's eyes widened. "Huh?"

"Democracy in action," Gerri added helpfully.

Palmer's mouth curled up flatly at the corners in a how-about-that expression. "Is that how you spend your school days," he asked, "trying to beat the curve?"

"Didn't you?" Gerri asked.

"When I was in school?" Palmer sat back and thought for a moment. Edith watched the shadows around his eyes deepen slightly. "We didn't get marked on a curve as such. I suppose there just wasn't all this jockeying for grades. We tried as hard as we could – which wasn't bad, you understand, not bad at all – but we didn't get too frantic about it."

"You would now," Woody put in heavily.

"How's that?"

"You would now." A mulish look came into the older boy's

eyes, as if determined to shove his way through to making a point, no matter what obstacles were placed in his path. Edith could see him figuratively dig in his heels and prepare to demolish anything his father put up by way of argument.

"I suppose so," Palmer said.

Edith suppressed a smile. Palmer had always had the knack of shifting quickly so as to leave his discussion opponent flat-footed and foolish. It was especially easy to do this to Woody, whose thinking was much slower than either his father's or his sister's. Edith found herself getting a bit peeved with her husband.

"Because of the emphasis on grades," she suggested.

Palmer looked up, not knowing whether she was supporting him or trying a flanking attack. "Yes, with the threat of being drafted as a kind of ultimate enforcement." He turned to Woody. "Which reminds me, how are your grades?"

Woody shrugged. Edith could see that this was exactly not the ground on which Woody wanted to stand. His grades had never been as good as Gerri's, or even Tom's. But it was Woody who stood to lose the most, at the moment, by poor grades.

"Can you translate that shrug?" Palmer asked.

"So-so. B's and C's. Mostly C's."

Palmer watched his older son for a long moment. "Is that good enough to get you in a decent college?"

"I don't know."

"Neither do I. But when it comes to college entrance, A's and B's have got to be better than B's and C's. Right?"

"I don't know."

"Sure you do." Edith watched Palmer pause and think of a new way of placing the matter before Woody. She decided to deflect him again, as she had done before.

"Of course, the war may be over by next year," she said then.

Palmer stared at her with some surprise. "Do you really think that?"

"It can't go on forever."

"One way or the other, it can," her husband said.

"One way or another?" Gerri asked. "What is that?"

"One way or another, we must have the kind of spending a war generates." Palmer sat back in his chair.

In the half-light, Edith thought, he looked rather distinguished. She could easily see how he had won the favors of that woman last year. The woman herself was quite attractive, and Edith could understand that she had found Woods so, too. Edith supposed the only woman who might not find him all that attractive was one who had lived for nearly twenty-five years with that cold, calculating banker's mind, utterly devoid of emotion, until she herself had grown cold and calculating.

So cold, Edith thought, that she had become a stranger to her own needs, thinking herself complete and satisfied doing what she had been doing, the deadly daily dullness of a life without emotional content.

"One way or another," Edith heard herself saying in a clear voice that was rather louder than the tone she normally used, "we have got to learn to stop living off murder."

The silence that followed this remark was broken by Gerri's thin, disembodied whistle. "From the book *Mommy Was a Commie*, by Geraldine Palmer," she said.

"Mamma was a comma," Tommy suggested and squeaked happily.

"Edith," Palmer began, "I have heard some pretty sil –"

"Tom was a bomb," Gerri suggested to her younger brother. Then, turning on her slower-thinking brother: "Woody is no goody."

"Edith," Palmer persisted, "I can't let that kind of thing go unchallenged."

"Are you challenging it?" she asked.

"I am."

"Just that? Just the formal challenge? Or are you going to present reasons?" Edith asked.

"First you have to exchange cards," Gerri announced, "and then name your seconds. I'm Momma's second."

"Who's Dad's?" Tommy asked.

Palmer glanced around the table. "Your mother and I will discuss it alone later."

"You meet behind the cathedral at dawn," Gerri suggested. "But first name your weapons."

"Damn it, Gerri," Palmer exploded, "must you turn everything into a TV skit?"

Gerri's eyes grew wide as she pushed the palm of her hand against her mouth. She froze in that position for a long moment. "Cut that out," Palmer commanded. "Edith, these children are getting way out of hand."

"Just me," Gerri amended.

"I guess I am, too," Edith added. She sat back in her chair.

She and her husband had had many small arguments in front of their children, reserving the big ones for later. But this was the first time a big one seemed to be getting out of hand before witnesses. She realized abruptly that of course they were not really arguing about the war at all.

"Well,' she began slowly, gathering momentum, "I don't think there's much point in postponing this one so the children can't hear it. One of them is vitally affected as of his next birthday, one of them will probably start dating draftable boys fairly soon, and the third one is only six years away from the draft. So..."

The silence was complete now. Even Gerri couldn't seem to bring herself to break it. Finaly Palmer stood up. "You'd think," he said in a deliberately very calm voice, "that you and I were about to decide the question of war, peace and the draft over the dinner table. I'm afraid it isn't up to us."

"It's up to everybody."

"Yes," he agreed. "That's true. Except there is a certain momentum for things, a certain rhythm or cycle or whatever it is. And the momentum of this war is established. It's a boulder rolling down a hill. It can be deflected a little. But it takes a very determined effort, a do-or-die effort, to halt it in its tracks without being overrun and killed. And I haven't seen any signs of anyone willing to stand up to the boulder and take his chances. Have you?"

"One person alone? It's not possible."

The children's eyes, Edith noticed, swung back and forth between their parents, following the interchange very closely, totally unlike the indifference with which they usually followed other conversations.

"Well, then," Palmer said, as if that finished the discussion.

"But people have to reach out to other people," Edith said. She could scarcely believe she was doing the talking. "People have to grab hold of each other. That's the only way they can be strong enough."

Palmer's pale gray eyes narrowed slightly. "Edith, what exactly are you talking about? Stopping the war? Or what?"

"That and everything else."

His mouth worked silently for a moment. She waited for him to speak. She knew, from their private arguments over the years, that although she could hold her own in concrete matters, his mind could outthink her on abstract things. She was prepared now for him to demolish her in a few sentences.

It had happened before, and it would not surprise her much if it happened again, even in front of the children. But it would hurt. Just once she wanted to be right about something, unassailably right.

"Isn't that what it's all about?" she asked. "To find that and make it strong as one can and hold onto it?"

His lips moved again, but he still hadn't spoken. He stood next to his chair, one hand on its back, looking slim and tall and terribly tired, or unhappy, or lonely, or all three. If she were capable of it anymore, Edith thought, her heart might go out to him. He seemed lost. But it was beyond her now.

Finally, instead of speaking, Palmer made a funny little gesture with the hand resting on the back of the chair, a kind of opening and outflinging, as if he had held seed in his hand and now he was scattering it, not sowing it, only wasting it.

"Well, I must run," he said at last. "I'm sorry."

"For what, Woods?" Edith wanted to know.

Their glaces sought each other. She wondered if he could read what was happening to her, what had been happening all this spring and what would inevitably go on happening until it broke them apart completely.

He nodded slowly. "Good night, kids. Edith." He went to the door of the dining room. "A late one tonight," he told Edith. "Don't wait up."

"Good night."

"Good night."

"Good night."

"Good night."

He left the room. The silence seemed to gather and grow. Edith put down her fork. All three children were industriously giving imitations of devoted eating, heads bent, eyes on their plates.

In its total lack of communication, Edith realized, this latest argument had been entirely too typical. She had never before been so bold in speaking her mind, perhaps because she had never before had any feeling worthy of bold expression. And as always, she had been left hanging in midair. In previous discussions she had usually been demolished by a clever twist of Woods' thinking. This time he had seemed rather to fall back, without seeming to, a kind of secret retreat, as if it had not been worth using his immense powers to demolish her, as if the zest of putting her down had somehow vanished.

Edith got to her feet. "Excuse me."

She left the room and headed down the long curving open flight of stairs to the main entry hall. Palmer was putting on his topcoat. The outer door was already open. A cool draft of March air blew in around them.

"Yes?" he asked, glancing up at her. She was standing on the second stair from the bottom, which put her a foot above him in height.

"I can't seem to let it all go that easily."

"All what?" His voice had the faint interest mixed with immense indifferences of a bank teller listening to some woeful tale of misnumbered checks and a missing stub.

"Woods." She paused.

"Yes?" The same patient indifference.

"Can you stop for one moment treating me like an applicant for a loan?"

He blinked. In the faint entryway light most of his face lay in shadow. Only his gray eyes looked alert, and even they seemed unable to stay for long on any one thing. They glanced at Edith, made a quick circuit of the area, then fixed on a plank in the floor.

"When I married you," she began again, "you were no banker. Now you're all banker."

"Is that so hard to understand?"

"All banker," she repeated. "Cold, disinterested in people, even in your own family. Interested, I suppose, only in banking."

"It's a common enough syndrome," he said drily.

"Can't you even discuss it without technical jargon?"

His eyes widened slightly. "Why are you so upset, Edith?"

"Because I feel I can't continue this way."

"What way?" He took hold of the doorknob.

"No!" The word seemed to rip out of her with painful force. "No, you are not going to turn this into another of your debating-society events. When I speak to you, I —" She cut herself off, aware that her voice had gone too high and too loud.

When she continued, her voice was under control again. "When I speak directly to you about my feelings, I will not be put off by this kind of technical-jargon, debating-team approach that turns every personal problem into some kind of socioeconomic thesis."

"I had no idea you —"

"Apparently," she cut in, "you have had no idea of what I

296

feel or need in many years."

He had been standing as if to leave. Now he closed the door and stood before it, as if barring her escape to the outer world.

"Nor any evidence from you," he countered, "that you were laboring under an immense load of dissatisfaction."

She watched his face, what she could see of it, for any sign of sarcasm. Evidently he actually meant it. He actually meant that he had had no clue to her feelings. For a moment she wondered what his face might look like if she referred to his shameful affair of two years ago, to his whoring around town while she worked to establish this home and fit them and their children into the fabric of this cold, hostile city.

But she had long ago decided not to mention the affair. He probably had no idea she knew of it. Time had robbed it of any but historical interest. There might have been a time when her knowledge could have been useful to her in forcing him to do something she wanted. But that time had passed. Like all guilty secrets, she reflected as she watched him, the passage of time made it possible to grow protective sheaths that blunted its sting.

"It can't have escaped you," she said then, "that our marriage has been dragging on in no more than perfunctory fashion."

"It hasn't escaped me," he admitted.

"Without your making any move to change it."

"I'm not alone in this marriage," he said. "If it's a perfunctory one, both of us are being perfunctory."

"It's possible, but—"

"And that if one of us had taken more of an interest in it, the other might have been heartened to follow suit."

Neither of them spoke for a long moment. Edith wondered suddenly if this were a bid from him for understanding or warmth. If it were, it came too late. And if it were simply one of his debating ploys, it must fail. She knew that even if she could find it possible to warm toward him again, he was too locked in ice ever to thaw. And if he were to make even a nominal move toward her, what of it? What would be so tremendous about it? What would she have then? Instead of a totally uninterested husband, she would have a half-uninterested one. She realized she was taking a dark view of it. The optimist would call the pitcher half full. But Edith knew it was half empty and draining fast.

"Let me put it this way, Woods," she said then, hoping her

voice was calm and logical-sounding. "I doubt if you really care to meet me halfway. And I doubt whether your halfway would be of interest to me. Is that clear?"

"Oh, yes. Quite clear."

"And what do you say?"

"Say?" He reached for the door knob again. "What does one say when the matter has been closed down tight and sealed off? Plead to have it opened again? Not likely."

She grasped the wrist of the hand with which he was reaching for the door. She started to twist, and he shook her off.

"I think I'd better go," he said.

"You..." She stopped and tried to control her voice. "You have given me nothing all these years," she managed to say then. Her voice sounded strangled with frustration, and she tried to ease the awful knot of tension on her throat. "And what infuriates me most is that I didn't even know it was nothing."

He gave her a polite stare. "Edith, it's getting late."

"I was so emotionally poor that I didn't even know I was being starved," she said. "I don't know which makes me angrier, knowing that or knowing how you have starved me, or knowing that you couldn't even have given me love if your life depended on it."

"Edith, this is terribly unfair. It's real hit-and-run. You know I have to leave."

"But that's it, isn't it?" she demanded. "That's about the size of it. It's just not in that banker's heart of yours."

She felt his hands on her shoulders. He seemed to be shaking her slightly back and forth. "Get hold of yourself," she heard him say. She tried to see his face, his mouth, but the light was bad. Was he saying words? Words came to her, but was he saying them? "Can discuss this calmly and..."

She lifted her arms in a violent upward movement that broke his grip. "Keep your hands off me," she whispered.

He reached for the door and got it open. The chill draft swirled around her legs. "Good night," he said.

"I've warned you, Woods," she said, maintaining her voice at a low level only by whispering. "You've been warned. I intend to have a life of my own."

"Certainly."

"I intend to make up for everything I haven't had. It's been a worthless life so far. I blame you for that, or at least half of it. But I don't do anything now to change it, I have no one to blame but myself. Do you understand me?"

"Certainly."

"It may have been easier for me to face emptiness when I was thirty. But I don't have that many years left now. Woods. And I refuse to continue throwing them away."

"Certainly."

"And stop saying 'certainly'!" she shouted.

He blinked again. It occurred to Edith that he had probably never seen her this way before, just as angry perhaps, but not voicing it. She waited for him to say something, knowing that his stance, with his hand on the open door, said anything that needed saying, and said it more honestly than words.

"Get out, then," she whispered.

"Certainly." A faint mocking look came and went in his cold gray eyes.

The door closed softly behind him. Edith leaned against it, as if to seal him out of the house forever. Then, moving quickly, she made her way up the stairs, past the dining room where the children perhaps were still eating dinner and directly to her bedroom. She closed the door behind her and sat down on the bed, trying to get control of her breathing.

It seemed very important to her to be able to do this. Breathing first, she told herself, then the rest of it.

68

The sun had already set behind the range of low hills that formed the western boundary of the nursery area. The very peaks of the greenhouses were still touched with a faint rosy light, but all the shadows had gone out of the scene, and in the front office the fluorescent lights burned hard and bluish.

The last of the salesmen had washed and driven off in his car. The last of the office girls had bundled up against the evening chill and gone out to the bus stop. The two caretakers smoked a last cigarette in the office and then switched off the overhead lights. They started on their rounds, carrying with them their time-block drums.

They were perfectly ordinary night watchmen from a reliable and well-known concern, working on a yearly contract. The main difference was that they were much younger than the typical night watchman, and they carried sidearms. The guns were seven shot Smith and Wessons firing ·44-magnum slugs capable of stopping a man at 200 feet by disemboweling him.

That and the unbroken perimeter fences, electrified with 4,000 volts, were the main differences.

Deep within the nursery complex, in that congeries of interlocking, intersecting greenhouses where green now changed quickly in the fading light to black, the thin mosquito's whine of an electric motor grew louder. The golf cart turned a corner at top speed, forcing the frail old man at the controls to haul himself erect against the sideways pull of momentum.

He hated this time of evening. No matter how he planned his time or checked his pocket watch or looked out at the sky, the late afternoon always seemed to catch him on its hip, alone and far away from his warm fire and the protection of his little home within a home, where the murderous night vapors could not reach him.

Don Girolamo steered the golf cart toward the steel door and touched the radio-control button. The door flew up, and the cart entered the room. The door slammed shut behind it. "Santo?"

"Si, padrone?"

Don Girolamo allowed himself to be helped from the car to the chair next to the fire. The cannel coal produced an immensely powerful glow of heat and gave a tiny touch of tar smell to the air, not unpleasant, and faintly reminiscent of wharves and fishing boats.

"My son has been summoned," Don Girolamo told his servant in Italian. "He is to arrive at any moment. Make certain he is not kept waiting. Have him ushered directly in to me."

"Si, padrone."

The effort of speaking so many words seemed to wind Don Girolamo. He settled back in the deep chair and concentrated on sucking life-giving oxygen into his lungs. After a moment, the effort of heavy breathing seemed to put him to sleep.

He dozed in utter peace, seeing visions of the little town of Terrasini, a fishing village on the northern edge of Sicily, to the eastern rim of the Golfo di Castellammare, not more than twenty-five kilometres west of Palermo. It was just before dawn. Already there was some light in the sky. The small, thick-sided, round-bottom boats were returning, a man standing near the stern of each one, sculling with long oars while his partner folded nets. The smell of tarred oakum was fat in the nose. One by one the boats arrived, and the men lifted off the baskets of fish. Silver bellies gleamed faint rose in the light of dawn.

Like most old people, Don Girolamo was not fully asleep. Through the mists of morning in Terrasini harbor he heard his son arrive with several other men. He kept his eyes closed and made certain his breathing remained regular. He waited and listened.

Someone gasped in pain.

"Keep it good and tight," his son, Vincenzo, said.

"Right." This was the trustworthy voice of the *cuscinetto*, Rocco Sgroi.

"He might faint again." The voice of that *cretino*, Gaetano Fischetti.

Again the gasp.

Don Girolamo thought for a moment. It could not be, he told himself, that his son had been stupid enough to bring someone here under duress. No one came here except members of the family. Not even Fischetti had ever been here before. No, once. Right after his son had married Rosalie. Never again. He was of the family, but Don Girolamo didn't like him.

Then how could Vincenzo have brought an outsider here?

"Did the security man see us?" Vincenzo asked.

"Just me," Rocco said. "He passed you and Shit-For-Brains and Tony on the strength of my say-so."

Vincenzo chuckled brutally. "He'll have his head handed to him by the old man. Don G. thinks his security's tighter than that."

"It is," Rocco agreed. "But this was a nephew of mine."

Feigning sleep, Don Girolamo tried to remember which of his night watchmen was related to Sgroi. He would have to go.

"Well," Gaetano Fischetti asked, "can we wake him?"

"You in a hurry for trouble?" Vincenzo asked. "You miserable little *pidocchio*, with that stiff-cocked *blatta* of a son of yours, making my Rosalie's life a shame and a misery."

"Don Vincenzo," Rocco interjected. "Klaman first, then the Fischettis."

"Klaman first," his *padrone* agreed. "I still think it was a mistake to bring Klaman to the old man. But, seeing what must happen to him, it can't matter much."

Again Don Girolamo heard the tight moan of pain. He was

pretty certain that Klaman was the silent member of the party, tape across his mouth and eyes, arm twisted up behind him and someone firm – Rocco, not Gaetano Fischetti – forcing up his hand whenever he felt Klaman needed a reminder. By now the arm would be numb with pain.

"I'm switching to his other arm," Rocco announced.

The whimper was all the more forceful, Don Girolamo felt, for being muffled by the tape. Rocco was a good man with reliable instincts.

"Santo," Vincenzo said, "can we wake *il padrone*?"

"Non lo so."

"He's trying to grab a little nap? Maybe we should give him an hour or so and come back."

"We have to take a chance," Rocco said. "Klaman is too hot as he is."

Vincenzo's deep, weathered voice crackled with tension. "I hate to stir up the old man. Well."

Don Girolamo felt his right hand being lifted from his lap. His son's lips pressed into the wrinkled back of his hand. Three times Vincenzo kissed his hand. Then: "Don Girolamo?"

The old man made his eyes open slowly. He nodded to his son and withdrew his hand. Slowly his glance shifted from Vincenzo to Rocco and from Rocco to Fischetti. In turn, each man ducked his head, bobbing it down as low as he could, like a Japanese greeting, and murmured something suitable. At no time did the old man look at Klaman.

He pointed his finger at Rocco and made a sideways smashing motion with the edge of his hand. Rocco stared at him for a moment, then nodded his understanding. He spun Klaman about, damp face blanked out by broad white patches of adhesive tape. Rocco's hand drew back, elbow bent. Then the arm shifted forward, moving from the shoulder only, the rest locked like a wooden brace. His fist connected with the sweaty point of Klaman's chin, just to the left of the Cary Grant dimple. Klaman's body arched backward as if a bow-string had been attached to him. At the point of maximum curvature outward, his immense belly hanging forward in mid-air, Rocco drew back his right fist again and buried it past the cuff of his coat jacket in Klaman's midriff. The body jack-knifed forward and collapsed in a neat pile at Rocco's feet.

"Sì, padrone," Rocco said.

"Now I can talk." Don Girolamo's voice was as dry as a cricket's whisper, all consonants, the vowels rustled over as unnecessary. It was Italian that only an Italian could understand. "You are all insane. You" – he swung on his son – "for involving me in this. You" – he turned to Rocco – "for letting him. The buffer does not let his man do foolish and dangerous things. You" – he turned on Fischetti – "for the depths of your terrible incompetence and the lechery and weakness of your son."

"You heard?" Vinnie Big asked in English.

"Weeks ago, *cretino*." The old man spat out the words in his full voice, then returned to speaking his oddly menacing, whispered Italian. "For weeks I have followed what Klaman was doing and what you were doing, both of you showing as much intelligence as a tick on a mule's back."

"This is unfair," Vincenzo began. "You cannot tell me you –"

"It is as if you and the fat Jew were a pair of toothless tomcats, circling each other in an alley, afraid to pounce, bite and kill because you have no teeth." The old man stopped suddenly and sucked in great rattling breaths of air. The other men stood listening to him in utter silence until he regained his breath again.

"Time and time again," Don Girolamo resumed in his dry rustling voice, the grating Italian giving off sparks as it moved, "I wanted to step in and end this foolishness. I knew this would destroy the respect your men pay you. It is obvious what has happened now. The Jew has shown you his evidence, and you have panicked."

"No such thing," Vinnie broke out in English.

"Only panic," his father continued icily, "could account for bringing the Jew here. He can only go one or two routes from here." Don Girolamo turned to Rocco Sgroi. "And you – I expected more of you."

Rocco nodded and hung his head slightly. Then, speaking softly in Italian, he said: "Don Vincenzo would have killed Klaman on the spot. I counseled against this then. I still counsel against killing. We must find a way to tie his hands and set him free to do our bidding."

"Ah, *si*!" A beautiful smile animated the dry face of the old man. A perfect set of dentures gleamed in the firelight. "Vincenzo, you heard?"

Vinnie Big nodded. His father could see how badly he took this support of the *cuscinetto*. But Rocco was safe enough from feeling Vincenzo's displeasure. "I heard," Vinnie admit-

303

ted. "The only question is, how?"

Don Girolamo closed his eyes for a moment. It pained him to see his aging son, to whom he had hoped to pass along all of the knowledge and power that was his, behaving in such an unsuitable way. He heard regularly from his sources how respected Vincenzo was, how able an "open" administrator, how just a decision maker, how feared by his enemies and loved by his friends, how successful in business, how crafty in making deals. All good, but when he saw his son at such close range as now, in the heat of panic, Don Girolamo realized that Vincenzo's reputation had been achieved largely under the protection of his father's reputation. On his own, the boy seemed unable to reason properly. His usefulness, even as a figurehead, was questionable.

This was such a simple problem really. It was a matter of knotting loose cords. None could be allowed to dangle. All must be firmly secured, if possible with one knot only.

The simplest solution was the most economical, Don Girolamo thought.

"Now, pay attention," he began, his voice fuller now. "Is the Jew still unconscious? Then here is what you must do."

69

Edith met Kimberley in a drugstore on Lexington Avenue not far from the Waldorf Hotel. Although she had left herself plenty of time, it was nearly six thirty when she arrived at the rendezvous. The sky over the city was turning dark blue.

Kimberley was seated at the soda fountain, sipping a long Coke through a striped straw. He grinned as she walked in the door in her flat-heeled walking shoes and golfing tweed skirt. "What the best-dressed picket will wear," he said, patting her hand. Neither of them felt quite right about showing any further degree of intimacy in such a public place.

"You look unusually good tonight," he said. "Kind of fresh and ... and excited."

"Just had a roaring fight with my husband."

"I don't somehow see you two in a real screamer. What about?"

"My life."

"Uh-huh. Small talk." He sipped his Coke and smiled to himself.

"I thought you'd have placards," Edith said.

"We pick them up on the line."

He paid for his drink, took her arm and guided her out of the drugstore. "Do you think there'll be any trouble?" Edith asked as he ushered her across Lexington.

"None predicted. These are nonviolent cats tonight. They have orders to fold up and lie down if the cops attack."

Edith made a grimace of distaste. "Why should they attack if the demonstration is peaceful?"

"Good question."

He led her to the northeast corner of Lexington and 50th Street, where a Hertz open-panel truck was parked. People, mostly of student age, milled about the truck, picking up sandwich signs and placards stapled to upright laths. Kimberley took a "MAKE LOVE, NOT WAR" sign. For Edith he chose a sandwich-board pair. The front placard read: "I DON'T WANT ANYBODY'S SON TO DIE IN VIETNAM." The back placard read: "PEACE AND FREEDOM BEGIN AT HOME."

"Do you buy the sentiments?" Kimberley asked.

"Certainly."

"I don't want you parading around in slogans you don't really dig."

"I dig," Edith said.

Giggling like juveniles, they moved quickly along 50th Street to the Park Avenue facade of the hotel and took their place in a line of more than two hundred people, moving in a stretched-out oval that the police were keeping several yards away from the main entrance of the hotel.

On the 49th Street side of the entrance, another oval of some two hundred people was slowly wheeling. The police had kept both ovals as close to the curb as possible to allow at least half the sidewalk's width for pedestrian traffic.

Near the entrance a television truck with rooftop camera was double-parked, but its floodlights were turned off. As Edith circled near it, she wondered if perhaps she would end up at the eleven o'clock news tonight. A Rolls pulled up to the entrance, and the doorman helped out an elderly couple Edith recognized, a savings-bank president and his wife she had been introduced to several times over the past few years.

"Good God."

"What's up?" Kimberley asked.

"I just had the most hideous thought. What if the dinner my husband's attending is at the Waldorf?"

Kimberley chuckled. "Want me to find out?" He handed her his placard. "Keep my place warm," he said and ducked out of sight around the corner.

The oval wheeled slowly in its restricted area. In a few minutes, Edith found herself back at the entrance. She watched a cab stop. A tall, gray-haired man in a dinner jacket got out first, then turned and helped out of the cab the woman with whom Woods had had the affair.

Edith saw that she seemed hardly changed at all. She hadn't seen Virginia Clary in more than a year, possibly eighteen months, and there was no reason for he to look very different. She was still fairly short, with immense dark eyes and short black ringlets. Edith saw that she was wearing a simple dress, ankle-length and cut low in front to show a generous cleavage. Once a whore, Edith thought, always a –

She stopped herself. The habits of a lifetime were almost impossible to break, she realized. That she, of all people, should be calling Virginia Clary a whore.

The thought of all the habits she would have to change now dismayed her as she plodded along on the slow moving line. The sight of the Clary woman dressed to the teeth while she wore a tweed skirt and walking shoes was also depressing. And the dour, joyless faces of her fellow pickets seemed to add the final touch of gloom.

Edith looked about her for a moment. Then she shrugged out of her sandwich sign and leaned it and Kimberley's placard against a lamppost. She headed east toward Lexington Avenue without looking back.

70

Rocco Sgroi, in addition to his many other attributes, was a humble man. Although he could claim a third-cousin relationship, twice removed, to Don Girolamo Biglioto and was in fact a second cousin of the Fischetti clan, he would never presume on blood ties so tenuous. He depended instead on his own competence, and for it the family had rewarded him richly.

Having deposited Vinnie Big and Tony Fish at two different busy corners to find their own transportation, Rocco was his own boss in what happened now, providing a heavy, legal layer of insulation between his activities and those of his *capo* – Don Vincenzo. Rocco garaged the Ford and picked up another one.

The new, featureless Ford sedan moved west now into the Chelsea district of Manhattan. As he drove, Rocco could hear a groan from the trussed-up body of Harry Klaman, lying on the floor of the back seat with a blanket over him. The wire on his ankles and wrists, the tape across his mouth and eyes would keep him relatively passive, Rocco decided.

He had already made a call from an anonymous telephone booth shortly after they had returned to Manhattan. The two boys were waiting for him in the shelter of a trucking garage doorway on Tenth Avenue in the twenties. Rocco slowed the car and opened the side door opposite him. The two boys hustled inside and sat beside him as he swung the car up Tenth and east on a street that ran in curves through a high-rise co-op apartment project. Both young men looked excited, but to Rocco they seemed bent on keeping their emotions repressed. He saw the excitement only in their eyes and the cautious sidelong glances they gave him.

Outlining the plan to the boys as he drove, Rocco steered the car east to First Avenue and began pushing northward into the timed cycle of the traffic lights. The glow of sunset was out of the sky now, at seven o'clock, and the worst of the evening traffic had passed. The anonymous Ford topped a rise at 40th Street and ducked into the tunnel that hid the U.N. buildings from view. Rocco gunned the car up past 50 miles per hour and managed to jump an entire cycle of traffic, coming out at 50th Street with a new cycle of green lights.

"Neat," one of the boys murmured.

"Gotta remember that," the other chimed in.

Rocco suppressed a smile and continued north until he reached an area of raw new high-rise apartment houses studded with mock terraces that signaled his entry into the fashionable East Side. Here white-collar people with pretensions could find one-and-a-half-room apartments in jerry-built skyscrapers for about half their monthly income. Rents of over $250 were common, Rocco knew, and secretaries making no more than $5,000 a year were willing to scrimp on everything else and crowd together, four to an apartment, for the upward-mobile advantages of an East Side address.

He steered the car west on a side street and ran it fast down a steep ramp to the basement parking garage. A short Negro attendant put down his newspaper.

"Take him out," Rocco muttered.

He watched the two boys work, observing with professional

307

detachment the economy of their movements. One circled behind the Negro before he had any idea of what was happening. The other brought his knee up into the Negro's groin. As he doubled forward in pain, the boy behind him kicked him in the buttocks and the boy in front kicked him in the face. From across the garage, over the sound of the Ford's motor, Rocco could hear a bone break somewhere in the Negro's body.

The boys pulled Harry Klaman from the back seat while Rocco pressed the button for the freight elevator. This was the riskiest part now, but since there were three passenger elevators in the building to take the bulk of traffic, the chances of meeting someone were cut down to reasonable odds. The fewer people involved in this, the better.

They hauled Klaman into the freight elevator and pressed the button for an upper floor. When they arrived, Rocco grabbed hold of the tape on Klaman's mouth and ripped it off. The sudden movement tore bits of skin from Klaman's lips. Rocco ripped the tape in half and pasted it over the electric-eye door-trip mechanism, causing the light beam to be blanked out. He pasted the remainder of the tape back over Klaman's bloody mouth.

"That holds the elevator here," he said. "Let's move."

They waited until Tippy answered her doorbell. Then they rode her back into the room on the strength of two knives with efficient-looking blades. Once the door was open, Rocco and one of the boys dragged Harry Klaman into the apartment and shut the door.

"What the hell is this?" Ben Fischetti asked.

Rocco's eyes jumped wildly, then located Ben on the bed. He still wore the ruffled shirt and bow tie of his dinner outfit, but he had shed his jacket, trousers and shorts. "Rocco, what is this?"

Rocco Sgroi's mouth tightened in a thin line of tension. No one had counted on this. Tony Fish had been certain his son was at the banking dinner. No one could have guessed he would stop by the broad's apartment for a quickie. "Just a little family visit, Ben," Rocco said, stalling long enough to let his mind work.

Give up? Bug out? What? Rocco drew on a pair of gloves and closed the door to the apartment behind him. He carefully wiped the knob. Now he knew what he had to do, and in many ways it was even better the new way than the old. He hoped Don Girolamo would see it his way. He especially needed the old man's support.

"Ben," Tippy said. "Tell me what's happening, Ben."

Rocco took the Minox from his pocket and fitted the flash attachment to it. Yes, the old man had to approve. He liked loose ends tied together neatly? This would be the neatest package yet.

"Ben?" Tippy asked. "Ben?"

Rocco picked up the telephone and dialed a number. "Plaza Hotel? Oak Room Bar, please." He waited. "Oak Room? Will you page Mr. Vincenzo Biglioto? Biglioto. Thanks." Rocco hung up the telephone and nodded to the boys. They put on their gloves.

"Ben?" Tippy cried.

71

"Favor of Almighty God upon these our undertakings," the minister intoned, "and move forward, secure in the blessings of good works."

Although he had by now heard perhaps thousands of goldy invocations, prayers, graces, benedictions, blessings and the like delivered by ministers, rabbis and priests at these dinners, Palmer's eyes still tended to glaze over at the first Name-drop.

By arriving an hour late, Virginia Clary had avoided the pre-dinner reception for dais guests. It seemed, as Palmer learned by consulting his printed program, that both of them were among the nearly fifty exalted persons on the dais.

His own presence up here, he realized as the minister droned on, was partly a measure of his position in banking. As the head of the largest commercial bank, he naturally would be seated on the dais, but there was a much more compelling reason as well. His presence tonight had to be given a certain amount of plain, ordinary exposure. The two forms of banking in New York State – commercial and savings – had been at each other's throats for so many years, with Palmer as a key figure during the final stages of the struggle, that the uneasy truce between the two groups could be given a much more lifelike look of permanence by publicly displaying Palmer's body at this gathering.

Palmer had refrained from glancing sideways past the ten or twelve people between them to look at Virginia Clary. Seeing her enter the crowded room had been enough auld lang syne for the moment. In the – what was it, eighteen months? – since they had spoken last, she seemed, if anything, to have gotten even prettier.

She had never been what he would have called a raving beauty. Her face had always been too extreme for that, her eyes and her cheekbones too large and the hollows beneath them too deep. In the interim since they had been lovers, Palmer realized, it had become acceptable for women to use quite a lot of eye makeup, even if they were rather high-ranking publicity executives in banking. Most women had taken the opportunity to make their eyes larger, darker and more striking in appearance. He had an idea that Ginnie had toned down her eyes in some subtle manner. She now presented a much less extreme picture, a more blended-in version of herself that went with her new position in life.

Palmer sensed, rather than heard, the "Amen" and the chairman's very brief remarks before the dinner was served. He glanced sideways at the chairman, in the center, caught the governor's eye, nodded politely, and let the waiter put a large iced coupe of cut fruit in front of him. Then he glanced in the other direction, away from the center of the dais, and nodded politely to a U.S. Senator and the chairman of the board of a large construction company. Farther along, almost at the end of the table, he saw Ginnie's dark curls bent slightly over her plate as she scribbled on a piece of paper, folded it and handed it to a waiter.

She had come a long way, Palmer decided. A number of women newspaper reporters had left journalism for public relations over the past decades, but probably none had done as well as Ginnie. Her first such job had been with Ubco. Palmer had inherited her when he arrived. She had proved to be possibly his only reliable ally in the bloody banking battle that followed and in his accession to the throne of Ubco. In the end to this day, Palmer was not entirely sure why she had done it.

Partly, he knew, it was because she was sure he would never leave Edith. Partly it was that she was fed up with commercial banking and felt her place lay with the simpler savings bank system, which dealt in the most primitive of banking transactions – savings, home mortgages and very little else. She called them "little people's banks". But also it was because she had seemed to fall out of love with him after the smoke of battle had cleared and she had seen the kind of infighting of which he was capable.

Palmer realized with a start that the waiter with the slip of paper was heading directly for him. He could feel his cheeks grow warm.

The waiter handed him the paper and stepped back a discreet pace or two. Palmer glanced at the familiar handwriting without reading it. He could feel his throat thicken. There was no reason for this. He had seen her handwriting hundreds of times before. He could pick it out of a thousand samples. Why should the sight of it now, after all this time, have any power over him?

"Do I know you from somewhere?" the note read. It was signed "Anxious."

Palmer's mouth quirked up at the corners. He dug around inside the pockets of his dinner jacket without finding a writing utensil. Seeing his dilemma, the waiter stepped forward and proffered a genuine Waldorf pencil.

"I'm in the banking game," Palmer wrote. He paused, trying to think of something funny, something light. Instead, he wrote: "If there's dancing, may I have the first dance?"

He watched the waiter bear this communication slowly along the dais to Virginia Clary. She smiled at reading it, then turned to find Palmer watching her across a dozen intervening faces. She shook her head from side to side and mouthed, "I'm sorry." Then she held up two fingers. Palmer nodded. They both began picking at their fruit cup.

So she had someone else, Palmer thought, someone who would get the first dance.

It was a little childish, he realized, to think that someone else wouldn't have appeared in the interim. She was a very attractive woman, and she met an awful lot of men in the course of her business day. Some of them had to be single or, if not, then interested enough to do what Palmer had once done.

Except, he remembered, that one of the other reasons she had broken up their affair was that she wanted to get married. Ginnie had been married once, he knew, and both her husband and her baby daughter had been killed in an auto crash which Ginnie alone had survived. He could remember her very clearly telling him that if they continued as they had, she and Palmer, she would never have the inclination to seek out anyone eligible for marriage. Obviously she had found him, or he her.

Palmer stabbed at a bit of pineapple with such savagery that

311

he started to topple the entire coupe. He recovered quickly and set it straight again.

Not just somebody else, he thought, but someone who wanted to marry her.

He knew he should be happy for Ginnie. He had always had nothing but the kindest feelings for her. And so, he told himself as he gave up on the fruit cup and pushed it away from him, I should now feel quite elated.

72

By eight o'clock, the job was nearly finished. It would have taken Rocco and the two boys a lot less time if it had been a simple thing, but there had been so many pauses and delays in setting up the pictures.

They had taken two rolls of Minox film, putting Tippy, Ben and Harry Klaman through just about every combination of positions and acts it was possible to fantasize. If left to his own devices, Rocco knew, he would have been satisfied with a few dozen changes in which the men visited various indignities on the girl. A simple man of simple tastes, Rocco's dream life gave him little background for a really artistic handling.

One of the boys, however, had apparently led an extremely rich and varied fantasy life, in which he had done about everything he could to both men and women. So by the time they had finished, Rocco had begun to feel vaguely unclean about the whole thing.

Then, too, Ben had given them a great deal of trouble in the beginning. He had blustered and bluffed and refused to pose. Rocco had been forced to show his gun with its long silencer tube and convince Ben of his utter indifference to using it.

"Okay," Ben had begged. "But leave the girl out of it, Rocco."

"She's right in the middle, Ben."

"She's not in good shape. She's a very upset kid. This could –"

"Shut up, Ben," Rocco cut in. "She's right in the middle, and you put her there."

"Whatever you want, I'll get it for you. But don't hurt the girl. She's sick. You could push her right over the edge."

"Yeah." Rocco laughed softly. "I could at that."

From the beginning, Klaman had been too happy to have

312

the tape and wires removed to make too many complaints. Then, too, he seemed to relish some of the things he was photographed doing to Tippy.

She had seemed to Rocco to be in a state of shock almost from the beginning. It was almost, he thought, as if she knew more than any of them how it would all end.

Now the ending was near. Rocco unloaded the second spool of film and pocketed it. The last batch of pictures had been strongly homosexual ones. Since he required only two at a time to be in each picture – the plan called for the pictures to seem to have been taken by the missing member of the orgy – a single snapshot might be misinterpreted. But the sequence, taken as a flow, with the identical setting of the bed and chair and the little red traveling clock clearly visible in each shot registering a slight change in time, made it an obvious record of a mixed straight-gay evening of fun.

"Ben," Rocco said, "wipe up and get your dinner clothes on and beat it for that bank party."

"I'm warning you, Rocco, if you hurt the girl, I'll –"

"Get dressed." Rocco's words were flat and not terribly loud, but they seemed to shut Ben up. Rocco had the feeling he was the kind of man who respected force and maybe even liked tasting it.

They finally hustled Ben out of the apartment by ten after eight. One of the boys slipped out on the tiny terrace and watched the street below until he saw Ben hail a cab and leave.

"Now we move real fast," Rocco said. "Wire up the heeb."

"Look fellas, I –"

Adhesive tape clamped off the rest of Klaman's protest. Still wearing gloves, Rocco stepped around the boys as they wired Klaman's wrists together. He reset the traveling clock to eight again.

He stepped back to survey the scene. Then he loaded the last spool in the Minox. "Tippy," he snapped, "down on your knees in front of the fat boy." He waited as she moved with sullen docility. Then: "Set him up with the the the shiv."

Rocco approved of the way Tippy had behaved through all this. Whether she was being posed in a position of submission or domination, whatever she was told to do, she fell into the pose with a waxy smoothness, like a well-fitted automaton. Her eyes were so blank of feeling that Rocco wondered if she were high on something. All in all, she seemed by training and preference the ideal victim.

One of the boys fitted his knife into Harry Klaman's bound hands. He stepped nimbly out of the way to avoid any sudden heroics from Klaman. Rocco nodded. "Turn that sweaty *punim* away from me, Harry, so I can't see the tape. Good. Now bend over a little as if you were gonna stab the broad. Good." He snapped four flash pictures as quickly as the strobe light would recycle, changing shutter speed very slightly between them to make certain he got his crucial photograph well exposed. Tippy turned to look at him.

"Okay," Rocco said. "Take him out."

The boy who had loaned Klaman the knife now removed it from his fingers and, holding the weapon by its blade, flicked its heavy case forward like a blackjack into the moist flesh above and behind Harry's right ear. His naked body started to sag. "Hold him," Rocco called. "This is the tricky part."

He motioned with the point of his chin to the other boy. "This is it, son."

The boy glanced at Rocco. It had been his fantasy life the trio had enacted. Now he seemed to falter for a moment. "Okay," Rocco said.

The boy moved in behind Tippy as she knelt there. He opened his knife.

The red traveling clock ticked. Behind the adhesive tape, Harry Klaman muttered unconsciously.

Tippy said nothing, even then.

73

The dinner dragged to an end by about nine fifteen. Palmer glanced at his watch and then sneaked a look toward the end of the dais where Virginia Clary sat. She had left her seat. Palmer considered this an extremely wise move, since most of the speeches were about to begin. But then, he told himself, she always did have good judgment.

Thirty minutes later, eyes glazed with boredom and smarting from the cigar smoke that seemed to have replaced the oxygen in the huge room, Palmer heard the last speaker draw to a close. He squinted up at the artificial stars in the ceiling as the chairman suggested that they were now free to enjoy themselves.

Palmer got up and spent the next fifteen minutes working his way off the dais platform. His progress resembled that of

314

an indecisive crab, moving sideways in spurts and rushes with small retreats along the way as people stopped him to register the fact of their presence.

"Seeing you again, Woods," a portly man with a long unlighted cigar kept assuring him as he pumped his hand. "Good to know that Ubco's not mad or anything."

"Thanks, George." Palmer had always been terribly suspicious of men, mostly politicians, who could always remember everyone's name. Now that he found himself able to pull off the trick, he began to suspect himself, too, of utter insincerity.

"Detroit merger fell through again," another man was saying now as he trapped Palmer's right hand and squeezed it. "But if you'd listened to me, Woods, you'd have gone the convertible debenture route and pulled it off. You can still do it, too, you know."

"Thanks, Bill."

Palmer edged his way past the governor without attracting his attention. In itself, this was something of a miracle. In an election year, few people within handshaking range of the governor escaped unshook.

"Oil lease situation off Baja California, Woods," a man in a tartan plaid dinner jacket was saying as he held Palmer's right hand in both of his. "But the whole depletion allowance question has got to be firmed up a hell of a lot more before we can think constructively about it."

"Thanks, Hal."

Eventually Palmer was able to step off the edge of the platform. He ran into the lieutenant governor, who pumped his hand rather vigorously and spoke for a few moments about the suggested tax changes being proposed over the next five years. Palmer thanked him, too, and moved on.

Within the space of five minutes' time, he had been greeted by another half dozen men in dinner jackets, one of whom introduced him to his wife. Two others took him sharply to task for the tight money situation, a third wondered whether the merger with the Westchester bank had fallen through, a fourth suggested the possibility of speculating in Cuban government bonds through a Swiss intermediary and a fifth wanted to know if it were true that Ubco's advertising was being shifted to another agency.

Palmer found himself with his back literally to the wall, near the entrance to the ballroom. He tried to locate Virginia again and failed. The orchestra began one of those interminable medleys in medium bounce tempo. Then he caught sight of her at the far end of the floor, dancing with a tall, somewhat burly-looking man with close-cropped dark gray hair.

This was the man she had promised the first dance to, Palmer believed, and she had made absolutely certain to find him in time for it, too. And what's more, he told himself, she couldn't care less whether I find her and ask for a dance or not.

And what's more, he decided, neither do I.

He started to make his way toward the cloakroom, when the elevator doors opened and a handful of men in dinner jackets burst noisily out into the hallway. One of them, a newspaperman who normally covered business stories, spotted Palmer and made for him.

"What do you make of it, Mr. Palmer?" he began.

"Hello, Al. Make of what?"

"The ... all the – Wait a second, you don't know there's a big fracas downstairs?"

"What fracas?"

"The other dinner," the newspaperman explained. "The Secretary of Defense is scheduled to talk to a bunch of top business brass and, Christ, Park Avenue's loaded with hippies and weirdos putting on a demonstration."

Palmer nodded. "Anything in particular they're protesting?"

The newspaperman, a shorter, chubbier man than Palmer, looked up at him with disbelief. "You putting me on, Mr. Palmer? The war. Vietnam."

"I get it." Palmer wondered if wisecracks were in order and quickly decided against such a course. "Well, I assume there are plenty of police."

"Hundreds. But me, I'm assigned to this lousy savings-bank di–" He stopped cold and eyed Palmer. "I didn't mean any disrespect, of course. But the action's downstairs, not up here."

"That's the story of our life in banking," Palmer said. Behind him, he could hear the band end the medley. "We're always the dull, quiet end of things. The excitement's always elsewhere."

The newspaperman again viewed him with disbelief. "You really are putting me on, aren't you?"

"Not I."

"At that dinner downstairs it's mostly top brass and space-type manufacturers. I bet Ubco pays the freight for half the

316

business they do."

"Is that a fact?"

"Figuratively speaking," the newspaperman added. Then: "How come you're not at that dinner?"

"Not invited. Invited to this one." Palmer had grown tired of the man's naïve line of questioning. He edged his way back into the ballroom with the journalist following him. "See you again, Al."

"Would you care to comment on the dinner downstairs?"

Palmer's face set in a bland expression. "I think ours tasted swell."

"You know what I mean, Mr. Palmer. About the demonstration and the rest of it. About the war."

"Al, I know you make your living this way, but doesn't it strike you as pretty idiotic to ask for a comment on something I didn't even know about till you told me?"

"So I'm an idiot," the man responded. "Now that you know, what about a comment?"

Palmer took a long breath. He knew how badly he had done up to this point, how unfair a position he had been put in, but he was damned if he would be drawn out by this moron. "I suggest you either stick to the story you were assigned, or else get back downstairs and ask your question there."

"In other words, you're telling me how to do my job?"

Palmer realized he had pushed the man into an emotional state that had little to do with what they seemed to be discussing. "Okay, Al," he said then. "You win. Take this down. Woods Palmer said, 'No comment.' All right? Friends again?"

"I suppose you think I'm some kind of boob you can—"

"Is this man annoying you?" Virginia Clary asked the newspaperman.

Palmer turned to find her standing next to him. "He's—"

"Al, if he's bothering you, I'll have him thrown out by six husky cops."

The newspaperman's eyes widened. "Listen, Ginnie, he's—"

"If there's one thing we won't stand for," she went on, "it's members of the public browbeating the press. Right, Al?"

"Ginnie"—Al's face twisted slightly with embarrassment—"this is Palmer, of Ubco."

Her eyebrows went up and she turned to Palmer. "I had no idea, sir," she said. "Then ... would you like this scrivener ejected by six husky cops?"

The vague bewilderment left Al's face with the knowledge

317

that he had been had. "Very funny, Ginnie." He gave her a look and walked away.

"Still making friends wher'ere you go?" Palmer asked in a light tone.

"Ever the public relations woman." She paused and looked him over at close range of a foot or two. "You haven't changed one iota. Not by a wrinkle. Not by a hair."

Palmer tried to see what it was about her that looked different and younger. He knew her to be forty by now, or perhaps forty-one, but to him she hardly looked more than thirty. It was probably, he thought as he watched her, the fact that she was not having an unhappy affair. Or instead, having a happy one. Or at any rate, was not mixed up with him.

"I do look better, don't I?" she said then.

"Quite remarkably. Not that you ever looked anything but good."

"If banking palls, try diplomacy. You're good."

"Only at telling the truth."

Neither of them spoke for a while. Then she said: "Were you the one who wanted to dance?"

He led her slowly through the throngs of people on the perimeter of the dance floor. A florid-faced man with a scarlet cummerbund grabbed Palmer's hand and detained him.

"Five percent tax-free municipal issue." he was saying. Palmer tried to concentrate on his words. "Archer fleecing," he seemed to say, "and archer filthily if potting wanes."

"Thanks, Ozzie." Palmer smiled and continued leading Virginia Clary to the dance floor.

"Does that mean yes?" she asked him.

Before he could set her straight, a thin man with brownish liver spots on his cheeks intervened, taking Palmer's hand to do so.

"Fortune paisley and Albert Hall," he said with terrible sincerity. "I know you healthy synonym when Peter flees."

"Thanks, Arthur."

They were on the floor now, and the band was playing a medley of tunes from the 1920s and '30s, all done up in campy rickty-tick tempo with much wah-wah brass, templeblock clacking by the drummer and the creamy moan of a reed section playing thirds.

Palmer went into his all-purpose fox-trot, holding her rather closer than he had intended to. The top of Virginia Clary's head came to his shoulder when she wore heels, and she did

318

now. When she tilted her head back to look at him, the disparity of their heights was adjusted slightly.

"The sleepless nights," she sang. "The daily flights. The quick toboggan when you reach the heights. I miss the kisses and I miss the fights."

"I wish I were in love again," Palmer added.

"I wonder," she said, letting the Rodgers and Hart song go its own way unaided, "if there is a snatch of song for every possible occasion?"

"They write enough of them," Palmer said.

She snuggled in slightly, or so it seemed to Palmer. Her breasts, large for a girl her size, felt as if she were wearing very little in the way of a bra. "No more pain," she sang as the song went into its release. "No more strain. Now I'm sane, but—"

"I'd rather be punch-drunk," Palmer finished.

"That's the second release. The first one is 'I'd rather be gaga.'"

"I didn't ask you out on the dance floor to get a lesson in Larry Hart lyrics."

"You didn't really ask me out at all. I had to shanghai you away from your journalistic friend."

"Yes. As for friends, who was that athletic-looking specimen who had the honor of the first dance with you?"

"Jimmy Kincaid."

"Representative Kincaid?"

She nodded. "With that build and that prematurely gray hair and the gift of blarney he's got, you may be looking at a future mayor or governor or Senator."

"He's still in his first term down in Washington, isn't he?"

"First things first."

"And you," Palmer went on, absolutely unable to control himself, "plan to be a future Mrs. Mayor, Governor or Senator?"

"The words 'I'll love you till the day I die,'" she sang as the song repeated again. "The self-deception that believes the lie. I wish I were in love again."

Palmer's smile froze on his face. He seemed unable to get rid of it. "I think you're trying to tell me something."

She nodded. "I'm trying to tell you I'm over you. And after this immensely long silence, I'm quite sure you're over me."

"Quite sure."

She hummed along with the song for a while. "Isn't this lovely?" she asked then.

319

"Marvelous."

"I mean, I mean..." Her voice died away.

He watched the way the lights shifted on her face as he moved her around on the dance floor. At one moment the hollows under her high cheekbones looked almost too dark. Then they lightened, and she looked happy. When they darkened again, she looked unbearably sad.

"Are you engaged?" Palmer heard himself ask.

"No."

"Then what?"

"Then please shut up. We're dancing."

"Believe me, sir," Palmer sang, "I much prefer the classic battle of a him and her."

"I don't like quiet and I wish I were in love again," Virginia finished.

"Are you?"

She looked up at him for a long moment as the band shifted into a Gershwin number. The lighting seemed to ebb. Her eyes grew darker. "Woods, does something give you the right to ask me all these questions?"

He shook his head. "I'm sorry."

"I'm glad you are." She smiled very slightly, hardly more than a faint hint of irony. "When you think how long it took me to comb you entirely out of my hair, I'm not likely to let you back in even an inch, am I? Even with those interrogator's eyes of yours. You made one hell of a good intelligence officer, didn't you?"

"But I didn't have people to question like you."

"I think I'd like to stop dancing, Woods."

"And rejoin Representative Kincaid?"

Her eyes flicked up again. "Are you jealous?"

"I —" He stopped dancing. They stood motionless in the center of the floor. "It's just dawned on me," Palmer said, "that I've been terribly rude to you, haven't I? And after you rescued me from that moron Al."

"Not rude. It's just that we seemed to have hit the wrong note."

"Not we. I."

He took her hand and led her off the dance floor. They stood for a moment. Palmer could see a man in one of those ridiculous white turtleneck shirts coming toward him, an investment banker he detested. He turned Viriginia Clary around so that he could seem not to notice the man in the turtleneck.

"I seem to be saying and doing everything badly. I got off on the wrong foot with Al, too," he told her. "I think I'm not quite myself these days."

"Trouble at the bank?"

"Nothing like that." He touched his temple. "In here. Questions. No answers."

She looked up at him for a long moment, trying to read his mind. Palmer knew that in other days she had been able to know what he was thinking often enough to impress him. Of course, they'd been very close then, he remembered, and now...

The man in the turtleneck fell into conversation with someone else. "What kind of questions?" Virginia asked.

"Harry Elder says I'm trying to run a class in philosophy instead of a board meeting."

"To Harry, any question that can't be answered with a dollar sign and a row if digits automatically becomes a matter of philosophy."

Palmer nodded. "He'll be sorry he didn't come tonight. He always liked you."

She nodded in return and stared past Palmer. "What's wrong with the boy wonder?"

Palmer turned to see Ben Fischetti, alone and terribly pale, gulping from a highball glass that seemed by its color to contain straight whiskey. Palmer noticed that one corner of Ben's mouth seemed permanently turned down in a peculiar tic. "Odd," he said. "Do you know him well?"

"Well enough."

Palmer wigwagged to the younger man. When Ben caught sight of the gesture and saw who had made it, the other corner of his mouth quirked down, and he jostled a third of his drink out of his glass onto the shoes of a passing state senator. Then, without pausing to make an apology, he came directly to Palmer.

"I'm sorry," he said by way of introduction.

"For what?" Palmer turned to Virginia Clary. "May I present Miss –"

"We've met," Virginia cut in. It seemed to Palmer that there was a plain note of chill in her voice.

"Uh, yes. Well." Ben stood there, shifting from one foot to another. He lifted one hand to scratch his cheek and seemed surprised that both his hands were clamped around the glass.

In trying to free one hand, he slopped more whiskey out of the glass.

"Everything all right?" Palmer asked.

"Uh, oh, of course." Ben took a desperate gulp and reduced the contents of the glass to about an inch of whiskey with an ice cube in it. "How's the, uh..." His voice died away.

"I beg your pardon?"

"I said, how's the muh –" Ben stopped and swallowed the rest of the drink. "The muh-merger. How's the muh-merger coming?"

His eyes were rounder than Palmer remembered. He wondered if Ben were afraid of him. He hadn't talked to him since that abortive lunch some weeks ago, at which time the performance Palmer had given might have frightened even a stronger man than Ben.

"If it isn't being too pre – uh – sumptuous," Ben was saying.

A faint line showed between Virginia Clary's glossy black eyebrows. "I think I ought to be getting back," she told Palmer.

"Can you wait just a minute more?" he asked. Then, without waiting for an answer, he turned to Ben. "I think it may go through," he said. "I'm not the final judge, of course. I suppose you're anxious to know whether you're going to be an officer of Ubco or not."

Ben's eyes flared alarmingly. White showed all the way around his irises. He got them under control after a moment. "Nuh-not at all," he said then. Then, hurriedly: "I didn't mean it that way. Of course I want to buh-be an officer of..." His voice seemed to fade out, even though his lips moved for a second more.

"I hope we can keep you at the vice-presidential level," Palmer said. He watched for a reaction. Very few would have surprised him – greed, eagerness, excitement. But he was unprepared for the flash of pure panic he saw. "Is everything all right, Ben?"

"Guh-great." Ben's mouth tightened in a hard line so that all the blood was pressed out of his lips. "Great," he said, taking pains to master the stammer.

"You and I will have to have some talks about the new-business work you've been doing. A good new-business getter is a tremendous asset to a bank."

"My God, I –" The instant the words left his mouth, Ben clamped his lips shut. "Oh," he said after a long moment, speaking very slowly and distinctly, "oh, I quite ... understand. I'm ... sure there are ... many things ... I ... have to learn."

The vertical line between Virginia Clary's brows had deepened. Palmer glanced at her and realized he couldn't detain her much longer. "Be talking to you, Ben," he said. He restrained the impulse to punch the boy lightly on the arm.

He piloted Virginia out of earshot. "Why is he so afraid of you?" she murmured.

"You noticed that? I'm damned if I know."

"He seemed frightened to death. Maybe it was of something else."

Palmer sighed. "It's probably all wrapped up in one of these philosophical things. Is the world getting more serious, or am I just getting too old to handle it?"

They were at a corner of the dais now. At a nearby table, the tall man with the gray hair was chatting with two other men. Palmer realized he had only a few seconds left before he'd have to return Ginnie to her party.

"Is there anything I can do to help?" she asked.

Palmer shook his head. He had wanted her to make such an offer, but he knew now that it wouldn't help. "I'll work it out," he said.

"Still very much the loner, aren't you?"

"Is that what I am?"

"The cat who walks by himself," she said. "And will one day walk right into a big fat trap." She looked at him. The frown line between her eyes went away for a second and then returned. "As a matter of fact, you're already in trouble."

"With what?"

"Are you really buying that bank?"

"Probably."

"Do you know Ben's background?"

"Yes."

"I'm the last person to blow the whistle on others," she said. "I don't believe in guilt by association. But this handsome young man gives off a terrible stench of trouble."

Palmer waved away her words. "I'm sorry to bother you with any of this, Ginnie. You were absolutely right. We are over each other. So, there's the good gray Representative over there waiting for you. It's been a pleasure."

"Damn it, Woods, you're walking out on me."

"Nothing of the kind."

She took his arm and headed him off toward the side door
323

of the ballroom. "I don't like being summarily dismissed," she said. There was a faint flush of red along her cheekbones.

She and Palmer passed by the elevator doors as one opened. "Starlight Roof," the operator said in a bored voice. "Going down."

Virginia steered Palmer into the elevator. "Kincaid can wait a few minutes. Buy me a drink downstairs?"

Palmer nodded. The elevator sank quickly. He felt his stomach rise against his diaphragm. It gave him a momentary feeling of breathless anticipation.

74

There were only a dozen or so people in the Oak Room Bar at this hour. Most of the regular patrons had either gone home or repaired to the restaurant for dinner. Don Vincenzo Biglioto, however, sat firmly ensconced slightly past the midway point of the bar where he had been sitting since approximately ten minutes before Rocco's telephone call establishing for all time Don Vincenzo's presence among disinterested witnesses.

Don Vincenzo had what the family referred to as *una scusa candida*, a white alibi, as opposed to *una scusa società*, one based on the word of family members.

He glanced around him at the dwindling group in the room. Earlier, he had struck up a very pleasant conversation with a well-to-do man his age, a visiting furniture manufacturer who had wanted to give himself a taste of luxury at the Plaza Hotel. This Mr. Feitlebaum, from Rocky Mount, North Carolina, had been a real Southern gentleman, Don Vincenzo felt, buying his share of the drinks over the most voluble of protests. In an expansive mood, Don Vincenzo had given Mr. Feitlebaum the name of several very exclusive restaurants where a mention of his – Mr. Biglioto's – name would produce instant, fawning servility on the part of haughty headwaiters and captains.

Now it was nearly ten o'clock, and Don Vincenzo was not only bored, he was very nearly drunk.

He realized, as he stared into the depths of his seventh Jack Daniel's and water, that spacing so many drinks so carefully over so many hours really didn't diminish their effect as much as he had hoped. Over the back bar, the mural of New York at night made him vaguely unsettled. He detested illusions.

324

On the other hand, he thought, what am I but an illusion? Unlike Rocco.

He was absolutely certain that Rocco had completed his job an hour ago at the very least. He could rely on Rocco to keep to his schedule. But it had been deemed essential that Don Vincenzo squeeze his alibi as far into the night as possible, in case the police got the time of the event slightly wrong. They had been known to place such times as much as an hour wrong either way.

The hour of death.

Don Vincenzo felt a faint shudder start between his shoulder blades and spread sideways to his armpits like a wave of icy water splashing on a winter shore.

He himself had not looked on death for many, many years now. It had been so long ago that he could hardly recall the precise occasion. Never once in this country had he involved himself personally in such matters. It had been preordained by the family that whatever else might conceivably be proved against the son of Don G., murder would not be one of them.

He knew his father had looked into death's face many times. His father had been tested on hundreds of occasions by the family in his youth, again and again putting his arm into the furnace for the good of all. He was pleased that the family rewarded deeds done in the old days by allowing him to remain isolated now from the sight of death. From a business viewpoint, it was very wise. In the old days, in the old country, as a greeen youth Don Vincenzo, too, had had his *tiro a segno*, his *allenamento*, his ... Rocco would know the words. His target practice.

Of course, the newer ones coming up had never been blooded, not even once. Someone like that miserable Ben Fischetti – for all his training as a soldier (and that was a laugh, wasn't it?) – had never killed.

Don Vincenzo started to pick up his seventh drink, then thought better of it. Later, not tonight, but much later, there conceivably could be questioning. It was virtually impossible for the police to make connections that quickly with the reality of what Rocco had done tonight. In all likelihood they would never make the connection, and the case would eventually be filed as unsolved. If any of them got a whiff of the truth, of course, an informer inside the force would report back to Don Vincenzo within twenty-four hours, and steps might then have to be taken. But to express it in numbers, the chances against

325

that were ninety-nine to one.

He glanced at his watch and saw that it was after ten o'clock. He gestured to the bartender with a twenty-dollar bill. "Keep it," he said.

"Thank you, *padrone.*"

"*Prego.*"

Don Vincenzo hoisted himself off the comfortable bar stool and started for the door. He stumbled once, but recovered immediately. He retrieved his coat from the hall checkroom, tipped the girl five dollars – giant tips made for total recall – and found his way slowly along the corridor, past the stairway to Trader Vic's and down the outer stairs to Central Park South. The doorman seemed to recognize him or, if not him, the smell of his money.

"A cab," Don Vincenzo said, stuffing another five into the doorman's breast pocket.

"Yes, sir!"

Don Vincenzo Biglioto drew a deep breath of the night air. To the east, across the street, the horse-drawn hansom cabs stood in a small row. Business was slow on week-nights. Beyond them the dark mass of Central Park gave the illusion of a country setting. For a moment, Don Vincenzo toyed with a fantasy of wooded hills and glades.

Che dolce. It was truly sweet, he told himself, to be utterly removed from the kind of things Rocco had to do for a living. Not even to have to think of such things was the sign of a good life, a fine life, one well worth living. He had only to maintain this illusion and all would go well.

Three squad cars, sirens wide open, roof lights flashing red and yellow, howled furiously along Central Park South, jumped the center stripe and roared east on the wrong lane.

Don Vincenzo felt that same twinge of creeping flesh along his back and shoulders. The cars were heading east at a tremendous pace. But surely there was no need for that if the body of one girl had been disc –

Sirens screaming and whooping, two cars pulled sharp right and hurtled south on Fifth Avenue. The other continued east on 59th Street, running red lights until it reached the corner of Park Avenue. Then it, too, turned south and headed downtown.

"What's the trouble?" Don Vincenzo asked.

The doorman shrugged. "Something at the Waldorf. Your cab, sir."

Don Vincenzo started to get into the cab. He took a last look at the quiet peace of Central Park and wished he could have spent more time in contemplation of it.

75

Kimberley was glad of only one thing. There were no horses. Horses scared him, scared most people on foot. Even the cops couldn't always control their horses. But for some reason the cops had seen fit to handle the whole thing with patrolmen.

Kimberley stood at the 50th Street corner, looking for Edith. He watched three police carry off a young man in leather trousers, buckskin jacket and bead necklace. The young man lay as limply as he could while the cops carried him through the crowd on the street into a waiting patrol wagon.

"Hey-hey, L.B.J.," the crowd shouted, "how many kids did you kill today?"

"Two, four, six, eight, why don't we negotiate?" the crowd yelled.

"Hey-hey, L.B.J., how many kid –"

Kimberley and the rest of the knot of demonstrators were huddled against each other, holding on to each other's bodies to keep from being separated by the pushing police and shouting in each other's ears to be heard.

"Six, eight, why don't we negotiate?"

"Freedom now!" a man screamed at the top of his voice.

"Freedom now!" the crowd responded.

"Freedom here!" the man howled.

"Freedom there. Freedom, freedom everywhere!"

From the south, somewhere in the direction of Grand Central Station, a large Hertz panel truck pulled up in the middle of the street in front of the Waldorf entrance. A dozen police in white riot helmets hopped off the tailgate of the truck, picked up long barreled pump guns and formed in a group as the truck drove away.

Kimberley saw that for several blocks in each direction the north-bound side of Park Avenue had been blocked to automobile traffic. Now the downtown lane on the other side of the mall was being blocked off. Squad cars were arriving singly and in pairs, and police were taking up stations at various corners as far east as Lexington and as far west as Madison. The entire area seemed to be cordoned off. He could find Edith nowhere.

Despite the noise and the glaring television lights and the crazy twiddling spokes of red glare from the roof lights of the squad cars, Kimberley had the sudden feeling they were all alone. The rest of New York seemed to have receded from this spot, as it to avoid getting involved.

"They have us isolated," a man shouted in his ear.

"Yeah. That's smart."

A woman started screaming so shrilly that it hurt Kimberley's ears. She was being dragged, limp, by a single cop, who hauled her upright at the rear door of the patrol wagon and shoved her inside.

"I'm hurt!" she screamed. "I'm hurt!"

The crowd's collective voice grew suddenly louder.

The police officer banged shut the door of the wagon and sent it on its way, siren moaning uneasily. A well-dressed man with a pipe in his mouth accosted the officer.

"There was no need to –"

Two cops lifted him by the armpits and hustled him out into Park Avenue, where another patrol wagon had drawn up, rear door open. They stuffed the well-dressed man inside.

A human chain had now been formed by the police. Demonstrators were being hauled along it from the rank of the crowd to the waiting wagons. One by one, the wagons filled and left. New ones pulled up for another load.

"It's all over," a calm, high man's voice suddenly thundered through a hand-held power megaphone.

Kimberley turned to see a white-haired man in plain clothes standing on the running board of a patrol wagon. "It's over, folks. You can leave by heading east for Lexington Avenue. There's a bus line there and an IRT subway station a block north. Or you can walk on to Fifty-third and get the IND trains. It's all over, so let's move it along."

A man and a woman dashed over to him, waving pieces of paper. Kimberley could hear one of them shouting something about a permit. Overhead, on the roof of the television truck, the camera swung to record the incident. Its zoom lens racked out to telephoto range.

"It's all over," the white-haired man repeated, his voice magnified by the megaphone. "Let's move along, folks."

Four uniformed officers picked up the two people with the permit papers and hustled them into waiting wagons.

"It's all over, folks."

"Freedom now!" a man yelped.

"Freedom now!" the crowd roared. They bulged dangerously out into the street at 49th, the mass of people surging across the sidewalk toward the patrol wagons. Kimberley saw a nightstick rise and fall, then another.

Kimberley looked for Edith among the few people heading east toward Lexington but failed to catch sight of her. Then he turned toward the street to see if perhaps the crowd had shoved her against her will toward the patrol wagons. He caught sight of her sandwich sign and his placard leaning against a lamppost.

A man clutched his face. The force of a blow had smashed his glasses and driven a sliver into his cheek. Blood spurted from the hole.

A girl lowered her placard sign and pointed the stick at the back of a policeman's head. She ran forward with the stick held like a lance. The blunt point of the stick buried itself in the flesh at the back of the cop's neck. He threw his arms out wide and pitched forward onto the asphalt.

Four policemen moved in as a solid phalanx, clubs swinging, until they reached the fallen cop. He had twisted sideways and was clawing at his hip holster, trying to free his revolver.

One of the cops watched him for a moment until he had worked the gun loose. Then the standing cop kicked the revolver free and picked it up. He stuffed it halfway into his tunic pocket. The patrol man lying on the ground grabbed his foot and pulled, spilling him to the ground.

Demonstrators and cops surged up over the two fallen policemen. The main mass of the crowd shifted sideways along the street from the corner of 49th toward the middle of the block.

Kimberley heard the short, sharp report of a handgun, muffled but distinct. For a brief instant the crowd fell silent. Then it panicked.

A woman in an imitation fur jacket scratched at the face of a nearby policeman. He swung his club in a short, tight arc and broke out her front teeth. She dropped to the ground and two men in civilian clothes trampled on her as they tried to run away.

Kimberley heard four shots in quick succession. The air filled with a thin, greenish smoke that drifted sideways in the breeze. People farther along the block were coughing and trying to cover their mouths with handkerchiefs. Kimberley smelled the gas. He dropped to the pavement at the base of the building and breathed through a folded handkerchief. His eyes filled with tears.

Police and demonstrators were reeling about in the gas now, flailing wildly. A heavyset older man in a black overcoat with a fur collar made his way to a policeman and spat in his face. The cop brought his knee up into the man's groin and toppled his sideways, bouncing his head on the kerbstone.

A young boy of about eighteen was kneeling on the asphalt, vomiting nearly into a sewer grating. A police officer grabbed his long yellow hair and hauled him, retching, to a patrol wagon.

A man with a broken placard stick tried to stab a nearby cop. He began to cough so violently that he dropped the stick. Kimberley lost sight of him through his own tears.

The lights had auras around them. Nothing looked the way it should, as if a mist were falling.

Kimberley could taste the gas through the folded handkerchief. In a few moments it would either blow away or he, too, would begin coughing. The twirling spokes of red light from the revolving squad car beacons looked like giant stilts hopping wildly through the night.

Far away, a woman was crying. Nearby, Kimberley could hear a man cursing very quietly, as if not wanting to be heard. Sirens in the distance grew louder, softer, louder.

"It's all over," a voice said in the amplified bellow of the megaphone.

"It's all over."

The sirens grew louder, nearer. Two ambulances pulled up near Kimberley. Their roof lights twirled.

"It's all over, folks."

"Freedom now!" a woman's voice shouted.

"Freedom here!" a man responded.

"Freedom there. Freedom, freedom everywhere!"

76

The area was deserted at this time of night. For most of its length, South Street lived in the shadow of the East River Drive near the bottom of Manhattan Island. Headlights off, the anonymous black Ford moved slowly between the pillars that supported the drive overhead. The car edged out toward the rim of the river.

The boy stopped the car. Rocco gestured to him and the other young man. They carried Harry Klaman's bulk between them and laid him on rotting timbers between two cast-iron stanchions. Beyond the wooden edge of the dock, the river flowed sluggishly.

Everyone except Klaman still wore gloves. Rocco gestured again, and both boys bent over Klaman. They tensed to roll him into the river. His eyes blinked wildly. With the adhesive tape on his mouth and the wire around his wrists and ankles, he knew he would sink to the bottom like an immense pig of lead.

Rocco shot each boy directly in the middle of the back of his head, just where the spinal cord ends in the slight bulge of the inion. The silencer tube squeezed the first shot into such a small sound that it failed to alert the other boy. When the slug meant for his brain tore through the silencer chamber, it made a somewhat louder noise, but not one that could be heard even a block away.

He had been the one, Rocco remembered, with the very dirty mind.

Rocco eased both boys into the river. They made small, anonymous splashes. Then Rocco hauled Harry Klaman back into the car, pulled the tape from his mouth and drove away. He had left the films with a friend, and he was eager to learn how they had turned out.

77

"That newspaperman friend of yours, seemed to think I had some connection with the other dinner," Palmer said. He had started a second drink in the Peacock Alley bar off Lexington while Virginia Clary still nursed her first Scotch and soda. He was aware that nearly fifteen minutes had passed since they had left the Starlight Roof and that, in all probability, Representative Kincaid would be furious with her. Neither of them had referred to this probability, however.

"Do you think he's right?" Ginnie asked.

"No. We probably don't bankroll more than a third of the companies there."

"Aw."

When she smiled, as she did now, her face lost its faint

shade of sadness, that look of original melancholy that had first attracted Palmer to her.

"If you're doing so well," she said then, "you really shouldn't bother with Fischetti's bank. The thought of Ben as one of your officers sends chills up my spine."

"Why? Is Ubco such a moral operation?"

She stopped to consider this. "You, personally, on your own, alone, are about as immoral a pirate as I have ever seen. I still haven't gotten over the way you pulled off that coup of yours a year and a half ago."

"You can't say I initiated it," he said defensively. "I was pushed into it."

"Pushed or fell. Nothing matters in one of those melees except who gets up off the canvas at the end and has his hand lifted by the referee. And you, my dear, were the only winner in sight."

"I hate to lose. So do you."

"Everyone hates to lose," she corrected him. "But someone has to, in order for someone to win. Or am I being too obvious?"

He nodded. "You still haven't explained what bothers you about Ben working for Ubco, with a nice chunk of stock. He's clean, neat, well spoken, well-educated, bright, attractive, clever and successful."

"He's all of that and one other thing."

"Yes?"

Virginia Clary sighed and finished the last of her drink. "He's owned, right up to his eyebrows. They have him in a lock, Woods. He's given up too many hostages ever to break away. A wife? Four children? Forget it."

"I presume we're referring to his father and his father-in-law?"

"Tony Fish and Vinnie Big."

"Good. Now we're closing in on what bothers me."

"They should, for starters."

"Why should they? What is so different about the way they do business and the way we do business?" Palmer signaled a waiter to bring a fresh round. "When I ask one of my esteemed associates about it, he mumbles something vague and old-school-tie and thinks he's made a statement. But none of them does make a statement. None of them can tell me what the real differences are."

She stared at her empty glass for a moment. "Isn't that a

terribly awkward question for someone like you to worry about? Suppose, God forbid, you got a true answer?"

"You're making fun of me," Palmer snapped. "Harry Elder tells me I'm in male change of life. Both of you are dodging the issue."

"That's true."

"Then what is it? Is it like bad breath?"

"Even your best friends won't tell you?" She smiled at him again, but this time the melancholy stayed in her face. "Am I a friend of yours, Woods?"

"Are you?"

"Why should I be?"

Before he could answer, the waiter brought fresh drinks and removed the old glasses. The delay caused Palmer to stop and think, his usual pattern, instead of blurting out the first thing that came into his head, as he had been tonight. "I suppose you're right," he said at last. "Why should you be my friend, after what happened?"

"Nothing terrible happened."

"Just a complete breakup between us."

"That wasn't terrible at all." She stirred her drink and then touched the little muddler stick to the tabletop, making a circle of liquid on its shiny surface.

"You reallly didn't want me in the shape I was in," she went on then. "I hated you at the end and was doing a bad job of concealing it. I don't hate you anymore. I know what it was then. It was hero worship. And when I found out you weren't the Parsifal you seemed, I felt you'd betrayed a dream, so I hated you. It only lasted a few months. Then I had a different problem. I missed you. Physically. Emotionally. Every way possible to miss a man. But that only lasted a few more months. It wasn't a prize year, for me. Not at all. Every time my telephone rang, at the office or at home, I was certain it was you. You. Calling. To say 'Let's get together again.' So that I could turn you down cold."

"I had no idea it –"

"Yes, you did," she interrupted. "You had to. Anyway, then, about six months ago, my mother died."

"I didn't kn –"

"It was in the papers. After I buried her, I gave up the old apartment we shared. I just had the Salvation Army come in and take away all the furniture. I moved. I redecorated. I met Jimmy Kincaid. I met other men. I felt a whole lot better. So I

333

sent you an invitation to tonight's dinner. Wasn't that the limit in stupidity?"

"Why should you th–?"

"And you accepted," she cut in, "which redoubles the stupidity to slam proportions. I was out of my mind to invite you, and you were insane to accept. How's Edith?"

Palmer blinked. "Fine. Or maybe not so. Why?"

"Still cleaving together, you two, through thick and thin?"

Palmer closed his eyes for a moment. "We're not on the best of terms."

"Is that news?"

"As a matter of fact, we're in much worse shape now than two years ago."

"Um."

He opened his eyes and made a brushing-away gesture. "Let's drop Edith, shall we? Let's get back to the question I asked you."

"Just like that?"

"If you don't mind."

"Whatever made you think I could give you an answer?" she asked.

Palmer gestured aimlessly. "You always could."

"That was then. This is now. We're not really tuned to each other's wavelength anymore, are we." It was a statement, not a question.

"Are we?"

She had started to sip from her glass. She put it down instead and carefully inspected it, as if she had discovered an ant somewhere within the amber fluid. Then she nodded very firmly. "We are."

Neither of them spoke for a moment. Then Palmer said: "I suppose I'm just a little desperate about all this, to be trying to unload it on you the first time I see you in a year and a half."

"Yes. I suppose." Her voice had gone cold.

After a while she got to her feet. "If the good gray Representative is still waiting up there, I'd like to be taken back."

"Of course." Palmer left money on the table and escorted her out into the corridor leading to the main lobby of the hotel. A heavyset, elderly man in a dark blue suit and dark gray overcoat bumped into Palmer as they emerged from the bar.

"Sorry." He started to push past.

334

"Hold it, Mulvey," Virginia said. "Still pushing voters around?"

The beefy man turned on her, his face chalky white. "What the hell do −?" He stopped, and a look of astonishment replaced the anger. "It's the Clary!"

"How goes it, James?" she asked.

"Are you telling me, girl, that you don't know what's occurring at the front of this hotel?"

"I saw demonstrators."

The heavy man shook his head sadly. "And to think there was a time when the Clary used to get to the scene faster than Homicide."

"What's happening out front?"

Mulvey jerked his double chin in the direction of the Park Avenue lobby. "Take a look for yourself, girl." He lumbered away at a fast clip.

Palmer smiled at her. "Still the darling of New York's finest?"

She shrugged. "Once a newspapergirl, always a darling."

They followed in the beefy man's wake, finding the various lobbies and public areas curiously deserted. They stopped for a moment to peek in the Sert Room and found that someone from Washington was in the middle of making an address.

Palmer listened for a moment but found it hard to distinguish between the man's discussion of defense needs and the equally profound insights of the speaker at the upstairs dinner. He knew intellectually that the two addresses were completely different. He knew that the caliber of the man from Washington was reputedly far above any local talent mustered for the dinner upstairs. He knew, in fact, that the failure to find distinguishing points was his own and could not be blamed on any of the speakers. And finally, he also knew that it didn't seem to bother him that it was his fault.

"I can accept the blame," he said aloud.

"For what that gasbag is spouting?" Ginnie asked.

They turned away from the Sert Room and started for the Park Avenue entrance. "Where is everybody?" Palmer asked. "Have the cops shooed them out of the lobbies, too?"

"No. They're keeping clear."

"What?"

They pushed through the revolving doors, still spinning from the momentum Mulvey had given them a few moments before.

The cool air felt soothing. There was a faant acrid trace of something in the air that Palmer couldn't identify at first. He sniffed twice. Ginnie took his arm. He could feel her fingers tighten on his wrist. She pointed toward the uptown corner of 50th Street.

Two ambulances formed an angle of protection around the few people left in the area. Interns were working over three bodies lying on the bare asphalt. The first was an elderly man in a fur-collared coat, whom they seemed to be trying to revive. A thick rill of blood trickled from the corner of his mouth. The second man had a large gash dug into the cheek below his eye. An intern was trying to stanch the flow of blood. The third patient was hidden from Palmer's view by two orderlies and a fireman with a pulmotor outfit. The fourth person lying on the ground, unattended, was a uniformed policeman. His hat had been laid over his face.

"Dead?" Palmer asked. "Good God!"

Ginnie nodded. The red revolving beacons on top of squad cars and ambulances crossed and crisscrossed again and again. With an anguished moan, a third ambulance arrived. Two girls in their late teens, whom Palmer hadn't noticed before, were escorted into the new ambulance. He couldn't see what was wrong with them, but they were sobbing.

A man in a white lab coat was talking to a police officer seated on the kerb holding his face in his hands. The intern was trying to get the cop to swallow something from a paper cup. The cop continued to shake his head and refuse.

An intern stood up next to the elderly man. His partner wiped the blood from the old man's mouth. The hand holding the plain white towel hovered for a moment, then draped the towel over the man's face.

High overhead, atop their trucks, television cameras continued to record the activity, but reporters were now down among the survivors, mingling with them, holding their microphones out to catch any words that might be spoken.

Virginia Clary looked at her tiny wristwatch. "They can still make the eleven o'clock news if they're using video tape," she said.

"Is that your only comment?" Palmer asked.

She blinked. "I ... I didn't mean –"

"Right." He turned her around and pulled her back into the lobby of the Waldorf. "Let's get you back upstairs to your friend Kincaid. I imagine he ought to be told what's been hap-

336

pening to some of his constituents."

"Look here, I–"

"Now I know what you meant about these deserted lobbies. Everyone's using the Lexington Avenue exits. Nobody want to get involved."

Palmer stopped in the middle of the lobby and stared around him. "I used to believe that it didn't take much to collect a crowd in Manhattan. But that's a lie, isn't it? The second anything violent happens, people scatter. Nobody wants to be a witness. Nobody even wants to know about it."

He put her in the elevator. "Take this lady back to the Starlight Roof," he told the operator. Ginnie was watching him with a look of disbelief mixed with anger as the doors closed between them.

Palmer started out the Park Avenue doors again, but stopped as he heard a burst of applause from the Sert Room. The speaker had barely finished when gentlemen in evening dress began to head for the cloakroom and their coats.

"Woods," a youngish man with rather long hair called. He was wearing a white turtleneck shirt. Palmer squinted in disbelief. He was sure he had seen, and avoided, this man at the other dinner.

"Super speech, eh?" the investment banker said.

"Weren't you upstairs, too?"

The man churned his hands about in a meaningless gesture. "On the move. Never give them a sitting target. Bit of a dust-up outside, eh?"

Palmer found that his fake British accent – he represented an investment group in England but, as far as anyone knew, had been born and educated in Milwaukee – and his longish hair and turtleneck shirt combined to make him as repellent as anyone Palmer had run into tonight.

He stared into the man's reddish face and found puffy signs of self-indulgence. "They were out there getting clobbered to protect bastards like you, Archie," he told the investment banker cheerfully. "Two of them got killed. A civilian and a cop. How was your din-din, old chap?"

The investment banker frowned – "Bad show, wot?" – turned on one heel and made for the cloakroom, where a double line of distinguished guests were already clamoring for their coats. Palmer stood to one side of the lobby, near the doors to Park Avenue, and watched them leave by the rear of the hotel. Evidently the word had gone around.

After a while, he went outside in his dinner jacket again. The night air had turned chilly. He watched two interns roll the elderly dead man onto a stretcher and lift him into one of the ambulances. The cop sitting by himself at the kerb now had company, a young Negro boy of about fifteen who was vomiting on his shoes in the gutter. The cop looked up and gave him a terrible, dead stare of disgust.

" 'Cha puking for?"

"Christ, man."

"I shot my buddy over you, kid." The cop stared belligerently at the boy but, getting no response, settled back on the kerb and stared at the asphalt in front of him. "Shot him dead," he muttered.

"He's no good to anybody now," a voice said behind Palmer. He turned to see the beefy Mulvey. "We get a few every year, you know," Mulvey went on. "Cops accidentally shoot one of their own in a raid or a shoot-out or a riot. It happens. The man who does the shooting usually resigns the cops within a year or so."

Palmer caught a faint whiff of the acrid smell again. "Tear gas?"

"Some new stuff." Mulvey made a face. "All-purpose riot-control gas. And these idiots cut it loose before they could pull their own men out of it. Gorgeous good planning."

"Was there a big mob?"

"I been playing with these pickets going on eight years now. It's my job," Mulvey said. "I can't hate the poor bastards. They're to be pitied. They don't like what they have, and they don't know how to get what they want . . ."

"It's the times," the beefy detective was saying. "In the old days, when a man hated the government he pulled up stakes and moved. My God, most of the world was settled that way. But you tell me: where are these poor bastards going to move to now? It's too crowded. Everything is big government. They've got to learn to live with it. They'll get nowhere eating their hearts out."

Palmer sniffed. The acrid smell had almost gone, or else he had grown accustomed to it. He started to walk south toward 49th Street, then remembered his coat was upstairs at the Starlight Roof cloakroom. As he turned around he ran head on into Virginia Clary.

"Oof!"

"Sorry."

"I hoped you hadn't run away," she said.

"Had a most illuminating talk with your friend Mulvey. I'm sorry I got angry at you before. Where's your date?"

"I told him I had to talk to you. He understands."

Palmer felt a twinge of alarm. "My God, understands what?"

"Understands we're good friends who haven't seen each other in a long time."

"I must say he's an awfully obliging fiancé."

"Woods, you are too obvious for words. We're not engaged."

"Then boyfriend."

"Yes," she admitted, "boyfriend. You're making me very sorry I came back down for you."

"Why did you?"

"I thought you needed help." Her dark eyes had a hooded look about them. "I should have known you never need help. Or never admit needing it."

Palmer watched her eyes for a moment. He started to tell her that she had been the one to refuse to help, when she said they were on different wavelengths. He thought of telling her that her remark about the television reporters having time to make the eleven o'clock news had angered him with its callousness. Instead he simply smiled and took her arm. They headed south toward the corner of 49th Street.

"What about your coat?"

Palmer shrugged. "Where can I take you?"

"My place?"

78

Sean was seated with Augie in one of the padded raspberry leather booths near the back of the place with a friend from Boston, a women's-wear buyer from one of the more expensive department stores there. They were joined at about ten thirty by another male friend, a buyer from a large specialty shop in Washington, D.C.

They had decided to make an evening of it and, by the time a third friend, a local department store manager, sat down in the booth with them, they had all had at least four drinks and were feeling just fine.

It was, Sean told himself hazily, a kind of an independence celebration. "What is it, you chaps? Independence Day? The

Fourth of June?"

Augie made a face. "Stop the Limey put-down. It's July, baby, and you know it."

"July?" Sean asked muzzily. "The June of July?"

This sent all five of them into paroxysms of giggling. "But seriously, folks," Sean went on in what he imagined was a perfectly hilarious Texas drawl, "mah wife, that's Lady Beagle, and me, we reckon to celebrate our ee-mancipation tonight in rill Texas stahl."

"Spare us, lovey," the Boston buyer sibilated.

"You chaps will brook no irreverence to your esteemed chief executive," Sean asserted, bearing down as heavily on the *s*'s as his companions. "Wot?" He narrowed his eyes and stared toward the front near the stand-up bar.

"I say." He shoved to his feet and made his way rather unsteadily toward Ben Fischetti. "I say, chappie. I say, old man. Pip, pip." He giggled as he stood there, unable to think of the next thing to say.

"Hello, Sean." Ben took a whiskey and soda from the bartender. "What brings you huh-here?"

"I'm always here. This is one of my little snugs."

Ben drank off half the highball. He paused for a moment, as if formulating his words very carefully. "Huh-have –" He stopped and waited. Then: "Have a drink?"

Sean picked the glass out of his fingers and led the way back to the booth. "Girls," he said, "this is Ben. Lovely man, but straight, so far."

The buyer from the nation's capital looked up at Ben and smiled very prettily. "Well," he said slowly, "nobody's perfect."

79

Edith was home by eleven o'clock and had tuned in the news on television just as the opening commercial for a stomach alkalizer ended and the announcer began to report the events of the day. She listened to three minutes on Vietnam, a minute in the President's new tax bill, two minutes on a cyclone that had cut loose in Arkansas and Missouri and a commercial for a headache remedy.

"Mom?"

She stared guiltily and turned to see her daughter Gerri in

the doorway, barefooted and in her nightgown. "You should have been asleep an hour ago."

Gerri nodded. "I couldn't sleep. Can I watch TV with you?"

"Just the news." Edith shifted sideways on the cloth-covered easy chair, and Gerri snuggled up next to her. The girl's thin body seemed terribly bony to Edith. She gave her a hug.

They watched two minutes on a fire that had gutted a Providence motel, a minute on a train wreck in Oregon, a minute on preparations for a new space shot at Cape Kennedy and two minutes on the spectacular marriage of two film stars, each for the fourth time. The news closed with half a minute on a fashion show in Paris at which the girls had modeled tinted vinyl dresses that were completely transparent, over chiffon underthings. All the views were long shots.

"Let's watch the local news," Gerri suggested then.

"Oh?" In her eagerness, Edith had forgotten that the first quarter hour was usually devoted to so-called national and international news. "All right. But then it's bed. Why couldn't you get to sleep?"

"Thinking."

"About what?"

Gerri squirmed and burrowed her head into Edith's side below her breast. "Things."

"Thinking about things. I see."

"War. Woody getting drafted, maybe. You and Dad fighting."

Edith swallowed twice and hoped the movement wasn't apparent to her daughter. "Which bothered you the most? Because it wasn't fighting at all, darling. Just a discussion."

"You do have a lot of discussions nowadays, don't you?"

Edith put her hand under Gerri's chin and lifted her head up to see her face. "Is that sarcasm? I'm well aware that we're not getting along."

Gerri grinned idiotically up at her. "The understatement of the century."

"Yes. Well, I don't expect you to understand it all. I don't. But it's something that happens occasionally in marriages." Edith paused for a moment to look at a commercial for a deodorant. "It's either serious or final or it isn't. I have no idea which kind this is."

The television screen showed a quick glimpse of a mouthwash, and then the local news program began. Edith watched the speaker from Washington, whom she had been picketing a few hours before, as he called for greater support for the war effort.

"Meanwhile, in front of the midtown hotel where the Secretary was speaking," the announcer said, "a demonstration was quelled by the police." The television screen showed the Washington man speaking, but no sounds came from his lips. Then the scene changed to a tantalizing view of a police patrol wagon moving off along Park Avenue. "Several injuries were reported," the announcer said as this was going on, "and there is an unconfirmed report of the serious wounding of a police officer." The screen showed the announcer reading from a sheet of paper. He paused and looked up into the camera lens. "At City Hall today, the mayor called on New Yorkers to help fight crime in the streets by –"

Edith snapped off the television set. "No fair," Gerri said. "Or was that all you wanted to see?"

"I simply didn't need to look at any more commercials to help me doctor my insides."

"But there's lot more news, too."

"I'm not interested."

"Just in the peace demonstration?" Gerri asked.

"All right. Yes."

"You were pretty hot about the subject at dinner, too."

"Yes."

Gerri sat up straight on the chair beside her. "You were there tonight, weren't you?" she asked suddenly.

Edith tried to choose a proper response. She decided she was too tired to evade. "Yes," she said. "I was picketing."

"How about that?"

"How about that." Edith nodded slowly. "It was frightening and boring, all the same time. Those people are not to be believed, Gerri. They are so solemn and glum that it's like a meeting of one of the penitential sects."

"No stomping and shouting?"

"A few tired slogans. A few chants, silly ones."

"You just don't dig the scene," Gerri said. "It's a whole new bag, Mom. Granny glasses and long dresses and hair parted in the middle and shoes that look like they were stolen from a nun. It's the solemn scene. You must have stood out like a swinger. Why, that skirt hits you right above the knee."

Edith smiled slightly. "I daresay."

"Did the cops make trouble for you?"

"No."

"Well, who got hurt?"

"I ... don't know." Edith stood up and put a little distance between herself and her daughter. "I'm afraid I ran away when it seemed to be heading for trouble."

"Oh."

Edith hadn't looked back at Gerri yet. When she did, the girl seemed lost in thought for a moment. Then: "But your friends stayed, didn't they?"

"Friends?"

"The people who brought you?"

"I suppose so." Edith shook her head. "I'm not all that clear about it. One minute it looked like trouble, and the next I was hailing a cab on Lexington and grateful that one stopped for me."

"Oh."

Neither of them spoke for a while. "Don't make it seem any worse than it was," Edith said then. "I deserted my friends. I admit that. Perhaps I just don't have the right to be in such places. If I'd been hurt, what kind of mother would I have been to you? And if I'd been subjected to publicity of some sort, it might have affected your father's work and our whole future."

"You remember that woman down South?" the girl asked. "The one who was shot to death driving a car? She had a family."

"Exactly. And—"

"Except that I suppose her kids were awfully proud of her anyway."

Edith frowned. "Are you suggesting that I should have stayed?"

Gerri's long, skinny arms folded down at the elbows, palms up and out like wings flapping at her shoulders. "I didn't suggest anything at all, Mom." she said with a great show of innocence.

"You know, your father's right. You children go too far sometimes."

"Just me. The boys pretty much toe the line." Gerri giggled. "It's all right about leaving the picket line. I mean, if it was a drag, why stay?"

"That's not why I left it," Edith reminded her.

"If you ask me, it's a good reason."

"I don't recall asking you."

Gerri made on of her God I-did-it-again faces. "Sorry about

343

that. Uh, do you want to call your friends and see how they did?"

"Why should – ? Oh." Edith thought for a moment. "Oh. I'm certain they're all right. I'll call you in the morning."

Gerri nodded. "Okay, Mom, I'm going to bed. You too?"

"I think so."

"Don't wait up for Dad," the girl said and pecked her on the cheek before bounding out of the room. "Night!"

Edith stood there, wondering whether she had lost the knack of knowing when her own daughter was being sarcastic, or whether she had grown paranoid and was reading hidden meanings into everything.

Considering how bright Gerri was, she decided, that last remark had undoubtedly been sarcasm.

80

Palmer and Virginia Clary had walked east as far as they could go along 49th Street. It seemed to Palmer that they had not stopped talking for very long, ranging mostly over the events of the night.

They started walking up First Avenue now, and Palmer found himself moving more slowly as the effort of the long evening began to make itself felt in his leg muscles. He glanced at an illuminated wall clock in the window of a watch-repair shop and saw that it was now now even half past eleven. It felt later in his legs.

At 58th Street they turned east again, crossing Sutton Place and stopping for a moment on a small dead-end pocket of street hardly five cars deep that led from the avenue east almost to the brink of the river. Virginia took them down a flight of masonry stairs to a tiny park that contained a few benches and an expanse of iron railing to keep loungers from falling down onto the rocks below that formed the edge of the river itself.

At this time of night, with the moon not yet up and the noise of traffic over the 59th Street bridge a steady rushing thrum, the pocket park seemed more isolated than ever. Palmer felt as if he were at the bottom of a shaft. High above him ranged skyscraper apartment houses and bridges that hurtled cars and trucks through the air. Across the black, oily expanse of the river huddled Welfare Island buildings in which the insane slept, or failed to sleep. Beyond, over Queens, a helicopter soared, its belly light blinking.

"Why here?" he asked.

She turned and pointed ot a small enclave of houses to one side of the tiny park. "I schemed and connived and waited patiently for that one, the little one with the mullioned windows. A savings bank owned it. The instant it went on the market I put in a high bid – too high – and snatched it right off the market again."

"You don't use the whole thing?"

"Ground floor and basement. That gives me two apartments to rent out."

"What kind of mortgage did you get?"

She made a face. "We've done so well pretending not to be bankers, I'd almost convinced myself of it."

Palmer laughed and turned back to watch the powerful flow of the dark river beneath them. "Harry Elder tells me he'd be hard put to find anybody who considers a banker a gentleman."

"Harry's right."

"He wants me never to forget we're dirty moneylenders."

Virginia Clary nodded vehemently. "Lower than the low. About the only thing lower is someone like me who does publicity for bankers."

He fumbled in the pocket of his dress jacket. He had not been cold during their long walk, but now he had begun to feel faintly chilly. "Do you have a cigarette?" he asked.

"Gave them up last year."

"My God, it was a salutary time for you, wasn't it? Me and tobacco in one fell swoop."

She was silent, staring at the river and then, downstream, at the southern tip of Welfare Island. "No comment?" Palmer persisted.

"Woods." She stopped and seemed to return to her mood of silence. After a while she sighed so softly Palmer barely heard it above the traffic noise from the Queensboro Bridge.

"Woods, what do you think when you got the invitation to tonight's dinner?"

"I thought: ah-ha, and similar sentiments."

"I'm serious."

"I ... didn't know what to think. I didn't have a thinking reaction. It was a visceral one, I suppose. I just wanted to go, that was all."

"What do you think now?" she continued.

"I'm still not thinking very much. Been thinking a great deal in the past few months about all sorts of depressing things. I suppose I'm afraid to think about this one because it, too, might turn out to be depressing."

"Well, that's frank enough. You weren't always that frank with me."

"I've gotten depressingly frank with myself lately. I see no reason to spare anyone near and dear." The moment he said that, Palmer tried to replay it in his mind to see if it meant more than he wanted it to. It did.

"You have my permission," Virginia said, "to retract the 'near and dear.'"

"No more mind reading."

"Sorry."

"My daughter Gerri mind-reads me. Apparently I am an open book."

"Only to women who—" She stopped.

"Who what?" he asked after a while.

"Who"—she turned away from him and moved down the rail a few feet—"who love you."

Neither of them said anything for a while. Then she moved still farther from him. "Why do you think I had them invite you?" she asked then.

"Wait a second," Palmer protested. "What about Kincaid? The other men you mentioned? What about the fact that we're over each other?"

She shook her head quickly. "You never did understand me, did you?"

"I guess not."

"When you sent in your dinner reservation, I sat at my desk and cried. Not for long. Just a minute or two." She turned toward him but kept the distance between them. "And when I saw you tonight, I nearly broke up all over again."

"But that talk in Peacock Alley?"

"That was just me, trying to be sensible."

Palmer took a step toward her. She retreated a step. In the overhead light of the park floodlamps, her cheekbones cast immense shadows that darkened most of her face. "You're going to have to explain it better than that," Palmer said then. "I've gotten very slow in my old age."

"There's nothing to explain. I did get over you. That much was the truth. I did get out and meet other men, lots of them.

346

Kincaid included. Some were nice enough. Doesn't that make sense? I was over you, but I was still comparing men to you. Perfectly understandable."

"No."

"Well, of course it is. Look, what sort of women have you been seeing this past year and a half?"

Palmer frowned. "I haven't seen any."

"You can tell me."

"I am," he said. "There hasn't been anybody since you."

She turned to look at the river. In the distance upstream, a small white cabin cruiser, its running lights reflected as shimmery smears, made its way south. The red of its port light looked like a tiny flame on the rippling water.

"How am I supposed to take that?" Virginia asked then. She had pulled her small dark otter jacket tightly together at her throat. Now her fingers let it drop, and the upper curves of her breasts emerged into the chilly night air. She clutched the jacket to her again.

"It wasn't meant to be taken any particular way," Palmer admitted. "I suppose you could say it took me as long to get over you as you took over me."

"Or that our affair was so unnerving, you just didn't want any of the bother ever again."

"If you like being negative about it, yes."

She smiled in a tentative way. "That did sound nasty."

"I don't mind."

"Some residual hostility," she mused. "I told you why I invited you to the dinner. But why did you come?"

"You didn't tell me at all," Palmer pointed out.

"Oh, but I did. Weren't you listening?"

He nodded. "I heard." Then, after a moment: "I decided to come because I wanted to see you again."

"So you could ask me questions nobody else will answer?"

"Yes. But that's only one reason."

She pulled her jacket tighter around her throat. "You must be freezing, Woods."

"Not quite."

"Come in the house and have a nightcap."

"Thank you."

He took her arm and led her up the stairs to the street level. "I had other reasons for wanting to see you again. I wanted to know how you were and how you felt and ... and I wanted to see how you looked. I wanted to hear your voice again. I thought maybe we might dance together. I wanted to feel you again. A lot of reasons."

She piloted them through the common yard of the row of buildings and up the short flight of steps to the ground floor of her house. "I missed you," Palmer heard himself say. "I didn't know how much I missed you until I saw that invitation."

"Come inside and get warm."

"Yes." He shivered slightly. "It's getting quite chilly."

81

The dark, anonymous Ford pulled to a halt about ten blocks north of the Park Avenue apartment house where Harry Klaman lived. Rocco glanced at his watch and saw that he had half an hour until midnight. He turned to look at Klaman, busy rubbing circulation into his wrists and ankles. A faint scab had crusted over the place on his lips where the adhesive tape had torn off flesh.

"Got the picture, Harry?" Rocco asked.

"Yes." Klaman paused for a moment in rubbing his wrists and pulled a handkerchief out of his pocket to mop his face. "I saw the photos, Rocco. I got the picture."

"You gotta sense of humor, too, Harry."

Klaman blinked. "Huh?"

Rocco opened the door on Harry's side. "Out. Walk home from here. No cabs. Understand?"

"Yes, Rocco."

"Good. From now on it's 'Yes, Rocco'. You don't breathe, you don't fart unless you clear it with me. Understand?"

"Yes, Rocco."

"By rights you should have been dead for hours, Klaman. But you're better for us alive than in a box. From here on in, you don't build so much as a shack without our say-so. Your whole business is our business. And any time you want to see what happens if you don't take orders, just watch. Now, out."

Rocco watched the heavy man leave the car. Klaman paused for a moment on the street. He turned back to Rocco.

"Is she really dead?" he asked then, in a pitiful voice.

"You'd better believe it. If you don't, just try pinning it on anybody. You'll do life for it, and the newspapers will get the juiciest sex scandal they ever handled."

"Okay, okay."

348

"Start walking." Rocco slammed the door shut and drove off down Park. He turned west on 72nd Street and crossed Central Park before stopping at an all-night drugstore on Broadway to make a toll call.

"Santo?" he asked when his call was answered. "Is he still awake?"

"*Si.*"

"Okay, give me an hour." Rocco hung up. He hated to disturb the old man's night, but he had his orders. Whatever happened, he was to make a personal report.

He wondered, as he drove up the West Side Highway toward the bridge, if Don G. would approve everything he had done. There had been no slipups. And the presence of Ben, unexpected though it was, knotted even more threads together than any of them had dreamed of.

He hoped the old man would approve. He had to, Rocco told himself. He had to approve and, if he did, he had to show his appreciation.

Sometimes, Rocco knew, Don G.'s appreciation was expressed with a generosity that could take one's breath away.

82

At midnight the Episcopalian church two blocks from the Fischetti home in Scarsdale pealed out the hour with enough verve to waken Rosalie. She glanced at the clock beside her bed. Then she got up and padded silently about the upper floor of the house in her bare feet, checking the children and looking for signs of Ben.

She went downstairs. Sometimes he got home so tired or drunk that he fell asleep on the living room couch.

She went into the kitchen and opened the refrigerator, gnawed by a terrible hunger. As she eyed the contents of the refrigerator, she reached for the breadbox and slid open the lid. Then she realized what she was doing and stopped. She slammed the refrigerator shut.

She padded back into the living room and read a magazine for a while. The hunger subsided. At twelve thirty she put the magazine away and picked up a book she had gotten out of the library. At one o'clock she laid it down and went upstairs to bed again. She had the distinct feeling that Ben would not be home tonight at all. The woman he kept on Ninth Street, the one from whose house she had seen him running that night, was probably no better than a whore of some kind.

Rosalie knew that she was living in a permissive society in which all kinds of lapses from conventional morality were possible. The magazines she read were filled to overflow with examples of infidelities and perversions that had become quite commonplace. The magazines were sorry about this state of affairs, Rosalie knew, and it angered them, but they continued conscientiously to report the most shocking of moral lapses again and again and again.

She supposed that if Ben had a mistress it was only right for her to have a lover, but she wasn't quite sure how she went about getting one.

She knew there were boys down in the village who talked a lot to her about such things. But they were terribly dirty young men who hardly ever washed. If there were one thing Rosalie knew she required in a lover, it was someone who showered regularly and brushed his teeth.

At one thirty she got up and went downstairs again to look up "deracinate" in the large dictionary.

83

"There's one idiot on my board who believes we shouldn't have anything to do with the Mafia because they have such a bent toward violence."

Palmer nodded to confirm what he had just said. He was on his third Scotch whisky, and he knew he was boring Virginia Clary to tears.

"As if man himself doesn't have a bent toward violence," he added then.

The room was a kind of library overlooking the river. One wall had been filled with bookshelves from floor to ceiling, but not all the shelves had books as yet. The rest of the room contained a large sofa – on which Virginia had curled up, glass in hand – a desk 'and an easy chair in which Palmer now sat. He felt he had begun to drone on and on, so he stopped.

"Man is more violent than any other animal," she said then.

"And the only one with the ability to decry it while practicing it. As if" – Palmer swung on, warming up again – "we weren't practicing violence out there in front of the Waldorf tonight to suppress those poor lunatic demonstrators. What have the annals of the Mafia or the syndicate or whatever it is to show that is any more callous or violent?"

"Only animal that double-talks," Virginia announced. Palmer realized she was no more sober than he. "Only animal who commits crimes no other animal would dream of committing and then calls such crimes bestial. He says of another man, 'He behaved like an animal.' But what he means is, 'He behaved like a man.'"

"He's the only animal who can talk."

"So he's the only who tells lies."

"Bravo," he shouted.

"Brava." She sat up straighter. "Let's have our sex straight."

"That's the best way."

"If you hate mankind that much," she said, finishing what was left in her glass, "why haven't you just blown your brains out?"

"Not my style."

"It's mine. I'm not that good a Catholic anymore to fear suicide."

"All right," he countered. "Why haven't you killed yourself?"

"Because there are too many sons of bitches in this world I want to take with me."

"Bravo," he said, "Brava."

"Don't you feel the same way?"

"I have no desire to change the world."

She nodded. "That's because it suits you as it is."

"Hell it does."

"The rich always perfer the *status quo*."

His eyes narrowed. "You really hate me, don't you?"

She walked with amazing steadiness to the easy chair. Then she knelt in front of him and put her head on his knees. "No, I don't."

"But damn it, what am I to do about this whole thing?"

"What whole thing?"

"The bank. The merger. The everything."

"Just face one thing at a time." She began to rub his thighs. "You're still in a state of shock about finding out that you're not much different from Vinnie Big. That's what's really behind all this questioning of yours. You already knew the answer. Big crime. Big business. To know that, you didn't need to see cops and picketers being killed to protect big business. You'd already done your own share of dirt, my dear. You'd shoved your own shivs. I'm not giving you any answers you didn't already know."

"You really do hate me."

She took his hand and squeezed it softly. "You already know the answer to that, too."

"Then how can you stand to be with me?"

"Corruption is man's native element," she said. "Conceived in sin. Born in corruption. To the manor born, so to speak. I occasionally give myself airs, but I'm still human and, thus, corrupt."

"Not really."

"I really do hope I'm less corrupt than some." She smiled up at him and the hollows around her eyes seemed lighter. "There are a few saints, of course. I'm not one. But I'm not as corrupt as you, for example. I haven't had the temptations."

"My life has been free of temptation."

This time she laughed. "You can speak, so you tell lies. You had power handed to you. It's a terrible temptation. If it had been handed to me, I wonder how corrupt I now might be."

"All power corrupts?" Palmer asked. "That's old hat."

He listened to his own words with the same fatal power he had always had of running back again over the tape recordings of memory. He realized he had done the same thing to Ginnie as he had to Harry Elder, with his talk of male menopause. He had taken both statements in and pooh-poohed them as old-fashioned. It was a move analogous in judo to meeting an oncoming opponent's headlong rush and, by moving sideways with a trip of the foot, to send him sprawling under his own momentum. It was a cheap trick actually, because it called for nothing from him but a certain shallow agility. It required no thought, no passion. It was a gimmick. He had been using ploys like this most of his life. They worked.

"Did you ever hear of something called male menopause?" he heard himself asking then.

"What Harry accused you of having?"

"Did I tell you that? I can't remember."

"I believe in self-questioning," Ginnie said. "I believe the rich don't ever do enough of it."

"You're sniping at me again."

"Not just the rich," she corrected herself. "We should all be Hamlets, now and then. Except that it gets to be a habit, doesn't it?"

"Questions. No answers." He touched her curly black hair.

352

"After a while you forget how to do anything but ask questions."

"Man is the only animal who gets in that bind."

He shook his head. "Rats in a maze, too." He toyed with a ringlet of her hair. "Do you think the forties are that dangerous an age for people?"

"They are for me."

"Do you think that if you realize your whole life's been a dead waste, it's too late in the forties to do anything about it?"

She sat up straight on the floor and stared at him. Her immense dark eyes were unwavering. "Don't give me that," she said. "You don't think your life's a waste. Not you."

"I was speaking, uh, rhetorically." He wondered if he should tell her about the scene with Edith. Then he decided it didn't really matter. He didn't need Ginnie's confirmation to know that Edith had been right.

"If I thought my whole life had been a waste until now," she said, "I would probably kill myself." She shook her head sideways. "No, I would probably kill somebody else. You, for example."

"Why would you kill me?"

"Because you're the most exasperating man I've ever known."

He made a self-deprecatory face. "Surely I have more memorable attributes. Aren't I the coldest man you've ever known? The least interested in people? The most compleat banker?"

Ginnie watched his face even more closely now. "Is that a self-portrait?"

"Does it matter who drew it?"

"Can't you ever answer a question except with another question?"

"Must I?"

They burst out laughing. She laid her head back on his knees, and he felt a strange sense of loss at not being as closely watched as he had been. He wondered why her scrutiny didn't seem to bother him, when almost everyone else's did, always had over the years. Even as a child he had rejected the watching helpfulness of teachers, parents, often even Hanley, his older brother. Ginnie had been perfectly right in front of the Waldorf tonight, when she had accused him of never needing help. Or never admitting he needed it.

353

He was, he supposed, everything Edith had called him. In addition to all of that, he was a loner as well. He had known this about himself for many years. He disliked cooperative ventures. He objected to having his works examined and then having help proffered. The only person who had ever been able to enforce help on him had been his father, for which he had never stopped hating the old man.

The only person whose help he had ever accepted, it seemed to him, had been Ginnie, and only, he remembered now, when in desperation he had had nowhere else to turn.

"Why do you suppose that was?" he wondered aloud.

"Mm?"

"Why did I—" He stopped short, realizing he had almost blurted it out. But why not? "I was wondering," he began slowly, "why I don't enjoy being helped by anyone but you."

She sat up again and smiled at him. "You can do better than that, Woods. You don't enjoy help? You positively despise and loathe it."

"A little less hyperbole might be even more helpful."

"Banker talk?" She wrinkled her nose. "Hyperbole is me mother tongue."

He shrugged weakly. "Even so, why do I trust you? Are you that great?" He watched her huge eyes for a moment. "I guess you are." He touched her chin with his finger, raising her face slightly. "You really are that great."

"Maybe not. But you think I am," she said, "and that's what interests me."

They watched each other for a moment. "You know," Palmer said then, "I had been thinking about you even before I got that invitation to the dinner. It's a little spooky. I had been thinking a lot of you just the week before."

"Is that all? What about all the aching months in between?"

"For a long time after we separated," Palmer said, "I nursed an awfully bent ego. It didn't seem possible that you could walk out on such a prize package."

"God, no," Ginnie agreed mockingly. "You had everything. A wife, three children. What more could a girl ask for?"

"And then I began to see the logic of your position."

She nodded. "You were always a great one for logic." She waved her hand as if brushing off a troublesome cobweb. "If I tell you a secret about yourself, Woods, will you promise not to hold it against me for telling you?"

"I promise."

Ginnie got to her feet and walked toward the window. Palmer turned to watch her as she stared up and out at the Queensboro Bridge overhead. "You hold onto logic as if it were a lifeline," she said. "But it's not. It's the tail of a tiger. And if you ever let go, it turns on you, and you get badly mauled."

"I don't und–"

"Well, try to," she interrupted. "Try to see what I mean. You are going into this whole thing with Ben Fischetti's bank by applying a strict line of logic. You ask the right questions, even though subconsciously you know the answers. Logic leads you to sillinesses. Of course there's a little difference between them and you, between what they do and what so-called legitimate businesses do. Trying to find the difference is like arguing about the number of angels who can dance on the point of a pin. Logic leads you into blind alleys like that, and you're left helpless, unable to act. What if you followed logic as capably as you can, and when it led you nowhere, relied on instinct? On emotion?"

He started to get up but found that his legs were too tired. He squirmed about in the chair. "In other words, I should listen to my built-in white Anglo-Saxon Protestant prejudices and turn down the merger."

She let out a small gasp of exasperation. "You're incredible. When it comes to listening to your heart, you're deaf. Do you honestly mean to sit there and tell me it doesn't really matter if you give Ben Fischetti's family a foothold in one of the largest commercial banks in the country? That you couldn't care less if Ubco becomes a shelter for them and a framework for their business schemes?"

"It's already a shelter and a framework for businesses at least as immoral as theirs. Perhaps more so."

"Then do you need one more rat in your cellar?"

"Huh?"

"Don't huh me, Woods." Her dark eyes slashed sideways at him in warning. "I'm asking a very simple question. Why can't you draw the line and say, very plainly: we have stopped accommodating every caller; we are no longer the town whore."

"That's a gorgeous thought. The bank as town whore." He watched her turn back to the window again. "But of course, we are, aren't we? Whatever a customer wants to do with his money, we accommodate him. Even if he's thirty million middle-class idiots who want to bankrupt themselves with

355

personal credit. We say yes, dear. Yes, got right ahead. Do it."

Ginnie turned a grin of pure triumph on him. "I feel like a teacher of retarded children," she said. "Can you really have got it?"

"But you've heard me say before we're not in business to make these moral distinctions. It doesn't matter to a bank, or it shouldn't, anyway, if a man wants to borrow a million to feed starving children or to make a new kind of jelly gasoline."

"Nonsense. Who ever heard of a bank lending money to feed kids?" She left the window and started to walk toward the far end of the room. Palmer watched the way her buttocks moved inside the long white dress. "All I'm asking." she said, "is that you exercise some common moral sense in the case of Fischetti's family."

"But what about all the other bastards?"

"One thing at a time."

"I'm serious," Palmer said. He straightened out in his chair. "Do you know what you're asking? If I draw the line at something like this, there are ten other things this week I should also refuse. And in the bank's portfolio at the moment there may be thousands of questionable deals I should also dig into and ... and ..."

"Extirpate?"

"Yes. Very good. Extirpate. Banks don't prosper by turning down business. And business ... is business. It occurred to me tonight that the dinner those people were picketing represented an awful lot of Ubco customers. Where does my responsibility begin and end? Shouldn't I logically end up on that picket line?"

"Now you see where logic leads you. The moment you let go its tail, you're in dreadful jeopardy." She walked back and stood in front of him. "I'm not suggesting anything so sweeping, Woods. It's the old thing of one problem at a time. Solve one thing. Then see what happens next."

"You sound like one of those tacky old ladies who writes advice to the lovelorn." He stopped, dismayed at the look on her face.

Palmer realized he had done the same thing again as he had done to her and to Harry Elder before. He had maneuvred her into an overextended position. "I'm sorry," he said quickly. "That was nasty. I didn't mean it."

"Didn't you?"

She turned and walked back to the chair across the room in

which she had been sitting before. "It's getting quite late," she said. "You should have been home by now."

"I don't think –"

"I do."

He stood up, feeling the fatigue in his legs. "I see." He walked a little stiffly past her chair to the door of the room. A short hallway led around to the right and out the front door.

He stopped at the doorway of the room. "Ginnie."

"Good night, Woods."

He touched the frame of the doorway. The wood, painted off-white, felt curiously firm and real to him. He saw his fingers clamp on the wood and hold tightly to it. The effort of clutching the frame made his arm muscles tremble. The tremor seemed to spread through his chest, wave after wave of catastrophe, like the onslaught of an earthquake.

"Ginnie."

Silence.

"Ginnie, don't send me away."

His voice sounded shaky. He turned toward her. She was seated only a few feet from him, her face turned up toward him, her large, dark eyes fixed on him.

"Please?"

She said nothing. He could feel his grip on the framework slipping. The strength seemed to be leaving his fingers and his arm. He could feel the tremors in his legs. His knees were buckling.

She reached out, as if to save him from sinking. "Woods?" He was on his knees, clasping the arm of her chair and looking at her.

Her face smeared away for a moment. Something was wrong with him. He could feel the tears welling up and running down his cheek. He blinked and tried to see her. Her face –

He buried his face in the soft folds of her lap. He could feel the white dress grow damp where his tears sank into it. He could feel her hand on his head, smoothing back his hair. She was saying something, but he couldn't hear it. Her voice smeared in and out. He lifted his head.

He blinked hard, trying to get her in focus clearly. "Don't send me away," he said then. "There's nothing out there. There never has been."

"It's all right."

"It's all in here with you," he said.

357

"Yes. All right, darling."

"Don't send me out there."

"I won't." She pulled his head down into her lap again and continued stroking him.

84

At three o'clock Edith turned off the television set and went to bed.

It was obvious to her that no matter when he got in, Woods could not justify his behaviour, even implausibly. He had met the Clary woman again, and they had picked up where they had left off. Only this time he simply wasn't bothering to be discreet about it. Well, why should he?

Edith supposeed it was just as well if Woods were the one to ask for a divorce. If she asked first, she knew, her bargaining position was far weaker. Divorce had been an accepted fact of life in her family, and she had listened to enough talk of it over the years to know that the one who wanted freedom most paid most dearly for it.

Not that Woods would be ungenerous. She and the children were already the beneficiaries of immense nonrevocable trust funds that had appreciated greatly in the rising market of the past five years. More than that, of course, there was support and alimony. She had her own money from her mother, but she was owed something for all the years he had used of her life. He would recognize that he had to reimburse her for the investment of her youth, which she had squandered on him. If he failed to recognize such a clear claim, the law would.

For a moment, as she lay on her bed with her eyes open, she toyed with the idea of setting a detective to work so that she could sue for a really magnificent settlement that would keep her terribly rich until her death. But to do that she would have to drag it into the courts.

They were both too civilized for that. Edith supposed, as she lay there, eyes growing heavier, that overcivilization was what had happened to their marriage. Too bad.

She was on a large bed, much larger than any she had ever slept on before. Kimberley was kissing her between her legs. She laughed and caught his head between her thighs and squeezed so hard she woke.

Kimberley would probably not want to see her again, not

after the way she had deserted him tonight. But on the other hand, he and she were already working together at Operation Boost. He shouldn't be too hard to bring around, if she felt like it.

She had him by the hand and was leading him down a long flight of stone steps that curved like the stairs in an ancient abbey or castle. When they got to her bedchamber with its flickering torches, he was white. He was not Kimberley at all. He was the attractive man at the butcher shop with the immense moustache who had given her that fierce, penetrating look last Monday when she had ordered the week's meat. His moustache felt coarse against her cheeks. His tongue choked her. She coughed and awoke.

Edith glanced at the clock and saw that it was only five minutes after three.

There was no need to woo Kimberley if she didn't feel like it, she realized. There were other men around. Now that she had started to bloom, no matter if it was a late start, she seemed to give off a budding odor that men understood.

85

The sleeping plants lay all about the little room with its perpetual cannel coal fire.

"A stroke of genius," Don Girolamo said in Italian. They kept their voices down for fear of waking Santo in the next room. "Your brain is my brain. Your heart is my heart. We are of one soul, you and I."

"Thank you, *padrone*," Rocco said.

"Your own alibi is prepared?"

"*Si padrone.*"

"Tell me, is there someone close to you whom you can trust? Some older man in the family whose mind is mature and orderly?"

Rocco shrugged. "I can search for one."

"Do so." Don Girolamo's voice dropped to a papery whisper. "My son is taking a prolonged visit to his native land. A father's heart tells me he will not return. And you will need your own buffer, my son."

Later, when he watched Rocco leave, he was truly sorry to see him go. He had found a younger man to replace Vincenzo, but where were the really young ones to come from? Not from the petty button men like the ones who had helped Rocco. They were fodder, not leadership material.

The old man sighed and settled back in the chair before the fire. He stared at the sheets of red-hot cannel coal as they flaked off in the flames. They used up the life-giving *ossigeno*, so did the treacherous plants.

All things were hostile in a hostile world. One had to be constantly, eternally on guard.

PART FIVE

Thursday

86

The paper, which was supposed to be delivered by seven thirty, hadn't yet arrived at eight in the morning, when Virginia Clary opened her front door to get it.

She pulled her dressing gown more closely around her and retreated into the house. She stood at the door of her bedroom and watched Palmer as he slept. His face looked terribly young. He showed no sign at all of baldness, of course, but it was more than that. She started to reach out and touch him, then decided to let him sleep.

He was going to be quite late today. He couldn't possibly go to the office in a slightly unpressed dress jacket and black tie. So there would be all the business of getting clothes from his home or going home to get them. Either way would be quite something to contemplate.

So it really didn't matter if he slept a bit more, Virginia decided. She went into the kitchen and closed the door. Then she leafed throught her small telephone notebook and dialed a number.

After twelve rings a woman answered the telephone. "Are you the people who are paid to deliver my *Times* in the morning?"

"This is the answering service."

"How can I speak to the newspaper delivery people?"

"You can leave a message, and they'll call you."

"They will like hell," Virginia said.

The woman at the other end of the line laughed. "You've called before?"

"You know, the *Times* gives these thieves an exclusive franchise in this neighborhood. I can't get anyone else to deliver the *Times* but these people. Tell them I'm writing the *Times* to complain."

"Yes, ma'am. Your name and address?"

Virginia gave them to her. "What's your name?" she countered.

"You don't need my name."

"I just wanted to be friendly."

"It's Alice."

"Hi, Alice."

"Good morning, Miss Clary."

"But I don't know the rest of your name."

"Alice May Janklow."

"Good morning, Miss Janklow. It seems to be a lovely morning."

"Yes, indeed, Miss Clary."

"Well, have a wonderful day."

"And the same to you."

Virginia grinned as she hung up the telephone. She switched on the radio and began making coffee. She left the small kitchen radio tuned to one of the local stations that gave nothing but news and newslike reports. As she measured water into the kettle, Virginia heard the early-morning voice of the announcer droning through a recap of yesterday's market closings.

"RCA up a half. And now, for our eight o'clock roundup of late news. The death toll in last night's peace demonstration has risen to three. Patrolman Horacio Muñoz, thirty-four, who was shot accidentally by his own gun in a scuffle, died on the scene. Albert Mittleman, sixty-eight, is also dead of a concussion. And a third man, who died early this morning at Bellevue Hospital, has been tentatively identified as Herman Pevney, whom police describe as an indigent in the vicinity of the riot. A full-scale police investigation has been announced by the commissioner after an early morning conference with the mayor. Meanwhile, the police were busy in another part of Manhattan. Summoned to a posh East Side apartment by building employees, they found career girl Dorcas Tipton, twenty-one, dead of seven stab wounds. The absence of any clear motive in the killing leads investigators to believe that this is the latest in a series of bachelor-girl murders that have plagued the East Side for more than a year now. The building's garageman, forty-eight-year-old Braden Johnson, told police it may have been the work of two young sex killers. The latest slaying took place only four blocks from one in early February, in which Elaine –"

Virginia switched off the radio and poured hot water into the top of the drip coffee pot. She wondered whether Palmer would be in the mood for anything to eat. She could not recall any time in their relationship when he had spent the entire night with her in a place that had a kitchen.

She walked back into the bedroom and tried to discern any signs of his imminent awakening. Eyes shut, he lay on his back, breathing deeply and peacefully, covers half off his naked body. She returned to the kitchen and poured herself a cup of coffee.

She wondered if she should be sick today and stay home from work. She wondered if he might like some lightly buttered toast brought to the bed on a tray with the coffee which, she remembered, he always took black. She wondered if he also mightn't be sick today and not go to the office.

The telephone rang almost directly in her ear. She winced and picked it up before it could ring again.

"Miss Carney, it's Eistein, from the papers. Miss Janklow says you're going to write a letter to the *Times*. Listen, there's no reason to do that, Miss Carney. I mean, one time the boy goofs up. I personally am on my way over to deliver to you the *Times* with my own hands right now this very minute."

"Of course, you understand," Virginia said, "normally I'm out of the house by now, and if I haven't seen the paper, it's simply no good to me."

"But this morning...?" The man's voice died away suggestively.

"This morning," Virginia said, 'I am staying home from work. It's such a lovely, lovely day, I'm planning to be sick."

"On such a day, Miss Carney, I personally am running all five blocks over to give you your *Times*."

"That's quite all right," she said. "You can walk."

LESLIE WALLER

The Banker

BANKING ON WITS

Woods Palmer is in at the deep end. He may be the new vice-president of the bank with the mightiest financial muscle in the free world. But he's up to his neck in political chicanery, industrial intrigue and internecine warfare of the competition.

There are no rules in the risk business. Just the players and the tricks of their trade – inside deals, political pay-offs, sexual blackmail, coercive PR, espionage, rumour . . .

Woods Palmer is gambling to win. With big money. And grit.

RICHARD COX

An Agent of Influence

When self-made millionaire Sir James Hartman's private plane disappears in Africa, his son Robert flies out to join the search.

His father's background – from lowly birth in Central Europe, to decoration for valour in the British Army and marriage into the British upper classes – is public knowledge. But Robert soon realises that there is much more to his father than was previously apparent. What really motivates Sir James and where do his loyalties lie? In the business empire he has built so brilliantly? Or with shadowy figures from his alien past?

From the bestselling author of *Ground Zero* and *The Columbus Option*, *An Agent of Influence* is a masterly thriller of international intrigue and terrifying authenticity.

All these books are available at your local bookshop or newsagent, and can be ordered direct from the publisher.

To order direct from the publisher just tick the titles you want and fill in the form below:

A Selected List of Fiction Available from Mandarin

While every effort is made to keep prices low, it is sometimes necessary to increase prices at short notice. Mandarin Paperbacks reserves the right to show new retail prices on covers which may differ from those previously advertised in the text or elsewhere.

The prices shown below were correct at the time of going to press.

☐	7493 0003 5	**Mirage**	James Follett £3.99
☐	7493 0134 1	**To Kill a Mockingbird**	Harper Lee £2.99
☐	7493 0076 0	**The Crystal Contract**	Julian Rathbone £3.99
☐	7493 0145 7	**Talking Oscars**	Simon Williams £3.50
☐	7493 0118 X	**The Wire**	Nik Gowing £3.99
☐	7493 0121 X	**Under Cover of Daylight**	James Hall £3.50
☐	7493 0020 5	**Pratt of the Argus**	David Nobbs £3.99
☐	7493 0097 3	**Second from Last in the Sack Race**	David Nobbs £3.50

All these books are available at your bookshop or newsagent, or can be ordered direct from the publisher. Just tick the titles you want and fill in the form below.

Mandarin Paperbacks, Cash Sales Department, PO Box 11, Falmouth, Cornwall TR10 9EN.

Please send cheque or postal order, no currency, for purchase price quoted and allow the following for postage and packing:

UK   80p for the first book, 20p for each additional book ordered to a maximum charge of £2.00.

BFPO   80p for the first book, 20p for each additional book.

Overseas   £1.50 for the first book, £1.00 for the second and 30p for each additional book
including Eire   thereafter.

NAME (Block letters) ....

ADDRESS ....

....

....